TWICE
ROYAL
LADY

D1158834

By the same author

Operation Kingfisher
Aphrodite's Island

TWICE ROYAL LADY

Hilary Green

R
buried
river
press

3165904515 7696

East Baton Rouge Parish Library
Baton Rouge, Louisiana

© Hilary Green 2015
First published in Great Britain 2015

ISBN 978-1-910208-33-5

Buried River Press
Clerkenwell House
Clerkenwell Green
London EC1R 0HT

Buried River Press is an imprint of Robert Hale Ltd

www.halebooks.com

The right of Hilary Green to be identified as author
of this work has been asserted by her in accordance
with the Copyright, Designs and Patents Act 1988

2 4 6 8 10 9 7 5 3 1

Typeset in Palatino
Printed and bound in Great Britain by
CPI Antony Rowe, Chippenham and Eastbourne

THE EMPRESS MATILDA, QUEEN OF THE GERMANS AND LADY OF THE ENGLISH

'Great by birth, greater by marriage, greatest of all in her offspring.'

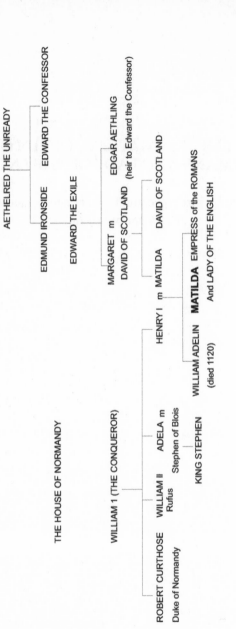

THE ROYAL HOUSE OF WESSEX

AETHELRED THE UNREADY

EDMUND IRONSIDE   EDWARD THE CONFESSOR

EDWARD THE EXILE

MARGARET m   EDGAR AETHLING
DAVID OF SCOTLAND   (heir to Edward the Confessor)

THE HOUSE OF NORMANDY

WILLIAM 1 (THE CONQUEROR)

ROBERT CURTHOSE   WILLIAM II   ADELA m   HENRY I m MATILDA   DAVID OF SCOTLAND
Duke of Normandy   Rufus   Stephen of Blois

KING STEPHEN   WILLIAM ADELIN   MATILDA EMPRESS of the ROMANS
(died 1120)   And LADY OF THE ENGLISH

1

UTRECHT, 1110

'I DON'T WANT to be married to that man. I don't like him!'

She was standing in the ante-chamber to the great hall of the castle of Utrecht, weighed down by the robes and jewels they had heaped on her. From the other side of the door she could hear the hum of hundreds of voices. There was a rustle of skirts close by and Sister Agnes knelt to bring her face on the same level.

'Hush, my lady! You must not speak so. King Henry is a great man, the ruler of all the Germans and soon to be Emperor of the Romans like his ancestor Charlemagne. He does you great honour in asking you to become his wife.'

'But I don't like him.' She could feel her lower lip beginning to tremble. 'He's old and I can't understand what he says.'

Sister Agnes had kind eyes and for a moment her lips curled in a smile. 'Twenty-four is not old. I know it seems like it when you are only eight, but remember, this is only a betrothal. By the time you are old enough to marry the difference will not seem so great. And you are a clever girl. You will soon learn to understand German, and to speak it. Just think, as King Henry's affianced bride, you will be a queen, and one day perhaps an empress.'

'But I don't want ...'

A hand gripped her shoulder and spun her round so that she was looking up at Reverend Mother Hildegarde. Her eyes were not kind.

'You don't want? When will you learn that your petty desires are of no importance? You have a duty. The King your father has decreed this match for you and it is your duty to him, and through him to God, to obey. Must I chastise you again, to break this rebellious spirit of yours?'

The door to the hall banged open to admit Lord Roger of Clare, whom the King her father had appointed to take charge of her.

'What is going on here? His Grace is waiting. Bring the Lady Matilda in at once.'

She looked at him and something opened in her mind, like a door to a lighted room. 'Lord Roger, it would not be fitting for a queen to be whipped, would it? It would be ... would be against the dignity of the throne.' She had heard the phrase somewhere and it seemed to fit.

Behind her she heard Mother Hildegarde give a sharp tut of disapproval, but Lord Roger bent his head. 'That is so, my lady.'

She pressed her lips together to still them and lifted her chin. 'Let us go, then. We must not keep King Henry waiting.'

The hall was decked with banners and the walls were draped with rich tapestries. The heat from hundreds of wax candles blew over her face as she entered and there were fresh, sweet-smelling rushes beneath her feet. On either side of the central aisle stood hundreds of lords and ladies in brilliantly coloured gowns, who doffed their hats and curtsied as she passed and whispered to each other. Ahead of her, on a dais, stood the man she must promise

8

to marry, King Henry of Germany, the fifth of that name. It was confusing. She knew one King Henry; her father, Henry of England, the first of that name; not that she had seen very much of him in her short life. Now there was this other Henry, a tall man with heavy dark brows and eyes that did not smile as she came towards him. She was not sure which of them frightened her more.

Her little procession reached the dais and the King stepped down to meet her. But instead of speaking to her, he looked across her head at Lord Roger and asked, in his heavily accented French, 'Have you brought the promised dowry?'

Lord Roger bowed. 'I have, Your Grace.' He snapped his fingers and four pages came forward, carrying between them two heavy chests bound with iron. They set them down and opened the lids. The chests were full of silver coins – 10,000 marks she had heard someone say.

King Henry nodded and the chests were closed and removed. Lord Roger said, 'And have you prepared the bride price as agreed, Your Grace?'

Henry gestured to a man in fur-trimmed robes who stood behind him and the man unrolled a scroll and began to read. She understood, dimly, that he was reading a list of lands and castles which now belonged to her, though she was not sure what she was supposed to do with them.

When the reading was finished Henry took hold of her hand. 'I, Henry of Germany, swear by God and on my honour that when you come to womanhood I will marry you. And in token of this I give you this ring.'

The ring was too big for her finger and the weight of the ruby in it made it slip round, so that she was afraid it would fall off. But she knew what she had to say. It had been drilled into her by the Archdeacon of Wilton, who was standing close behind her.

'I, Matilda of England, promise by God and on my honour that when I come to womanhood I will marry you.'

She heard a sound, as if the people behind her had been holding their breath and now let it out in relief. Then the archdeacon stepped forward and she knelt beside Henry while he pronounced a blessing. When he had finished, Henry took her hand again and led her up onto the dais and seated her on a throne to the right of his own. It was too high. She had to hitch herself up onto it and her feet did not touch the ground, but that did not seem to matter. Everyone in the hall was cheering and she realized they were cheering her. For the first time, she smiled.

Trestles were brought in and boards laid across them and covered in gleaming damask. The assembled company arranged themselves on benches alongside them. Serving men and women carried in silver bowls and platters and flasks of ale and wine. A whole suckling pig was brought in on a spit and set before Henry, and one of his squires carved slices for him and for her. There were barons of beef and roasted fowls and haunches of venison and mounds of bread to soak up the juices. Each dish was accompanied by a different sauce, with strange flavours she had never tasted before. Lord Roger, seated on her right, leant over to murmur, 'You must taste everything, but then you can send the dish to one of the guests as a sign of favour.' He told her which lords and ladies to honour in this way, but dish after dish kept arriving until she felt her stomach would burst. The smoke from the candles got in her eyes and the heat made her feel sleepy. Henry laughed and joked in German with his courtiers, but no one had much to say to her and after a while she felt a desperate need to empty her bladder. She looked round for Sister Agnes but she was nowhere to be seen.

At last King Henry rose to his feet and all the lords and

ladies rose, too, to bow or curtsey as he swept out of the hall, with his pages and squires following. Then, to her relief, Sister Agnes reappeared and took her to a small room off the hall, where a chamber pot was waiting for her.

After she had relieved herself Lord Roger came in and beamed at her. 'Well done, my lady. You conducted yourself perfectly. I shall report as much to the King your father.'

'Am I a queen now?'

He continued to smile. 'Not quite yet. There will be a coronation, but the date for that has not been set. It will be some months ahead, I expect.'

She was not sure whether to be disappointed or relieved. After a moment's thought she said, 'I think I should like to go home now.'

She heard Sister Agnes catch her breath and Lord Roger's smile faded. He said, quite gently, 'This is your home now, my lady. You will live at King Henry's court and be attended by his people, until you are old enough to marry.'

She stared at him in consternation. It was too much. She was worn out and her head was throbbing. She could not hold back the tears any longer.

'I want to go home! I want to go home!'

The betrothal took place at Easter and the date of the coronation was set for 25 July, in the cathedral of Mainz. She was given a suite of rooms in the palace and Archbishop Bruno of Trier came to prepare her for the ceremony. She liked Bruno. He had a gentle manner and, although his expression was grave, there was a smile in the depths of his brown eyes. He brought with him a young monk, Brother Lothar, who was to teach her German, and Father Bouchard to be her personal chaplain. Learning had never been hard for her. In the convent she had learned to read and write in French and Latin and her lessons had been the most enjoyable part of her day. She quickly picked up German and was praised by her teachers.

She was given three German noblewomen as her ladies-in-waiting. They made a fuss of her and told her stories. She did not always understand them but they made her life much more pleasant than the strict regime of the convent. She was given everything she asked for – sweetmeats; a puppy; a white pony to ride. There were pages and servants to attend her. She even had her own household knights, boisterous young men who spent their time hunting and jousting and playing jokes on each other. Whenever she appeared among them they fell silent and bowed, but after she passed by she heard them start laughing again and she could not help wondering if they were laughing at her. She was intrigued and alarmed by them in equal measure, because the only men she had known up to now had been priests or the solemn-faced nobles who advised her father.

Reverend Mother Hildegarde had gone back to her convent in Wilton but Sister Agnes was still with her. She loved Agnes. Since she was sent to the convent at the age of three to be educated she was the nearest thing to a mother she had known. Sometimes she thought about England, and about her real mother, the Scottish Princess Matilda who was now Queen of England. She could remember, just, the time when she lived at court and her mother came every day to kiss her and play with her; but then she was sent away to the convent and her mother became a rare visitor. She did not miss her, or the convent. She no longer asked to go home.

She saw very little of Henry. Archbishop Bruno explained that he was much occupied by affairs of state.

In his father's time there had been unrest and rebellion. Henry had joined the rebels himself and been crowned while his father was still alive. When the old king died the kingdom was left in disarray and Henry had to restore order and justice. She was happy that he was so occupied. She had no wish to spend time with him.

One day she was sitting at her lessons when one of her ladies came in to say there was a young noblewoman in the ante-chamber who desired an audience with her.

'Who is she?'

'Her name is Adeliza of Louvain, madam.'

She looked at Bruno for guidance and he nodded.

'Well, I suppose you had better ask he to come in.'

To her surprise the girl who entered was scarcely older than herself. She was fair-haired and pretty but her face was pale and she looked nervous. She came forward and fell on her knees in front of Matilda.

'My lady, I beg you to intercede with the King your husband on behalf of my father, Duke Godfrey. He supported the old king during the rebellion, because he thought that was where his duty lay and since your lord, King Henry, took the throne he has kept him in prison. He repents of having raised his sword against him and wishes to swear allegiance. My lady, we hear that he is in poor health, and while he is absent we are undefended. Wicked men attack our estates and steal the cattle and the produce. The burden is too great for my mother and her health, too, is failing. In the name of the most merciful God, I ask you to speak to the King on our behalf and beg him to release my father.'

Her eyes were full of tears and Matilda felt very sorry for her. She looked to Bruno again for advice. 'Can I? Would the King listen to me?'

Bruno bent towards her. 'It has long been regarded as

fitting for a queen to intercede with the King on behalf of his subjects. I think at this time he would wish to be seen to please you.'

The prospect frightened her. She whispered, 'But how? What do I have to do?'

'You must go to him when he is in council. I will show you when and where. You must kneel and clasp his knees and repeat what Adeliza has told you. You must ask him, out of love for you, to show mercy.'

'Out of love for me?' She had seen no sign that Henry loved her, but she trusted Bruno. She turned her face to Adeliza, who was still kneeling. 'I will do my best ... but I can't promise.'

Adeliza caught her hand and kissed it. 'Thank you, my lady! A thousand thanks! I am sure the King cannot refuse you.'

Next day, on Bruno's instruction, her ladies dressed her in her finest gown and he led her through the palace to the great hall where the King held council and dispensed justice. He was seated on his throne, surrounded by a dozen or so richly dressed men, with scribes and squires and pages hovering in the background. He had a map on his knee and was frowning down at it.

A steward announced, 'Your Grace, the Lady Matilda desires audience.'

All the men turned to look at her. Henry looked surprised, as if it took him a moment to remember who she was. She was trembling, but Bruno gave her a little push and she walked forward, holding herself erect as she had been taught, and knelt at his feet. She laid her hands on his knees and felt a flutter of nerves at the liberty.

Henry put the map aside and said, quite gently, 'What is it you would ask, my lady?'

'Sire ...' Her voice was shaking but she pressed on. 'I

come to intercede with you on behalf of the Lady Adeliza of Louvain. You have her father Count Godfrey in prison. He repents of lifting a sword against you and begs your forgiveness. His wife is ailing and his land is undefended, and wicked men are stealing his cattle and his crops.' She raised her eyes and found that Henry was looking at her with interest, as if seeing her properly for the first time. Emboldened, she went on, 'I beg you, sire, show mercy and let him go.'

He reached down and took her hands and raised her to her feet. 'My wife-to-be, it would not be right for me to refuse this first request. Count Godfrey shall be freed, provided he is willing to take the oath of fealty to me. You may tell Lady Adeliza that she can expect her father home very soon.'

She caught her breath in delight. She had never imagined it could be so easy. 'Oh, thank you! Thank you!' She wanted to run back to Adeliza, who was waiting outside. She took a few steps, then remembered where she was and turned back to curtsey. He was watching her with a smile.

'You may go.'

She made herself walk back up the length of the hall to where Bruno was waiting. As she reached the door she heard voices behind her, and a little laughter, but it was not unkind. Bruno congratulated her and Adeliza fell on her knees and kissed her hands.

'My lady, thank you! We shall always be in your debt – always!'

As they walked back to her own rooms she asked Bruno, 'Will the King always do what I ask him?'

He shook his head. 'I fear not, my lady. There are bound to be times when necessity forces him to say no. But you have made a good start. I think he will always listen to you, if you speak as persuasively as you did today.'

*

On the day before her coronation Roger Pole came to see her. He had remained at King Henry's court but had spent most of his time in discussion with him and with his council.

'Are you ready for tomorrow?'

'Yes – I think so.'

'You have been told what will happen and what you must do?'

'Yes.'

'Just remember, my lady, that you are twice royal, both through your father's line and through your mother's. He is son to the great William of Normandy, who conquered England, but your mother is the daughter of the sainted Queen Margaret of Scotland, who was sister to Edgar Aethling, the chosen successor of King Edward, whom they call the Confessor. Their father was Edward, the son of Edward Ironside, and through him they can trace their descent back to Cerdic, who founded the line of the kings of Wessex. So in you the blood of the ancient kings of England is united with that of the present royal line. When you walk through the cathedral tomorrow to your own coronation, let everyone see that you are a true queen, by blood as well as by marriage.'

As she entered the cathedral next day she tried to live up to that injunction and carry herself like a queen, but the robes and the jewels they had decked her with were even heavier than they were for her betrothal and it seemed a very long walk from the great west door to the high altar. The cathedral was packed. Princes and lords had come from all over Europe to see her crowned. Henry was already there, enthroned on a dais in front of the altar. She reached the steps up to the dais but as she tried to climb her toe caught in the hem of her robe and she nearly fell. Luckily, Archbishop Bruno was just behind her. He caught her and lifted her bodily to the top of the steps and seated her on the throne next to Henry's.

The service seemed interminable. She had been taught exactly what to expect and what to do, and her grasp of Latin was good enough for her to follow most of what was being said or sung, but after a while she found it hard to concentrate. Her back and neck ached from the effort of sitting up straight. She longed to change her position but she knew she must not fidget. The sceptre was put into her hand and then the sign of the cross was marked on her brow and breast with the holy oil. For a moment she forgot her discomfort in the realization that she was now the Lord's Anointed, no longer a mere mortal but one chosen by God to rule. The crown was set on her head. It was very heavy and slightly too large, so that it rested on her ears, and she was afraid that if she moved it might fall off. Then the lords who owed allegiance to Henry came forward one by one to do homage to their new queen. The first one to kneel in front of her was quite old. He had grey hair and a straggly beard and she heard his knees crack as he lowered himself and she almost giggled. It seemed ridiculous that he should kneel to her. But then she remembered the holy oil and was serious again. He placed his hands between hers and repeated the words of the oath and she responded as she had been taught. His place was taken by another and then another. She knew the names of some of them but most were strangers.

At last it was all over. The choir sang a joyful anthem. Henry rose and gave her his hand and together they walked in procession down the aisle. Then they were out in the sunshine and the streets were lined with cheering people.

The following day Sister Agnes came to her with tears in her eyes. 'My lady, I come to bid you farewell.'

'What do you mean? Where are you going?'

'I am going back to the convent, madam.'

'To England?'

'Yes.'

'You can't! I want you here.'

'My lady, it is the King's command. All your English attendants are to leave.'

'All of you?'

'Yes, madam.'

'But I shall be all alone.'

'No! You already have your German ladies, your pages and knights. You will soon find that you are among friends.'

She stamped her foot. 'I don't care about them. I want you here. I forbid you to go.'

'We must. It is the King's command.'

'I shall speak to the King. I shall tell him he can't send you away. He has to do as I ask.'

She turned and ran from the room. At the entrance to the King's apartments, a chamberlain forestalled her. She tried to push him aside.

'Let me pass! I am the Queen! I want to see the King.'

'You Grace, forgive me. The King is not here. He has gone hunting.'

Tears rose in her throat. 'But I need to talk to him.'

'Later, madam. When he returns I am sure he will be happy to listen to you.'

'But I need to talk to him now!'

Lord Roger came quickly along the corridor. 'My lady, you must come back to your own rooms. Your people are waiting to take their leave.'

'No! They are not to go. I won't let them.'

He looked down at her kindly but shook his head. 'We have to obey the King's command. He wishes you to be attended only by his own people, so that you will learn more quickly to speak his language and understand the customs of the country.'

'Are you going too?'

'Yes, my lady. I must. Now, come with me, please, and say goodbye.'

They came in one by one to kiss her hand, the servants and attendants who were sent with her from England. Agnes was the last. There were tears in her eyes as she bent to kiss her cheek, but Matilda turned her face away. *'I am a queen,'* she told herself, *'and queens don't cry. Let them all go! I can manage without them.'*

Later, she watched from the window as they mounted horses or mules and rode away. The last link with England was broken.

2

WORMS, JANUARY 1114

MATILDA LOOKED AT her reflection in the polished bronze mirror and smoothed the white linen of the close-fitting gown over her hips. The body she saw in the mirror seemed unfamiliar. There were new curves and she could see the rise and fall of her breasts as she breathed. Magda, her waiting woman, slipped the overgown over her head and arranged its folds. It was dyed a deep rosy purple, a colour she knew was called mazereon, and elaborately embroidered with gold thread. Over that, Magda draped a robe of fine wool the colour of mulberries. It, too, was embroidered with gold and the edges were trimmed with grey fur. Finally, she covered her hair with a veil of fine white linen. Matilda noticed that her hair was different, too. When she was very young it was fair, but now it had darkened to the colour of ripe hazelnuts.

Her stomach was churning with a mixture of excitement and trepidation in equal measure. She was twelve years old, and today was her wedding day. There were questions she needed answers to but no one to ask. She said, 'Am I ... will he ... will the King be pleased with me?'

Magda patted her arm. 'Never fear, my lady. No man

could want a more beautiful bride.'

It was not what she really needed to ask, but she knew no way of framing the question. So she took refuge in petulance. 'This veil doesn't feel right. I'm afraid it will slip.'

Magda clicked her tongue. 'Leave it be, my lady. The crown will hold it in place.'

One of her ladies-in-waiting opened the door of the chamber. 'Your Grace, they are ready below. It is time to leave.'

'Very well. Bring me the crown.'

A page entered, bearing the crown on a velvet cushion. He knelt before her and she took it and placed it on her head. It fitted better now and she was more used to the weight. She moved into the ante-chamber, where her ladies sank into deep curtseys, and two more pages took up the trailing hem of her gown. They descended the staircase and crossed the great hall to where the procession was waiting at the foot of the steps. Her household knights were already mounted, except for the youngest, whose name was Drogo, a quiet, fair-haired young man, more thoughtful than the others. He waited by the bridle of a pure white palfrey, whose saddle and bridle were of scarlet leather ornamented with gold. He knelt as she approached and looked up at her with a smile.

'I wish you joy, Your Grace.'

He made a stirrup of his clasped hands, she put her foot into it and he lifted her effortlessly into the saddle. Her master of horse gave a signal and the procession moved off.

The streets of the town were crowded. Men lifted children onto their shoulders to see her pass; women hung out of windows and threw flowers into her path. She smiled and nodded to left and right. In the course of more than three years she had learned what was required of a queen.

She had learned much more than this. Since her coronation she had lived in the city of Trier on the River Moselle, where the cathedral was famous for its schools. Students came from all over France and Germany to learn there and her education continued to be overseen by Archbishop Bruno, one of the most learned men in the kingdom. German was now her first language, but she could still read and speak the Norman French she was brought up with, and her Latin was fluent. More importantly, she had been instructed in the complex problems that beset her future husband's realm and in particular the conflict that existed between him and the Pope over church policy. Henry had spent most of those three intervening years in Italy, attempting to come to some agreement with the Pontiff.

'I don't understand,' she said once to Bruno. 'Why is the Holy Father angry with the King?'

Bruno sighed. 'It is complicated, my lady. Let me try to explain. Here in Germany it is the custom to elect our bishops, but the King has been able to exert considerable influence over the choice. Then, once the election has taken place, it is the King who invests the bishop with the symbols of his office, the ring and the crozier, and he expects the bishop to do homage and swear fealty to him in return for the lands he holds. The Pope believes that this is a matter for the Church, not the King, and the investiture should be performed by himself or by a papal legate. His Grace your husband refuses to give up the privilege.'

'But if the bishop holds lands from the King,' she said, 'surely he must swear fealty. Otherwise he would be like a prince in his own little kingdom and the King would have no authority.'

'It is a question of priority. Which should come first, the

bishop's duty to the King, or his duty to God? There are those who believe, myself among them, that duty to God must always take precedence. '

She had thought about this for some time and then interrupted her lesson to say, 'In the Bible, we are told that when the Pharisees showed Jesus a coin with Caesar's head on it and asked Him if it was right to pay taxes, he answered that they should render unto Caesar the things that were Caesar's and to God things that were God's. Isn't that the answer to the problem between the King and the Pope?'

Bruno had looked at her with a smile of surprise and a shake of his head. *'Out of the mouths of babes and sucklings!* You are wise beyond your years, madam. But I fear the solution is not as simple as it sounds.'

Not long afterwards they heard that Henry had taken the Pope and all his attendant prelates prisoner at Ponte Mammolo and forced His Holiness to concede his right to continue to invest his bishops with the ring and crozier, and to crown him Holy Roman Emperor. But as soon as the Pope was free again he rescinded the permission and excommunicated Henry. It was too late, however, to undo the coronation.

But that was not what she was thinking of as she rode towards the cathedral. She might be a queen and an empress; more importantly she was now a woman. She had had her first bleeding and the time had come for her marriage to Henry to be consummated. She had seen little of him since her coronation. He was with her at Bamberg where they celebrated Christmas a few days earlier, but though she took her place beside him during the feasting they were never alone. He was still a stranger to her and she dreaded what would happen when the ceremony was over.

The cathedral was packed. Dukes jostled for position with archbishops; bishops rubbed shoulders with counts; lesser members of the nobility squeezed themselves behind pillars and into corners. From the great west door she could see that the King was already enthroned before the altar. Archbishop Bruno led the procession that conducted her down the long aisle to his side. Henry rose and turned to look at her and she was relieved to see that he seemed satisfied, but there was something else in the look that disturbed her. The service proceeded, but she could not focus her mind on it. She knew that she should be praying fervently for the success of her marriage, but it felt as if it was all part of a dream. She spoke her vows automatically. The Archbishop of Worms pronounced a blessing, the choir sang a psalm, and then it was over and Henry turned to face the congregation and offered her his hand. She placed her own on it and the contact sent a quiver through her nerves so that she almost withdrew it, but the people were waiting and the two archbishops were leading the way down the aisle. She walked beside her husband out of the cathedral and into the winter sunshine and the cheering crowds in the square.

Henry had ordained that the celebrations should be the most magnificent in living memory. In the great hall of his castle, hundreds of noblemen and ladies squeezed onto the benches that lined the long tables. In the places of honour there were five archbishops, thirty bishops and five dukes. Men and women of lesser rank crowded into the gallery overlooking the hall to watch. To a fanfare of trumpets, the feast began. Bowls of rich broth were followed by quails' eggs and fish with a spicy sauce called Egerdouce. It was sixteen years since Count Stephen of Blois returned from the Holy Land – returned in disgrace, branded a coward by his own wife for abandoning the siege of Antioch – but nevertheless bringing with him tales of the exotic food served at the court of the Emperor Alexios in Constantinople. Since then he had been followed by other lords and knights, returning victorious from the conquest of Jerusalem, bringing in their train merchants with stocks of precious spices. Now every nobleman wished to have a cook who understood the use of these spices, and Henry was not to be outdone. Next came goose, with a sauce flavoured with nutmeg and cinnamon, and pheasants with ginger. After these had been consumed there was another fanfare and the *entremets* were carried in shoulder high by a relay of serving men. Peacocks and swans in full plumage, with gilded beaks and wearing crowns upon their heads, were processed around the hall, to murmurs of amazement. Great pies came next, stuffed with all sorts of game and poultry, their crusts elaborately sculpted to look like castles and gilded with egg yolks and saffron and sprinkled with sugar-coated caraway seeds. With them came jellies in jewel-bright colours, custards and blancmanges. When these had been consumed the climax of the feast was reached as the 'subtlety' was paraded round the room. It was a fantastic confection of sugar and marzipan made to look like a giant marriage bed garlanded with roses. Duly admired, it was broken up and shared among the guests. The feasting concluded with sweetmeats and hippocras, wine sweetened with honey and flavoured with spices.

She was used to feasts now, albeit not quite as elaborate as this one. She tasted tiny portions of each dish put before her and dispatched them to carefully chosen guests. She no longer relied on Henry or Bruno to tell her who should be favoured in this way. Over the months she had observed the members of Henry's court carefully. She knew who the loyal retainers were, who should be rewarded, and who the waverers were, who might respond to flattery. As the meal progressed she was aware that Henry was watching and after a while he leant towards her.

'You have learned well, my lady. I am impressed.'

She felt herself blush and lowered her eyes.

During the meal minstrels played and troubadours wandered the hall, improvising songs to flatter the ladies. Between each course, tumblers and jugglers performed and clowns recited riddles and told jokes. She tried to keep her mind on their antics, to blot out the thought of what must happen later. The guests were on their best behaviour. There was no shouting or brawling, but as the hippocras circulated there was more laughter and the jokes became bawdy. They were not intended for her to hear, and most of them she did not understand, but the expressions on the faces frightened her.

At last Henry rose to his feet and she knew she must do likewise. She had drunk more wine than usual and her legs felt unsteady. Two processions formed, men in one, women in the other with her at the centre, and they left the hall to the sound of cheers and suggestive comments. Swept along by her companions, she was conducted to the private apartments above and into a room dominated by a huge double bed. It was bright with wax candles and perfumed with frankincense and when the sheets were turned back she saw that the mattress was sprinkled with rose petals. Her ladies-in-waiting crowded round her, giggling, and helped her to undress and put on her a nightgown of linen so fine it was almost transparent. She longed to ask the questions that had been churning over and over in her brain, but she could not find the words. They were saying things like, 'Oh, the King has got a treat in store for him! A pretty little thing like you,' and, 'You're a lucky girl, with such a fine strong man for a husband. He'll take some satisfying, I warrant! You won't get much sleep tonight!'

Finally, they put her into bed and snuffed out most of the candles. In desperation she grasped the hand of one, Lady Anne, and begged, 'Don't leave me! Stay a little while.'

Anne giggled and said, 'I don't think His Grace would be very pleased to find me here!' Then she sobered and squeezed her hand. 'Don't worry. It will all be over soon.'

They left and she lay flat on her back, with her arms to her sides, rigid with fear. Brought up by nuns and educated by celibate clerics, there had been no one to tell her what to expect. She had seen the dogs that roamed the castle, of course, but she told herself that surely it could not be like that between men and women. She could hear men's voices approaching, singing and laughing. Then the door opened and Henry came in. He stood looking at her for a moment, then he snuffed out the last candles so that the room was lit only by the fire in the hearth. He came to the side of the bed and threw off the heavy furred robe, which was all he was wearing. She had never seen a naked man before and the sight of his erection terrified her. She shut her eyes, and felt the bed shift under his weight.

'Come!' he said. 'It is no good pretending to be asleep.'

She opened her eyes again and found him looking down at her. His eyes glittered in the firelight.

He nodded. 'Well, madam? Shall we go to it?'

He grasped the hem of her nightgown and pulled it up to her throat. Then he pushed back the blankets and she was mortified at the realization that he was looking at her naked body. He put his hand between her thighs and pushed her legs apart. Then he lowered himself onto her and she smelt his breath, heavy with wine, and his sweat. His weight seemed to crush the life out of her. Then the pain came, as if her body was being split open. He thrust into her and the pain was worse. She would have cried out but she did not have the breath. He grunted and thrust, again and again, and then at last he gave a groan and was still. For a long moment she wondered if he was going to lie on her all night and thought that if he did she would be dead by morning. Then he rolled off, got out of bed, farted, reached under the bed for a pot and pissed noisily into it. Finished, he picked up his robe and turned to look at her.

'I wish you good night, my lady.' And with that he lumbered across to the door and disappeared into the next room.

For a long time she lay without moving, fearing that he would come back. Then she began to weep, but silently. She wanted no one to come in and ask her what the matter was. Her whole body hurt and there was a wetness between her legs that she was afraid to investigate. Eventually she cried herself to sleep.

In the morning Magda came to her. 'Well, my lady?' she said cheerfully. 'How is the new bride this morning?'

Suddenly Matilda was ashamed, ashamed of her ignorance, of her tears. It must be the same for all women, she thought, so she would not let anyone see her distress. She summoned her pride and said, 'Well enough, I thank you.' Then Magda pulled back the bedclothes and her courage deserted her. She screamed. 'Look! What has he done to me?'

There was blood on the sheet.

Magda laughed. 'That's nothing to worry about. That is your badge of honour. It will be shown to the court to prove that you were a virgin. Now, get up and let me wash you.'

Trembling, she asked, 'Where is the King?'

'Gone hunting.'

That was some comfort. A new thought came to her. She understood that she was expected to give Henry an heir. Perhaps what happened last night need not be repeated. She asked, 'Am I with child now?'

Magda laughed again. 'Bless you, madam! It's too soon to tell. That must be as God wills, but we shall not know for a week or two yet.'

That night she knelt at the end of her bed and prayed that something would happen to keep Henry away. It seemed her prayers were answered, for though she lay awake and trembling for a long time he did not come. He did not come the next night, or the next. She was almost beginning to believe that he had no intention of repeating the act she dreaded, when the door to the connecting room opened and he came in. This time she knew what to expect. She turned her face away and gritted her teeth and the pain was less, though she was still not healed. He thrust and thrust, then came with a roar and pulled himself out of her.

'By the mass! I might as well fuck an effigy in the churchyard! Are you made of stone, woman? Have you no human feelings?'

It was too much. She burst into tears, but they were tears of anger as well as pain. 'I? Have I no feelings? How can you ask that? It is you who has no feelings! Otherwise you would not hurt me so.'

He drew back. 'Hurt you?'

'Yes, you hurt me! How can you be so cruel?'

He glared at her for a moment. Then he grabbed his robe and went back to his own room.

Next day, two doctors arrived. She was in her solar, trying to read, while her ladies sewed and gossiped.

'We have orders from the King to examine the Queen,' one of them said. 'Pray prepare her.'

Magda took her into the bedroom, laid her on the bed and pulled up her skirts. She struggled up and pulled them down again.

'What do they want? What are they going to do?' she demanded. But Magda's hand on her shoulder forced her back and when the doctors approached the one who seemed to be the senior said severely, 'We have our orders from His Grace. Pray do not force me to call your women to hold you down.'

The examination left her weeping with rage and humiliation. The doctors bowed themselves out of the room without explaining their conclusions. When they had gone she grabbed Magda's hand.

'Why? Why did they do that to me?'

Magda frowned. 'The King must be dissatisfied. You know your duty as a wife. Have you done it?'

'Yes! Yes … but he was not pleased. I don't understand why.'

Magda patted her hand. 'I have a friend – one of the King's waiting men. He may hear something. I will try to find out.'

Later that day, when she was undressing her for bed, she whispered, 'My friend overheard the doctors talking to His Grace. It seems he is concerned that you may be incapable of being a proper wife to him.'

'Incapable? But I let him do what he wanted.'

'Well, we have evidence of that. The blood on your sheets. He cannot put you away on those grounds.'

'Put me away?'

'If the marriage was not consummated His Grace could apply to the Pope for an annulment.'

'Then what would happen to me?'

'I imagine you would be sent back to your father in England.'

'But it was! It was! He cannot deny that.'

'The doctors will have been able to verify that you are no longer intact. You need have no fear on those grounds. But it may be that the King is worried that you will be unable to give him an heir. If you were to conceive, that would put an end to the matter.'

From then on her ardent prayers were that she may already be with child. A week later it became apparent that she was not.

Henry came to her room.

'I have spoken to the doctors who examined you. They tell me that you are too young to bear a child and if you were to quicken it might result in your death and that of the babe.'

She had prepared her answer. 'Forgive me, sire. I am young and ignorant about these matters. I am sorry if you are dissatisfied, but I beg you not to send me back to my father. It would cause a great scandal and he would not be pleased. He is a powerful ally and I think you need his goodwill.'

His eyes narrowed but he gave a small smile. 'Whatever you lack in bed, I am told you have an astute brain and an understanding of affairs that is beyond your years. You have just proved that. The doctors suggest that I should abstain from congress until you are a little older. The time will come, they think, when you will be able to provide me with the heir I need. So for now I will not force you to a duty you find so distasteful.'

The relief was so great that she almost burst into tears. 'Your Grace, your kindness is such that I cannot find words to thank you. I promise that I will try to fulfil my duty. A little time is all I ask.'

'Have no doubt, madam, that the time will come when I shall require you to make that promise good. Meanwhile, though you may not be able to fulfil the duties of a wife, I require you to fulfil your role as a queen. From now on I expect you to be at my side, both in council and at ceremonial events. It is time you learned how the affairs of the kingdom are regulated.'

Next day he sent for her. He was sitting behind a large table, on which maps were spread, and several of his closest advisers were with him. He dismissed them and indicated that she should sit opposite him. She had a sudden impulse to build upon this new trust, to prove to him that she was worthy of it. She sank to her knees.

'Your Grace, may I ask a boon?'

'Ask.'

'You have imprisoned Adalbert, the Archbishop of Mainz, in your castle of Trifels. I have been told that he was once one of your most trusted advisers. The citizens of Mainz have petitioned me to beg you to release him. Will you grant me that?'

He frowned. 'Adalbert had good reason to be grateful to me. I made him arch chancellor and then archbishop, and how did he repay me? He sought to put his relatives in positions of power. He occupied castles to which he had no right, and stirred up rebellion in Saxony. And he supported those who deny my right to exert my authority over the bishops.'

'But I have heard that he repents of the wrongs he has done you. He is an old man, and much weakened by his imprisonment. My lord, would it not show you to be a merciful and magnanimous ruler if you were to release him?'

'Who has been telling you all this?'

'It is Archbishop Bruno, who you know has been my

tutor and my counsellor since I came here. He is a good man, and a wise one.'

'Bruno?' He raised his eyebrows. 'I am surprised. I thought he and Adalbert were at odds regarding the investiture controversy.'

'Perhaps they were, my lord. But Bruno believes that by imprisoning him you have given other great men of the realm cause to fear that the same could happen to them. Do you not think, sire, that by keeping him in prison you may be provoking others to rebel? But by showing mercy you may reconcile them to you?'

He looked down at her in silence for a moment and she felt a pang of fear. Had she presumed too much on her position? But he wanted her to take up her role as queen, and this was one of its proper functions. At last he smiled and reached out his hand to raise her.

'Very well. Let this be my wedding gift to you. Adalbert shall be freed, as long as he is prepared to confirm his loyalty to me.'

Some days later Adalbert was shown into her presence. It was obvious that he had been much weakened by his brutal imprisonment. His hair was white, he was pale and gaunt and leaned heavily on a stick, but he fell to his knees and kissed her hand.

'My lady, I owe you a great debt. If I can ever serve you by giving council or in any other way, you may call on me and I will do whatever is in my power.'

She raised him with a smile. It was good, she reflected, to be a queen and be able to influence the lives of powerful men.

3

ITALY, 1116

THE MONTH OF March was not the ideal time to cross the
Brenner Pass. The snow was still deep on either side of the
road and a bitter wind blew off the mountains, but Matilda
revelled in the excitement of travelling through such
spectacular scenery. These were the first real mountains
she had even seen. And this was only the start. Soon she
would see Venice and Rome, and perhaps meet the Pope.
Henry was riding ahead of her, surrounded by his household knights and a gaggle of squires and pages. Behind
was a train of nobles, lords spiritual and temporal, with
their attendants, and behind them the mules and pack
horses carrying equipment and supplies. Contingents of
men-at-arms formed a vanguard and a rearguard. It was
not such a great force as the one which Henry took with
him on his last expedition, but it was impressive enough.

She had her own knights riding ahead and behind,
together with grooms and pages and three ladies-in-
waiting. They were not enjoying the expedition. She
could hear them complaining about cold feet and numbed
fingers. She looked behind her. Their noses were red, their
fine complexions roughened by the wind.

She turned in the saddle. 'Stop moaning! When you hear me complain, I give you leave to do likewise. Until then, be quiet!'

Their eyes widened but they bent their heads in obedience. Two years had passed since her marriage and she was no longer a child to be pampered and reassured. She had learned to assert her authority. She turned back and caught the eyes of the knight who rode closest to her. He grinned, and she grinned back.

'Come on, Drogo! I'm tired of plodding along. Let's have a gallop!'

She pulled her chestnut palfrey out of the line of horses and kicked her forward. She was a spirited creature, her favourite, and required no extra urging. They cantered fast alongside the line, spraying up snow into the faces of the King's knights. Someone shouted a protest, then quickly fell silent as he saw who it was. Drogo followed hard on her heels. When she drew level with Henry she checked her speed and he looked up from conversation with one of his advisers.

'Is something amiss, my lady?'

'Nothing, Your Grace. Exercise to warm the blood. I trust Your Grace is in good spirits?'

He looked at her and smiled. 'Well enough, I thank you. But have a care. Do not let your horse stray off the road. The drifts are still deep.'

'I shall, my lord!' She turned her horse's head and cantered back to her place in the line. Henry's companions, taking their cue from him, watched her go with indulgent smiles.

She and Henry had learned to like each other over the passage of the two years. He had not come to her bed again. She knew he had mistresses, one of whom, at least, had given him a daughter. She imagined that they were able to please him in ways she was only just beginning to guess at. She had no objections to this state of affairs. He could have as many mistresses as he wanted if it kept him out of her bed. But there lurked always at the back of her mind the thought that at some point in the future she would be required to provide him with an heir. Meanwhile, she was learning what he required of her as his queen. At every important event she had been at his side; she attended council meetings; frequently she was asked to petition him for grants of money or land to religious houses; she had co-signed charters giving special privileges to cities or monasteries; on several occasions she had been able to reconcile erstwhile opponents to him.

It had been a turbulent time. The kingdom was still far from settled. Rebellions in different provinces had occasioned pitched battles and Henry had suffered two severe military defeats. Worse still, the dissension in the Church had grown stronger. There were demands for reforms giving the bishops greater independence. They were led by Frederick, Archbishop of Cologne, and had culminated in a final act of defiance. Though Henry had been officially excommunicated some years ago, the sentence had never been read in Germany, until Frederick pronounced it in April of the previous year, thus formally freeing all his subjects from their allegiance. Now it was vital to come to some accommodation with the Pope. Hence the expedition on which they were now engaged.

Henry had a pretext for another incursion into Italy. As emperor he already commanded the allegiance of the citizens of Verona and Padua. Now the Countess who ruled Emilia and Tuscany, another Matilda, had died and left him all her lands. She was an autocrat who had left rebellion simmering in her cities. He planned to establish his authority, not through force but by conciliation. Matilda knew that this was partly her doing. In the council chamber where the policy was agreed, her voice had as much influence as that of Henry's older advisers.

The streets of Rome were lined with cheering crowds. It was Easter 1117, and the Emperor and his wife were going to the great basilica of St Peter's to be crowned. Matilda sat beside her husband in a barge decked out with embroidered hangings and garlanded with flowers. It was unfortunate that they were unable to ride over the bridge across the Tiber, but a garrison left behind by the Pope was in control of the Castel St Angelo, which would have made crossing by that route a very dangerous undertaking. It was a pity, also, she reflected, that the crowning would not be performed by the Pope himself. Henry had sent conciliatory messages ahead, but as he approached with his army His Holiness had found it expedient to retire southwards to Monte Cassino. Instead, the ceremony would be performed by the Archbishop of Braga, Maurice Bourdin. She tried to quell a sense of disappointment. It was not important who officiated. From now on, she would be recognized as Empress and Queen of the Romans.

It had taken a year to get to this point, but it had been a successful year. She reminded herself of the triumphs, and of the great cities she had seen. They stayed for a short while in the palace of the Doge of Venice; then the royal party with all its hangers-on moved on to Padua and Mantua, where Henry's policy of conciliation paid dividends and earned him loyal followers. At the castle of Canossa they had been greeted with a long poem, praising him for his wisdom and mercy and her for her beauty and gentleness. It was only when they had started to head south that things had not gone according to plan. But what did it matter that the Pope had fled? Apart from the garrison in St Angelo, the city was at their feet and she was about to become an empress.

On the far side of the river they walked in procession to St Peter's. Matilda gazed in awe at the towering façade but it was the interior that left her breathless. The long central nave was bordered by marble pillars and the sheer height of the gabled roof made her feel dizzy, while the glitter of gold reflecting the light of hundreds of candles dazzled her eyes.[1] At the climax of the long, elaborate ceremony the crown which was placed on her head was even heavier than the one she was required to wear at her first coronation, but she had grown since then and exercise had made her stronger, and she was able to walk down the aisle beside her husband with her head erect.

Out in the streets her eyes were dazzled afresh by sunlight and her ears were filled with the clamour of the crowds. She had heard murmurs that Henry had paid out large sums of money to guarantee this joyous reception but she had dismissed them. If it was true, so be it. It was all part of the struggle for power, and right now they were winning.

The following weeks were filled with the kind of routine she had become used to. Together with Henry she adjudicated on disputes, heard petitions and granted charters. There was another celebration, too. Henry had arranged the marriage of his natural daughter, Bertha, to Count Ptolemy of Tusculum, thereby strengthening his influence in that area. Matilda was not shocked by the news. Henry was not alone among the kings of Europe in producing and acknowledging illegitimate offspring. Her own father was renowned for the number of his conquests. The sons and daughters of kings, even if born on 'the wrong side of the

---

1. This is not the St Peter's that we know now, but an earlier construction.

blanket', were still useful pawns in the power game.

By Pentecost, the most pressing disputes had been settled, agreement with the Pope seemed no nearer, and the heat in the city was becoming oppressive. To celebrate the festival Matilda processed with Henry from St Peter's to the Basilica of Santa Maria Maggiore. They wore their crowns, to remind the citizens of where their loyalty should lie. By the time they reached the basilica she could feel the sweat running down her spine and she had a headache that threatened to split her skull. As they entered the basilica the sudden shock of the cool, dark interior made her head swim, so that she had to reach out to catch hold of her husband's arm.

He looked at her in alarm. 'What is it? Are you ill?'

'It's nothing ... the heat. I shall be all right in a moment.'

He took her arm and supported her as they walked towards the thrones prepared for them in front of the altar, and by the time they reached them she had recovered. Later that day, however, he came to where she was sitting in the cool cloisters of the monastery where they had taken up residence.

'I am worried about you. You look pale.'

It was the first time he had shown such concern and she was touched. 'There is no need. It was the heat, nothing more.'

'Well, you need suffer it no longer. I have had enough of this city. Tomorrow we go north, back to Canossa.'

Canossa was perched on the top of precipitous cliffs on the flanks of the Apennines. After the dust and heat of Rome the verdant slopes of the mountains were as welcome as gentle rain on parched ground and Matilda felt herself revive like a flower left too long without water. It was clear that Henry felt the same. In Rome he had grown increasingly morose and ill-tempered, but now he declared that he had had enough of official business and was going to attend to his own pleasure. And to Henry pleasure had only one meaning – the hunt.

No one was surprised when she expressed her intention to join him. Years ago, soon after her marriage, she had become aware that ladies of the court frequently rode out with the hunters, so at the next opportunity she ordered her pony to be saddled and her knights to mount up, ready to ride with them. When Henry saw her, he was furious and peremptorily ordered her back to the castle. Matilda, mutinous, had watched the hunt depart and then called her knights to follow with her. The young men, disappointed at losing a day's sport, hesitated only briefly. It was not difficult to track the sound of horns and baying hounds and soon they were on the heels of the hunters. Suddenly the barking of the dogs rose to a crescendo and the horns sounded a different call and the whole company set off at the gallop. Matilda set her heels to the pony's sides and galloped after them. The pony was a willing beast, as excited by the noise and the other horses as she was, but it was too small to keep up and soon she was left far behind. Even her knights, carried away by their own momentum, were out of sight. Furiously, she cut at the pony's rump with her whip and in response it dropped its head and bucked, almost unseating her. The sound of the horns faded into the distance and she found herself alone. She urged the pony forward, but after a few paces she realized that it was lame. She dismounted, looped the reins over her arm and turned to go back the way she had come – except that she no longer knew which path to take. Brambles tore at her skirt and a low branch whipped across her face and she swallowed back tears of pain and fear. The forest was huge and she was completely lost.

There was a sound of hoofbeats, a cry of alarm and then Drogo flung himself off his horse and came to her side.

'My lady, forgive me! I should never have left your side. Please tell me you are not badly hurt.'

The look in his eyes almost unleashed the tears she was struggling to repress. Instead she took refuge in anger.

'How dare you ride away and leave me? I might have been killed.'

'Forgive me!' the young knight repeated. 'I know I was wrong to leave you. I will accept any punishment you give me, if only you will say you are not injured.'

'Of course I'm not. It's this stupid pony. He can't keep up and now he's lame.' But in spite of her efforts the tears spilled over and she felt them running down her cheeks. 'I'll have to walk back.'

He shook his head. 'No, my lady. There's no need for that. You can ride back on my courser.'

She looked at the tall, black horse and shook her head. 'I can't ride him. He's too big.'

'I will lead you.'

She considered the offer doubtfully. 'We are a long way from home. You can't walk all that way, leading me.'

'I could walk to Jerusalem and back if it would do you service, madam,' he replied.

She looked at him, flattered and amused in equal portions by his words, and was suddenly overtaken by giggles. For a moment he looked awkward, then he laughed with her.

'Then if you will permit it, I will mount behind you. My horse will carry us both easily.'

So in that manner they had returned to the castle. It was by ill luck that Henry had been forced to abandon the hunt, because his horse was lame, and rode into the courtyard immediately behind them. The sight of his young queen,

41

her gown torn and muddied and her face scratched, seated in front of Drogo and encircled by his arms, sent him into a fury. He ordered her to her rooms and it was only her tearful intercession that saved Drogo from being turned away to seek his fortune where he might. Nonetheless, Henry sent his physician to examine her and make sure that she was not seriously injured and the following morning she was attended by no lesser personage than the King's master of horse. Henry had come to the conclusion that, since she had shown herself determined to participate in his favourite sport, it would be more fitting for her to be suitably mounted and taught to ride properly. She learned quickly and showed herself an adept and daring horse-woman and now, whenever the King rode out, she was at his side. Drogo, meanwhile, had become her most devoted servant and was never far behind.

So today she rode out with the rest of the court and soon they were deep into the forest in pursuit of wild boar. The trees were dense and the paths through them narrow and winding, making it easy to lose sight of each other. Matilda found herself separated from Henry, forging her own route towards the sound of the hounds. A fallen tree trunk barred her way, but her mare jumped like a stag and she did not hesitate. On the far side there was a shallow ditch, overgrown with brambles, which tangled round the mare's forelegs. She pitched forward, somersaulted and Matilda flew through the air. In the endless second before she struck the ground she had time to fear that the horse would come down on top of her. Then there was only blackness.

She regained consciousness to the sensation of being held in strong arms. A voice was saying, 'Please, my lady, wake! Mary, Holy Mother, preserve her. Let her not die! Madam, I beg you, open your eyes!'

She opened them. Drogo's face gazed down into hers

and she was suddenly aware of how blue his eyes were. They are the same colour as the sky, she thought hazily. His face was pale and creased with anxiety, but as she stirred he caught a sharp breath of relief.

'Praise God! You are alive! I was so afraid ...' He looked suddenly abashed and began to loosen his hold on her. 'Forgive me, my lady ...'

She reached up and gripped his sleeve. 'No, don't let me go. Hold me!'

She saw him moisten his lips, hesitating, but his grip tightened again and he murmured, 'Don't be afraid. I am here. You are quite safe. Are you hurt?'

She considered the question for the first time and responded, 'No, not badly hurt. Just shaken, I think.'

They looked at each other. Something was stirring deep in her body, a sensation she had always tried to suppress as sinful, but now it did not feel like a sin. Later she was never sure whether she kissed him or he kissed her, but his tongue on hers was like liquid fire and the heat of it surged through her whole body. Then he pulled back with a gasp, his eyes wide and scared.

'My lady, forgive me! I never meant ... it was no disrespect....'

She came back to the reality of what had happened with a jolt. Her mind was in tumult. Had he insulted her? Had she demeaned herself? Who was at fault here? He removed his arms from round her and she staggered to her feet. He remained kneeling and there were tears in his eyes.

'Forgive me,' he whispered again.

She straightened her gown and brushed dead leaves from her shoulder. Looking down at him she said, 'We will not speak of this again. You will tell no one. You understand?'

His relief was written in every line of his face. 'No one,

my lady. Trust me, I shall never speak of it. Only let me continue to serve you.'

She felt a sob catch in her throat. 'What would I do without you? You are my most faithful servant ... my most faithful friend.'

He rose. 'Let me be that always. It is all I ask.'

She nodded, unable to speak, and turned away to where her horse was grazing peacefully, as if nothing had happened.

4

CANOSSA, 1117-18

IN THE DAYS that followed it was remarked upon by Henry's courtiers that Matilda was more devoted than ever to her duties as his consort. She was at his side when he sat in council; she was with him at dinner when he entertained his vassals and potential allies. She flattered those who held back out of pride, flirted with those who wavered out of doubt, was cold to those who presumed too much. She attended mass every morning and took the sacraments, and at confession she admitted to such minor transgressions that her indulgent confessor gave her the lightest of penances. As Christmas approached she was everywhere, consulting with the cooks, employing minstrels and jongleurs, overseeing the decoration of the great hall. Henry's Christmas court was the most glittering occasion seen in those parts for many years. When the musicians struck up for dancing after the feast she led the measures with such grace that all eyes were fixed upon her. She danced with one lord after another, but never looked in Drogo's direction. Only in the privacy of her own apartments, with none but her ladies-in-waiting as witnesses, she was given to fits of abstraction, gazing out of the window or staring blankly at a book without taking in a word. These episodes were interspersed with sudden outbursts of irritability, which occasionally ended in tears.

The twelve days of Christmas were only just over when news came from Rome and Henry called a council.

'Pope Paschal is dead and those whoresons have elected John of Gaeta to succeed him. He is calling himself Gelasius II. He has always been a supporter of those renegade bishops who are seeking to deprive me of my rights I must go to Rome immediately and get rid of him, and ensure the election of someone who will support my claim.'

With Henry gone, Matilda's moods became more volatile than ever. One evening, when she was being prepared for bed, Magda gave a deep sigh as she brushed her hair. Matilda raised her eyes from her lap.

'What ails you? Are you sick?'

'No, madam. I was thinking of a friend I had when I was a young girl.'

'What about her?'

'She fell desperately in love with a young man who was one of her father's squires. Of course, there was no question of marriage. He was far beneath her in rank. She tried to forget him, but it was useless. The more she tried to behave as if nothing was amiss, the more miserable she felt in her heart of hearts. And the young man, too, pined in secret. He lost all his pleasure in his usual pursuits and was frequently taken to task for neglecting his duties. His friends began to fear that he had contracted some illness that was slowly stealing his life away.'

She put up her hand to still Magda's, but lowered her eyes again. 'What became of them both?'

'I hardly like to say, madam, lest you should disapprove.'

'Tell me.'

'The young lady had a faithful servant who saw how she was suffering, and one night she brought the young man to her bedchamber so that they could ease the pangs of love in each other's arms.'

'But that was a sin ... was it not?'

'In the eyes of the Church, perhaps. But I do not believe it was a sin in the eyes of God. After all, why has he put into us the desire, the need, for love? St Paul instructs us to love one another, because love is of God, does he not?'

'But carnal love?' She was trembling.

'God created our bodies as well as our souls. He implanted these desires in us. Why should a poor girl or a poor boy pine away for want of a few moments in each other's arms? It is all very well for nuns and priests to abjure the pleasures of the flesh, but to my mind it is a sin to let another human creature suffer for want of a little kindness.'

She got up slowly from her stool and turned to the bed. 'And what became of your friend and the young man?'

'They had great joy in each other. It could not last long, of course. The lady's father had already chosen a husband for her and she had to go to him – but she told me that she never regretted her decision, for she had known the pure happiness of love fulfilled, and it was a memory she could treasure all her life.' As Matilda slipped off her robe and climbed into bed she added, 'There is a young man in like case here in the castle. He droops and pines and his friends fear for his life. Perhaps, madam, you could counsel him. Shall I send him to you?'

She met the older woman's eyes and read encouragement. Desire and conscience struggled briefly. 'Send him. I will do my best to ease his mind.'

A short time later there was a faint knock at the door.

She sat up and drew the sheet to her chin. The bed curtains were open and the room was lit by firelight and starlight from the window. In a voice hardly above a whisper she called, 'Come in.'

Drogo slipped into the room like a shadow and stood just inside the door. 'You sent for me, my lady?'

'I am told you are in need of counsel, and comfort.'

'Indeed, madam. In dire need.'

'Come closer. I will help you if I can.'

He moved to stand by the bed. 'I am sore wounded. No one but you can staunch the bleeding.'

'Then let me try.'

His limbs were hot and he trembled as if in the grip of a fever, but when she felt his body pressed against her own something surged up within her as if a dam had broken. She clutched him close, her mouth seeking his, and the kiss was so fierce that she felt her lips bruised, but she did not draw back. His hands moved over her body and then he broke the kiss with a gasp, to fasten his mouth to her breast. She had never experienced this desire, this urgency of need before and when his hand slipped between her legs she opened to him eagerly. There was no pain this time, only a sense of triumph as she took him into her and heard his sob of joy as he came.

Afterwards, they lay gazing into each other's eyes in the light from the fire. He whispered, 'I am yours, body and soul, now and for all eternity.'

Her joy drained away like water from a leaking vessel. 'You must not say that. You know it cannot be. Our paths must take different courses.'

He reached out, his hand gripping the back of her neck, his expression suddenly fierce. 'Do not tell me that this is the first and last time! You cannot be so cruel.'

'No! I did not mean that. Only that we cannot be

together always. The time must come ...'

'Until it does, let us seize whatever happiness we can find. That is all I ask.'

'Yes,' she whispered. 'Let us do that.'

In the weeks that followed he came to her every night. With the King absent it was not difficult for Magda to smuggle him up to her room. She existed in an animal world, where thought was banished and only the senses were real. By day she performed her duties with such serenity that no one suspected any change, but she moved and spoke like an automaton, living only for the night to come. She continued to go to mass and take the sacraments and her confessor still found no cause to chide her. Her mind was closed to all thoughts of the future, or to any danger to her immortal soul.

Too soon, a herald arrived with a message from her husband. Henry was on his way back. With the same unnatural calm, she ensured that the castle was prepared for his arrival. He swung down from his horse, kissed her hand formally, and turned to his steward.

'Call a council meeting for tomorrow morning. There is much to discuss.'

'I have secured the election of Maurice Bourdan as Pope Gregory VIII,' he told the assembled noblemen, 'but Gelasius remains in the Vatican and many are calling Gregory the anti-pope. God rot their heretical souls! However, there are more pressing concerns. I have news from Germany. The bishops are fomenting rebellion and the men I left in charge are losing control. It is imperative that I return with all possible speed. The Queen will remain here as my regent.'

There was an intake of breath from the men round the table. A girl of sixteen years to be given such power!

Matilda's only thought was that Henry would be out of the way again.

Henry continued. 'She will require help and advice, of course. Philip, as imperial chancellor for Italy, you will of course remain here. I will also leave my chaplain, Hartmann, to assist the Queen, and Judge Iubaldus will be on hand to advise on matters of law and custom.'

'When do you plan to leave, my liege?' one of the courtiers enquired.

'In ten days from now. I plan to be in Augsburg by Easter.'

The next morning Matilda was suddenly seized by a bout of nausea. Magda brought a basin for her to vomit into and wiped her lips afterwards.

'Is this the first time you have sickened like this?'

'Yes. I must have eaten something bad last night.'

Magda's expression was taut. 'Perhaps. Tell me, when was your last flux?'

'My last flux? I don't know. I always forget. But you should know.'

'God help me, I should remember! Fool that I am, I should have taken note.'

'Oh, I know when it was. It was the day the King killed that great boar. I did not hunt with him because my stomach was griping and I was angry because I missed it.'

'Not since then? That was before … before I first brought Drogo to you.'

Matilda stared at her, and the churning in her guts had nothing to do with her earlier nausea. 'You don't think … '

'What other explanation can there be? You are not so innocent that you do not understand.'

'I am with child?'

'God help us, yes!'

'But I can't … What can I do? I cannot have a child!'

'Think. Have you lain with your husband?'

'No! Not since we were first married. You know that.'

'Then you must make sure that you lie with him before he leaves for Germany.'

'Lie with Henry? I cannot.'

'You must! He is going away. Who knows when you will see him again. We can say the child came early. He will not know any different.'

'But I cannot bear to lie with him.' She was weeping now.

Magda took her by the shoulders and shook her. 'If you value your life, you will. And not just your own. Do you imagine Drogo would be allowed to live if the truth came out? Or me?'

She stared up into the older woman's eyes. 'But how can I make him lie with me? He never comes to my room.'

Magda's grip relaxed and she knelt to bring her eyes level with her mistress's. 'He will come gladly enough if you let him see you are willing. You know well enough what power you have over men. Drogo is not the only one who would give half his fortune to bed you. I have seen you smile and flirt and draw them to you.'

'But it means nothing!'

'Not to you, perhaps. But use those wiles on the King and he will be as enthralled as they are.'

'The doctors told him he should not bed me in case I quickened. They said I was too young to bear a child.'

'But you are not too young now. The Church states that a wife owes a duty to her husband, and he to her. Tell the King that it troubles you that you have not fulfilled that duty. He longs for an heir. He will not hesitate.'

She felt bile rising in her throat again. 'But to let him touch me … to let him do that …'

Magda got to her feet and regarded her with something close to contempt. 'Do you imagine you are the only wife who has to close her eyes and grit her teeth? You have experienced the delights of love, now it is time to pay the price.'

'What about Drogo? What must I tell him?'

'Tell him it is finished. Now you have to be a wife – and a queen.'

That evening at dinner she leant close to Henry, feeding him choice morsels from her own plate, touching his hand and whispering in his ear. He had been drinking, but he was not drunk. To begin with he seemed amused; then she saw a different look in his eyes, a mixture of lust and suspicion. He pulled her close to him and muttered, 'What game are you playing? What is it you want of me?'

She forced herself to meet his eyes and smile; then she lowered her lashes in pretended embarrassment. 'My lord, I am afraid you will think me forward and shameless if I tell you what is in my mind.'

'Tell me.'

She had prepared in advance what she was going to say. She drew a breath and made herself continue. 'I have been thinking, it is now four years since we were wed. In all that time you have been a most gentle and understanding husband. You have not demanded of me those duties that a wife owes her husband. But now, my conscience troubles me. The Church teaches that there is a marital debt owed between husband and wife. I believe it is time that I began to pay that debt.'

He took her chin in his hand and forced her to look at him. 'Is this your own desire, or has some priest urged you to it?'

She swallowed and responded with an effort, 'It is my own wish, sir.'

'Then your wish shall be fulfilled.' To her alarm he seized her hand and pulled her to her feet. All round the great hall conversation ceased and men rose in consternation. It was against all custom for the King to leave in the middle of the feast.

He waved them back into their seats. 'Eat, my friends, drink and take your ease. I have more pressing business to attend to.'

He almost dragged her out of the hall and up to his own bedchamber. His squires were at his heels, ready to attend to his needs, but he dismissed them and turned to her.

'So, at last you come to understand your duty as a wife as well as a queen. Let us see how well you can fulfil it.'

She had schooled herself to this. She must not seem too eager. He must believe that she was still without experience. But she must make sure that the act is accomplished. If she seemed unwilling, he might yet decide that there was more pleasure to be found elsewhere. As his fingers fumbled with the laces of her dress, it was not hard to seem shy, and when he had undressed her to her shift she clasped her hands across her breasts in a gesture of defence that he saw as modesty.

'Come now, there is naught to be ashamed of. We are man and wife and such shame has no place between us.'

He picked her up bodily and carried her to the bed and then there was no need for pretence, for he was oblivious. He was not so brutal as she remembered, but he did not, as Drogo had always done, take pains to arouse her before he entered. Her gasp of pain was not simulated but, mercifully, he came quickly and it was all over. Afterwards, instead of rolling off her and getting up, he propped himself on his elbows and looked down into her face.

'So, my queen, now we are truly one. I have waited a long time for this day. The pity is, we have only a few days before I must leave you.'

'Yes,' she answered breathlessly, 'it is unfortunate. But at least you may leave me with a lasting memento.'

He laughed aloud. 'Pray God it be so! But I fear one night may not be enough.'

It was not just the one night. He came to her bed the next night and the next, until she pretended exhaustion and begged a night of uninterrupted rest. That evening she made sure that his wine cup was kept filled and when he eventually staggered off to bed she was fairly sure that she was safe for the time being. As soon as the castle had settled to sleep, Magda brought Drogo to her bedchamber. He was deathly pale and the look in his eyes reminded her of a trapped animal.

'The King has been with you, these last nights. Has he forced himself upon you?'

'No. It was at my wish.'

'Why? Magda said you have to tell me something. What has happened?'

'Can you not guess?' She was furious with him for his failure to understand. 'I am with child!'

He stepped back as if she had struck him. 'With child? My child?'

'Whose else?'

'What shall we do? If the King finds out ...'

'Do you not understand yet? That is why I had to persuade him to lie with me.'

'You will pass the child off as his?'

'What else can I do?'

He backed away from her, shaking his head. 'He will never be deceived. The child will not resemble him.'

'We must pray that it resembles me. Henry is desperate

54

for an heir. If it is a boy, he will be quick to acknowledge it.' She moved to him and grabbed his arm. 'Do you not see? It is our only chance. And with the King away, we can have more time together.'

He pulled free of her. 'No! We have sinned most grievously. This is God's punishment. I cannot lie with you while you are with child. The Church forbids it. And I can never claim the child as my own. I shall go away. I must find somewhere where I can repent and try to expiate my sin.'

'No!' She flung herself at him, clutching him round the neck. 'You cannot leave me! How can I bear this on my own?'

'That will be your punishment. You will bear the child and for the rest of your life you will have to pretend that it is Henry's. How could I stand by and watch that? I can have no part in it.' He detached her grip and moved to the door. 'Farewell. By morning I shall be gone.'

'No! No!' she sobbed, stretching out her arms to him, but the door opened and closed again and she was alone.

Henry departed for Germany and Matilda kept to her room, giving out that she was ill. It was not far from the truth, since she continued to suffer violent bouts of vomiting. She let it be known that Drogo had been given leave to return to Germany with the King, to visit his mother who was ailing. No one could tell her where he really was.

As the days lengthened her sickness eased and she began to resume her duties. Letters were dispatched to Henry to tell him that his wife was expecting their child, and messages came back which assured her of her husband's delight in the news. At night, she continued to weep secretly, desolate in the absence of Drogo, but by day she forced herself to seem content in the expectation of the birth, and little by little, as the child grew, she began to find comfort in the thought that she carried some remembrance of their love.

It was midsummer when a messenger arrived from England and sought a private audience. His face was grave and she felt a tremor of fear.

'Well? What news do you have for me?'

'Madam, I fear I bring sad tidings. Your lady mother is dead.'

'Dead! When?'

'In May, madam. I am sorry that the news has not reached you before, but the King your father is campaigning in Normandy and it took some time for word to reach him. Then messages were sent first to Germany. It was not understood that you had remained here, rather than travelling with your husband.' His eyes dropped to her protruding belly. 'I see now that it would not have been wise for you to attempt the journey. Please believe me that I am greatly saddened to be the one to bring you such distressing news.'

She rose and walked away to gaze out of the window. She could hardly remember her mother but she recalled her as a beneficent presence in her childhood. Since she was sent to Germany there had been regular letters assuring her of her mother's continuing concern and prayers for the welfare of her soul. She knew that she could never have confessed her sin to the woman many regarded as a saint, but there had been some comfort in the thought that one pure soul was interceding for her. Drogo had spoken of God's punishment. Suddenly she found herself asking if this was the beginning. She dismissed the messenger without looking at him and went up to her bedchamber. There she threw herself down on the bed and gave way to a storm of weeping.

Abruptly, the sobs gave way to cries of pain and Magda, who had hastened to her mistress's side, caught her arm in alarm.

'What ails you? Madam? Where does it hurt?'

'My belly ... the child ... argh! What is happening?'

Magda pulled up her skirts and cried out in shock. The coverlet was drenched in blood. She ran to the door and shouted to one of the waiting women. 'The midwife! Fetch the midwife! Hurry!'

By the time the midwife arrived an object which resembled a skinned rabbit had been hastily swathed in a towel and carried away. Matilda lay ashen faced and shivering but she was no longer weeping.

Magda stooped over her, wiping her face with a damp cloth. 'Rest now, my lady. It's all over.'

'It is dead, is it not?'

'Yes, madam. So small, it could not live. But take comfort. There will be others.'

She moistened dry lips. 'No. It is God's judgement on me. I have sinned and I am justly punished.'

5

GERMANY, 1119-25

MATILDA RODE INTO Augsburg at the head of a splendid entourage and was greeted with acclaim by the citizens who lined the streets. Her reputation had preceded her and they knew her as 'good Queen Matilda', the pious ruler who dealt justly with high and low. But this was not the high-spirited girl who had ridden out of the city with her husband four years earlier. This was a woman who was every inch the Queen Empress and bore herself with fitting gravity. Henry met her at the city gates and greeted her with suitable ceremony and they rode in procession to the cathedral to give thanks for her safe arrival. Then they went on to his castle, where a great feast had been prepared. It was not until the last sweetmeats had been consumed and the last draught of hippocras swallowed, and the attendant lords and ladies had gone to their lodgings and the household knights had spread their pallets among the rushes and the debris on the floor to sleep, that she and Henry were able to retire to the privacy of the solar above.

He waved away the squire who offered more wine and seated himself opposite her. It struck her that he had aged since she last saw him. There were lines around his eyes and mouth that were not there before. They regarded each other in silence and she knew what it was that hung in the air between them. To speak of it was hard, but to remain silent would have been like leaving an open wound to fester.

She said, 'I am sorry about the child.'

He shook his head. 'It was not your fault. It was the will of God. It seems He has decreed that I should not beget an heir.'

She stared at him with a mixture of shock and relief. 'How can you say that? There is still time.'

'No. I have consulted with several learned churchmen. As a boy I sinned by rebelling against my father. I had myself crowned while he was still alive. God has turned his face against the Salian house. After my death the crown must pass to someone more worthy.'

The release of tension made her shiver. For a moment she could think of nothing to say. Then she murmured, 'Well, God's will be done.'

He shifted in his chair and she thought she saw him wince.

'Are you well, sir?'

'Well enough. I should be better if those rebellious bishops could be brought to heel.'

'This matter of the investiture – is it still unresolved?'

'They still insist that only the Pope or his legate can invest them with the symbols of their office.'

'Can you not find a compromise?'

'Why should I? I am a divinely anointed king. It is right that I should have supreme authority over all my subjects.'

'At least Gelasius is dead. But your choice as Pope, Gregory, has not been much help.'

'Bourdon? God rot him! He has skulked around in

southern Italy and never attempted to establish himself. So now we have to deal with the very man who pronounced my excommunication, Guy of Varenne – Pope Calixtus II as he calls himself now.'

'The prospects are not good, then.'

'You might expect that, but Calixtus is no fool. He wants a resolution to the problem as much as I do. He has suggested a meeting. He is going to hold a council at Rheims and suggests we might meet at Mouzon while he is in the area.'

'Have you agreed?'

'Reluctantly. But I shall take a big enough force with me to make sure he understands I am negotiating from a position of strength. I want you with me. From the reports I have had from Italy, your insights could be valuable.' He got to his feet with a groan. 'It's late and you must be tired. I'll say good night.'

She rose too. 'My lord, are you sure you are well? Are you in pain?'

'A griping in the guts. It's nothing.'

'What do your physicians say?'

He gave a mirthless grin. 'They tell me not to eat so much.'

At the door of her bedchamber he took her hand and kissed it formally. 'Good night, madam.'

'Good night, my lord.' She made a curtsey and went to her solitary bed, where her waiting women undressed her. Magda was not one of them. She had been given a generous pension and sent back to her family.

'God's blood!' Henry was pacing the floor of the solar in his castle at Mouzon. His face was purple with rage. 'Does he expect me to come to him as a penitent, barefoot and clad only in my shirt, as my father did to Pope Gregory?

I'll see him burn in hell before I do that!'

Matilda waited for him to pause for breath and then asked, 'The Pope will not negotiate?'

'Negotiate? He is not even here. It seems when he saw that I was bringing the army with me he fled, like the craven coward he is, fearing that I intend to take him prisoner, as I did with Paschal at Ponte Mammolo.'

'Ponte Mammolo?'

'Oh, you won't remember it. You were only a child at the time. It was before we were married. Paschal refused to crown me as emperor unless I renounced the right of investiture. It was the only way to make him see sense.'

'I do remember now. Archbishop Bruno explained it to me. So Calixtus is gone?'

'Yes, damn him! And he has renewed the sentence of excommunication and appointed Adalbert as papal legate. Adalbert of all people! He has never forgiven me for shutting him up in Triers. He—' He broke off abruptly and clutched his stomach with a groan. His face had gone from red to ashen and he staggered to a chair and collapsed into it.

She turned to an attendant page. 'Fetch the King's physician. Quickly! Quickly!'

The boy ran out and she went to kneel by her husband's chair. 'What is it? Are you sick?'

'This pain in my belly! Is it any wonder I cannot digest my food when I am so plagued by these intransigent priests? Am I never to be allowed to govern my own kingdom in peace?'

'You must try to be calm. It avails naught to get yourself into such a rage.'

The physician arrived and diagnosed an excess of choler. He recommended blood letting but Henry would have none of it. Under protest he swallowed a bitter-tasting draught carried by the doctor's apprentice and slowly his colour returned. The doctor left and, seeing Henry in a calmer mood, Matilda decided the moment had come to speak.

'You know, do you not, that the King my father suffered the same difficulties over investiture that you do? But many years ago now he arrived at a compromise with his bishops.'

'A compromise? A surrender!'

'Not so, my lord. True he gave up the right to invest with the symbols of spiritual power, but the bishops must still do homage to him for their temporal rights. They are still his vassals.'

He grunted but made no other comment. She persisted. 'Perhaps it might help to consult with him. He may be able to suggest a way forward.'

'And let the world see me running to my father-in-law because I cannot control my own realm?'

'No. Surely it is a sign of strength to confirm your friendship. Our countries have long been allies. I am the living proof of that.'

He looked at her from narrowed eyes and she braced herself for a new outburst of fury, but instead he said, 'The arrangement works? Your father has suffered no loss of power by it?'

She spread her hands. 'I know only what I learn in letters from England. But I know that the peace he has made with the Church has allowed him to turn his attention to other matters, such as putting down rebellion among his Norman barons.'

Henry brooded for a moment. 'Very well. I will send an embassy to England. They can consult with the King your father and report back.'

'My letters tell me that he is presently holding court

in his castle of Gisors. That cannot be more than seventy leagues from here. If he could be persuaded to meet us halfway ...'

'No! Calixtus will see it as a sign of weakness if I have to go running to Henry. I cannot afford that.'

She stood up. 'I could go. The monastery of St Quentin is roughly halfway between here and Gisors. It is well known as a place of pilgrimage. No one would be surprised if I should choose to visit it. And if my father were to chance to make a pilgrimage there at the same time ... Well, surely it is natural that a father might wish to meet with his daughter after so many years.'

Henry gave her a long look. Then he said, 'They told me when I married you that you were clever. They were right!'

Some days later Henry's steward came to the room where Matilda was sitting with her ladies-in-waiting. They were working at their embroidery, embellishing copes and altar cloths for use in the royal chapels. She was reading *The Monologian* of Archbishop Anselm of Canterbury, a meditation on the nature of goodness.

The steward coughed apologetically. 'My lady, there is a man outside who begs an audience with you.'

'What sort of man?'

'An itinerant preacher, madam. A very rough sort of fellow. But he insists that you will know him. His name is Norbert.'

'Norbert! Of course I know him. He was one of the emperor's chaplains when I first came to live here. Send him in at once.'

The figure who entered was very different from the man she remembered. Then, although nominally a canon in holy orders, he was as worldly and as finely dressed as any of Henry's courtiers. Now, to her horror, he was dressed in a filthy robe of rough homespun wool and barefoot, and he was so thin that the bones of his face seem to protrude through his skin.

With an effort she recovered her self-possession and rose to greet him. 'You are most welcome. But I see that you have fallen on hard times. Please sit and I will send for food and drink.'

He shook his head, smiling. 'Thank you, madam, but I have no need of either. I have fallen indeed, but fallen into the arms of our Lord. He sustains me in my every need.'

'Then, sit at least and tell me what has happened to you since you left my husband's service.'

He seated himself in the chair which one of her ladies brought over. 'I am surprised that you remember me. You were only a girl when I left with your husband to visit the Pope, the first time he went into Italy.'

'I remember you well. You were always kind to a girl who was far from home and among strangers.'

'I am glad of it. You ask what has happened to me. You know, of course, that on that expedition your husband took His Holiness prisoner at Ponte Mammolo. That was a cause of grave distress to me. I could not reconcile myself to the idea that God's appointed could be so shamefully treated. It was then that I began to consider leaving the emperor's service. A few months later I was riding alone through the forest when a terrible thunderstorm broke. My horse was frightened by the noise and threw me. I must have lain unconscious for a long time, for when I woke my clothes were completely soaked through, but I knew that God had spoken to me. I was like St Paul on the road to Damascus and I knew God had a purpose for me. I returned to my home in Xanten and placed myself under the authority of Abbot Cono. By the grace of God I was ordained to the priesthood soon after. Since then I have travelled the world preaching His word.'

'But you look so thin and your clothes are so worn. Won't you let me help you? At least I could see that you had a new habit, and some shoes.'

He shook his head again. 'The Bible tell us that we should take no thought for our life, what we should eat, nor for our bodies, what we should put on. I thank you for your offer but that is not why I came. I have a message for you.'

'A message? From whom?'

'From Drogo, who was once your knight.'

'Drogo?' For a moment she could not speak. For more than a year she had been making cautious enquiries about his whereabouts, but to no avail. She saw that her ladies were listening, though they pretended to be absorbed in their work. She stood up. 'Come with me. We will talk privately.'

She led him to her private chapel. There she turned to him. 'What message have you for me?'

'That Drogo is well and has turned to God. He is one of my followers and plans to take his vows and enter a monastery.'

She turned away, clasping her hands together to still them. 'What has he told you of what passed between us?'

'Nothing. But he told me that he thought it might ease your mind to speak of it.'

For a moment she said nothing. Then she dropped to her knees before him. 'Father, will you hear my confession?'

The abbot of the monastery of St Quentin received her with due respect and she was shown to a room in the guest house. It was well furnished. The bed curtains were brocade and there were tapestries on the walls depicting biblical scenes; a fire burnt in the hearth and a servant brought warm water for her to wash her hands and face and then served a meal which had nothing to do with monastic austerity. Her ladies murmured among themselves as they ate, but she was restless and too much on edge to enjoy the food. Her father had sent messages promising to meet her but she knew only too well how easily he could be distracted by some dissension among his vassals, or even, she suspected, the prospect of good hunting. She had no real memory of him, except as a distant and slightly frightening presence. He had been given the nickname of Henry Beauclerc, because he had been educated by churchmen and could read and write and understand Latin, but the letters they had exchanged had been formal and gave no indication of his feelings. She knew him only by reputation as a brave leader in battle and a wily negotiator in the council chamber.

Dusk was falling when she heard the clatter of hoofs in the courtyard below. Looking down, she saw him ride in with a small escort of knights. He dismounted but from this height she could not see him clearly. She had only an impression of a thickset figure of medium height, who nevertheless moved with energy and agility. Henry disappeared into the building and she was left to wait for a summons. It was possible that, after his journey, he might not wish to meet her until the next day. She could only try to school herself to patience.

The bells rang to call the monks to vespers and she heard the muffled sound of their voices singing the holy office. Then the lay brother who brought their dinner tapped at the door.

'Madam, the lord abbot asks that you will attend him in his solar.'

She bade her ladies remain where they were, wrapped a cloak round her shoulders and followed the man along the cloister to the abbot's house. He knocked on a door, then bowed and moved away. From inside a voice louder and gruffer than the abbot's instructed her to enter. She hesitated, straightening her shoulders and adjusting her veil, which the breeze had disordered. In the brief pause she reminded herself that she was a queen and an empress. Then she pushed open the door and went in.

Henry was standing in front of the fireplace. He was wearing a knee-length woollen tunic dyed a deep blue and his travelling cloak of Italian red lined with squirrel fur was thrown across the back of a chair. She saw that his dark hair was streaked with grey and his face was weathered to the colour of leather. For a moment they looked at each other in silence. Then it occurred to her that the character of a dutiful daughter was likely to serve her better than that of the Queen Empress. She curtsied and lowered her eyes.

'My lord father.'

He crossed to her and raised her. 'Daughter, welcome. I trust you are in good health?'

'I am, sir. I hope the same is true for you.'

'Well enough, I thank you. Pray, be seated. Will you take some wine?'

She sat and thanked him and he poured wine for them both from a flagon on a side table.

He said, 'I hear good reports of your conduct. You have proved yourself a worthy wife to the emperor.'

'I hope so.'

'Is your husband well?'

'He suffers from a disorder of the stomach. His doctors diagnose an excess of choler.'

'He should be bled.'

'He has been, much against his will. But it seems to have given little relief. He is greatly troubled in mind by this continuing dissension over the matter of investiture.'

'Ah!' Henry nodded and stretched his legs to the fire. 'I can sympathize with him there.'

'But you have reached an agreement with your own bishops, have you not?'

'I thought I had, until the Pope held this last council in Rheims. Then he had the gall to consecrate Thurstan as Archbishop of York without any reference to me and without any requirement to pay homage.'

She frowned. This was not what she hoped to hear. 'Does that mean the compromise has broken down?'

'Not permanently. Sooner or later this whole matter has to be resolved, but in this respect I believe your husband the emperor and I can help each other.'

'That is good news! It is what my husband desires also. That is why I am here.'

'You can tell him that he has my support. If we show a united front, Calixtus may be more willing to come to the negotiating table. But tell him this also. The only way to find a resolution is by compromise. We shall both have to put aside our pride.'

'I will tell him.'

They were silent for a moment. Then she said, 'I was greatly distressed to hear of my mother's death.'

'Indeed. It is a great loss. She was a woman as close to sainthood as it is possible for a mortal to be. It pained me deeply that I was so hard pressed in Normandy that I was unable to attend her funeral.'

'I know how difficult it must have been for you. But since your great victory at Brèmule you must be in a stronger position.'

'I am, thanks be to God. But there are still enemies

who would be yapping at my heels if they saw any sign of weakness. Louis of France is always ready to support anyone who challenges me. That is why I must seek to strengthen alliances wherever I can. I have it in mind to marry again.'

'Marry!' This came as a shock. 'To whom?'

'I am in discussions with Count Godfrey of Louvain to wed his daughter Adeliza.'

'Adeliza!' The image of a young girl, distraught and tearful, rose in her memory. 'But ... she is so young. She is hardly older than I am.'

'Quite. Young enough to bear children.'

'Children? But you already have – ' She stopped herself. Henry's many illegitimate children were an open secret, but not relevant here. 'You already have an heir. How does my brother William Adelin?'

'Well, thank God. I have arranged a marriage for him too. He is to wed Fulk of Anjou's daughter.'

'Fulk! But I thought he was a sworn enemy.'

'He was, but a substantial sum of money convinced him to change sides. He plans to make a pilgrimage to the Holy Land and he needed the cash. Louis has finally accepted William as my heir and he has done homage for our territories in France, so the succession is secure.'

'So, what need is there for you to re-marry?' She could not prevent herself from speaking, though she did not understand why the idea should distress her.

Henry chuckled. 'A king must have a consort, and the girl is comely. And a man cannot have too many sons.' His expression became serious again. 'On the subject of children – you have not given your husband an heir yet.' He fixed her with sharp, dark eyes. 'Are you barren?'

She felt the colour rise in her face and forced herself to answer calmly. 'No, I am not. There was a child, a few months after Henry left me in Italy as his regent. It did not live.'

'Ah.' Her father looked relieved. 'These things happen and we must bend to the will of God. But if there has been one child there can be more. Yet this must have been some time ago – two years at least.'

'But for most of that time I have been in Italy and Henry has been in Germany. I returned less than a month ago.'

'Of course. There is time yet, then.'

She decided not to mention Henry's surprising decision with regard to the succession. That was a problem that could be put off for years.

Her father stood up and yawned. 'It is getting late and I'm sure we are both tired. I will wish you good night, daughter.'

She rose too and he took her hand and kissed it, then kissed her on both cheeks. 'I am glad we have had this meeting. I have left it too long. Perhaps soon you can visit me in England.'

'I should like that.'

'Then we must arrange it. Good night.'

She dipped a curtsey. 'Good night, Father.'

Messengers rode backwards and forwards between the two Henries and the Pope and slowly the outlines of a compromise began to emerge. Matilda was glad to find her husband more amenable to reason, but she was also concerned. He seemed to tire quickly and the pains in his stomach were getting worse.

A year passed and at the beginning of Advent another messenger rode into Henry's castle at Goslar. Matilda was standing by a window, watching the last autumn leaves drifting to earth, when her husband's steward came into the room.

'Madam, the King your husband desires your presence in the solar.'

One look at Henry's face told her that something bad had happened.

'I have grave news from England,' he said. 'Your brother William is dead.'

'Dead? How?'

'Drowned. It seems he was returning from Normandy with your father after receiving the homage of the barons there. A sea captain, the son of the very man who captained your grandfather's ship when he conquered the English, begged the King to travel in his new ship, which he boasted was the fastest yet built. Your father refused since he had already embarked many of his people on a different vessel, but he gave permission for William and his friends to sail in the *White Ship* – that was the name of the new one. No one seems to know exactly what happened, but the ship struck a rock and capsized. There were only two survivors.'

'And my brother was not one of them.' She found her way to a chair and sat. She had not seen her brother since they were babies, so there was no sense of personal loss, but the implications of the news were too many to take in at once. As an afterthought, she crossed herself and murmured, 'God rest his soul.'

Henry supplied an automatic 'Amen'.

'My poor father! It will be a terrible blow to him.'

'The letter speaks of his unassuagable grief. He refuses all comfort. And William was not the only one lost. His half-brother Richard and his half-sister were also drowned.'

'What comfort could there be? The death of Richard and the girl will sadden him, but they were not legitimate. William was his only heir.'

'That is the crucial point, as far as we are concerned.

Who is next in line for the succession?'

'I am his only other legitimate child – but the English barons will never accept a woman as ruler. The only other claimant will be the other William, William Clito, the son of my Uncle Robert, whom they call Curthose.'

Henry grunted. 'That won't please your father. He and Robert were at each other's throats for years until your father overcame him at Tinchbrai. He still has him in prison There can't be any love lost between him and Clito.'

'And Louis of France has always preferred Clito. This is going to make the situation in Normandy very unstable again.'

'Best we can hope for is your father goes ahead with his marriage to Adeliza and gets himself another son as soon as possible.'

'Perhaps.' She shook her head. 'I don't know. An infant son could never rival Clito for the throne.'

'Then pray that your father lives long enough to see him grow up.'

Her father was obviously thinking along the same lines. Early in the new year a letter arrived from him.

'My father has married Adeliza,' she reported to her husband.

'Good! Best thing he could do,' Henry responded. 'Godfrey of Louvain has been loyal to me ever since I released him from prison.'

'At my intercession,' she could not resist pointing out.

'As you say. The point is, the marriage strengthens the alliance between our two countries.'

She sighed and shook her head. 'Perhaps. But I feel sorry for Adeliza. Poor girl. I fancy she will have little joy in the match.'

Negotiations with the Pope dragged on but the need

for a settlement was becoming ever more urgent. Henry's status as an excommunicate allowed any dissatisfied baron or prelate to promote rebellion. He was still troubled by recurrent pains in his abdomen and was less combative than before. With wry humour, Matilda reflected that he had no stomach for fighting.

They had not long returned to Goslar when an embassy arrived from Henry of England. He wished Matilda to visit him.

'Do you want to go?' her husband asked.

She considered. 'It is not an attractive prospect. I have no happy memories of my childhood there, and no friends that I can remember. And I do not look forward to meeting my father again in his present frame of mind. I hear he is still inconsolable and given to violent changes of mood. But I am curious. England is the land of my birth, after all.'

'And you are Henry's only legitimate child. So far there seems to be no sign that Adeliza has conceived.' He sat forward in his chair. 'Do you suppose he might be considering appointing you as his heir?' His eyes brightened. 'That would unite the two kingdoms. Imagine! We would rule an empire greater even than Caesar's.'

She neglected to point out that the Roman empire stretched into eastern lands far beyond their control. Instead she said, 'And who would rule after us, since you have decided that God has turned his face away from your line?'

Henry slumped back. 'True, true. But all the same I think you should go. You owe your father that much.'

She made her preparations with mixed feelings. There was no question of crossing French territory to reach Normandy. King Louis' hostility meant that she would never be granted safe conduct through his realm. Instead she must go through Flanders; then at Barfleur her father would have a ship waiting to take her across the narrow sea. Her only experience of a sea crossing was when she came to Germany as a child of eight and her memories were not reassuring. Those, combined with the disaster of the *White Ship*, meant that she looked forward to the voyage with considerable trepidation. It was a relief when word came from Flanders. Count Charles would not permit her to pass through his territory. As a vassal of the King of France he did not wish to offend his overlord. The visit had to be abandoned.

Finally, the prolonged negotiations with Rome looked like bearing fruit. A meeting was arranged at the city of Worms between Henry and three representatives of the Pope: Lambert, Cardinal Bishop of Ostia, and two other cardinals, Saxo and Gregory. After long deliberations an agreement was reached. Henry would have the right to invest the new bishops with their temporal authority, symbolized by the giving of a sceptre, and they would then receive the tokens of their spiritual authority, the ring and the crozier, from a papal legate. Henry's excommunication was rescinded.

Afterwards, Henry grudgingly admitted to relief but he was far from happy. 'My great ancestor Charlemagne would never have given in. '

'At least you have the right to be present when new bishops are elected,' she pointed out. 'That way you will still have great influence. It is the same compromise that was arrived at in England and it seems to have worked well enough for my father. And now that you are in communion with the Church again we can concentrate on bringing those rebellious barons to heel.'

Over the ensuing months Henry criss-crossed his domains, suppressing rebellions, calming dissent, restoring order, and Matilda was at his side constantly. Meanwhile her father's difficulties in Normandy proliferated. Fulk of Anjou decided that his interests were best served by allying himself with the opposition and married his other daughter, Sybilla, to William Clito. Pressed on both sides by Anjou and Louis of France, Henry of England invoked his alliance with Germany and the emperor responded by sending troops to Metz, on the French border. While Louis' attention was distracted, a small force of English knights achieved a victory at Bourgthéroulde which finally ended the Norman rebellion. Her father capitalized on the situation by persuading Calixtus to annul Clito's marriage.

They celebrated the Christmas of 1124 in Strasbourg, but it was obvious to Matilda that her husband's health was failing. The physicians prescribed bleeding and cupping and purging, but the remedies only served to weaken him. He was relying more and more on a concoction of poppy juice to ease the pain, but he refused to remain in one place. As travel became easier with the arrival of spring, the court moved to Mainz and stayed briefly in Henry's castle of Trifels. There, one night, he called her to his bedside.

'I fear, wife, that my time on this earth is short. God has ordained that I shall have no successor of my blood. When the time comes, much will rest on your shoulders.'

She felt an icy chill settle somewhere in the centre of her body. 'You must not speak like that. You are yet a young man. You will recover. I pray every night to the Holy Virgin to restore you to health.' She was speaking the truth. Over the years she had come to love him. It was not the love of a wife for a husband, but for a friend and companion and a safe stronghold in time of trouble. She could not bring herself to consider what might happen to her if he died.

75

He shook his head. 'I think not. I believe the time has come for me to lay down the burdens of the flesh. You must be prepared. To that end, I wish you to take into your safekeeping the imperial regalia, the symbol of my authority.'

'But to what end? What do you wish me to do with them?' He had drunk poppy and she could see that he was on the edge of sleep. She grasped his hand. 'Henry! Speak to me. Who do you wish to name as your successor?'

'You must do as you think fit. Listen to good advice and God will guide you.'

It was useless to pursue the matter. He was already asleep. But he had given his orders. The locked chest containing the imperial crown and sceptre were brought to her chamber within the hour. Sleepless, she forced herself to consider the possibility of his imminent death and the question of the succession. She knew that by tradition the rulers of Germany were elected by the great landowners, lay and clerical. But Henry inherited the throne from his father and the Salian dynasty had ruled for several generations. How much importance would that have in choosing his successor? She went over in her mind the possible candidates. There was his nephew Frederick of Swabia, eldest son of his sister Agnes, and Frederick's brother Conrad – but Conrad had just left on a pilgrimage to the Holy Land. Frederick rebelled once, but he had been reinstated and was travelling with the court. He seemed to be the only candidate, but she was unsure whether the barons would accept him. Should she proclaim him as Henry's heir? But he had made no such choice. 'Take advice and God will guide you.' It seemed he was as undecided as she was. On that thought she eventually fell asleep.

Next day Henry seemed stronger and insisted on continuing his progress. They took a ship down the Rhine, heading for Utrecht. When she asked why he responded, 'As long as I control Utrecht we have a port from which ships can sail to England. I cannot allow the likes of the Count of Flanders to come between me and my main ally.'

Much work was in progress in Utrecht. Wharves and warehouses were being constructed along the newly canalized river. Henry insisted on inspecting them, but he was clearly in great pain. They were standing in a loading bay, watching a cargo of wool being unloaded, when he suddenly sagged to his knees. His face was deadly white and his lips were blue.

'Help me, someone!' she cried. 'Send for the King's physician.'

Some of his courtiers lifted the King and laid him on a sack of wool. She fell on her knees beside him, chafing his hands, pierced by a sudden terrible fear.

'Fetch the King's chaplain! Quickly!'

Frederick pushed through the throng and knelt on his other side.

'Uncle, I am here. Speak to us. Name your successor!'

Henry's eyes flickered open. He looked from her to his nephew and his lips moved. She bent closer to hear him. He seemed to summon strength from somewhere and whispered, 'Frederick, I commend my wife into your care. You are my heir.'

There was a stir in the crowd surrounding them and a young priest shouldered his way to her side. To Matilda's immense relief he carried a small box, which she knew must contain a phial of holy oil.

'I was called for. I was told that there is someone who needs—' He broke off, overwhelmed by the sudden realization of the identity of the man lying before him.

'I thank God who sent you. My husband is in sore need of grace.'

She stood up and the priest took her place. Leaning over Henry, he urged him to make confession of his sins, but the King did not appear to hear him.

'I urge you, for the saving of your soul, to make the act of contrition. Do you truly repent of all your sins?'

She watched, holding her breath. Henry's eyes flickered and his lips moved. It was impossible to tell what he was trying to say, but the priest took it as assent and pronounced the words of absolution. Then he took the oil from its container, unstoppered the bottle and anointed Henry's eyes, nose, mouth and ears, murmuring 'Through this holy anointing, may the Lord in his love and mercy help you with the grace of the Holy Spirit.' He had hardly finished when she saw an indefinable but unmistakable change in her husband's features. The priest saw it, too. He bent his head close to Henry's, listening for any sign of breath, then laid his ear against his chest. He looked up and shook his head and began to recite the prayer for the dead.

When he ceased there was a silence, as if all present were holding their breath. With a shock Matilda realized that they were waiting for someone to take control. Practical necessity came to her aid. She gave orders for Henry's body to be removed to the nearby church; the necessary messages were sent to his household; necessary formalities were put in train. The same cold practicality got her through the ensuing days. The King's body was prepared for burial. His heart and entrails were interred with due ceremony in the cathedral of St Martin in Utrecht. Then the cortege proceeded up the River Rhine to Speyer, where he was to be buried in the cathedral beside his father. Messengers galloped throughout the realm and beyond, carrying the news, and the great men of the land assembled for the funeral. It was the greatest gathering of nobles and prelates the country had seen since their wedding over ten years ago.

They had not come primarily to pay their respects to the old king, but to ensure that their interests were served by the choice of the new one. It was time for alliances to be made, for factions to coalesce, bargains to be struck. It was generally accepted that Henry's dying words appointing Frederick as his heir referred only to his own lands and possessions, not to the crown itself. No one asked for her opinion.

When the ceremony was over she retreated to Trifels and for the first time she had a chance to think about the consequences of what had happened. All through a long night she struggled with the question of what part she should play in the coming debate. Henry had placed the royal regalia in her charge. Did he mean that she should be the one to choose his successor, or had he just given them to her for safekeeping? Did he intend Frederick to take his place? Should she try to impose him on the assembled nobles as the new king, and if she did would they accept him? She was not even sure that he would be the right choice. He had shown himself capable of vacillation when it came to the important matters of the realm. She twisted and turned on her pillow, but when sleep eventually came it brought no solution to her problems.

Next day Archbishop Adalbert rode out to the castle and begged audience. She had never felt the same animosity towards him as her husband. Indeed, she had secretly been of the opinion that he had much right on his side in his struggle to reform the practices of the Church. Since she petitioned Henry for his release he had always treated her with kindness and respect; in fact she had sensed an almost fatherly affection. She received him gladly.

That same fatherly concern was manifested in his behaviour now. He offered his condolences for her loss, asked after her health and promised that he would do whatever he could do to help in any way. His kindness broke down her last barriers of reserve.

'I am greatly troubled,' she confessed and told him about her conversation with Henry and the consignment of the regalia into her keeping. 'I do not know what I should do now. Did he mean me to choose the next king? If so, who should it be?'

Adalbert smiled gently. 'Let me lift that burden from your shoulders. It is clear to me that the King gave you the royal regalia for safekeeping, to be handed over when the time came. It is not for you to choose who should succeed him. By long tradition the ruler is elected by the chief men of the realm. Give the insignia to me. I will keep it safe and when the election is over I will bestow it on the new king at his coronation. You need have no further anxiety.'

For a moment she hesitated. Then she recalled Henry's words: 'Listen to good advice and God will guide you.' Adalbert was a man of God. This must be the guidance she had been waiting for. She handed over the chest containing the regalia and he set off back to Mainz, where the election would take place.

It was not until much later that she understood how relinquishing the symbols of kingship had weakened her own position. Under the guidance of Adalbert, the nobles chose three of their number as electors: Leopold, margarve of Austria, Frederick of Swabia and Lothar of Supplinberg, one of Henry's most turbulent subjects. It was Lothar, no friend to her, who was chosen as king.

Alone in Trifels Castle she contemplated her future. Would the lands she was endowed with on her betrothal to Henry still be hers now he was dead? Even if they were, would she be able to protect them from the rapacity of the barons? Bitterly she recognized how much stronger her position would have been had she not accepted Henry's belief that God did not intend him to have children. It had served her own inclinations at the time, but now she saw how much she had lost by it. In the cold early morning hours it began to dawn on her that she was now dependent on Lothar's goodwill and her fate was in his hands. As long as she retained her position as the dowager empress, she presented a threat to him and a focus for opposition. He would have to dispose of her somehow. He might decide to give her in marriage to one of his adherents, as a reward for support or to ensure his loyalty; or she might be given the option of taking the veil. Either choice revolted her. To be married again to a man she could not love was insupportable; but she could not reconcile herself to the life of a cloistered nun. From the age of eight she had been the cosseted and spoilt bride of a great king; for the last ten years she had been a queen and an empress, and the trusted consort of the ruler. Now she was alone and vulnerable. She was twenty-five years old, and the future seemed to hold neither hope nor comfort.

6

WINDSOR, JANUARY 1127

'I, David, King of Scotland, do swear by Almighty God and on this Holy Relic, that should King Henry die without further issue, I will faithfully defend and support his daughter, the Lady Matilda.'

Enthroned beside her father in the great hall of Windsor Castle, Matilda surveyed the assembled nobility of England. The Archbishop of Canterbury had already taken the oath, as had all the bishops. Now it was the turn of the great secular lords, led by David, her mother's brother. King of Scotland in his own right, he also owed fealty to Henry for his English lands and attended his court. She smiled down at him as he knelt, his hands placed between her own. Since she returned to England he, of all the nobles at her father's court, had shown her the greatest sympathy and kindness.

As the next man stepped forward there was a disturbance.

'My liege, I protest!' Anselm, the abbot of Bury St Edmunds, thrust himself in front of the King. 'As lords spiritual, we should be next to take the oath.'

Matilda suppressed an exclamation of irritation. The

order of precedence had been agreed after much discussion, and it infuriated her that these overweening clerics were constantly attempting to claim superiority over the men of noble birth who ran the kingdom. She had had enough of the constant war between Church and state in Germany.

Henry glowered at Anselm. 'It has been decided. No more argument! Stand aside and let Earl Robert make his vow.'

Robert stepped forward and knelt. Matilda welcomed his oath of fealty as she had David's. One of Henry's bastards, he had been brought up at court and had proved himself one of the ablest and most loyal of their father's knights. As a result, he was now one of Henry's most trusted councillors and had been rewarded with the earldom of Gloucester. Tall and broad shouldered, he had his father's sharp dark eyes. He had the reputation of being invincible in battle and in the tourney, and he had also inherited Henry's astute intelligence and tactical sense. Some years older than herself, he was another who had welcomed her and shown her affection when she arrived.

One by one, some with better grace than others, the rest came forward, knelt, and spoke the words of the oath. She watched the faces. Some of them were already familiar, others were strangers to her. She was under no illusion that they were swearing of their own free will. Henry had summoned them from all over England and Normandy to attend his Christmas court and had refused to let any of them depart until they had taken the oath.

It was almost a year since a message reached her at Trifels that the King her father wished her to join him in Normandy. She had not hesitated but had gathered together all the valuables she could carry: the resplendent jewels given to her over the years by her husband the emperor, together with two crowns worn by him on various occasions, and most treasured of all, a reliquary containing the hand of St James. They had not been in the chest containing the royal regalia and so had not been handed over to Aadalbert. With these and a small escort of loyal knights, she had slipped out of Trifels and ridden for the border. Henry had sent an escort to meet her and take her to him at Rouen, where she had been greeted with cheers and flowers. It had felt then as if her troubles were over.

In the months that followed she had realized that her father's court was not the peaceful harbour she had imagined. Adeliza had not produced the longed-for heir and Henry's temper was becoming more and more uncertain. Normandy was constantly harassed by threats of invasion from neighbouring dukedoms, with the support of Louis of France, and the victory at Bourgetheroulde had bought only a temporary respite. The death of William in the *White Ship* had put an end to his marriage to the daughter of Fulk of Anjou, and lost Henry a valuable alliance. With the succession still in doubt, only the King's prowess in battle and cunning in keeping his unruly vassals under control prevented the kingdom from disintegrating.

During the course of the year she had got to know her father for the first time. He was not an easy man to get close to, but she had come to respect his many abilities. First and foremost, of course, he was a warrior and a great commander, but it was away from the battlefield that he showed his real talent. He controlled the mighty barons of England and Normandy by promising rewards of land and honours but never actually handing them over. His anger was a force to be feared and a man could lose his favour with an unwise word, and between that danger and the promise of preferment he kept them in a state of constant uncertainty. To those whom he trusted he was generous and they served him with unshakable loyalty. Besides Robert, one of the most favoured was Brian fitz Count, another bastard, fathered by Count Alain of Brittany, who was once married to Henry's sister Constance. He too had been brought up at the English court and readily admitted that he owed everything to Henry.

Henry was not called 'Beauclerc' for nothing. He was well educated and understood the value of education in others. For this reason he had surrounded himself with a number of clever men from humble backgrounds and promoted them to high office, much to the fury of his nobles, many of whom could neither read nor write. As a result, the administration of the affairs of both England and Normandy was far more efficient than before, to the benefit of the King's treasury.

There seemed, however, to be no solution in sight to the problem of the succession. Adeliza welcomed her with delight when she first arrived, recalling fond memories of how she had interceded on behalf of her father all those years ago, but her joy had quickly given way to tears.

'I am so afraid! The King so longs for a child. I fear he will put me away because I am barren and find some pretext to divorce me. And then what will become of me?'

'He cannot do that,' Matilda had responded, but without much certainty. 'The Church would not allow it. Tell me, does he … come to you frequently?'

'Oh yes! Almost every night when he is not away on campaign. But … but …'

'What?'

'I don't like to say it. It seems disloyal.'

'Say what?'

'Sometimes he … he cannot … he said it is my fault, that I do not do enough to excite him, but I do try to please him in every way I can. I am not one of those women who

... who has learned to do things ...'

She broke off and Matilda put her arms round her. 'I understand what you mean. It is not your fault. You are not a whore. If Henry can only perform the act with such a one, then he must do without legitimate children. God knows, he has plenty of bastards! He has squandered his seed and perhaps this is God's way of punishing him.'

In spite of all this, she enjoyed her time in Rouen. Henry's court was sophisticated. There were musicians and minstrels, and learned men to talk to, and she had been free from the constant need to plan and scheme to thwart her husband's enemies and to travel around the kingdom to quell rebellion. Then, in September, Henry had brought her to England. She had heard rumours about the climate and the food, and they were all true. It seemed to her that it had rained constantly since their arrival. The food was monotonous and the wine all but undrinkable – though that did not seem to deter most of Henry's courtiers. More importantly, she had the impression that they did not regard her with the respect due to her rank. To them, she was no more than the King's widowed daughter. The title of Empress and Queen of the Romans meant nothing to them. She had found it hard to accept their unceremonious manner towards her and as a result she was aware that they thought her proud and lacking womanly modesty.

Now, at last, that was being changed. As she sat beside her father and listened to nobleman after noblemen pledging their loyalty and support, she felt that her proper position was being recognized.

Spring arrived at last and for the first time she began to appreciate the country, with its rich pasture and fertile fields, but the sunshine was uncertain and she was always cold. They were in Henry's castle in Winchester when she was summoned to his presence. He was in one of his famous rages.

'God damn him! The treacherous villain!'

'Who, my lord?'

'Clito! My misbegotten nephew! He has married the daughter of Rainer of Montferrat. She's kin to Louis of France. He's my brother's son! Why does he try to thwart me at every turn?'

'You have had his father imprisoned for years, since you defeated him at Tinchebrai,' she pointed out. 'It isn't surprising that Clito hates you.'

Henry merely growled. 'Traitors, both of them. And now Clito is Count of Flanders – right on the borders of Normandy and just a day's sail from the English coast.'

'And his father is being kept at Devizes,' she mused. 'Too close to the south coast. Clito might be tempted to invade to release him.'

'Good point.'

'Why don't you send him to Robert of Gloucester's stronghold at Cardiff? Robert can be trusted to keep him safe.'

Henry gave her a sharp glance. 'You're quick to grasp strategic necessities. That's good. You'll understand what I am going to say next. It's time we arranged a new marriage for you.'

She felt a physical jolt, as if the air in front of her had suddenly become solid. She had known since her husband's death that this was likely to be her fate. A young widow with royal blood was too great an asset to be wasted, but until today Henry had not mentioned it and she had begun to hope that he had other plans for her, or at least that she might be given some choice in the matter.

'Marriage?' she said cautiously. 'Who did you have in mind?'

'I have had embassies from Lotharingia and Lombardy asking for you, but I have told them I have other plans. You will marry Geoffrey of Anjou.'

'Geoffrey?' For a moment she could not think who he meant. Then the realization hit her like a drench of icy water. 'Fulk's son? He's only a child, surely!'

'He's fifteen, soon to be sixteen. Old enough to father children.'

She stared at him in unbelief. 'You expect me to lie with a boy of sixteen?'

'I expect you to do your duty as a daughter, and as a wife. I've spoken to the boy. He's intelligent, answered my questions with wisdom beyond his years. And he is comely enough, if that matters to you. They call him *"le bel"*.'

'In that case he is probably vain and spoilt.'

'He's a splendid horseman and adept with arms of every kind. He will make an excellent knight.'

'He is not even a knight yet?'

'That can be remedied very quickly.'

'But he has no title, no lands.'

'That, too, will be changed very soon. His father, Fulk, has been offered the hand of Melisande, the heiress of Baldwin of Jerusalem. He will be King of Jerusalem and he will leave Anjou to Geoffrey.'

'He may hope that.' In her mind's turmoil she seized upon any negative point that offered itself. 'But will the lords who hold Jerusalem accept him?'

'Whether they do or not does not matter to us. Geoffrey will be Count of Anjou.'

'A count!' She drew herself up and fixed her father with a haughty stare. 'I am an empress! I will not lower myself to marry a mere count.'

'You were an empress,' Henry responded dryly. 'Now you are just a widow and my daughter – and as such you will do as I bid you.'

'Never! You will have to drag me to the altar in fetters – and even then I will refuse to speak the vows.'

He did not fly into a rage, as she expected. Instead he said grimly, 'So be it. This marriage will take place. Until then you may keep to your chambers.'

He called for one of the men-at-arms who guarded the door and bade him conduct her to her room. She recognized that a refusal would only result in a humiliating defeat, so she went without another word.

It was tantamount to a prison sentence. She was not allowed to leave her rooms for any reason. Her ladies-in-waiting and her servants were dismissed and replaced with others she did not know, so there was no one she could confide in, no one to carry a message for her. Not that she could think of anyone who might help. She was painfully aware that she had no real friends in Henry's court.

After some days her half-brother, Robert of Gloucester, came to see her.

'Sister, I beg you to yield to our father's wishes. You know as well as I do that people of our rank and position are not free to marry where our fancy takes us. We have a duty to consider the wellbeing of the realm.'

'But a boy of fifteen!' she exclaimed. 'Surely our father could have chosen a more suitable candidate.'

'It is a strategic necessity. Anjou borders Normandy. It must be under the control of someone who has ties to us, not someone who might choose to help the rebellious barons, or form an alliance with Louis of France against us.'

She clamped her jaw shut. 'There has to be another way. Does not our father have a bastard daughter he can farm out to this boy count?'

Robert gave up, shaking his head. Her next visitor was her confessor.

'Daughter, you are committing a mortal sin by defying your father. Be advised by me. Make yourself conformable to his will.'

Then a letter arrived from Bishop Hildebert of Lavardin. She had met him in Rouen and developed an affection for him. He was a gentle and wise teacher and reminded her of Bruno, who was her tutor as a child. In the letter he chided her for causing her father so much distress by her disobedience and begged her to abide by his wishes. She sat with the letter in her lap and, for the first time since the confrontation with Henry, she wept. It was an admission of defeat.

She was escorted to Rouen to be betrothed to Geoffrey by Robert and Brian fitz Count. As they rode south from Winchester she maintained a stony silence, repulsing all attempts at conversation. That night they were entertained in Southampton Castle by William, Count of Aumale, nicknamed *'le gros'* for his huge girth. He set out a magnificent feast for them but she hardly touched her food and as soon as possible she retired to the solar. Her ladies, cowed by her mood, grouped together and whispered, while she sat apart. After a little while, Robert and Brian came in. Robert drew a stool close to her chair and looked earnestly into her face.

'My dear sister, it saddens us both to see you so downcast. I understand that this match is not one you would choose, but it is the King's decree and we have no choice but to obey.'

Brian brought a stool to her other side. He was a good-looking man, with golden brown hair that curled onto his forehead and hazel eyes which normally held a glint of mischief; but tonight he was solemn.

'Madam, please believe me, I favour this marriage no more than you do. There are many men I could name more deserving of your hand. But it is as Robert said. We must obey the King. But I beg you, do not turn your face away from those who would be your friends and would offer what comfort they can.'

She looked at him and remembered that he himself was married to a much older woman. It was a marriage arranged for him by Henry and had brought him the lordship of Wallingford, giving him, a landless boy, a castle and an income. It had made his fortune, but it could not be a love match. From his expression she guessed that he understood her distress and she realized how churlish her behaviour must seem.

'Forgive me, sir. I did not intend to inflict my evil mood on my companions. I know that you mean me nothing but good. As you say, we are all the King's subjects and must do as he commands.'

He took her hand and kissed it and she felt a shiver of pleasure, such as she had not known since the loss of Drogo. 'I ask only to be allowed to lighten your burden on this journey. It is little enough, but all I can offer.'

The next day, on board ship, he sat beside her and entertained her with accounts of adventures in Henry's service. He was a well-educated man with a lively wit and before long she found herself first smiling and then laughing aloud. That night, in Henry's castle at Barfleur, he revealed a new talent. He had a fine light baritone voice and sang to his own accompaniment on the lute. He sat by her and sang softly, as if for her ears alone. It was a ballad, on a theme much loved by minstrels everywhere: the sad plaint of a knight in love with lady far above his station.

When he finished she said, 'That is a lovely air, and one I have not heard before. Is it new?'

He smiled. 'Very new, my lady. It was only written last night.'

'Last night? By whom … you mean you …' She understood abruptly what dangerous waters she had ventured into. She looked down at him. 'You understand I am to be betrothed. Whether I like it or not, I will never betray my future husband.'

He sighed and nodded. 'I understand, my lady. Neither of us is free to fulfil their own desires.'

As they rode towards Rouen, he was always at her side, while Robert rode ahead with the vanguard of her escort. But next morning she saw him from her window in conversation with her brother. It was obvious from their manner that they were engaged in a vigorous argument. Finally Robert made a sharp gesture of command and Brian turned away angrily, but from then on he kept a distance between them.

At Rouen Castle she saw her future husband for the first time. True to his reputation, he was a remarkably handsome youth. His russet hair shone in the sun like a bronze helmet and his eyes were the colour of summer skies; his features were regular and his figure slim and athletic. It was not hard to see why he was nicknamed *'le bel'*. Nor was it hard to see from his bearing that he delighted in the admiration he attracted. She took an instant dislike to him.

She went through the ritual solemnity of the betrothal stony-faced and with her head held high, and scarcely looked at her future husband. She had vowed to herself that, though she had been forced to go through with the match, he would have no joy of it.

In June of the following year Henry ordained a great knighting ceremony in Rouen. The cream of the nobility of Normandy and Anjou had assembled and the town was overflowing with their entourages, plus the merchants and small traders who were always attracted to such events in the hope of making a quick profit. The streets were decked out with banners and flowers and vivid with the colours of men's cloaks and women's gowns, as the citizens tried to ape the fashions of the nobility.

Matilda sat beside her father in the centre of the great cathedral. She was dressed in a bliaut, a style of gown in the latest fashion, which fitted closely to her upper body and then spread into a full skirt, a style that suited her slim figure. It had tight sleeves to the elbow which then opened out into a trumpet shape. The gown was in a delicate shade of green and she wore a girdle embroidered with gold round her waist. Over it she wore a mantle of darker green, richly embellished with gold stars and moons. She would have liked to wear her crown, but it had been made clear to her that it would not be appropriate. Instead a simple gold fillet held her veil in place.

In front of them, on the steps leading up to the high altar, Geoffrey knelt, clad in a simple white robe. His head was bent and in the candlelight his hair shone like polished copper. She knew that he would have been there, keeping silent vigil, all night and for a fleeting moment she felt sympathy. He must be chilled and aching in every limb, but he knelt on, unmoving. The murmur of voices from the crowd filling the nave fell silent as the archbishop and all his attendant clergy entered and the mass began. When it was over Geoffrey rose and turned to face the congregation. Henry stepped forward to face him. His two sponsors, his father and another nobleman, handed him the sword and shield, which had been lying on the altar. Geoffrey knelt again and repeated the words of the oath of knighthood, promising to be loyal to his lord, a brave defender of the weak and to treat all women with courtesy. This last provoked in Matilda a grim internal smile. Henry struck him on the shoulders with the flat of his sword.

'I dub thee Sir Knight.'

The congregation cheered, trumpets sounded and the ceremony was over.

Next day there was a tournament to celebrate the occasion. Galleries of tiered seats had been erected in an open field outside the city gates. Matilda took her place beside her father in the centre of one of them. For that occasion she was dressed in blue and silver. All round her men and women were chatting and laughing. The sun was shining and there was an air of festival but she sat like a statue, allowing no sign of either pleasure or distress to show in her face. It was a talent she had cultivated over the past year. She knew that people were beginning to call her haughty and arrogant, but she did not care. She wanted everyone to see that this marriage was not of her choosing. Henry, meanwhile, laughed and joked with those around him.

A trumpet sounded and the knights who were to take part in the tournament rode into the arena and dismounted to bow to Henry. All eyes were on Geoffrey and she could not help but follow their gaze. He was splendidly dressed and accoutred. He was wearing a hauberk of closely woven rings of steel, shoes of iron with golden spurs, and a helmet studded with precious gems, which glittered in the sunlight. Having made his bow, he turned to his horse and vaulted into the saddle without touching the stirrups – no mean feat in full armour. The crowd cheered and he acknowledged the applause with a wave.

'Vain, as I thought,' she said to herself.

At either end of the field there were banks where bushes of broom were in full flower. As Geoffrey cantered back towards the lists a young woman stepped forward and held up a sprig of bloom. He reined in and leaned down to her, took the sprig and fixed it in his helmet. Matilda understood that he would fight wearing this other woman's favour rather than asking her for one. The implications would not be lost on the watching crowd.

There was no denying that he acquitted himself well in the mêlèe that climaxed the proceedings. He was fighting on the weaker side, but he succeeded in unhorsing a giant of a man from the opposing team. It went without saying that he would be awarded the prize for the most successful knight. It would have been easy to give way to the excitement of the occasion. She had watched many tournaments before and had always found them thrilling. But this time she forced herself to remain impassive throughout, determined not to give him the satisfaction of seeing that she was impressed.

That night there was a banquet and she found herself for the first time seated next to him, unable to avoid conversation. The sprig of broom was now in his hat. There was no point in trying to ignore it.

'I see you still wear the favour you were given earlier,' she said.

He gave her a charming smile that did not quite reach his eyes. 'It brought me luck today so I shall wear it always as my badge of honour. It is called in Latin *planta genesta*. I think from now on I shall call myself Plantagenet.'

She lifted her shoulders in a gesture of disinterest. 'As you please.'

He reached across and tried to take her hand, but she withdrew it and clasped it in her lap. She saw him flush and his lips took on a childish pout. She thought, I was right. He is spoilt and petulant. He expects everyone to fall at his feet. Well, he will learn that I am not so easy to impress.

He said, 'Why are you so cold? Do I not please you? If we are to be married you must be kinder to me than this.'

After the meal there was dancing. Normally this was something she would enjoy, but tonight she was forced to lead the dance with Geoffrey. He danced well but showily, with many extra flourishes and athletic leaps. She did not attempt to match him but paced through the measures with what she hoped was both dignity and grace. As he led her back to their seats he said in an undertone, 'Can you not smile? Am I to have to put up with your ill manners after we are wed?'

She met his eyes. 'I see nothing to smile about, sir.'

He threw down her hand and turned away, and for the rest of the evening he danced and flirted with all the most beautiful women in the room. When other members of the court asked her to dance she pleaded exhaustion and kept to her seat.

7

ROUEN AND ANJOU, 1128-29

THE WEDDING TOOK place one week later. Once again, there was a great feast and she was powerfully reminded of her first wedding. She recalled her anxious fears about what was to follow and thought bitterly that she looked forward to the night to come with just as much dread, though for very different reasons. Now she understood only too well what was expected of her. She ate little and drank less, but she saw that Geoffrey was draining his goblet with a frequency that told her he was as uneasy as she was. When at last the final sweetmeats had been consumed, her father brought the feasting to a close with a jovial remark about not keeping young lovers from their bed. He was perfectly aware of her unwilling compliance in the match, but he was determined to behave as if nothing was amiss.

Her ladies took her up to the chamber that had been prepared for them and helped her to undress, but there was no giggling or ribald jokes this time. Her demeanour made it clear that such things would not be tolerated. When she was in her nightgown she dismissed them, but she did not get into bed. Instead she knelt at the prie-dieu in the corner of the room.

'Merciful God, guide me tonight! I have made vows before you to obey this man, who is now my husband, but must I prostitute myself to a boy who cares nothing for me, nor I for him?'

There was no answer, and she expected none. Outside there was the sound of drunken male laughter, then the door opened and closed.

'You can get up off your knees. The time for praying is over.'

He was in a night robe, his face flushed with alcohol, his hair tousled. She got up and their eyes met.

He said, 'Take off your robe. I want to see you naked.'

'No.'

'Take it off! I am your husband and I command it.'

She held his gaze. 'And if I refuse, what will you do? I will not submit without a struggle and I do not think my father will be impressed if he sees me tomorrow with bruises on my face. Or do you plan to call your servants to strip me? How the court gossips will relish that story!'

He stared at her for a moment in impotent fury. Then he said, 'Very well. Get into bed.'

She knew she had no choice but to comply and he stripped off his gown and climbed in beside her. She noted that he had an erection, but it was an uncertain one. He reached out and fondled one of her breasts and suddenly she was seized by a vivid recollection of Drogo's touch, and of the quivering delight which it aroused in her. But the memory only served to increase her repulsion. She pushed his hand away and pulled her nightgown up to her waist.

'Do what you must. Just get on with it.'

He climbed on top of her and pushed a hand between her legs. 'You frigid cow! You're as dry as a stone.' She made no reply. He attempted to enter her, but his penis had gone soft. He rubbed at it with one hand, swearing under his breath. Then he grabbed her hand and pulled it down. 'You do it!'

She snatched her hand away. 'If you are not man enough, don't expect me to help you. I am not your whore.'

He made another frantic effort and then rolled off her. 'So be it. Why should I want to fuck an ugly cow like you? I can have any pretty girl I want.'

'Then go to one,' she responded. 'But think what the gossips will say tomorrow.'

He was silent. They were in Henry's castle, so he did not have a room of his own to retreat to. The realization dawned on both of them that they were bound to spend the night together. He turned his back on her and she allowed some of the tension to drain out of her limbs. It was a mercy, she reflected, that no one would expect to be shown a bloodied sheet in the morning.

Neither of them slept much that night. Once she thought she heard him weeping. She nursed a sense of bitter triumph, mixed with misgivings about the final result. Towards dawn she turned her thoughts to practical details. He rolled restlessly onto his back and she said, 'Wake up. We need to talk.'

'I am awake,' he growled. 'I haven't slept all night.'

'Neither have I. But now we have to think about today. Listen …'

'Why should I listen to you?'

'Because I am ten years older than you. Because I have been a queen and an empress, the consort of one of the most powerful men in Europe. I have more experience of ruling than you will ever have.'

'So? What are you trying to say?'

'First, if you value your manhood, you must behave as if everything last night had been to your satisfaction. So you must appear your normal, happy, confident self. If you sulk everyone will guess what the problem is.'

'I'm not a fool. Don't treat me like one.'

'Very good. Next, we must both behave as fits our rank. In a day or two your father leaves for the Holy Land and you will be Count of Anjou and I, God help me, will be your countess. We have a duty to show all your vassals that we are fit to govern them. If they guess what is wrong between us they will have no respect for either of us. My father has made this marriage to give him secure frontiers on the south of his domains. There are enough rebellious barons on both sides to seize upon any excuse to rise up. We have to present a united front. Do you understand me?'

He glowered at her for a moment. Then he said, 'Very well. Look to your own behaviour. It is not my gloomy face that will give the game away.'

He was a better actor than she expected, laughing and joking with the other men over breakfast, but neither he nor she made any attempt to assume the role of loving newly-weds. Any one of their immediate entourage would have seen through the pretence immediately.

The celebrations went on for days, with jousting and hunting by day and feasting at night, and they played their parts as expected of them. Only when they retired to bed were the masks discarded. On the first occasion she anticipated the coming night with foreboding, but Geoffrey made no attempt to repeat the fiasco of the night before. He turned his back on her without a word and soon began to snore.

While the festivities continued, news came that occasioned further celebration. William Clito had been killed in battle. When Henry announced this there was a cheer and a babble of excited voices. Undercover of the noise, he turned to her.

'Make me a grandson, daughter, and no one will dare lift a sword against us!'

On the final day they all gathered in the cathedral to pray for God's blessing on Fulk's enterprise. He was to set out for Jerusalem with his entourage of chosen knights as soon as the service was over. Outside the great doors, he bowed to Henry, embraced Geoffrey and kissed Matilda's hand. Then he swung himself into the saddle, a trumpet sounded and the whole cohort clattered off towards the city gates. She looked at Geoffrey to see if he was moved by his father's departure, but instead he looked triumphant. He was now Count of Anjou.

At the final feast Henry presented gifts to all the knights who had travelled from far and near to take part in the tournaments. There was an atmosphere of raucous good cheer. For everyone concerned except the two central figures in the proceedings, it had been an unqualified success. But as soon as the meal was over Geoffrey requested a few minutes' private conversation with her father. She watched them suspiciously as they withdrew into the solar. Surely he could not intend to complain about what happened on their wedding night? No, she convinced herself, he could not do that without laying himself open to ridicule. When he reappeared, his handsome face was contorted with fury, and her father had the satisfied look she knew meant he had had the best of an argument.

As soon as they were alone she said, 'Something is wrong. What is the matter?'

He turned to her, glowering. 'You and your father have taken me for a fool! I was promised the castles along the border, the ones confiscated from Robert of Bêlleme, as part of your dowry. Now Henry is refusing to hand them over.'

She suppressed an ironic smile. That was so typical of her father. He promised and then withheld at the last moment. There was no point, however, in adding fuel to the flames. She said, 'I think perhaps what my father intended was that the castles should pass to us on his death.' She laid the lightest emphasis on the 'us'.

'On his death! That could be ten, twenty years from now! I want those castles under my control.'

She decided there was no point in prolonging the argument. 'Well, there is nothing to be done about it now. Perhaps with time we may be able to change his mind. We should get some sleep now. We have a long ride ahead of us tomorrow.'

The journey to Angers, the principal seat of power for the Counts of Anjou, took eight days and in each village or town they were greeted with cheers and flowers. It was easy to resume the mask of royalty. She had had plenty of practice. She smiled and nodded and accepted the tributes offered to her with dignity. Geoffrey, on the other hand, was quickly bored. He wanted to be off hunting or practising in the tilt yard. He urged them on through the welcoming crowds and resented any hold-up. To her relief, they spent the nights in the manor houses of minor nobility or failing that in inns. Either way, there was little privacy and no likelihood of a repetition of their wedding night.

In Angers itself the whole populace turned out to welcome their new count and his countess. The façades of the houses along the main street had been draped with costly tapestries and choirs waited for them at every corner to sing songs specially composed for the occasion. Flowers were thrown down from balconies and their horses trod over carpets of petals. At last they reached the fortress, its grey bulk poised on its hill above the River Maine. As they rode over the drawbridge she looked around her, at the place that would be her home for the foreseeable future. Within the massive curtain walls there was the usual agglomeration of outbuildings – kitchen, stables, smithy, bakehouse and so on, and on one side a garden with vegetable beds and fruit trees. Beyond these rose the walls of the keep, the central hall flanked by two towers. It was a well-built castle, though far smaller than the ones she lived in with the Emperor Henry, or indeed those belonging to her father.

Grooms came running as they entered the stable yard and led the horses away. The house servants were crowded into the great hall to welcome the master home. It was clear that Geoffrey was well liked, at any rate within his own household. Her own reception was more guarded. She guessed that her reputation for haughtiness had preceded her but reckoned that it was no bad thing for them to be somewhat in awe of her. She had brought only a small entourage. There were half a dozen knights whose loyalty she trusted, but she had left behind the ladies who had attended her at her father's court. They were Henry's choice, selected to be her jailers when she refused to comply with his wishes, and she felt no affection for them. She had brought only a girl called Eloise, the daughter of one of Henry's knights, to be her waiting woman.

Looking round the hall, she noticed signs of neglect. The rushes that covered the floor had not been changed for a long time and mixed in with them were bones and scraps of food and, her nose told her, piss and dog excrement. She remembered that Fulk had been a widower for some years and the castle had obviously lacked the oversight of its chatelaine. More evidence was presented when they sat down to eat. The food was plentiful, but not well cooked and carelessly served, and the pages who served it were grubby and unkempt. She made mental notes of work to be done.

The private rooms for the family members were situated in the two towers flanking the hall. When they had eaten she was conducted up the narrow spiral staircase to the one she would share with her husband. There was a big bed in the centre of the room, a chest for storing clothes, a table and a couple of stools, and in one corner a small stack of straw pallets. Now that Geoffrey was a knight he had squires to attend him. They would sleep on the pallets and the only privacy the married couple would have would be afforded by the heavy brocaded bed curtains. That evening she noticed that Geoffrey was drinking heavily and guessed that he was trying to bolster his courage. She was proved correct. As soon as her maidservant had helped her undress and withdrawn, he stamped in with his squires in tow. The curtains were closed but she heard him mumbling and guffawing with the boys as he undressed.

Then he said roughly, 'Now get out, both of you. Go and find somewhere else to sleep.'

They giggled and murmured good nights and she heard the door close. Then Geoffrey flung back the bed curtains, ripped off the covers and without preamble threw himself on top of her. She forced herself to lie still. With sudden vivid recall, she remembered Magda's scornful tones telling her that she was not the only woman who had to grit her teeth and shut her eyes. So this was to be her fate. This time he succeeded in entering her and gave a shout of triumph. He thrust and thrust and to her dismay she found her body responding of its own accord, so that her hips pushed upwards to meet him. It was not pleasurable, but yet it felt somehow right, even necessary. It seemed to take a long time before she felt him ejaculate, with a choking groan, and even then he continued to lie on her, panting. Finally he pulled himself out and raised himself on his elbows.

'There! So now you know you are wedded to a real man.'

She looked up into his eyes and replied coolly, 'Quite. So now you have proved that to your own satisfaction there will be no need to repeat the experiment.'

'Oh yes! I intend to repeat it every night. You can look forward to that!'

There was only the one bed, so they had no choice but to share it. Soon he was snoring, but she lay awake while the pattern of moonlight from the unshuttered window moved across the floor. This would be her new life and somehow she had to make the best of it. It seemed she had no choice about how she passed the nights, but the days were still her own. She must concentrate on what they offered and put the rest to the back of her mind, like a nagging tooth that can be forgotten when the attention is elsewhere.

She woke when he climbed out of bed and shouted for his squires. At least he had the sense to pull the curtains closed before they arrived. She waited until he had dressed and left before she got up and called for Eloise. She had decided how she was going to spend the day. For now she would concentrate on her role as chatelaine. Wider matters of the governance of her husband's domains could wait. Geoffrey, she learnt without surprise, had gone hunting. As soon as she had broken her fast, she sent for the steward and gave her orders. By midday the floor of the hall had been swept and scrubbed and fresh rushes mingled with sweet herbs had been spread. Meanwhile, she made her way to the kitchens to interrogate the chief cook. He had heard, vaguely, of the spices she had been accustomed to in her time as queen and empress, but made it clear that he had no wish to trouble himself with such foreign concoctions. She picked out a scullion who looked more intelligent than the rest and sent him off into the town with precise instructions. He returned with some of the ingredients she had ordered and a message that a certain merchant would be happy to supply the rest as soon as he could get a message to a colleague in Marseilles. Next she inspected the kitchen gardens and found, as she expected, that much of the ground had been allowed to revert to weeds. She castigated the gardener and gave him a list of herbs, culinary and medicinal, that she expected him to sow. That night, at least the food had some savour and the page boys had clean hands and tidy hair. Geoffrey did not notice any difference, or at any rate he did not remark on it, but he clearly enjoyed his meal. He had had good hunting and was in a good mood.

At bedtime he kept his promise and fucked her energetically. It was the only word she knew to describe it. There was no love involved. It was as mechanical as the mating of dogs. It happened every night until her monthly flux came on. When she told him that he would have to abstain, he glared at her.

'You are not with child, then?'

'It seems not.'

He slammed his hand against the bedpost. 'By God, I have been doubly cheated! The castles and revenues your father promised are not forthcoming and I am shackled to a barren wife!'

She forbore to remind him that, according to the ancients, conception was more likely to occur when the woman had some pleasure in the process. He continued to glower for a moment, then he turned and strode out of the room. She learnt later that he left the castle and spent the night somewhere in the town. After that he rarely came to her bed. It was an open secret that he had a mistress, a young widow reputed to be extremely beautiful. She did not protest.

Once his lust was being satisfied elsewhere, they were easier with each other. He had little experience in the routine administration of the affairs of his new domain, and less patience. She had been learning these skills from the age of twelve. It seemed that Fulk had left these matters to a small group of clerks and Geoffrey was happy to follow his father's example. She summoned the treasurer and insisted on going over the accounts. In this she was taking a leaf out of her father's book. He had put her half-brother Robert and Brian fitz Count in charge of a similar audit in Normandy, with results that were beneficial to his treasury. She wished wryly that she had their services at her command.

The dispensation of justice was another duty that Geoffrey preferred not to bother himself with. Very soon the first plaintiffs presented themselves at the castle. A minor lord had a complaint against another for hunting on his land. A peasant had died without issue and there was a dispute over who should inherit his holding. A merchant in the town was accusing another of defrauding him. Geoffrey tried to pass the decisions down to local bailiffs or merchants' guilds. Matilda knew that this would only store up trouble for the future, so she offered to adjudicate on his behalf. When matters arose which he had to deal with himself, she offered counsel and he took it, reluctantly at first, but then with grudging appreciation.

As the months passed, Geoffrey's true character revealed itself. He had a superficial charm that drew people to him, but he was also given to outbursts of unreasoning rage. She often recalled the legend that one of his ancestors married a mysterious woman called Melusine, who was in fact a devil, giving rise to the family's appellation of 'the devil's brood'. There were times when it seemed fully justified. She was forced to acknowledge, however, that in the one quality which was more important than all others for someone in his position, he excelled. He was a consummate warrior. He was a superb horseman, and unequalled among his peers for his ability with lance and sword and an excellent shot with the crossbow. Not only that, but he had that indefinable brilliance that made men glad to accept his leadership. In a world where authority depended on military power, he was well equipped to rule.

She made a point of going to watch him with his knights in the exercise yard at the castle, where they practised swordplay or tilted at the quintain. It was an essential discipline for knights in preparation for battle. A ring of straw hung from a post in the tilt yard and each man in turn rode at it at full gallop with his lance couched and attempted to thrust the weapon through the centre of the ring. If he missed and hit the ring instead the quintain pivoted and the knight received a nasty blow on the back of the head from a heavy sack at the other end of the arm. Geoffrey never missed.

Once she had established her position with his household she had more time to herself and when next he planned to hunt she declared her intention to come with him. He demurred, saying that she would get hurt, or be in the way. She insisted and he was forced to concede that she was as good a rider as he was, and no less daring in the pursuit of their game. He was amazed to discover that she could fire a crossbow, a skill she learned from her first husband's master-at-arms. When she first took up the weapon, he was inclined to mock her.

'A crossbow is about as useful to a woman as a distaff would be to a man.'

'You think so?' she responded. 'You might recall that a woman can wield one of these to good effect. My own half-sister, Juliana, almost killed our father with a cross-bow bolt when he besieged her and her husband in their castle of Breteuil.'

In spite of this easing of their relationship, Geoffrey made his dissatisfaction with the marriage clear at every opportunity. It was not only what he regarded as her frigid-ity in bed. Her father's failure to hand over control of the Norman castles was a constant irritant. He was building up to one of his famous rages and finally found an excuse to vent it when an embassy from Henry arrived bearing a charter document. It was not an important matter, merely a grant of money to the abbey of Fontevraud to be paid out of rents from farms in London and Winchester, but it required her signature to authorize it.

Geoffrey watched without comment, but when the ambassadors had left he demanded, 'Why you? Why not both of us? These are matters of royal prerogative. If I am to rule jointly with you when your father dies I should be signing such documents as well.'

She hesitated, aware that they were on treacherous ground. 'I do not know if the English barons are yet ready to accept an Angevin lord as their king.'

He rounded on her, his face contorted. 'What do you mean? Does your father rule or not? It is for him to decide who should rule after him, not them.' He slammed his fist on the table. 'I have letters from my father. The lords of Outremer have accepted him and he is married to Melisande. When Baldwin dies he will be King of

Jerusalem – perhaps even before that. Am I to be nothing more than a paltry count for the rest of my days?'

She regarded him in silence for a moment. His handsome features were flushed with anger and he looked like a spoilt child who had been denied a treat. Suddenly her patience snapped. This boy was not fit to rule a kingdom. She stood up. 'Yes, my father rules and it is for him to decide. It seems that at present he does not see you as a future king.'

After that he refused to speak to her for several days.

Their sexual relations continued to be the main source of tension. He bedded her from time to time, usually in a mood of revenge for some imagined slight, but as the months passed and she failed to conceive she began to believe that she might, in truth, be barren. When her monthly flux arrived yet again, she brooded gloomily on the memory of her affair with Drogo and its after effects. She knew that she had committed a grave sin and wondered if this was God's punishment. She reminded herself that she had confessed to Norbert and received absolution. That should mean that she had been forgiven. Norbert, after all, was one of the holiest men she had ever met. His reputation had grown steadily since their meeting at Mouzon and he was now the abbot of a new monastery at Prémontré. Surely, she reasoned, if anyone could release her from God's displeasure it would be him. Her father's injunction haunted her. 'Make me a grandson and no one will dare to lift a sword against us.' She knew, only too well, how greatly her position in Germany had been weakened by her failure to produce an heir. Had she had a son, she might now be the empress dowager, acting as regent for her child, in a position of power and security; instead of being married to this spoilt boy.

One day he walked into the solar, where she was reading, and announced, 'Rosanne has given birth to a son.'

Rosanne was his mistress. She realized that this was something she should have expected, but nevertheless the news came as a shock. She tried to assume a manner of calm detachment.

'Congratulations. I hope she and the child are both well.'

'Both flourishing.' His face had the expression she had seen before, when he had vanquished all comers in a tournament. 'So you see, it is not me who is at fault.'

She should have seen that coming. She bent her head over the book and said nothing.

He went on, 'Since this seems to be the only son I am likely to get – until Rosanne gives me another, of course – I have decided to bring him here to live in the castle. I want him to be brought up in a fitting manner.'

This was not unusual. Her own half-brothers were brought up at her father's court. But it was a blow. She said, 'Surely it would not be wise to separate him from his mother so soon. You must wait until he is weaned, at least.'

'Why? Rosanne will come with him. I shall put her in the room in the other tower, the room I slept in before my father left for Jerusalem.'

She put the book down and rose slowly to her feet. They had come to a crossroads. 'You will not.'

'I shall! Who will stop me?'

'No one. But if you do, I shall not be here. I shall return to my father and you can kiss goodbye to those Norman castles and any faint hope you ever had of succeeding him.'

'Go then!' he shouted. 'Go! I shall be glad to be rid

of you! This whole marriage has been a cheat and a deception.'

The cavalcade that left the castle and rode towards the Norman border was very different from the one that arrived a year earlier. Geoffrey refused to send a proper escort with her. She had half a dozen knights for protection and her chaplain and Hugh, her steward, and Eloise. It was in this poor state that she returned to her father's court.

8

ROUEN AND ENGLAND, 1129-32

HENRY WAS PREDICTABLY furious, but his anger was directed as much at Geoffrey as at Matilda. He was incensed by the fact that he had allowed her to travel so poorly escorted, and he had been irritated by Geoffrey's constant demands that he surrender the castles and recognize him as joint heir to the throne.

To her he said bitterly, 'So you could not do the one thing I needed of you. If he had got you with child it would not matter that he has thrown you out. Is he sterile, or is it you?'

'He did not throw me out! I left because he wanted to bring his mistress and his bastard to live in the castle.'

Henry grunted. 'Well, that answers one question. The fault does not lie with him that you have not conceived.'

She bit back an angry rejoinder and turned away. It was true that she had failed in the one crucial service she could have performed for her father and her country. But her father did not refer to the matter again. Adeliza, too, had failed to produce the longed-for heir, and it seemed likely that he did not wish to delve too deeply into the reasons for that.

As soon as the opportunity arose, Adeliza took her up to her own chamber. She grasped her hands and exclaimed, 'My dear, I am so sorry to see you back like this. Tell me what went wrong. Was he brutal to you?'

She sighed wearily. 'Not brutal, no. Unfeeling, perhaps. But he is only a boy. Perhaps I should have made allowances.'

'But he must have done something terrible to make you leave him. What was it?'

She related the cause of that final quarrel and Adeliza put her arms round her. 'Of course you couldn't allow that. How can he ever have imagined that you could?'

She shook her head. 'I have had time on the journey to think, and I realize now that I was at fault too. I was cold to him in bed. I never wanted to marry him and I vowed he should have no pleasure in the match, so I have only myself to blame if he never came to care for me. If only I had conceived ...'

'If you knew how often I have said that to myself! Why can I not give Henry the one thing he craves above all others? But it must be God's will, and I try to accept that.'

'I wonder. You told me once that the fault could lie with my father, not with you. I cannot give myself the same excuse. Geoffrey is potent, he has proved that. The fault is mine, and I believe it is God's judgement for my sins.'

'Your sins? What sin could you have committed that God would punish you so?'

She hesitated, but the longing to unburden herself was overwhelming. 'It was a long time ago. I was just a girl, but I knew very well that what I was doing was wrong. There was a young man, one of my knights ...'

'You let him make love to you?' Adeliza's eyes were wide with shock.

'I encouraged him. I loved him so much and we had so

much joy in each other … but then the terrible thing happened. I conceived.'

'You conceived? Then you are not barren.'

'I was not, then.'

'What did your husband say?'

'He was not with me. I was in Italy, he had returned to Germany. I told him the child was his … but it did not live. So you see, I committed a mortal sin and this is my punishment.'

'Then you must confess and seek absolution.'

'I did, years ago. I thought I had been forgiven but now …'

Adeliza squeezed her hand. Compassion had taken the place of shock in her eyes. 'Perhaps you should seek advice from someone else, another priest. It may be that there is something you can do, some penance …'

She smiled bitterly. 'I thought I had served my punishment in my husband's death and my marriage to a man I cannot love. It seems I have not.' She got up. 'Does it not seem to you, Adeliza, very cruel that we women are seen as having no value except as breeding stock? We have no more say in the matter than cattle, penned up to be serviced by whichever bull our master has selected.'

Adeliza put her hand to her mouth. 'Matilda, have a care. That sounds like blasphemy. The Bible tells us that the woman must be subject to the man.'

'The Bible as written by a man!' she exclaimed.

'You must not speak like that! The Bible is God's word, not that of mortal men!'

She bowed her head. 'You are right. I am prone to the sin of pride. I have been told that often before. I must struggle to correct myself.'

Contrary to her expectation, it seemed Henry valued her for more than just her potential as a brood mare.

Over the next months he made a point of involving her in the business of rule. She travelled with him around Normandy, and when he returned to England she remained in Rouen and resumed to some extent the role she had fulfilled as consort to the emperor. It appeared that her father was intent upon associating her in the minds of his vassals with the governance of his domains. To what end he never made clear, but she knew that the problem of the succession preyed on his mind. For her own part, she brooded in private moments over Adeliza's suggestion that she should seek counsel from a priest, but she was loath to confide in any of the churchmen in Henry's entourage. Far too often, in her experience, the assumption of holy orders was seen as a way to achieve advancement in the secular world, rather than as a way to escape it.

When Henry returned to Normandy, ambassadors arrived from Geoffrey. After the audience her father sent for her.

'Would you like to guess what that insolent puppy is demanding?'

'A divorce? An annulment on some far-fetched pretext?'

'Quite the contrary. He wants you back. He said you are his lawful wife and should be returned to him at once.'

She tried to quell a rising sense of panic. 'What did you tell them?'

'That he failed to treat you with the respect due to my daughter and you will remain with me.'

She drew a breath of relief.

'Thank you, sir.'

Some days later word reached them that Geoffrey intended to set out on a pilgrimage to Compostella. Henry ground his teeth in fury.

'That boy will do anything rather than stay at home

and tend to the affairs of his county. I shall write and tell him to abandon the idea.'

'I doubt,' she said with some asperity, 'that Geoffrey will be inclined to listen to your wishes in the matter.'

'Then who will he listen to?'

'Perhaps if he could be convinced that he will do God's will better by remaining at home than by undertaking a pilgrimage ... Perhaps Bishop Hildebert might have some influence. He has acted as intermediary before.'

'Hildebert? Yes, you are right. I shall write to him and tell him to write to Geoffrey conveying my extreme displeasure.'

In due course word came back from the bishop that Geoffrey had abandoned the idea of the pilgrimage. She remembered that it was Hildebert who advised her to give in to her father's demands and marry him. She could not rid her mind of the thought that she was being punished for her earlier sin and that perhaps she was compounding that sin by refusing to return to her husband. What would Hildebert expect her to do now? She wrote to him, asking for counsel.

He wrote back:

My dear daughter in Christ,

I have been greatly saddened by your breach with your husband. I am aware of the circumstances and it is clear to me that it is Geoffrey who is most to blame. I have written to him, begging him to put away his mistress and do everything in his power to reconcile himself with you and with your father. But I must also beg you to reconsider. It is written in the Bible that a wife should be conformable to her husband's will, and you do ill to set your own desires above the instruction of Holy Writ. You say in your letter that you are troubled in your conscience

117

and afraid that you may have deserved God's displeasure.
It would ease your mind to confess yourself to a man of
God and perhaps to take some time for prayer and con-
templation. My advice to you is to go on retreat for a time,
perhaps a month, and I would suggest that you could not
do better than to go to the abbey of Bec-Hellouin. The
abbot there, Theobald, is a holy and wise man who will
give you good counsel. Meanwhile, I commend you to
God's blessing. Hildebert.

She told her father that she needed time to consider
her future and received his permission to absent herself
from court. She rode south, across the River Loire, with a
handful of attendants and an escort of men-at-arms, and
came to the wooded valley where the abbey sat amidst
fertile pastures and fields of wheat. She was received
with courtesy, lodging was found for her escort and she
was given a simple room in the guest quarters. For some
days she was content to allow the simple routine of monastery life to soothe her. She was not required to get up
in the middle of the night to attend matins, or lauds, but
she attended the services of prime and terce and sext and
nones and vespers. Her favourite service was compline,
sung just before the whole monastery retired to bed. She
spent the intervening hours reading. She could not go into
the library, which was reserved for the monks and where
any female presence would cause a great disturbance, but
books were brought to her and she read in the cloisters or
the garden. At the back of her mind always was the recollection of Hildebert's words. 'It would ease your mind to
confess ...' Eventually she found enough courage to beg
a private audience with Abbot Theobald and, under the
seal of the confessional, she spilt out the story of her affair
with Drogo and its consequences.

When she had finished, Theobald was silent for a moment. When he spoke it was not in the voice of condemnation that she feared, but one of gentle consideration.

'It was a sin, certainly. But you were very young and it was a long time ago. I think, perhaps, you have already been punished enough. But you have confessed also that you are prone to the sin of pride and it is that that you must address. In the Bible we are told that pride goeth before destruction and a haughty spirit before a fall. It is that spirit that made you so unwilling to subject yourself to marriage to a man you thought beneath you. You must learn to conquer that. Go back to your husband and make yourself compliant to his will. That is the way of salvation.'

Some weeks after her return to Rouen, Henry sent for her. He had a letter in his hand.

'Your husband writes that he wishes you to return to him and he will receive you with all honour and treat you as befits your station as his wife and my daughter. It seems he has been in correspondence with Bishop Hildebert, who has persuaded him of the error of his ways and he wishes to make amends. What do you say to his proposal?'

She bowed her head. The thought of returning to Geoffrey still repelled her, but she knew now where her duty lay. 'That must be as you decide, my lord.'

'True, but I would like to know your thoughts on the matter. Are you prepared to go back?'

'On certain conditions. He must put his mistress away, and the child too. I know he has acknowledged him and wants him brought up in a fitting manner, but I do not … I cannot have him growing up in the castle. It would be too bitter a reminder. I'm sure there are noble families among Geoffrey's vassals in whose household the boy could be brought up. It is not an uncommon arrangement – as you know yourself.'

He acknowledged the sally with a smile and said, 'That sounds reasonable to me. And if Geoffrey undertakes to do that, and to behave honourably in future, you would be willing to return to him?'

'If it is also your wish.'

'It is true that I should prefer it. The alliance with Anjou is crucial, and I still have hopes of a grandson. But the decision is not so simple. When you returned from Germany I made all my principal English vassals swear that in the event of my death they would support you and any children you might have in the matter of the succession. Now some of them are saying that I promised that I would not marry you to a foreigner without consulting them first.'

'Did you promise that?'

He shrugged. 'I may have said something of the sort. But no one raised a dissenting voice when I betrothed you to Geoffrey, so I took it that I had their consent. Now, however, I think it would be politic to make sure that we have their full agreement before returning you to him. We will go back to England and I will call a full council so they cannot afterwards pretend that they were not consulted.'

'And if they decide against it...?'

Henry gave her a grim smile. 'They won't, if they know what's good for them.'

The council met in Northampton on 8 September. She found it strange to be back in England. It was the country of her birth but she had spent so little time there that she felt she was among foreigners. Even their Norman French had a different accent and it was occasionally interspersed with words from the old English language, which she had never learnt. It was a relief to find her uncle, David of Scotland, there. He seemed to have a special affection for her as his sister's child. He drew her aside and asked, 'Is this truly what you wish? I would not like to see you forced to return to a man who treated you so disgracefully.'

'If I am honest, Uncle, I think I was as much at fault as he was,' she answered. 'It will be best for everyone if I go back.'

As Henry predicted, there was little argument from the assembled lords. They knew Henry's temper too well to oppose him openly. She was to be returned to her husband, provided that he gave an undertaking to treat her honourably. She had the impression that most of them had little interest in her fate. In fact, she suspected that they would be glad to have her out of the way. They treated her with scant respect, and she responded with frosty dignity. Before they were allowed to leave, however, Henry extracted from them all a new oath of fealty to her and her sons, if any should be born.

Letters were dispatched, laying down the conditions for her return. By the time Geoffrey's replies, undertaking to honour the stipulations of the council, had been received the autumn was well advanced and sailing conditions were unfavourable. Henry had no intention of risking his one remaining legitimate child on the sea that claimed the life of his son, so it was decided that they would remain in England for the winter. Her reunion with her husband would have to wait until the spring.

The citizens of Rouen were lining the streets in their finest clothes once again. Henry had sent heralds round the city to ensure a good turnout to welcome his son-in-law. It was late May and the sun was shining and the bells in all the churches were ringing. Geoffrey arrived at the head of a glittering cavalcade, mounted on a pure white Spanish courser. Henry met him at the city gates, but Matilda watched him ride into the courtyard from an upper window. It was over two years since they parted, but she was unprepared for the change in him. It was partly that he had grown a beard, close clipped and as red-gold as his hair. It made him look older, but there was more to it than that. He was no longer a pretty boy. He had grown into a very attractive man. His behaviour was different, too. He acknowledged the cheers of the crowd with waves and smiles, but with a new-found dignity. He was not showing off, as he did when they first met. She felt an unexpected stirring of excitement at the thought that they would soon be reunited.

They met in the great hall of the castle. She was wearing vermilion, with an overmantle of cloth of gold. He was in a blue tunic embroidered with silver thread, white hose and a mantle of deeper blue lined with white satin. He dropped on one knee before her and kissed her hand.

'Madam, I have done you great wrong and I beg your forgiveness.' The words were a formality but they were gracefully pronounced.

She raised him and their eyes met, and she was reminded of how intensely blue his were. There was a challenge there, but beneath that she detected an offer of a truce. She said, 'The faults were on both sides, but they are in the past. Let us look to the future.'

'With all my heart,' he responded and kissed her on the lips.

There was the usual feasting in celebration and she was reminded of the two previous occasions when she had sat through course after course in dread of what must follow when the meal was over. Tonight her emotion was not one of fear. She was nervous, but there was something else, a thrill of anticipation, which disturbed and excited her. She noticed that Geoffrey was only drinking in moderation and wondered what that portended.

At last the feasting ended and she was escorted up to the same room where she spent that first disastrous night with Geoffrey. She wished suddenly that she had gone to him in Angers, or better still that they had met halfway, in a castle they had never visited before. When her women had undressed her and left, she sat looking at her reflection in the polished steel of her mirror. What did he see when he looked at her? That first night he called her an ugly cow. Poets and courtiers had praised her noble ancestry, her learning and her piety. Some had called her beautiful, but usually those who had never seen her, or only at a distance. It was conventional flattery, nothing more. But she could not, in all honesty, call herself ugly. Her chin was perhaps too square for feminine prettiness, but her skin was clear and showed very few lines. Her hair was thick and a lustrous brown and her eyes were large and fringed with dark lashes. What was more, she still had all her teeth. She was thirty years old, but her body was slim from hours spent on horseback or practising with the crossbow; her stomach was flat and her breasts full and firm. She told herself he had no reason for complaint.

The door opened and he came in. She stood and they looked at each other, and she saw that he, too, was uncertain. She remembered that he had demanded, on that first night, to see her naked and she had refused. With a swift, fluid movement she unfastened her robe and let it fall to the floor. His lips parted in a silent gasp, then he copied her and stood naked. There was no uncertainty about his erection this time. In the candlelight his body was sleek and golden and she was gripped by a sudden urgent desire to feel it pressed against her own. She moved to the bed and got in and he joined her and pulled her to him. His body was warm, his skin silky under her hands. He leant down and kissed her mouth and her pulse began to race. He had learned much in the intervening years. It crossed her mind that Rosanne had taught him, but she dismissed the thought. He began to caress her, but she was overcome by a need that must be satisfied at once. She wound her arms round him and dragged him onto her, her nails digging into his back. It was not a gentle coupling, but fierce as one between wild animals. When he entered she matched him thrust for thrust. She felt him ejaculate and then her own body contorted in a spasm of ecstasy.

When it was over they lay still, panting, until eventually he drew himself out and rolled onto his side. They looked into each other's eyes. He murmured, 'So, I am wed to a lioness. What fine cubs we shall breed together!'

She smiled. 'I think we may have already begun.'

9

ANJOU, 1133-35

HER PREDICTION WAS proved correct. They were in his castle at Le Mans when her pains began. Geoffrey was absent, dealing with some minor disturbance. It was not an easy birth. The child was late, and unusually large, but as the waves of pain engulfed her she told herself that she was finally expiating her sin. Geoffrey, warned by a messenger on a lathered horse, galloped into the courtyard and raced up the narrow stairs just in time to hear the baby's first cry. The midwife held the swaddled child up to him.

'Praise God, sir. You have a fine, healthy son.'

He gazed wonderingly at the child in his arms. 'My son! I have a son.' Then, a little belatedly, he turned to her. 'How do you, wife?'

'Well enough, thanks be to God. Bring him here to me.'

He laid the bundle in her arms and she looked down at the child's face. It was red but not wrinkled and wizened as she had seen other newborn children look. He opened his mouth and gave a loud, demanding yell. Geoffrey laughed. 'He has his grandfather's temper.'

She thought, Or his father's, but dismissed the idea. Instead she said, 'We will call him Henry. It is only fitting.'

'Henry.' He considered for a moment. 'I had thought of Fulk, after my father, but no, you are right. Henry he shall be.'

The child was baptised in the cathedral by Bishop Guy of Ploermel. His patron saint was St Julian, to whom the cathedral was dedicated, and Matilda gave a richly embroidered pall to cover the effigy of the saint in gratitude for her safe delivery. The older Henry was overjoyed with the news and sent gifts and blessings.

During the intervening nine months they had not been idle. Slowly they had rebuilt the shaky partnership they had begun to construct during the first year of their marriage. She had learnt much from her father while with him in Rouen about the administration of a kingdom and she applied those lessons on a lesser scale in Anjou. Disputes were settled, taxes collected, Geoffrey's treasury swelled. But many of his barons resented the new regime and he frequently had to ride out with his knights to impose order. In the early days she went with him and earned the respect of the men by her willingness to share the hardships of sleeping on the cold ground and eating the same rations. Usually, the sight of Geoffrey's banners and his accompanying band of well trained knights and men-at-arms was enough to bring the recalcitrant vassal to heel; but sometimes a show of force was not enough and they had to fight. On these occasions, she was often seen wielding her crossbow to good effect.

When her pregnancy was more advanced she had to stay behind, but Geoffrey still turned to her for advice. They were not lovers, in the full sense. At the beginning they coupled fiercely every night, but the teaching of the Church forbade intercourse once it was known that she was with child and their relationship was now one of comrades in arms, albeit shot through with suppressed desire.

As soon as she was healed after the birth, he came to her bed again and the old passion flared up, but within weeks they discovered that she was pregnant again. She was amazed by this sudden fecundity after so long without conceiving. King Henry was back in Normandy and Geoffrey was still forced to go campaigning at regular intervals, so it was decided that she would be safer in Rouen. She went willingly. It was a place where she had always felt at home and she was glad to be with her father again. He was delighted with his grandson, and with the prospect of another on the way. She noticed that he was putting on weight. He had always had a good appetite but now he tended to gorge himself to repletion. She recalled the physicians telling her first husband that he should eat less and felt a tremor of alarm, but Henry seemed to be in good health. He farted and belched more than before, but did not give any sign of being in pain. She told herself that she was worrying needlessly.

She was still in Rouen when her second labour began. This time it was clear early on that it was not going to be straightforward. The pains were acute, but they went on and on without result for two days. Then, unaccountably, they ceased and she was terrified that the child might be dead – but in a few hours they began again, more violently than ever. The midwife crouched at the end of the bed, urging her on.

'Take courage, my lady. Bear down! Call upon St Anne, who gave birth to Our Lady. Ask for her aid.'

She pushed and screamed and begged any saint who might be listening to end her suffering, but she was exhausted. It came into her mind that she might be dying. It was not infrequent for women to die in childbirth. Her ladies clasped her hands and mopped her brow with rose water and dimly she could hear them praying. The midwife called for oil and dipped her hand into it, and she screamed again as she felt the hand thrust into her distended vagina.

'The child is the wrong way round. I must try … Ah, there! Now, my lady, one more effort …'

She had no more strength to scream but she did not want to die. She thrust downwards and something inside her seemed to split apart, and the child erupted into the daylight in a smother of blood and mucus. She hardly heard them saying that it was another boy.

She was dimly aware in the hours that followed of being washed and given watered wine to drink and sips of soup. She heard the midwife murmuring something about 'too much blood'. Then the fever started and she lost all grasp of reality. When she next regained consciousness her father was at her bedside, clasping her hand, his face furrowed with tears.

'I am dying, am I not?' she whispered.

'We must pray to the Holy Mother to save you,' he answered. 'I have prayed and paid the monks of the abbey to say masses for you. We must trust in God.'

She forced herself to concentrate. 'I have bequests to make. I need to give away what I own to those who will make good use of it. Fetch a scribe.'

He protested that there was no need but she insisted. The scribe arrived and she listed her jewels and her lands and dictated that they be given to various abbeys and churches. Then she said, 'Father, I have one request of you. Let me be buried at Bec-Hellouin.'

'Bec-Hellouin? No, no. You must lie beside your great ancestors in the cathedral here. Your place is with Duke Rollo and William Longsword.'

'No!' She twisted restlessly on her pillow. 'I implore you, Father. It is my last wish. Let me be buried there among those holy monks and let them say masses for my soul.'

He sighed deeply. 'Very well, since you desire it so. It shall be as you wish.'

Whether it was Henry's prayers or the masses he had paid for no one could tell, but miraculously she did not die. The day came when she had the strength to ask, 'The child – did it live?'

'It did, my lady, God be praised.'

'Is it a boy or a girl?'

'A boy, my lady.'

'And does it thrive?'

'It does. The wet nurse says he is a lusty child.'

'Has he been baptised?'

'He has, madam. He was given the name Geoffrey, after his father.'

'Good, good.' She nodded, but she did not ask to see him.

Her father postponed his return to England to stay with his two grandsons. His pleasure in them was undisguised but it seemed to her that he gave them more attention than he spared for her. She was lethargic and unable to feel any pleasure in the new baby. Geoffrey, meanwhile, was occupied with an incursion by some of the Norman lords on his border and could not leave the battle to come to her. She felt abandoned. The thought which she once expressed to Adeliza, that most men regarded women as having only one use, to breed them heirs, returned with augmented force.

Slowly her strength returned. When autumn brought an end to the fighting season, Geoffrey wrote that he longed to have her at his side and eventually she felt sufficiently recovered to make the journey to Le Mans, where he was quartered. She brought her two sons with her and he greeted all three of them with joy.

'God be praised you are safe! It broke my heart that I could not come to you when you were in such danger, but if I had those grasping barons would have stolen half our lands.'

That night he came to her bed but she repulsed him. 'You do not know how close to death I came bearing our last child. I have no wish to risk myself like that again.'

He was not happy, but he reluctantly acquiesced, with the proviso that this would be a temporary arrangement only, until she fully regained her strength.

Winter passed. One fine spring day a stranger rode into the courtyard with a small retinue. Geoffrey brought him to Matilda, who was sitting in the garden while little Henry and his nursemaid played with a ball and baby Geoffrey slept on a rug nearby.

'My dear, this is William Talvas. He is the son of Robert of Bellême and we were childhood friends, but we have not met for years.'

She frowned. 'Bellême? Your father fought against my father at Tinchebrai. You are the son of a rebel who is in one of my father's prisons?'

Talvas bowed. 'It is true, my lady. My father was unwise enough to rebel against King Henry and paid the price. My hereditary lands have been confiscated ever since.'

Geoffrey broke in. 'William wishes to reclaim the castles confiscated from his father. He has done nothing wrong and I do not see why he should suffer.'

'Those castles were given to me as part of my dowry. Have you forgotten that?'

'Together with others, but we have never been given possession of them. If I had had them under my control I would have been able to put down that attack by the

Norman lords without the slightest difficulty. Now I propose to back William's demand that the castles be returned to him and that we be given full control over the others.'

'You have asked before. You know the answer. He will not yield them while he lives.'

'Then by God I shall take them by force! They are mine by right. Robert was one of my father's vassals and now William is one of mine. I shall not only demand the return of our property, I shall require Henry to do fealty to me for them.'

She stared at him in disbelief and then she laughed. 'You must be out of your mind! My father will be furious.'

'Furious or not, I intend to have those castles.' He came closer and squatted beside her. 'Think, Matilda. This is our sons' inheritance. If we do not protect it, it will be lost to them. If your father should die, what protection would we have from those rapacious Normans? Your father may have made us allies in theory, but you know as well as I do that the Normans hate us Angevins. We have been at each other's throats for generations. While your father lives he may be able to keep them under control but after ...'

'Why need we worry about that now? My father is in the prime of life. He will live to see his grandsons grown up.'

'Perhaps. But you know as well as I do how suddenly a life can be cut short. An unlucky blow from a sword, a crossbow bolt, or a sickness ... we are all mortal. We owe it to our sons to protect their inheritance.'

She sighed. 'It will mean going to war against my father.'

'Not if Henry gives in.'

'Well, write to him again – but in the name of God don't mention the question of fealty.'

As she expected, the request was refused out of hand. Deaf to her protests, Geoffrey assembled his knights and his men-at-arms and marched for the border. Word came that one of the Norman border lords, William of Ponthieu, had risen in rebellion against Henry and he and Geoffrey had joined forces, and that Henry had returned to Normandy and taken the field against them. Geoffrey sent a message urging her to raise further reinforcements and join him.

Over a long, sleepless night she wrestled with her divided loyalties. There was a time when she would not have considered siding with Geoffrey against her father, but things were different now. She had two sons to consider and their future welfare was her primary concern. If Geoffrey was defeated what would become of them? She reminded herself that her father had twice bound her to an unwanted marriage for his own political ends. All he wanted from her was an heir. Now he had two but he still refused to fulfil the promises he made at her wedding. She had another life now, and it was time to look to the future. In the morning she sent out demands to all Geoffrey's vassals for further levies of men and arms and as soon as they were assembled she rode to join her husband at the frontier.

The months passed in one indecisive skirmish after another until winter brought the fighting season to an end. When they returned to Angers, Geoffrey made it clear that he expected to resume normal sexual relations and she reluctantly acquiesced.

As Advent approached she started to prepare the castle for the Christmas celebrations. One evening as dusk was falling a messenger rode into the courtyard on a lathered horse and almost collapsed as he dismounted. Brought into the great hall, he fell on his knees before her.

'Gracious lady, do not be angry with me for the news I bring you.'

She looked down at him. His clothes were caked with mud and his face was grey with fatigue. A cold fist clenched on her gut. 'What news?'

'Madam, forgive me. The King your father is dead.'

10

ANJOU, 1135-36

THE SAME PRACTICALITY that served her well when her first
husband died came to her aid now. The messenger was
sent off to the kitchens with instructions that he be fed
and given a bed. Then the enormous implications of the
news overcame her. Geoffrey, alerted by a page, ran in and
found her sitting with her face in her hands. He knelt by
her and gently drew them away, but her eyes were dry.
She gazed at him in blank unbelief.

'It is not possible. He cannot be dead.'

'How did it happen? Was he killed in battle?'

'No. A sudden illness. That is all the messenger knew.'

'When did this happen?'

'Five days ago. The man has ridden almost day and
night to reach us.'

He stood up, crossing himself. 'God rest his soul. You
will mourn him, of course. We may have come to blows,
but he was your father. You will want to arrange masses
for his soul ...'

She rose abruptly. 'There will be time to mourn later.
I have been thinking. I must move quickly to claim the
throne.'

'The throne of England?'

'Of course, where else? We must leave for England at once.'

'No! We must secure our position in Normandy first.'

'Once I have England, Normandy will follow.'

'Not necessarily. Your father held both, but only after he had conquered his brother Robert and taken Normandy from him. If we go to England and leave the situation in Normandy unresolved, the Norman lords may choose someone else to rule. Once I am established as duke we can go to England without fear of trouble in our rear.'

'You?'

'Us. Obviously as my wife you will be the duchess.'

She looked at him and felt exasperation tinged with pity. 'I am Henry's heir. I shall be queen and duchess in my own right, not as your wife.'

His face darkened. 'And me? Do I have no rights?'

'Of course, as my husband you will have a place of honour. You will be my consort.'

He made a dismissive gesture. 'The English barons will never accept a woman as ruler.'

'They are oath sworn to me and to my son.'

'Your son is three years old! They won't accept him as king.'

'Then I will rule as regent until he is of age. You know very well that Henry never meant you to be king.'

'Henry is dead! His intentions no longer matter. We must forge our own destiny.'

She ran her hands over her face, pushing back the hair that had escaped from under her veil. 'We are acting like the foolish hunter who sold the bear's skin before he had killed the bear. First we must get to England and gather the support of the barons. Then we can discuss titles and lay claim to Normandy.'

'No, we must have Normandy first.' He turned to her urgently. 'Can you not see? If I leave Anjou those Norman lords we have been fighting will pour over the border and seize everything. I will not risk my birthright to be your consort in England. We must act now. At the very least we must secure our borders. You must assert your rights over those Norman castles.'

She laughed bitterly. 'I had other news to give you, but I was going to keep it until Christmas. I am with child again.'

Guigan Algason, the castellan of Argentan, met them in front of the city gates. Heralds had gone ahead to warn him of their approach and the gates in the massive walls were wide open. He fell on his knees beside Matilda's palfrey and offered her the keys on a silk cushion.

'Madam, you are my liege lady now that the King your father is dead. The castle of Argentan is yours, as are Exmes and Domfront, which are also under my stewardship.'

She thanked him and rode through the gates with her husband at her side. Algason might welcome her out of duty, but he knew as well as she did that the citizens might feel differently. They were followed by a large force of knights and men-at-arms, together with their squires and pages, and the smiths and butchers and bakers and all the hangers-on who make up an army. The castle could accommodate their personal entourage of clerks and chaplains and ladies-in-waiting and servants, together with their household knights, and the other prominent men found lodgings in the city. The common soldiers had to make camp in the fields outside. It was winter and there were no crops to provide them with sustenance. They soon resorted to stealing livestock and raiding grain stores and looting outlying villages. It could only be a matter of time before trouble broke out between the Norman citizens and their uninvited Angevin guests.

They had been in the city only three days when a young man wearing the colours of Robert of Gloucester rode in in the company of two men-at-arms. He introduced himself as Leofric of Shaftesbury, clerk in the earl's household.

'My lord of Gloucester has sent me, my lady, to offer you his deepest sympathy on the death of the King your father, and to assure you of his loyalty and support.'

'I thank you, and him.' She indicated that he should sit and leant towards him eagerly. 'Was the earl with him when he died? I know nothing of the circumstances.'

'He was, my lady. We were at Lyons-la-Forêt, the King's favourite hunting lodge.'

'I know it well. Was the King in good health?'

'So it seemed, and in good spirits too. He was looking forward to some good hunting. The first evening he partook of a dish of lampreys, always a favourite of his.'

'And one that always disagrees with him! His physicians have told him to avoid them.'

'I know nothing of that, madam. In truth, he made a plentiful repast, refilling his trencher several times. Then, in the middle of the night, he was taken with a powerful colic and began vomiting blood. His physicians were called and every treatment they could suggest was tried, but alas to no effect. Very soon it was obvious that His Grace was weakening.'

'Was a priest with him?'

'Indeed, madam. None other than the Lord Archbishop Hugh of Rouen was with him for three days. My lord of Gloucester instructed me to tell you particularly that your father confessed his sins and received absolution. He pardoned all exiles, revoked sentences of forfeiture and gave instructions for his body to be buried in Reading Abbey. Having thus eased his conscience, he made a peaceful and godly end.'

'May God rest his soul.'

'Did he name his successor?' Geoffrey broke across her murmured prayers. She looked at him in exasperation. Would he never learn when to speak and when to keep silent?

Leofric shook his head. 'My lord, I know nothing of that. It was not part of the message I was given to bring to you.'

'What arrangements have been made for conveying his body to England?' she asked, before Geoffrey could interrupt again.

'It has been embalmed and the entrails buried in the priory church of Notre Dame Du Pré. The lords who were with him, including my master, have taken an oath that they will not part company until they have conveyed his coffin safely to its last resting place. When I left, they were preparing to set out for Caen to take ship for England.'

She took a ring from her finger and extended her hand. 'I thank you for bringing me this news. It has eased my heart to know that he died in a state of grace. Take this as a token of my gratitude.'

Leofric kissed her hand and bowed himself out of the room. As soon as they were alone Geoffrey gave vent to some colourful curses. She said, 'What did you expect? Even if he did make his intentions clear, would we have been told the truth? But now we have a breathing space. Nothing will be decided until after the funeral. We must set out for England immediately.'

'No! We dare not leave until we are sure that Anjou

is safe. First we need to establish our control along the border. I am going to claim the remaining castles we were promised. I'll give them into the charge of Juhel de Mayenne. He's loyal and has a just claim to them. In return I shall ask for a promise of support if we need to call on him later. Then we need to get oaths of fealty from the leading Norman lords. After that, when we are sure that our backs are guarded, we can set out for England.'

She chewed her lip in indecision. 'If I am to claim the throne, I must be in England when the barons meet for my father's funeral. But it is a bad time of year for sailing. It may be that there will be a delay in taking my father's body across the narrow seas. But we cannot afford to wait for long.'

'Trust me! Juhel will be installed in Ambrieres within days and then we can move. Anyway, who else could they choose? Are there any other claimants?'

'It would have to be someone with the blood of the first William in his veins. Clito is dead. Who else is there? Henry's sister Adela is married to Stephen of Blois. She has sons. The eldest is Theobald, I think. The second is another Stephen. He was at court when the first oath was taken to support me and he swore, along with the rest. He has charm. He is a bit like my father, ready to eat and joke with anyone, regardless of rank. I think my father was quite fond of him. And of course the third son, Henry, is Bishop of Winchester.'

Geoffrey spat. 'Blois! That nest of vipers! They have been our enemies since time began. We need to know what is happening in Caen. I shall send a reliable man to keep an eye on those lords who are accompanying the coffin.'

Geoffrey left to claim the remaining castles. While he

was absent his spy returned with news.

'The weather has prevented the lords from taking ship. They are waiting in Caen, but I have heard disturbing rumours. Some of them met with Norman lords at Lisieux and discussed the question of the succession. It seems they favour Theobald of Blois.'

She leapt to her feet. 'Traitors! Oath breakers! I will have their heads for treason when I am queen and they will burn in hell for their sin.'

Geoffrey returned triumphant just before Christmas.

'Juhel de Mayenne now holds the castles of Ambrières, Gorron and Châtillon-sur-Colmont – and what's more William Talvas has seized Seès and Alençon. At least we control the border area now.'

'Then we can leave for England at once.'

'Is there any truth in the rumour that the English lords have offered Normandy to Theobald?'

'So I have heard. That makes it all the more imperative for me to assert my authority. The traitors hold honours on both sides of the narrow seas. They will not wish to owe allegiance to two different lords. Once I am queen, they will soon abandon Theobald.'

'Even if I agreed with you – which I don't – it is impossible to set out for England now. All the reports speak of terrible storms. It would be madness to try to cross until they abate. You said yourself that nothing will be decided until Henry is buried. At least wait until after Christmas.'

Christmas was celebrated with as much state as could be managed at short notice and the festivities were marred by outbreaks of fighting between Normans and Angevins in the city. The twelve days were not over when another messenger arrived. The weather had cleared and the cortège with the King's body had left Caen, but word had crossed the Channel in the opposite direction. On 22

December in Winchester Cathedral, Stephen of Blois had been anointed King of the English by the Archbishop of Canterbury.

A letter from Robert of Gloucester brought further details. Amongst his other honours Stephen held the lordship of Boulogne, through his wife, who was also called Matilda; and he happened to be there when news of Henry's death was received. While his older brother was negotiating with the knights accompanying the King's body for possession of Normandy, he had gathered a small force and braved the weather to cross to England. He was refused entry to Dover, which belonged to Robert, but pressed on to London, where he was received with acclamation. The principal source of London's wealth was the wool trade with Flanders, most of which passed through the port of Boulogne, so the citizens were delighted at the prospect of the same overlord holding both cities. Stephen promised them valuable concessions, including nominating London as a commune, which would give them much greater freedom to manage their own affairs. So all the leading burghers had done homage to him and promised their support. From there, Stephen had moved quickly to Winchester, where the royal treasury was held, and with the aid of his brother, the bishop, persuaded William Pont de l'Arche, the treasurer, to hand over the keys. Robert wrote:

This having been achieved the usurper then set out to persuade the Archbishop of Canterbury to crown and anoint him as king. The Archbishop was loath to do so because of the oaths we had all sworn to you and your son, but Hugh Bigod, the Earl of Norfolk, and two other knights, swore that they had heard your father on his deathbed release all his subjects from their oath to you and name Stephen as his successor. To my knowledge, neither Hugh nor the other two were present at the time, though they were among the King's followers, but the Archbishop believed them and took that as sufficient grounds to proceed with the coronation.

I have learned that upon news of your father's death, many of the lesser barons, freed from the fear of his retribution, and seeing no one at hand to take over the rule of the kingdom, seized the opportunity to settle old grievances and grab for themselves disputed lands, so that the country lapsed into anarchy. Many men longed for a strong ruler to bring order to the chaos. Stephen has thus drawn to him many of the great men of the kingdom and his position is such that, unless you can bring a sufficient force to unseat him, he must prevail. I beg you to believe me, madam, that you have my undying loyalty, but for the present I can do nothing to advance your cause.

Matilda rounded on her husband. 'You see? This is what our delay has wrought. If I had done as I wished and gone straight to England the people would have seen that the succession was secure and I could have put a stop to that lawlessness. Now, let us gather our forces and set out before the usurper makes himself stronger yet.'

Geoffrey shook his head obstinately. 'I dare not leave Normandy yet. You have seen how unpopular we Angevins are. If I take my troops to England the Normans will rise up and we shall lose all that we have gained.'

She gazed at him in disbelief. 'You are refusing to help me to prosecute my just claim to the crown? You will not join your forces with mine?'

'Not at present. When I have Normandy, then we can think about England.'

'You put being Duke of Normandy above my right to the throne?'

He looked back at her with narrowing eyes. 'Why not? You told me yourself that your father never intended me to be king. I should rather take what I can get than waste my energies pursuing a hopeless quest.'

'Then I shall go alone!'

'Don't be a fool! You do not have sufficient men to mount a campaign. It would be madness to challenge Stephen, who has all the resources of England behind him, with such a pitiful handful.'

'Then come with me!'

'No! You must have patience and wait until we are ready. With Normandy at my command we can raise enough men and money to mount a proper campaign. Besides,' he softened his tone, 'have you forgotten you are with child? How can you think of risking yourself in battle until after the birth?'

She sent for Alexander de Bohun, the captain of her household knights. Over the recent years she had been carefully building their numbers, determined never again to have to rely on Geoffrey for an adequate escort. But they were still a small force by comparison with his army.

'My husband refuses to help me to drive out the usurper who has taken my throne. Can we muster sufficient forces to attack Stephen?'

He shook his head sadly.

'It is impossible, my lady. You know yourself how few we are in comparison to the numbers the usurper could bring against us. It would be suicide to attempt it.'

'But my brother, Robert of Gloucester, would raise his people in my support. I am sure of that.'

'It is not enough, madam. Without my lord Geoffrey's assistance we would be fools to proceed.'

*

She had no choice but to remain in Argentan. In Anjou a dissident baron, Robert of Sablé, raised a rebellion and Geoffrey was forced to return to suppress it. Matilda paced the castle battlements in frustration as she waited for his return. Then just after Easter one of the spies she had dispatched to report on what was happening in England arrived and begged audience.

'King Stephen—'

She cut him short. 'You mean the usurper Stephen!'

'Forgive me, my lady. I have become accustomed to referring to him as king. Otherwise it would be obvious that I am in your service.'

'Very well. Go on.'

'He summoned all the lords to his Easter court. Before them all he produced a letter from Pope Innocent approving his assumption of the throne. All had sworn fealty to him, save only your brother, the Earl of Gloucester. He has always refused to present himself at court, in spite of many summonses from Stephen. This time … forgive me, madam … this time he went. He did homage and was received with great kindness and rewarded with lands and privileges.'

'I do not believe you. He would never betray me like that.'

'I can tell you only what I have gleaned from talking to men about the court, madam. But I believe it is true.'

She turned away, determined not to show weakness, but she could not stop her tears. 'The traitor! The traitor!'

A letter arrived from England. At first she did not recognize the seal; then she remembered that it belonged to Adeliza. With a shock she realized that she had not given a thought to the other woman's fate since Henry's death.

To the Empress Matilda, Countess of Anjou, and rightful Queen of the English; from Adeliza, widow of Henry, King of England.

My dear friend – I cannot address you as daughter, though my marriage to your father would give me that right. You were a queen long before me and I have never forgotten how you interceded with the Emperor, at my urgent plea, to release my father. I have hoped to welcome you to England to take up your rightful place, but now the usurper Stephen sits on the throne and you are not here to oppose him. If only you would come, my dear friend, there would be many who would welcome you with open arms – myself among them. We have been too long without a just ruler. Freed from your father's authority the petty barons all round the country have taken the chance to expand their power. Old injuries are avenged, disputed land is seized, brigands and masterless men terrorize the country and the people cry out for law and justice. That is why so many are prepared to bend the knee to Stephen. By putting down revolts and imposing his rule he is making himself stronger with every day that passes.

If you were to show yourself I do not doubt that the people would rally to you, and I should be glad to do what little I can to help. You will know well the weak position of a widow who has not produced a child to inherit her husband's powers. I have retired to the convent of Wilton Abbey, but I still retain the lands and properties granted to me by your father and I am willing to use their revenues to help your cause. But you must be here. Without your presence the usurper will consolidate his gains and we shall be unable to unseat him.

I long to embrace you as my friend, my daughter as the law would have it, and my queen.

Geoffrey was still occupied in Anjou. There was nothing she could do in response to this plea.

She had one consolation. On 22 July she gave birth to a third son and named him William, after his illustrious grandfather. This birth was easier and she was convinced that this was due to the intercession of the Holy Mother, to whom she had prayed fervently. She wanted to make a thank offering, but for some days she could not decide on an appropriate gesture. During her lying-in, her mind returned to the child she had lost so many years ago in Italy and that necessarily brought back memories of Drogo. Norbert had told her that he had become one of his followers, so she assumed he was at the monastery of Premontré. Slowly an idea grew in her mind. She would found a new abbey on land she held nearby in the forest of Gouffern, and who better than Drogo to be its first abbot. Norbert, she knew, was dead and his place as abbot had been taken by Hugh, who was the chaplain who accompanied her on her journey to Utrecht for her betrothal to the emperor. She called her secretary and composed a letter to him. She asked him to send some monks to form the nucleus of a new foundation, which she would endow, and suggested Drogo as a suitable man to take charge of it. She remembered Hugh well, and felt sure that he would comply with her wishes. The letter giving his assent arrived quickly and she gave orders for building to begin.

She was up and about the normal business of the household when her steward informed her that a monk by the name of Brother Drogo wished to be admitted to her presence. She had intended the new abbey as a thank offering to God, and some form of reparation to Drogo for the destruction of his career as a knight in the emperor's service. It had not occurred to her – or perhaps, she thought afterwards, she deliberately ignored the possibility – that it would provoke a meeting between them. Her heart began to thump and for a moment she considered telling the steward that she was not available. But that would be the ultimate betrayal. She gave orders for him to be brought in and dismissed her attendants.

He stood before her, his eyes cast down and his hands hidden in the sleeves of his white robe. She looked at him and felt a physical shock. She would not have recognized him. He was very thin. His cheeks were hollow and the hair that remained around his tonsure was sparse. She remembered that the Premonstratensian order imposed a life of great austerity.

Her throat was dry and it was a struggle to speak. 'Welcome. I trust you are in good health.'

His eyes flickered up to hers briefly. 'I am, my lady. I pray that the same is true for you.'

'I am well enough. You will know that I have recently given birth to a son.' This time his gaze held hers for a fraction longer and she knew that he was thinking of the child that might have been theirs. She went on, 'I wish to make a thank offering to the Virgin for my safe delivery. It is for that reason that I wish to endow a new foundation for your order.'

His tone was formal, without emotion. 'It is a noble enterprise and one worthy of your great piety. I come to thank you on behalf of my community.'

'You must know, too, that my father has recently died and that the throne that should be mine has been usurped by my cousin. I hope to win God's favour to secure a happy enterprise in my struggle to regain it.'

'You may be assured, madam, that our prayers will be offered daily to that end.'

'I wish you also to pray for the soul of my father and for the well-being of my three sons.'

'All these will be remembered every time we pray, in gratitude for your bounty.'

They were both silent for a moment. She sought for some way of prolonging the conversation. 'I hope you have found everything in order in your new home.'

'We have all that we could wish for. Your grace has made ample provision.'

'If there is anything else, do not hesitate to ask.'

'There is nothing more. As you know, we live very simply.'

She hesitated and then rose to her feet. 'Will you bless me before you go?'

There was a fractional hesitation. Was he remembering, and asking himself whether either of them had any right to ask blessing from the other? Then his priestly vocation reasserted itself. 'Assuredly.'

She knelt and felt his hand on her head, the touch so light as to be almost imperceptible. He intoned the words of the blessing and she stood up.

'If that is all, my lady...?'

'That is all.'

He made a slight bow and moved towards the door. With a rising surge of emotion she added, 'God go with you, Drogo.'

He turned and met her eyes properly for the first time. 'And the blessing of God remain with you, my lady.'

Then he was gone.

In September Geoffrey began to implement his plan of reducing the Norman strongholds one by one, until all the lords decided to submit and accept him as duke. He had found new allies, including the powerful Duke William of Aquitaine. He captured the city of Carrouges and advanced towards Lisieux, but here he met with determined resistance in the shape of an army led by Waleran of Meulan, one of the Beaumont twins, who were leading supporters of Stephen. At the beginning of October a messenger galloped into the courtyard of Argentan Castle and dropped to his knees in front of Matilda.

'My lady, I bring word from Lord Geoffrey. He is in dire need of support. He is besieging the castle of Le Sap, but his men are sick and he fears he may have to retreat unless help comes. He begs you to bring your knights to his assistance.'

Her spirits sank at the summons. She had barely recovered from William's birth and the prospect of a long ride through hostile territory was daunting. She sent for Alexander de Bohun, however, and ordered him to marshal her forces. The next morning she rode out at the head of her household knights and men-at-arms. Even before they came in sight of Geoffrey's camp, their nostrils were assailed by a terrible stench and as they rode in the reason became apparent. Men were lying between the tents, helpless and groaning, and the smell of excrement was overwhelming.

Alexander looked at her grimly. 'The bloody flux. I feared as much.'

Beyond the camp they could see that the walls of the castle had been breached and there was fighting going on amongst the rubble, but only a small force appeared to be engaged.

'It looks as if the main work is over,' Alexander commented. 'Our forces are victorious and what remains is just a mopping-up exercise.'

'I pray you are right,' she responded. 'It is clear that most of the men are in no condition to fight.'

They rode on towards the tent where Geoffrey's standard was flying, but as they reached it they heard a confused commotion and a small group came running towards them from the direction of the castle walls. They were carrying someone on a makeshift litter. One of them carried a helmet and her breath caught in her throat as she recognized the sprig of broom which Geoffrey still used as his emblem. She leapt down from her horse and met them as they reached the tent. Geoffrey was white with pain, his teeth clenched to choke down moans he could not quite suppress. One of his feet was bare and blood was pulsing from a gaping wound.

'What happened?' She caught his squire by the sleeve.

'A javelin, my lady,' the boy panted. 'Thrown from the battlements. It pierced his shoe and went right through his foot.' He turned aside, pressing his hand over his mouth as if about to vomit.

They were waiting for her to take command. 'Carry him into his tent. Fetch the surgeon. Fetch clean water and bandages.'

It was obvious from the smell that Geoffrey had not only been wounded but had succumbed to the sickness laying waste his army. His attendants laid him on the bed and begin to strip him of his filthy clothing. She looked at him and felt only revulsion. He was sobbing and swearing, all his charm and courage gone. She turned away and went to the entrance of the tent to greet the surgeon.

There was a stir amongst the crowd around the tent and William of Aquitaine pushed his way through. She had met him briefly, when he passed through Argentan to join Geoffrey.

'Praise God you are here, madam. Our case was perilous before but now it is a hundred times worse.'

'Perilous, sir? It seemed to me as we rode in that the castle had been taken.'

'Taken, yes, but a few of the garrison are still holding

out in the keep. It was one of them who threw the javelin that wounded Lord Geoffrey. How does he?'

The last question was addressed to the surgeon, who looked up briefly. 'If we can stop the blood he will do well enough.'

'Do what you can. He must be ready to travel by morning.'

'Travel?' she demanded. 'Travel where?'

'Away from here, back to your own land. Waleran de Meulan is hot on our heels and we are in no condition to withstand another battle.'

'I saw that. Is it the flux?'

'Yes, and more than half the men are suffering from it. It is as much as they can do to stand, let alone fight.'

'I cannot order the retreat without my husband's agreement. Summon all the captains to a council. We will meet with them as soon as the surgeon has finished here.' She turned back to the bed. 'Are you succeeding?'

'I have washed the wound with wine and packed it. I will bandage it and we must hope that it is enough to stop the bleeding. I will prepare a draft for my lord to ease the pain.'

'No poppy!' Geoffrey ground the words through a clenched jaw. 'I must stay alert. Our position is dangerous.'

She stooped over him. 'Take the draft. I am here, with William and your other captains. If you agree we must withdraw, I can see that it is done in good order – as far as is possible.'

He hesitated and then nodded. 'But not until I have spoken to them. They must know the order comes from me.'

The surgeon sent his apprentice to fetch the necessary ingredients and while they waited she asked, 'What has brought about this terrible sickness among the men?'

151

He pursed his lips. 'It is ever thus with an army in the field of battle. The men must live off the land. The crops have been devastated by the fighting so all that is left is the livestock – sheep, cattle, horses, dogs if there is nothing else. The men have no skill at cooking, and they will not wait to satisfy their hunger, so the meat is eaten half cooked, without bread or salt. The human stomach cannot tolerate such a diet for long.'

The captains of the army assembled and it was quickly agreed that a retreat was the only option. Geoffrey was in no condition to give orders by that time, but they accepted that Matilda spoke for him. Before dawn next day tents were struck and wagons loaded and the army straggled out of camp and headed south towards Argentan. Matilda gave instructions for her knights to form a rearguard, but she rode beside the litter in which her husband was carried. In spite of the surgeon's draft he could not suppress his groans and he was so pale that she feared for his life. It was an ignominious end to the campaign. Many of the men were in such dire straits that they had removed their braies and rolled their hose down to their ankles to give free passage to the trickle of filth, and their track was marked by a trail of dung, as if a herd of cattle had passed that way. Those that were too weak to walk were either carried by their stronger companions or left by the wayside. They could expect little mercy from the local inhabitants, for the Angevins had made themselves hated all through the region. Stories of atrocities abounded and they were accused of desecrating churches and raping nuns. William assured her that Geoffrey issued an edict threatening death to anyone convicted of such horrors, but the rumours still persisted.

They forded the River Don and as they climbed the rising ground on the far side she heard shouts and the clash of swords behind her. She cantered back to where she could look down on the river and saw a contingent of Norman knights in fierce conflict with her own men. The baggage train was still making its cumbersome way across the ford and the Normans were attempting to capture it. Already one of the carts had been diverted and dragged back to the far side of the river, but Alexander's knights were defending vigorously. With the horses fetlock deep in the water, there was vicious hand-to-hand fighting going on. She dismounted and grabbed the crossbow which she carried hooked to the pommel of her saddle, aimed and fired. A Norman clutching the bridle of one of the carthorses cried out and slumped backwards into the river. She reloaded and fired again and another Norman fell off his horse. Her knights took fresh heart and began to drive the remaining opponents back, until suddenly the Normans broke and rode for their own side of the river. Some of her own men started in pursuit but Alexander ordered them back, knowing they could be riding into an ambush. The drivers of the baggage carts whipped their horses up the bank towards her and Alexander led his men after them.

When he reached her he said, 'I am sorry, my lady. They took us by surprise. They were laying in wait in the shelter of that band of willows. They have taken one wagon. Do you want me to take the men and try to recover it?'

'No. You are needed here to protect the main force against further attacks. Do you know what was in the wagon they have stolen?'

He made a wry grimace. 'I fear it was the one containing my lord's state robes and jewels.'

She almost laughed. It seemed a fitting conclusion to the whole disastrous episode.

11

ARGENTAN, 1136-37

By the summer's end they were back in Argentan and there was nothing more to be done but wait out the winter and prepare for the next campaign.

As the months passed, Matilda's life began to settle into a routine. Argentan was a pleasant enough place to live. It was a rich city, and well defended by solid walls with sixteen towers, within which the castle itself was surrounded by its own battlements. She knew it well. It was a favourite with Henry because of the skill of its armourers, and he had settled his personal hauberk makers on lands in the vicinity. The Norman population accepted her as their natural suzeraine and once Geoffrey's army had been dispersed for the winter there were no grounds for dispute. She resumed her usual duties, overseeing the administration of the area, while Geoffrey concerned himself with affairs in his own county. There were days when she began to think that perhaps life as the Countess of Anjou and Normandy was sufficient and the prospect of being Queen of England seemed a distant dream.

Her principal care was for her three boys, and particularly for Henry. He was now a sturdy 4-year-old, active and strong willed, in need of strict discipline. She undertook his education herself, determined that he should learn to be a scholar as well as a soldier, like his grandfather. He was intelligent but impatient, and it was hard to keep him at his books for long. When he was a little older she would employ a schoolmaster, but for now his lessons provided a focus for her own active mind. His other training she handed over to her master-of-horse and her master-at-arms and both reported him an apt pupil. She had less interest in the other two. William was just a baby and could be left in the charge of his wet nurse. It was Geoffrey, the middle son, whose birth nearly cost her her life, whom she found it hardest to care for. He was a fretful, sickly child, constantly whining and given to violent tantrums. In the end she decided that he should be sent away to be reared in another noble household and he went to Saumur to live with the Goscelin family, long-time allies of the counts of Anjou.

She watched over the rest of her household, too, and took a particular interest in the young men who came to train with her knights. They were landless boys for the most part, second and third sons, whose only hope of pre-ferment was through their prowess at arms. She watched them in the tilt yard and when she noticed any who seemed to have potential she offered them a place in her entourage, with the promise that if they proved worthy she would make them knights.

With the arrival of spring Geoffrey's spies reported that Stephen had landed in Normandy with a large force. Geoffrey immediately summoned all his vassals for a new campaign, determined to put together an army to equal his rival's. While he waited for them to gather they heard further news. Stephen had come to an agreement with Louis of France to accept him as Duke of Normandy, and his son Eustace had done homage to Louis in his father's stead. Also, he had reconciled himself with his brother Theobald, thus neutralizing a possible threat from Blois.

Worse news followed.

'That turncoat William of Aquitaine has gone over to France. He has even betrothed his daughter Eleanor to that milksop of a son of Louis.'

'That is ill news, indeed,' she said, but could not resist adding with a wry smile, 'Young Louis may end up regretting the match. From what I hear Eleanor is not only so beautiful that she turns every man's head, but a very strong-minded young woman. He will have his hands full.'

'Never mind that!' he snapped. 'We have to deal with Stephen before he makes himself too strong. We must march immediately.'

This time she went with him. She could not face more months of waiting for news. Initially they advanced unimpeded. Stephen was occupied with imposing his authority over a number of rebellious local lords in the north of the duchy. They reached Lisieux and occupied the castle of Livarot. They had not been there very long before word came that Stephen was moving to attack them.

Standing on the battlements with Geoffrey, she watched his army pitch camp in the surrounding fields. They were numerous and well equipped and she realized, with a tightening in her gut, that they were going to have to withstand a long siege.

'Oh!' She caught her breath. It felt as if someone had stabbed her. 'Look there!'

'What is it?'

'Over there. That is Gloucester's banner. I knew he was a traitor but I did not think he would take the field against us.'

'God rot him! Just let me meet him on the battlefield.'

156

'You may yet have the chance, if they decide to try to storm the castle.' She continued to survey the field. 'Whose banner is that?'

'William of Ypres,' her husband replied. 'He's a mercenary from Flanders. His men are probably the best trained and equipped in the army, but I hear rumours that he is not well liked by the Norman lords. There have been disagreements, even fights.'

'That could be good news for us.' An idea began to form in her mind. 'Perhaps we could encourage it.'

'How?'

'I don't know yet. But there must be a way ...'

Later she summoned two young squires from her household. They had come to her notice on several occasions because their daring and irrepressible sense of mischief had got them into trouble.

'Piet, you speak Flemish, do you not?'

The boy looked uneasy. 'I do, madam. My mother was from Flanders, but pray do not hold that against me.'

'I do not. I have a mission for the two of you and that ability may be useful. Listen ...'

She outlined a dangerous escapade, which they accepted without hesitation.

The following day, patrolling the battlements with Geoffrey, they heard a sudden outcry from the Norman camp.

'What's going on?' Geoffrey asked, and hurried to a point where he could overlook the centre of the camp. She joined him and others flocked round them as the noise rose to a crescendo.

'By God, they are fighting each other!' Geoffrey exclaimed. 'It looks as if Stephen's men and the mercenaries have come to blows.'

As they watched the fighting spread, as men from each

157

contingent threw themselves into the fray in support of their comrades. Swords were drawn and fierce duels broke out all round the camp. Then they saw Stephen erupt from his tent with his squires and men at arms. He strode into the mêlée, shouting commands, and little by little the fighting subsided, but there were bodies on the trampled grass.

Geoffrey was exultant. 'Truly, God is on our side! If feelings are running that high they will never hold the army together for the length of a siege.'

The two young squires were waiting for her in her chamber.

'You have achieved more than I ever imagined,' she told them. 'And you will be amply rewarded. How did you do it?'

They exchanged grins. 'It was easy,' one said. 'We slipped out of the postern gate just before dawn and hid among the bushes by the river bank. We had seen that the Flemish squires water their horses at a different point from the Normans, so we waited close to where they always come. When it got light they started to bring the horses down to the river. We waited until two of them came on their own and then we jumped on them and tied them up and took their clothes.'

'It wasn't difficult,' Piet chimed in. 'They weren't expecting trouble. We told them there were crossbow-men watching from the battlements and if they shouted and drew attention to themselves they would be shot. Then we took their horses and went into the camp. We were wearing Flemish colours and no one thought to challenge us. We joined a few lads who were hanging around waiting for orders and I got talking to them. It was obvious they were just spoiling for a fight with the Normans. Then Rollo here spotted the squire of one of the Norman lords rolling a barrel of wine towards his tent. So I said, "Come on, lads. Let's have a bit of fun. Let's take his wine off him." They caught on at once, so we waylaid him, grabbed the barrel and started to make off with it. Of course, he immediately set up a yell that the Flemings had stolen his master's wine and in no time half a dozen of his fellows came rushing out after us and a real punch-up started. Then two Norman knights came out of their tent and started laying about them with the flat of their swords, trying to break up the fight. Then a couple of Flemish knights appeared and when they saw the Normans with their swords out they drew their own and attacked them. And after that more men joined in and more still. It was chaos!'

'But you got away unscathed?'

Rollo took up the tale. 'Once they were all busy knocking the devil out of each other we started to run away. Some of the Normans came after us, but the tents were quite close together and we were running along a narrow alley between them. We still had the barrel, so I rolled it down towards the lads chasing us. It caught two of them and knocked their legs from under them and the rest got tangled up with the ones on the ground and that gave us enough time to dodge out of sight among the tents. We waited for a bit, but by that time there was so much fighting going on that no one took any notice of us. We ran for the river, grabbed our weapons and cut the two Flemings loose and headed back to the postern. Ranulf had agreed to wait there and let us back in, so here we are.'

She felt a stirring of excitement which she had not known for months. 'You are both brave and audacious young men and well deserve the best reward I can offer. Tomorrow you shall both be knighted. You have my word for it.'

They gazed at her wide eyed. It was indeed the greatest reward they could imagine. Rollo blushed to the roots of his hair. 'Madam, it is an honour to be of service to you. We ask for no more reward than that.'

'Nevertheless, you shall have it. And more. Here ...' She drew from her fingers two rings set with rubies. 'Wear these as a sign of my gratitude.'

They fell on their knees and kissed her hands and she knew that there would be at least two young knights in her household who would be willing to lay down their lives for her.

The effects of the fight were greater than any of them could have hoped for. Next morning they saw that all round the enemy camp different contingents among the Norman forces were striking their tents and loading equipment onto carts. By midday the places they occupied were nothing more than patches of trodden grass.

'By God!' Geoffrey exclaimed. 'Stephen has lost half his army.'

A day later envoys from Stephen came to the castle under a flag of truce. She received them with Geoffrey in the great hall of the castle.

'Well?' Geoffrey asked when they had made their obeisances. 'What does your lord want with me?'

'Sire, King Stephen offers generous terms. He has affairs of his own to attend to in England and would be glad to resolve the present conflict. He offers a truce, to last for three years, and in return he will pay you a pension from his own estates. Do you accept?'

They retired to the solar to confer.

'We cannot accept!' she insisted. 'It will be tantamount to accepting Stephen's right to the throne.'

'Let us not be too hasty,' her husband replied. 'Our resources are stretched to the limit, you know that. The men are weary of campaigning and the summer is drawing to an end. We cannot hope to gain much more territory for now. If we take Stephen's offer it will give us time to restore our forces and prepare for a new advance. And the money he offers will help to recruit men and equip them.'

She saw the force of his argument and the truce was duly signed. Geoffrey withdrew his troops to Carrouges.

There was one more piece of news before the summer was out. King Louis of France was dead and had been succeeded by his mild-mannered son. There was no way of guessing which side in the conflict he would support.

One day Matilda's steward came to her to say that an itinerant friar was waiting in the hall and begged to speak with her. She told him to bring the man to her chamber. He was barefoot and dressed in the brown habit of a friar, but his voice when he spoke had the accents of a courtier.

'Madam, I have a boon to ask. Will you dismiss your ladies so we can speak alone?'

She sent the women away and the friar threw back his hood to reveal a face she remembered.

'I know you. What is your name?'

'I am Leofric of Shaftesbury, madam. In the service of the Earl of Gloucester. I came to you once before with a message from my master.'

She got to her feet. 'Gloucester! What is a servant of that traitor doing in my castle?'

He knelt. 'I beg you, madam, do not judge too quickly. I bring you a letter from my lord your brother. He sent me disguised like this for fear it should fall into the wrong hands.'

He took a folded parchment from the purse at his belt and held it out. She recognized the seal as Gloucester's. She broke it, unfolded the letter and read:

161

To the Empress Matilda, Countess of Anjou, Rightful Queen of the English and my dearly beloved sister.

I know you must believe that I have betrayed you, but I beg you to let me state my case. I held out against the usurper as long as I could, but when there was no word from you, no sign that you intended to come to England and enforce your rights, I had to appear to yield. If I had not done so, I should have lost all my lands and any power I possess to aid you, should you require my help. Believe me, I did homage with a heavy heart and I am prepared to retract it at any sign from you.

I have not returned to England with Stephen, but have remained here in Caen, which as you know is my ancestral home, where I have a strong castle. Here I have been joined by several others who hate the usurper as much as I do. There are others in England who I know will rise for you the moment you set foot on the shore. But we must bide our time until our friends have laid the foundation for your return. Be patient, but meanwhile please be assured that I am, as I have always been, your loving brother and devoted servant.

12

CARROUGES AND CAEN, 1138-39

PATIENCE WAS, INDEED, what she required. Another long winter passed, while she was occupied with maintaining order in the border lands between Normandy and Anjou and Geoffrey was raising and training recruits for a new campaign in the spring. She had her hands full, as sporadic fighting broke out all over the disputed territory between her lands and those still loyal to Stephen. In Lent Ralph, the lord of Esson, rose in revolt and she had to send Alexander de Bohun to suppress him. They brought him back to Carrouges in fetters, and she had him kept in her dungeons until he agreed to hand over his castle.

Envoys went back and forth between her and Robert, disguised as friars or merchants. From one of them she heard that Stephen had taken this local fighting as a sign that the truce had broken down and sent William of Ypres and Waleran Beaumont back to Normandy to restore order. Then just after Easter came news that raised her spirits. Her brother wrote:

I have decided that the time has come to make it clear to Stephen where my loyalties lie. He suspects me already and not long ago I narrowly escaped an ambush laid for me by William of Ypres. I have, therefore, sent him a formal 'diffidatio', repudiating my oath of fealty. It means, of course, that my lands and castles will be forfeit, but Bristol, which is my main stronghold, is well defended and provisioned and I do not doubt that it will withstand any attack. But we must move soon, while our friends are still in control of their own castles. You must persuade your husband to bring his powers to join with mine and then I do not doubt we shall be victorious.

She sent to Geoffrey, urging him to move north with his army, but he responded that he could not leave Anjou yet. It was June when he finally arrived, bringing with him the strongest force he had yet mustered. She showed him Robert's letter.

'Now are you convinced? We must move now, or it will be too late.'

He gave her the impatient, almost contemptuous look she knew too well. 'How do you imagine we are going to march an army through Stephen's territory to reach your brother? Waleran holds Falaise, which lies right across our path. If we are to reach Caen we first have to reduce Falaise.'

'Then let us do so!' she exclaimed.

They marched north, but news from Caen caused them to change their plans. Waleran and William of Ypres had been joined by a large force of knights sent to help them by Ralph of Vermandois, Louis of France's uncle, and they were laying waste the area around Robert's stronghold. Further progress seemed impossible and they withdrew to Argentan.

A letter arrived from Adeliza:

I have news. I am married again, to William of Albini, who is a strong supporter of the usurper Stephen. It is not a match of my choosing, but I think Stephen suspects my loyalty. He is afraid that I might become the focus of rebellion against him and wishes to prevent that by putting me in the charge of a man he can trust. It is not as terrible as it might have been. William is not a cruel man and we are quite comfortable with each other. I believe we may come in time even to love each other.

Do not imagine that this lessens my affection for you or my determination to help you. But you have not shown yourself in England and I begin to believe that you have no intention of claiming the throne. If that is so, I must content myself with living under the usurper – but I long for the day when we might embrace each other again.

God keep you and prosper you in all things.

Your loving friend, Adeliza

Hot on the heels of this letter came another, this time from Robert:

My dear sister

I fear we may have lost our chance to drive the usurper from power. Our friends in England have not waited for my signal, but have risen up in the expectation that I will bring you to join them. Stephen proved too strong for them. In the West Country he has attacked my liegemen and taken Castle Cary from Ralph Lovel and Harptree from William fitz John, though thank God he did not attempt Bristol. Godfrey Talbot raised his forces on the Welsh border but he, too, was overcome and Shrewsbury was taken and the entire garrison put to the sword. Stephen has even taken Dover from my castellan Walcheran Maminot. He rewards his supporters with earldoms and generous grants of land and money.

At the same time your uncle, David of Scotland, attacked and took several northern cities, and could we but have been there to threaten the usurper from the south we might have prevailed, but as it was he has been defeated in a great battle in Yorkshire. Letters come daily from friends in England begging me to return and bring you with me. We must move soon or all may be lost.

At her insistence Geoffrey marched his army northwards again, and this time they reached Falaise. They encamped around the city, cutting off all aid from outside, and the mangonels went to work, battering the walls, but the city was impregnable. Every time a breach was made it was fiercely defended and their troops were driven back until the damage could be repaired. It was a summer of drought and the harvest was poor. The Angevins laid waste the countryside around, but Falaise was well stocked and had deep wells that did not run dry. As day followed day of blazing heat Geoffrey's men became disheartened. Sickness broke out in the camp and the number of deserters grew.

As the leaves started to turn and the days shortened, Geoffrey made a decision. 'It is enough. We are doing no good here. Tomorrow we break camp and head for home.'

'No!' It was a cry of desperation. 'We cannot abandon the struggle now. Surely the city cannot hold out much longer.'

'Nor can we,' he replied. 'There is not a blade of wheat or a grain of flour left for miles around and all the cattle have been slaughtered or have died of starvation. I will not wait to see my men cut down by the flux as they were outside Le Sap. We leave tomorrow.'

'Very well,' she said. 'You may return to Carrouges if you wish. I shall go to join my brother in Caen.'

'Are you mad? How do you think you will get there?'

'We shall ride at night, by the back roads. Waleran is cooped up in Falaise. Maintain the siege for one more day and we shall be in Caen before he realizes I am not with you.'

'We? Who is this "we" you speak of?'

'I shall take my own knights with me, and I shall take Henry too.'

'You will not! You will not take my son on this fool's errand.'

'He is our son, and he is also heir to the throne of England. If we are to prevail it is necessary for him to be there with me, so people can see the succession is secure. They may have doubts about a woman as queen but they will accept me as regent.'

'And if you and he are captured by Waleran's men, what then? He will hand you over to Stephen as a prisoner, or hold you as a hostage to prevent me from claiming Normandy.'

'No, there is no danger of that. It is the last thing Stephen would want. Think. I am his cousin and the King's daughter. Imagine his dilemma if I were to be captured. He cannot with honour act against me. If he imprisons me it will inflame opinion and draw more supporters to my cause. As long as I am here in Normandy people can believe I have no intention of claiming the throne, but once I am in England they will have to make a choice. Stephen would far rather have me out of sight and mind than shut up in one of his dungeons as a rallying point for all the disaffected elements in the country.'

Geoffrey considered for a moment, then he shrugged. 'Do as you think best. I have my hands full here.'

'And you have no intention of bringing your forces to support my claim?'

'I have told you, not until I am sure of Normandy.'

She regarded him with bitter contempt. 'Then we part here, tonight. Henceforth our ways are different. You will maintain the siege long enough for me to get to Caen?'

'One day longer. No more than that.'

She called her knights together and they made their preparations. They muffled the horses' bits and the metal of the stirrups and wrapped heavy cloaks over their armour so no chance gleam of reflected moonlight would betray them. As darkness fell, as quietly as possible, they mounted up and left the camp. Henry rode in front of her, held securely between her arms. He demanded at the start to ride his own pony, until silenced by a sharp slap. They rode all night, keeping to the byways, and by dawn they were in sight of the walls of Caen. The countryside here, too, was desolate; the farms were deserted and there were no cattle in the fields. Like Geoffrey, Waleran had laid waste the whole area in an attempt to force Robert to yield. And like Geoffrey, he had been forced to give up.

She sent a small party of knights forward under her banner to announce her arrival and when she followed the castle gates were opened and Robert stood in the courtyard to welcome her. They embraced and then he knelt and kissed her hand.

'My dear sister and my queen, welcome! I have dreamed for so long of your coming.' He looked past her at her retinue. 'You have come with such a small escort! Your husband follows with the rest of your forces?'

She shook her head. 'I fear not. He refuses to leave Normandy and nothing I can say will persuade him. I bring you what help I can – myself, my knights – and my son, King Henry's heir.'

She saw him come to terms with it and then he bowed gallantly. 'Then you bring me what is most needful. Our English friends will rise for you. What need have we of Anjou?' He knelt by Henry, who was clinging to her skirts, half asleep and fretful. 'My prince, welcome! I have wanted for a long time to meet my nephew.'

He brought forward the three men waiting behind him and introduced them. 'You know our brother Reginald of Dunstanville, of course.'

Reginald was another of King Henry's bastards and she had met him at her father's court. He knelt and greeted her in the same terms as Robert. The other two were Baldwin de Redvers and Stephen de Mandeville, who both hailed her as queen.

When she had rested they held a council of war. All agreed it was too late in the year to mount a campaign. She must endure another winter of waiting.

With the new year came surprising news from Adeliza. Theobald, the abbot of Bec, had been elected as Archbishop of Canterbury.

'Incredible!' Robert exclaimed. 'Henry of Winchester must be beside himself with rage. He must have assumed that the post would be his.'

'According to Adeliza's letter the election was held while Henry was absent, overseeing the ordination of deacons,' Matilda said. 'But this must be good news for us. I have met Theobald. He is a good man. I believe he will be on our side.'

'Perhaps,' Robert said, 'but I wouldn't be too sure. Waleran of Meulan is the patron of the abbey of Bec. I don't mind betting that he persuaded Stephen to elect Theobald, so as to have his own man in a position of power.'

In their endless discussions of the best way forward it was suggested that she should make an appeal to the Pope to recognize her as the legitimate heir to Henry. So as soon as the passes over the Alps were clear she sent to Bishop Ulger of Angers and asked him to go to

Rome and speak on her behalf. After a long wait his answer came in a letter carried by one of his canons.

To the Dowager Empress Matilda, Countess of Anjou and daughter of King Henry, greetings.

I fear I have but little comfort to offer you. I pleaded your cause to the utmost of my ability before His Holiness, but King Stephen had also sent an emissary in the form of Arnulf of Sees, the son of Bishop John of Lisieux. He is a man of subtle intellect and a persuasive tongue. He argued that the main question to be decided was whether you are, in fact, King Henry's heir and that the matter of any oaths sworn to you are subsidiary to this. His main argument turned on a slander that I fear will pain you deeply; that your father's marriage to your mother was unlawful because she had once worn the veil of a nun and therefore you are illegitimate. I am sorry to tell you that Pope Innocent neither accepted nor rebutted this charge, but refused to give judgement either way, or to adjourn the matter to a later date, so the question remains unresolved. He did, however, accept the gifts sent to him by Stephen and has written letters confirming him in the possession of the throne.

She crushed the parchment between her hands and threw it to the ground.

'How dare they slander me like this? And slander my sainted mother and my noble father? I have heard these rumours before and I know them to be untrue. My mother was sent to the abbey of Wilton to be educated by her Aunt Christina, who was the abbess at that time. I remember her telling me that Christina was a cruel disciplinarian, who sometimes forced to her wear the veil in order, she said, to protect her from the lascivious Normans. But when she was alone she threw it off and stamped on it. It was never intended that she should be a nun. It is a question that was raised at the time of her marriage to my father, but it was resolved to the satisfaction of Archbishop Anselm. If that saintly man had had any doubts he would never have officiated at their wedding. And now it is dragged up again to keep me from my rightful place.' She threw herself into a chair and covered her face with her hands. 'In the name of God, I swear that all I have ever tried to do is to be a dutiful daughter and all I ask for is my right and my bounden duty to my father's people. Is this the end of all my hopes?'

Robert squatted beside her and took her hand. 'Take courage. All is not yet lost.'

She looked at him bleakly. 'Is it not? Our friends are defeated and every day the usurper makes himself more secure – and now this …'

'Not all our friends are defeated. We still have powerful voices that will be raised in our favour.'

'Whose? Who is left except we four?'

'You remember Bishop Roger of Salisbury?'

'Of course. He was my father's chancellor and his closest colleague. They called him the first man in England after the King. But he has declared for Stephen, has he not? Are you telling me that he might come over to our side?'

'I have every reason to believe it. He was devoted to your father and I have heard him express the deepest affection for his children.'

'It is true. I remember him as a very kind man. When I was little he was almost more of a father to me than the King. But affection is not enough.'

'True. But before I left England I had spoken with

him several times and he gave me the impression that if it came to a choice between you and Stephen he would always take your side. Since then Brian fitz Count has kept up the contact and he writes to me that Bishop Roger is less and less contented with Stephen's rule – and he is not alone.'

'Not alone?'

'You spent so little time in England once you were grown up. Perhaps you were never fully aware of how much power and influence Bishop Roger and his family had. His two nephews, Alexander and Nigel, were both important officers of the royal household until they, too, were elevated to bishoprics, Alexander at Lincoln and Nigel at Ely. Not only are they princes of the Church, through your father's favour they have become great land-owners and the keepers of several important castles. They hold Sherbourne and Devizes, Malmesbury, Salisbury, Sleaford and Newark. In short, they are among the wealthiest and most powerful men in England. Between them, under your father's rule, the whole administration of the affairs of the country was in their hands.'

'And you think they may be ready to turn against Stephen?'

'He does not trust them as your father did. Why should he? They are not beholden to him as they were to Henry for their good fortune. My guess is that he would prefer to be rid of them and put his own men in their places. They understand this and would rather see you on the throne.'

'So what are we waiting for? What do we do next?'

'We must have further assurances that if we move they will come out on our side. And there are others, less important but nevertheless useful adherents, whom we must woo to our cause. My agents in England work constantly to win them over. Meanwhile, I shall look for others here in Normandy who can be persuaded. Be patient a little longer. Our time will come.'

There was one good thing to come out of these months of waiting. Robert and the young Henry had taken to each other strongly. Henry hero worshipped his warrior uncle, whose prowess with sword and lance was greater than all challengers, and Robert found him brave and steadfast in his determination to master those same talents, and quick-witted in his understanding of tactics. He brightened Matilda's day by telling her what a noble king her son would one day make. With the addition of her followers, the castle was full of knights and men-at-arms, who would grow quarrelsome if not kept occupied. Robert made sure that they had little time on their hands. They practised swordplay and rode with lances at the quintain in the tilt yard. Waleran had given up the siege and returned to England, so they were at liberty to ride out in the surrounding countryside without fear of being ambushed. They went hunting whenever the weather allowed it. She envied the men their constant activity. Sometimes she rode out with them, or practised with the crossbow, but she tired more readily than before. She had given birth to three sons in as many years and it had taken its toll. There were few other women in the castle, other than serving girls, and none that she felt any affinity with. She passed much of her time reading but her temper grew shorter and she had less and less patience with idle chatter.

Just after midsummer her hopes received another devastating blow. A messenger came from England with letters for Robert. He read the first and threw it aside with a shout of fury.

'Not this too! Are they all fools?'

'What is it?' she asked.

'The bishops have been arrested.'

'All of them?'

'Salisbury, Lincoln, Ely – the ones I told you of. It seems there was some kind of brawl at Stephen's Whitsun court at Oxford – a quarrel between Roger of Salisbury's men and those of another lord that ended with swords being drawn. Stephen used it as a pretext to have Roger and Alexander arrested and demanded that they hand over their castles. They refused and Nigel fled and took refuge in Devizes.'

'Stephen would have been within his rights, if they came armed to his court and caused an affray,' she pointed out. 'Or do you think there was more to it than that?'

He shrugged. 'Who knows?' He turned to a second letter and exclaimed, 'Ah, this makes it clearer. Brian fitz Count writes that Waleran of Meulan and some others accused the bishops of being prepared to hand their castles over to you if you were to land. No wonder Stephen took the first chance he got to clip their wings.'

'Have they handed over the castles, as he demanded?'

He glanced down the letter. 'Yes, damn them! It seems he threatened to starve Roger and hang his son if Devizes was not handed over. The castle was held by Roger's mistress, the boy's mother, and she handed over the keys rather than see her son hanged. After that, he threatened and bullied all three of them until they gave in.'

'So our last hope disappears,' she murmured. 'It seems the four of us are trapped here. We do not have the forces to break out and recapture all your Norman holdings, let alone what you have lost in England through espousing my cause. For my own part, I cannot return to Anjou, having parted finally with my husband. Truly, I begin to believe that God has turned his face away from me.'

Reginald had listened in silence, but now he said, 'This

may not be as bad for us as it seems at first. Stephen will have done himself no good by attacking the church. It may well turn other powerful churchmen and even the Pope in our favour. What we have lost on the one hand we may gain on the other.'

Evidence of this came in a new batch of letters. Brian fitz Count wrote that Stephen's brother, the Bishop of Winchester, now recently appointed papal legate and therefore the leading prelate in the kingdom, had summoned him to appear before a church council to answer for his attack, arguing that the bishops should have been tried before a church court. Through some clever casuistry by the Bishop of Rouen, who came to the King's defence, the confiscation of the castles was allowed to stand, but Stephen was forced to do public penance for this attack on the Church. *'Henry of Winchester may be as worldly a bishop as any of the others,'* Brian wrote, *'but he is also determined to stand up for the rights of the Church against the throne. And his attitude will be shared by many others.'*

He was very quickly proved correct. A letter arrived from none other than Bishop Henry himself, inviting her to come to England and assuring her that the throne could be hers in a matter of months. It was followed by a letter from Adeliza:

Dear friend and daughter in God,

The moment has come. All through the kingdom the unrest against Stephen's rule grows stronger. My husband supports the usurper, but I retain control of my castle of Arundel. If you can make landfall on these shores I can offer you a safe refuge until you are able to claim the crown.

Matilda showed the letter to Robert and the others and

Reginald said at once, 'That is all we were waiting for. If we do not move now we may as well give up all hope.'

Robert looked from one to the other and they all nodded agreement. 'Very well. But it will not be easy. Stephen's ships control most of the south coast and the approaches to Bristol. We must find a safe place to land our troops.'

He dispatched riders to carry messages to friends in England, asking them to survey the coast and report back on possible harbours. The answers were not encouraging. Dover, Rye, Winchelsea and Southampton were all firmly held by Stephen's supporters and his ships patrolled constantly. To land any further west would mean a long ride through hostile territory to reach Arundel. For hours they pored over the map, until Matilda said, 'Arundel is on the River Arun and not far from the sea. Is the Arun navigable?'

'Only for small craft,' Robert replied. 'It would be impossible to land a large force there.'

'Then let us take a small ship and as many men as it can hold and go direct to Arundel. If you are right and our friends will rise in support when they know I am in England, the rest of our forces can follow when they have secured a harbour for us.'

'I have a suggestion,' Baldwin put in. 'Let me stage a diversion. Stephen took Corfe Castle from me, but I learn that it is only lightly defended. I will take my men and land at Wareham and I do not doubt but I shall be able to retake Corfe. That way, you will have a port of entry in the west when you need it.'

The plan was agreed and all necessary preparations put in train. After some discussion it was decided that Henry should be sent back to his father, under the care of Reginald. She resisted the idea at first but Robert persuaded her that it would be foolish to risk the capture, or even the death, of the heir to the throne. She tried to seem light-hearted as she said goodbye to him, promising him that he would join her in England very soon, and he went off quite happily, largely because this time he was allowed to ride his own pony – for the first few miles at least.

Baldwin and his men left in August and by the end of the month they heard that he had reoccupied Corfe and that Stephen was already moving west to besiege him. The moment they had waited for was at hand.

13

ENGLAND, 1139

As THE SETTING sun cast long shadows across the water, a sleek galley nosed cautiously into the mouth of the River Arun. Seated in the stern beside her half-brother, Matilda looked up at the huge castle mound silhouetted against the paling sky, with the sharp outline of the stone-built keep at its summit. In front of her, crammed on the thwarts, were the carefully selected knights they had brought with them, some from her own household, some from Robert's. Behind them, two other craft were packed in the same way. In all, they had brought with them 120 men – a small force with which to mount an invasion. In total silence, with muffled oars, they crept up the river. They were all aware that they could be sailing straight into an ambush. Then from just ahead of them a lantern was waved, then covered, then waved again and Robert let out a sigh of relief.

'There's the signal. Pull together, lads.'

The rowers bent to their oars and the ship glided forward until with a gentle bump it came alongside the landing stage, where three men were waiting. Ropes were thrown and tied off and a gangplank was laid across the gap; then Robert handed her up onto it. A hand reached out to steady her as she crossed and she set her feet on English soil for the first time in seven years. The three men fell to their knees and the leader introduced himself as Adeliza's seneschal.

'My mistress bids me welcome you as our most noble lady and our queen. She is waiting to greet you in the hall.'

He led the way through a gate in the surrounding palisade, across the bailey and up the steep slope of the motte. They passed through another gate and the doors of the keep were thrown open. Adeliza stood at the entrance, outlined against lamplight from within. She curtsied, and then embraced Matilda with tears in her eyes.

'I have so longed for this moment! At last England will have her rightful queen.'

The hall was full of people, the men and women of her household, and as Matilda entered they all knelt. Adeliza said, 'My friends, let us hail our queen!'

A shout went up and some of the more important members of the household pressed forward to kiss her hand. Then Adeliza led her up to the dais at the end of the hall and seated her in the place of honour, while servants quickly set up the trestles and boards in the body of the hall ready for a feast. Warm wine was served and a succession of delicacies but, while her knights tucked in, she ate little. The sea crossing had been boisterous and she had never been a good sailor. At last she was conducted up to a room at the top of the keep, where Adeliza's women were ready to help her undress. As she drifted on the edge of sleep she wondered if she should be feeling triumphant or just very afraid. All she could be sure of at the moment was a great relief that at last the long wait was over. The die was cast, and her fate turned on what might happen in the coming weeks.

*

As soon as they had broken their fast next morning she sat down with Robert and Adeliza to make plans.

Robert began. 'As far as we know, Stephen is still heading for Corfe, but as soon as word gets out that you are here, as it must, he will turn round and come to confront you. By then, I must be in Bristol.'

'Bristol?' Adeliza queried. 'Surely you will stay here and give your protection to Lady Matilda.'

He shook his head. 'I must join up with my main force in Bristol. All our friends are in the west and it is from there that the war against Stephen must be waged.'

'Then let me come with you,' Matilda said. 'If it is as you say, I must be there too.'

'No. It is too dangerous for you to travel with such a small escort as we have with us. You must stay here with Adeliza until I am able to fetch you.'

'But how will you get to Bristol? As you say, Stephen will be heading this way. You might meet him on the road.'

'I shall take the small lanes and tracks which only the local people use. Stephen will be on the high road, to make the best speed. I shall take my own men with me and we will ride fast. With luck, we shall be in Bristol before he realizes I am not still here with you.'

'And us?' Adeliza asked. 'What are we supposed to do?'

'Your husband supports Stephen, I know. Is he with him now?'

'Yes.'

'If he returns and orders you to hand over the castle, will you defy him?'

She swallowed, but nodded. 'I will. He knows that I stand with Matilda. She is here at my invitation. I will not give her up.'

'Well said! And if it should come to siege?'

'The castle is well provisioned, and not easy to attack.'

'Then if necessary you must hold out until I am able to raise sufficient forces to rescue you.' He got to his feet. 'I must be on my way. The longer I delay, the greater the danger for all of us.'

They watched him ride out with his most trusted knights. Adeliza turned to her. 'Will he get to Bristol?'

'We must pray that he does. If he is taken our cause is lost.'

'What do we do now?'

'Post sentries to watch the road, arrange the disposition of our men in the event of an attack, check the provisions – and then we wait. It will not be long, I imagine.'

She was proved correct. Two days later a sentry shouted down from the roof of the keep. 'Horsemen on the road!'

She ran up the twisting staircase that led to the roof, Adeliza behind her. Henry's widow spoke the truth when she said the castle was not easy to attack. It was set on rising ground, protected on one side by the river and surrounded on the other three by flat, marshy land criss-crossed by small streams. The one road leading from the edge of the forest to the massive stone gateway in the outer fortifications was built as a causeway over the marsh. Looking north they saw a company of horsemen ride out of the forest and come to a halt. Behind them came a close formation of knights, at the centre of which flew Stephen's banner. As they watched, a single horseman rode forward and drew rein in front of the army. He was wearing a hauberk but no helmet and even at this distance she recognized him.

'So, there he is, the usurper!'

Stephen sat on his horse for a few moments, staring

towards them, then turned and rode back to his knights. Orders were given and the men spread out along the edge of the rising ground and began to pitch tents. She turned to look towards the river and saw that two ships were already moving in to blockade it.

'Is there any way through the marshes?'

'No. The only way in or out is either the road or the river.'

'So, the ground is too soft for cavalry, or to bring up siege engines, and the distance is too great for archers or mangonels to be effective. Stephen's only hope is to starve us out. The question is, how long is he prepared to wait?'

There was a stir among the men on the road and three knights rode forward, one of them carrying a lance from which a white banner streamed. 'Ah, there is the answer. He is hoping to persuade you to give me up.'

By the time the three emissaries entered the great hall she was seated beside Adeliza on the dais at the far end. She recognized the leader, a stocky man with grizzled hair and a scar on one cheek, from her time at her father's court. His name was Gilbert de Clare.

He bowed to Adeliza. 'My lady, I bring greetings from King Stephen.'

Adeliza replied, 'Greetings to you, my lord. What business has Stephen with me?'

'The King wishes you to hand over to my custody the oath-breaker and rebel Robert of Gloucester, whom you are sheltering in your castle.'

Matilda suppressed a smile of elation and relief. Robert must be safe in Bristol.

Adeliza's expression was defiant but a faint tremor in her voice betrayed her nervousness. 'Earl Robert is no longer here.'

Gilbert's eyes narrowed. 'Not here? I require proof of that.'

Matilda cut in. 'My lord, your manners do not match your station. You are in the presence of two queens. It behoves you to act with more humility.'

He glanced sideways at her. 'Lady Adeliza was indeed queen while King Henry was alive ...'

'And King Henry being dead I am now your queen, as his only rightful heir. I require you to treat me as such.'

He returned his gaze to Adeliza. 'King Stephen also requires that you relinquish the Lady Matilda into his custody.'

The tremor was more pronounced as she answered, 'Lady Matilda is here as my guest and at my invitation. We have long been friends and it is natural that I should offer her hospitality. Stephen has no right to demand that I hand her over to him.'

Matilda looked him in the eye and when she spoke her voice was icy. 'You have your answer, my lord.'

He looked from her to Adeliza with contempt. 'You may have cause to regret this defiance, madam.' And he turned to walk out of the hall.

Her voice stopped him in his tracks. 'You have not been given leave to go, my lord. You do not leave the royal presence until given permission.'

He hesitated, then turned back. She rose to her feet. 'I am an empress and your rightful queen. You will pay me due deference or you may live to regret it.'

She saw him calculating the possibilities. In the end he bowed stiffly. 'Madam.'

'Tell the usurper Stephen that I am come to claim the crown which is mine by right and in accordance with the oaths given to me by all the lords of England and Normandy – including you, Lord Gilbert.' She extended her hand, palm down, and he had no option but to kneel and kiss it. 'Now you may go.'

He glared at her, then turned on his heel and stalked out of the hall, followed by his two companions.

Adeliza turned to her. 'You are magnificent. I have never had your courage.'

She squeezed her hand. 'You did well enough. You might have given me over to him. I thank you for your loyalty.'

'What will Stephen do now, do you think?'

'He knows now that Robert must be in Bristol. He will not want to waste time besieging us while Robert makes himself stronger in the West Country. I think we shall see another embassy before long.'

Once again, she was proved correct. Next day another group of men rode up to the gate under a flag of truce. This time, the identity of the leader took her by surprise.

'My lord bishop! I did not expect to see you here.'

Henry of Winchester's manner was as smooth and urbane as if he were making a normal courtesy call. 'Madam, I am delighted to see you well. It seems that Lord Gilbert did not deliver my brother the King's message very tactfully. I am here to assure you that he means you no ill.'

'Then he will have no objection to my remaining here with the Lady Adeliza. And he will withdraw the force with which he has, for some unknown reason, attempted to surround us.'

Bishop Henry smiled and glanced behind him at his escort. 'These matters are best settled quietly between friends. Can we speak privately?'

Adeliza conducted them into the solar and sent a page for wine. Matilda turned to confront the bishop. 'It was by your instigation that I am here. What do you intend now?'

He made a reassuring gesture. 'Let me explain. Shall we sit?'

When they were seated and the wine had been poured, Adeliza dismissed the page and Henry said, 'I beg you to trust me, my lady. I have your best interests at heart. Am I not right in thinking that rather than being cooped up here, grateful as I know you are for the Lady Adeliza's hospitality, you would much prefer to be with Lord Robert in Bristol?'

She gave a brief, mirthless laugh. 'Indeed, but what I should prefer and what is possible are two different things.'

'Suppose it were possible?'

'How? Why should Stephen let that happen?'

'Consider his position. He cannot contemplate an attack on the castle. For one thing, it is impregnable, except by undertaking a long siege. And for another, you and Adeliza are ladies of high rank and honour, and moreover you are his cousin. An attack on you would be seen by all men – and by the Church – as against all the laws of honourable behaviour. I have convinced him that it is Earl Robert who is his chief opponent and it is in the west that he must concentrate his forces. I have suggested that, rather than leave you here, where you may draw any malcontents to support your cause, it would be better for him if you were with Earl Robert, thus concentrating all the opposition in one place. He has listened to my arguments and as a result he is prepared to offer you a safe conduct and an escort to take you to Bristol.'

'And as soon as I leave here, he will be able to renege on the agreement and take me prisoner.'

'No. For two reasons. One is that he has no wish to keep you as a prisoner. I repeat, any attack on your person would only serve to alienate all men of goodwill and draw more supporters to your side. The second is that I myself will accompany you, until such time as you can be

185

handed over to Earl Robert or his representative.'

Adeliza reached out to grasp her hand. 'It is a trap. It must be. Stay here with me, where you are safe.'

She released herself gently. 'If I stay here, I may be safe but I can be of no help to Robert or the rest of our friends. There is nothing I can do shut up in this castle. I trust Bishop Henry. I do not believe he will betray me.'

Henry said, 'It may help to convince you if I tell you that I know for a fact that Earl Robert is safe in Bristol. I met with him on his way there.'

'You met with him? How? He was planning to travel secretly by little used roads.'

'As I guessed he would. But I knew he would have to pass through my lands, so I set watchers on all the tracks. Their reports enabled me to intercept him. We spoke only briefly, but I was able to assure him of my continued support and to promise him that I would do all in my power to bring you to him.'

She drew a deep breath. 'Very well, my lord bishop. If you can, indeed, persuade Stephen to give me a safe conduct, I accept. And I thank you for your intervention on my behalf.'

'I act not only on your behalf, but on my own and on the behalf of the Holy Church, which my brother has unjustly attacked in arresting my fellow bishops.' He stood up. 'I will return now to make the necessary arrangements. Can you be ready to leave tomorrow?'

'I can.'

Early next morning a company of armoured knights clattered up the road to the castle gate. At their head were two men. Bishop Henry was one. With surprise Matilda recognized the second as Waleran of Meulan. Stephen had sent one of his most trusted commanders to escort her. He brought with him a milk-white mare, richly caparisoned, for her to ride. She embraced a tearful Adeliza and mounted. Horses had been found for her small band of knights and they took their places behind her. They rode down the causeway into the forest, where Stephen's army was already striking tents and packing wagons with equipment. No one attempted to challenge them and soon they were on the high road leading west.

They passed the first night of the journey at Wolvesley Castle, Bishop Henry's palace in Winchester. At Calne, Waleran turned back but Henry stayed with her until they reached the borders of Robert's lands. Here they found Robert waiting for her with knights of his own household. He greeted her ceremonially, kneeling to hail her as queen. Henry declined the invitation to continue to Bristol as Robert's guest and rode back towards Winchester.

The following evening they came into view of Robert's castle in the protective embrace of the Rivers Frome and Avon. He had spent a great deal of money and energy in rendering it one of the greatest fortresses in the country. The stone blocks for the curtain walls and the keep with its four towers were brought by ship from Caen and unloaded at a dock protected by a water gate. A second well-defended gate gave access from the road. Within the walls of the bailey were kitchens and bakehouses, smiths' forges, stables for the horses, gardens full of vegetables and fruit trees and houses for the men and women who served him. To reach the keep it was necessary to pass through a second gatehouse in another wall. In places the walls were so thick that three men could lie end to end on top of them. It was easy to see why Stephen had concentrated on taking over outlying castles but had never attempted Bristol itself.

As they dismounted in the inner courtyard, two women came out of the main entrance to the keep. The elder was thickset, with greying hair and a strong, bony face. The younger had Robert's dark hair and a pretty, dimpled face. Robert greeted them both with obvious affection and then turned to her.

'Madam, I present my wife Mabel and my youngest daughter, who is named after her mother.'

Both women curtsied and the elder said, 'My lady, you are most welcome. We have waited long to greet you as our rightful queen.'

The younger one blushed and managed only to murmur, 'My lady.'

Robert's wife led her into the great hall, where the household was assembled to greet her, and then took her up to a chamber in one of the towers. Two waiting women followed, one plump and comfortable, the other little more than a girl. They were introduced to her as Berthe and Hawise.

'I do not doubt that you are tired after your long journey, madam,' Mabel said. 'There is warm water here for you to wash and your chest will be brought up to you directly. There is wine and fruit for you to refresh yourself, but when you have rested we shall offer you something more substantial. I will leave you now, but if there is any-thing you require Berthe or Hawise will get it for you.'

There was something brisk and overbearing about her hostess's manner that she found annoying. She was obvi-ously accustomed to giving orders. It was not hard to see why Robert had been prepared to leave her in charge of his castle and his lands while he was in Normandy.

Robert had laid on a great feast to welcome her and there were minstrels and jongleurs to entertain them, but she was too tired after the long ride to want anything more than a bed where she could relax in safety. Very soon there would be more dangers to face, greater perhaps than any she had yet known, but for now she could sleep in peace.

Next morning she had just finished dressing when a page appeared with a request from Robert to meet him in the great hall. She found him in the company of two men, and at the sight of one of them her heart gave a jolt. It was Brian fitz Count, who told her stories and sang her love songs to lighten her mood on the way to her betrothal to Geoffrey, twelve long years ago. Robert sent him away, she remembered, and on her last, brief visit to England, when she left Geoffrey, he was absent on his estates in Wales, so they had not met since. His curly hair was cut closer now and his face was leaner; there were hollows in his cheeks that suggested he did not eat enough; but his hazel eyes were as bright as she remembered them. He came forward quickly and dropped to one knee.

'Gracious lady, I have dreamed of this moment. All I am and all I have are yours to command.'

She gave him her hand to kiss and found her voice a little husky as she replied, 'Dear Sir Brian, I am glad to see you again. I thank you for your loyalty.'

'In that, madam,' he said as he rose, 'I have never wavered. I have no doubt that you are the only true heir to your father's crown. That a woman may inherit is established in Holy Writ. In the book of Numbers it is written that the Lord decreed that the daughters of Zelophehad had the right to inherit their father's land. In the same spirit I swore to uphold your right, and I will never be forsworn.'

Robert chuckled softly. 'You see, sister? Our friend has become a scholar in the years since you last met.'

'I would never have doubted his learning,' she replied, 'whether it be Holy Writ or the songs of the troubadours.' She caught Brian's eye in sign that she had not forgotten.

Robert turned to the second man. 'I believe you have not met Miles Fitzwalter. Miles is sheriff of Gloucester and castellan of Gloucester Castle.'

Miles was older than Brian, a solid oak of a man with broad shoulders and a mane of grey hair. Robert said, 'Brian and I are oath sworn to you already. Miles wishes to do homage also. Shall we proceed?'

'I shall be happy to accept his fealty,' she answered.

A chair was set for her and Miles knelt and placed his hands between hers and swore to be her liege-man of life and limb and to protect her against all enemies. Looking into his eyes she sensed that once sworn, he would maintain his faith to the last breath.

The ceremony over Robert called for wine and they retired to the solar to sit in council.

'We can do nothing until we know Stephen's next move,' Robert said. 'I do not think he will attempt to confront us here, but Harptree and the other outlying castles are at risk. Meanwhile, we must make sure of as many allies as we can.'

'Trowbridge is ours,' Miles said. 'My son-in-law Humphrey de Bohun will see to that. And Pain Fitzjohn, who is sheriff of Shropshire and Herefordshire, is married to my other daughter Cecily. Between us we hold all the marcher country between here and Wales.'

'And we can be sure of support from the Welsh princes,' Brian added. 'My holding of Abergavenny has brought most of them onto our side.'

'As far as numbers of men goes, we have my troops plus a contingent of mercenaries under Robert fitz Hubert, and the Angevins who came with Lady Matilda. There is no question of challenging Stephen to a pitched battle. All we can do for now is to keep hold of those towns and castles we have and hope that others will come over to our side.' Robert turned to Brian. 'Your castle of Wallingford is one of the most important. It gives us a foothold further east and control over the crossing of the Thames. It must be held at all costs.'

'Indeed.' Brian got up. 'And to that end I must be on my way. I must be on hand in case Stephen decides to attack us there instead of coming to Bristol.'

As they watched the two men ride away with their escorting knights she said, 'It was good to see Brian fitz Count again.'

'I know he was eager to see you,' her brother replied. 'I believe he has been half in love with you all his life.'

'Oh, surely not!' she exclaimed. 'What could he hope from that?'

'Nothing at all. I don't believe he would have wished for anything more.'

'What do you mean?'

'I have never really understood Brian. I think he has enjoyed his romantic attachment to you, partly because it could never have any physical outcome. He has been married to Matilda of Wallingford for years, as you know, but she is old enough to be his mother and there has been no issue. I think he has little love for women in the flesh.'

'Is he a lover of men, then?' she asked in surprise.

'No, there has never been any suggestion of that. Whatever Brian's desires may be, he seems to prefer chastity. If he were not such a doughty fighter I would say he should have been a monk.'

It was spoken lightly, but she sensed that her brother wished to crush any notion she might have of a romantic dalliance with the count. She responded with a hint of acidity, 'You need have no anxiety for the state of my heart, brother. Two husbands, one dead and the other alive but absent, are quite enough.'

'What do you think of Miles?' he asked.

'I like him. He seems honest and steadfast.'

'I hope you are right. I confess until today I had my doubts. He seemed loyal to Stephen from the start and Stephen responded by making him one of his constables and giving him Gloucester Castle. But he assures me that he was only biding his time until you and I were back in England.'

'Perhaps he is wiser than some of our other supporters, who rose up prematurely and have suffered in consequence. But is it not difficult for you, that he holds Gloucester Castle when it is part of your fief?'

He shook his head. 'It isn't. The castle is property of the crown, not mine. It was one of our father's favourite residences. So in point of fact, it is yours.'

'Of course. I had forgotten.' She considered. 'I believe we can trust Miles. There was something in his look that gave me confidence.'

'Well, let us pray that you are right. We need every man we can get if we are to put you on the throne.'

The pleasant sensation of security she enjoyed the previous evening evaporated quickly. It was clear that victory over Stephen was not going to be as quick or as easy as she had been promised before she left Normandy. They were not left in doubt about Stephen's next move for long. A rider clattered into the courtyard with a message from Brian. Stephen had appeared in front of his castle at Wallingford and was preparing a siege.

'God damn him!' Robert muttered. 'We must hold Wallingford at all costs.'

Fear dragged at her heart. It was not the castle she feared for, it was Brian. 'We must send him aid, at once.'

'No. Do not worry yourself. Wallingford is a strong fortress and Brian will have made all the necessary preparations. He will hold out without our help.'

That night she prayed with greater vehemence than usual. For the first time she was acutely aware that men were preparing to lay down their lives for her. Next morning she confessed herself to Robert's chaplain.

'If it comes to open war, I shall have a great burden of guilt for the lives that will be lost. Am I wrong to press my claim?'

'It is the usurper Stephen who must carry the guilt if that happens,' she was reassured. 'It was your father's wish that you should succeed. To that end he made all his vassals swear to uphold your right. It is those men who have broken their oath who will suffer God's anger.'

Days passed without news. Then Robert's spies reported that Stephen had grown tired of being encamped outside Wallingford. He had built two counter castles to contain the defenders and left a contingent of men to hold them, but he himself was coming west with his main army. It seemed his sights were set on Trowbridge, but in a surprise diversion he attacked and took Miles's castle at South Cerney. He then headed for Malmesbury, held for Robert by the mercenary captain, Robert fitz Hubert. When word reached Robert from that city he exploded with rage.

'God's blood, is there no faith in men? That traitor fitz Hubert has handed the castle over to Stephen without a blow struck.'

'I never trust mercenaries,' she commented. 'Most of them would sell their services to the devil if the pay was better. But now there is nothing to stop Stephen advancing on Trowbridge.'

'Miles will deal with him,' Robert assured her. 'He will not allow his daughter and son-in-law to suffer.'

In the event, Miles took a more daring gamble. He

gathered his forces and cut across Stephen's rear to reach Wallingford. While Stephen was encamped in front of Trowbridge a messenger brought word to Bristol that the counter castles had been overrun, the men left to defend them either killed or taken prisoner, and the siege had been lifted. She breathed a sigh of relief in the knowledge that Brian was no longer in danger. Miles, meanwhile, took the opportunity to capture Hereford.

Her supporters were growing in numbers. John fitz Gilbert, once her father's marshal and the castellan of Marlborough, came to offer his homage, as did a number of local lords and several Welsh princes. But as the days passed she grew more and more restless. She had always been used to command. From the age of twelve she was a queen, and then an empress, and even after her second marriage she was Countess of Anjou with her own household and her own responsibilities. She had lands and the rents and taxes they produced. Now she might be hailed as a queen but she was a guest in another man's house and dependent on him for her every need. Robert was always kind but she found it hard to accept that she had no authority. Robert's household was renowned as a centre of learning and culture and there was no shortage of men with whom she could discuss works of theology or secular poetry, and every evening minstrels played and sang in the great hall. But this only served to remind her of her lessons with Henry back in Normandy. She missed her son acutely and worried that he would not receive the education or the discipline that he needed.

As always, when unable to find any occupation to fill her days, she became irritable and quick tempered. The main source of friction was her relationship with the Countess Mabel. She had been so used to giving orders that she forgot sometimes it was Mabel's role to organize her household and she gave instructions only to find them countermanded.

Matters came to a head over the small question of spices in cooking. As before in England, she found the food served in the castle bland and uninteresting, so one day she made a foray into the kitchen and lectured the cooks on the virtue of the exotic spices she learned to like in Germany and introduced into Anjou. The head cook listened mutinously and when the meat arrived at the table that evening it was exactly the same as before. Frustrated, she threw down her knife and exclaimed, 'Can no one in this country cook food that has some flavour to it?'

Mabel turned her head and gave her a long look. Then she said coldly, 'I regret, madam, that the meal does not please you, but I would remind you that we are in a state of war. It is winter and much of the countryside has been laid waste by rival armies. The peasants are on the verge of starvation. Thanks be to God, we are in a better case here, but we should be grateful that there is still meat on the table.'

She felt the colour rise in her face. How dared this woman speak to her like this? She rose to her feet. 'I would remind you who it is to whom you are speaking. I am aware of the privations of war. It has been my constant experience through much of my life. I have never found that it prevents a clever cook from adding a few herbs to a dish. But since you are satisfied, madam, I will say no more.'

She left the rest of her food uneaten and walked out of the hall, aware of the buzz of consternation as some of the men and women eating at the long tables rose to their feet and were commanded back to their places by Robert. She knew she had committed an act of great discourtesy in leaving before the meal was over, but to have remained would have been intolerable.

Robert came to find her in her private chamber. 'Sister, it does not become you to quarrel with the hospitality you are offered here.'

She looked at him and was furious to feel sudden tears well up in her eyes. She swallowed them back and answered, 'Forgive me. I was lacking in courtesy just now. It is not the food ... though I am still convinced it could be more palatable if only the cooks would listen to me ... but that is not important. I am just ... just so tired of this endless waiting, with nothing to do. I am not one of those women who can sit all day and sew and gossip. I have not been bred to it. I must have occupation. Do you not understand that?'

He sighed. 'That is all very well, but you must understand that we can do nothing until we have drawn more supporters to our side. I am tired of waiting, too, but we must be patient. Meanwhile, will you try to make your peace with Mabel? You are alike in so many, many ways, both noble ladies, born to authority. You must not quarrel.'

'I will try,' she promised. 'I will apologize to her and ask her forgiveness.'

She did as she had promised, though she found it very hard; Mabel accepted the apology stiffly but they still were far from at ease with each other.

Miles, paying one of his periodic visits to Bristol, found her standing at the battlements on top of one of the towers.

He bowed and said, 'I was told I should find you here. But the wind is cold. Would you not rather be inside, by the fire?'

She gave him a brief, wistful smile. 'The caged bird is warm and well fed, but do you not think it would rather have the freedom of the open air, however cold?'

196

'You feel yourself caged? I am sorry to hear that. For myself, I should rather be here than out there.'

He gestured to the view spread out below them. It was true that there was little to attract the eye. It had been a wet November and the low-lying ground on either side of the two rivers reflected the grey sky in myriad puddles; while further away the fields were brown and the trees bare of leaves.

She shrugged. 'I spoke metaphorically. You must bear with me. I lack occupation, that is all.'

'Ah.' He nodded. 'If I can pursue the image further, perhaps you need to spread your wings.'

'If only it were possible!'

'May I suggest a solution? I know that your brother has brought you here to be under his protection, but it seems to me you might prefer to live in your own castle.'

'My castles are all far away across the sea.'

'Not all of them. Gloucester is but a short ride from here.'

'Gloucester?'

'It was your father's. Stephen gave it to me to hold for him, but it belongs to you. It is ready and waiting for its rightful lady to claim it.'

'But it is yours, your home, as Bristol is Robert's. Your wife is the chatelaine.'

'No. She knows as I do that we are only holding it till you require it.' He took her hand and bowed his head over it. 'I beg you, my lady, gladden us with your presence. You will be as safe there as you are here and you will be able to direct the affairs of your domain as you would in Anjou or Normandy.'

The suggestion was put to Robert, who agreed to it with, she sensed, some relief. Two days later Miles returned to escort her and she rode out through the gatehouse followed by her retinue of knights. At Gloucester she found the great hall decorated to receive her and a warm welcome from Miles's wife Sibyl and their two youngest children Mahel and Lucy. Sibyl was a small, plump woman with dark hair and blue eyes and a gentle manner quite unlike the authoritarian Mabel. Matilda knew at once that she would be happier here.

She was now able to establish her own household. She had brought Hawise with her. She had found her efficient and amenable, and when offered a permanent position as her waiting woman the girl accepted with alacrity. Also with her was a young monk, Thurstan, whom she had taken on as her secretary. Sibyl had recruited three young women, daughters of local lords, to be her ladies-in-waiting. Miles's son-in-law, Humphrey de Bohun, came to pledge allegiance. He had been her father's steward and originally served Stephen in the same capacity but now he renounced his duty to the usurper and offered his services to her instead. Together with the knights she brought with her from Normandy, they formed the nucleus of a new court.

Once she was safely installed Miles proceeded with his next plan, an attack on the town of Worcester, taking the knights she had brought with her to augment his own troops. While she and Sibyl were still waiting for news of the outcome, the prior of the monastery of Llanthony Secunda came to visit. Some years earlier Miles had transferred the canons of the Augustinian Priory at Llanthony in Monmouthshire, which came under his jurisdiction, to a site near Gloucester and set up the new house. The prior was a man of ascetic appearance and gentle manner, but that day his expression was severe.

'Madam, I am deeply troubled by the effects on the ordinary people of this fighting. Is it not possible to find some solution to this conflict?'

'Certainly,' she replied. 'Let Stephen renounce his spurious claim to the throne and acknowledge me as his liege lady and the fighting will stop at once.'

The prior sighed deeply. 'I fear there is little likelihood of that. Can we not find a compromise?'

'What compromise is possible?' she demanded. 'Hark ye, sir. Do you accept me as the rightful Queen of England?'

'You know I do, madam. If it were not so I should not be here now.'

'And do you believe that God fights on the side of right and justice?'

'Assuredly.'

'Then perhaps He will teach Stephen the error of his ways. Until that time, we must fight on.'

Sibyl asked, 'Is there some particular incident that is worrying you, Father?'

The prior was silent for a moment. Then he said, 'There is, but I hope I shall not offend you in telling it. Yesterday two young men, canons of Worcester Cathedral, came to me to ask for refuge at the priory. They told a story that distresses me greatly. It seems that when the citizens heard of the approach of your army they were in such fear that many of them sought refuge in the cathedral, bringing all their furniture and other belongings with them. The numbers were such that the priests could hardly make themselves heard during the services above the weeping of the women and the crying of infants. The clergy, anxious about the safety of the cathedral treasures in the event of an attack, decided to remove them. They took down and hid the gold cross on the altar and the statue of Our Lady. The attack began while they were singing the service of prime. The monks clothed themselves in all the most precious vestments, rang

199

the cathedral bells and walked in procession through the town, carrying the relics of St Oswald, but the attackers were unmoved by the sight. The castle garrison fought back and for a time it seemed the attack might be beaten off, but then it was resumed with new vigour. Your Angevins broke down the gates and rampaged through the town, burning and looting as they went. The castle held out, but the town has been destroyed.'

'And Sir Miles, my husband?' Sibyl asked.

'I have no knowledge of his welfare, madam.'

Matilda turned a cold gaze on the prior. 'As I said, Father, we are at war. If the citizens and the garrison of Worcester had submitted to me as their rightful queen they could have avoided all this destruction. And as a point of fact, it was not only "my Angevins" who were involved. Miles had his own troops with him as well.'

He looked apologetic. 'I can only relate the story as it was told to me, my lady.'

'With a great deal of exaggeration, I have no doubt,' she said. 'When Miles returns we shall hear the true story.'

'I have no reason to disbelieve the two men who have fled to my priory.' The prior drew himself up. 'Now, if you will permit me, I shall leave you. I shall pray that this terrible destruction may be brought to an end soon.'

She responded proudly to his tale, but later that night she lay in bed with a heavy heart. Her confessor had told her that all blame rested on Stephen, but she could not get the image of the terrified women and children huddled in the cathedral out of her mind. Miles returned next day, uninjured, and her knights were triumphant. They had captured much booty and brought prisoners, whose ransom would swell the small payment they had been getting from her depleted coffers. She told herself that this was war, and war had always been like this.

Winter closed in but the fighting went on. Stephen tired of besieging Trowbridge and withdrew. Rumour had it that the barons fighting at his side were not prepared to sustain a long siege. But he did not leave the area unmolested. He reinforced the garrison at nearby Devizes and laid waste the countryside for miles around.

Miles's holdings around Gloucester were larger than she at first realized, extending well into the borders of Wales, and all these were now in her possession. These areas had not suffered the depredations of war and she found herself once again in the position of managing her own estates, with rents and tithes coming in. As she had always done, she set about visiting outlying farms and forests, assessing the condition of the land and the animals and the competence of the minor lords who held the land in fee. Miles had husbanded his resources well, and she found little to criticise. Her admiration and affection for him grew daily. Though formidable in battle, he was gentle and even tempered at home and treated her with respect tempered with an almost fatherly concern. It was something she had never experienced before. She had never known her father when she was growing up, and after they were reunited his moods were far too volatile to promote the sort of trust she felt for Miles. In gratitude, she enfeoffed him with the castle of St Briavel and the whole of the Forest of Dean.

At midwinter they learnt that Bishop Roger of Salisbury had died. However hostile he might once have been to Stephen he seemed to have repented, for he left all his treasure to the King. Over Christmas all fighting ceased, as the Church decreed, and they celebrated it with as much festivity as circumstances allowed. On her knees at night she prayed that the new year would bring an end to the stalemate.

14

ENGLAND, 1140-41

As IF TO offer her new hope, there was unexpected news from the far west. Reginald, her other half-brother, who remained behind in Normandy, had gathered a new force and landed in Cornwall. Here he had married the daughter of William fitz Ralph, a local baron, and thus gained possession of several castles. Delighted, she dispatched messengers bearing a charter, signed by herself and witnessed by Robert and Miles, creating him Earl of Cornwall.

It was not only in the West Country that Stephen's rule was shaky. The next area to revolt was East Anglia. Hugh Bigod rebelled, though he did not come out openly in her favour. Much more significant was the rebellion of Bishop Nigel of Ely. One of the three powerful bishops who once ruled England under King Henry, he was the only one who had maintained his hostility to Stephen. Now he declared for Matilda and defied the King from his bishopric. Ely was not easy to attack. It was an island, surrounded by marshland, and Nigel had a castle at Cherry Hill and another guarding the only road at Aldreth.

One night, as dusk was falling, a horseman appeared

at the gate of Gloucester Castle. He was ragged and filthy, and his horse was close to foundering. When he was brought into the hall she almost dismissed him as a vagabond but although his legs seemed ready to buckle under him he managed a courtly bow.

'Madam, forgive my appearance. I am Nigel, Bishop of Ely, and I have come to ask for refuge.'

He was exhausted and close to starving. It was not until he had been given food and found clean clothes that she was able to ask for his story.

Bishop Nigel shook his head wearily, as if he could still hardly believe what had happened. 'Stephen built a bridge of boats across the marsh. And someone, I believe it can only have been one of the monks from the monastery, showed him the only ford across one of the rivers. He mounted a surprise attack and captured both castles and their garrisons. I managed to escape through the fens with nothing but the clothes on my back. I ask you of your charity to take me in.'

'Your story fills me with anger and despair,' she responded, 'but you are welcome to stay here as my guest for as long as you wish.'

Robert rode in one day, fuming. 'That misbegotten son of a dog, fitz Hubert, who gave up Malmesbury to Stephen, has had the impudence to get a few of his Fleming mercenaries together and seize Devizes Castle.'

'Devizes has been Stephen's since he took it from Bishop Roger,' she pointed out. 'Fitz Hubert is your man. Why are you so angry?'

'Because fitz Hubert wants to hold it for himself. He's trying to establish himself in his own fief. But he won't last long. John the Marshal reckons that castle belongs to him, so I've sent him off to sort fitz Hubert out.'

A week later John himself came to her to report success.

'What have you done with fitz Hubert?' she asked.

'Hanged him. He was a blasphemer and a monster who tortured his prisoners. He had the cheek to ask me to submit to him! He deserved all he got!'

She turned away, shaking her head. The country was descending into anarchy. Deputations reached her daily from city burgesses and bailiffs of once-productive estates. Trade was at a standstill; so many of the peasants had died of starvation that there were not enough left to till the land; famine stalked the countryside. The killing had to stop. Stephen, too, must be suffering, she reasoned. Forced to traverse the country from end to end, putting down one rebellion after another, he must be tired and longing for peace. Perhaps the time for negotiation had arrived. She sent a message to Bishop Henry, asking him to act as mediator. At length she received a response. Stephen had agreed to send representatives to a meeting at Winchester at Whitsun if she would send hers. She asked Robert to join her at Gloucester to discuss the proposal.

'I don't like it,' Miles declared. 'Why should we trust Henry? He's Stephen's brother.'

'It was Henry who invited me to come to England,' she pointed out, 'and he arranged to escort me from Arundel to here. He means us no ill.'

'It doesn't make sense,' Miles objected. 'What's in it for him?'

'For a start, I think it still rankles with him that Theobold of Bec was chosen as Archbishop of Canterbury instead of him,' Robert said. 'And he was genuinely angered when Stephen arrested the three bishops. He thinks Stephen is interfering in church business, and he won't tolerate that.'

She sighed. 'This struggle for power between the Church and the monarchy seems to have dogged me all my life. My first husband, the Emperor, spent all his energy fighting to retain the right to invest bishops. After I am crowned I must try to find some permanent solution. But just now it seems to be working in our favour. We must take the chance and go to Winchester.'

'Not you!' Miles and Robert spoke with one voice. Robert went on, 'We can't run the risk. Stephen may be desperate enough now to take you prisoner, or even have you assassinated. I will go, with Miles and Brian fitz Count.'

She saw the force of his argument and reluctantly agreed.

'What terms are we prepared to accept?' Miles asked.

'That will be up to Henry to negotiate,' she said. 'But we have justice and Holy Writ on our side. I am convinced that the Church must back my claim. Tell Henry that I do not fear an ecclesiastical judgement.'

Robert and Miles were gone for several days and returned grim faced.

'Stephen was represented by his queen and by the Archbishop of Canterbury and Henry himself purported to be acting on his brother's behalf. We gave him your message and he asked if Stephen would also agree to be bound by the decision of the Church. The answer was an emphatic no. It seems Stephen still thinks he can win and he won't concede anything.'

She sank into a chair. 'Then there is nothing for it but to fight on. I had great hopes of support from Theobald of Bec. But it seems he has chosen to throw in his lot with Stephen.'

As the summer passed, her frustration grew. One inconclusive engagement followed after another. Stephen moved to dislodge Reginald from Cornwall and appointed his own earl, Alan of Brittany. There was some fierce fighting, but Reginald held on and Alan was unable to establish himself. The county remained in the Angevin camp. Stephen returned to Worcester and used it as a base for attacks in the area, including one on Robert's property of Tewkesbury. Robert had a magnificent house there, which was burnt to the ground. In revenge, Robert attacked Bath, but his forces were ambushed and there were heavy casualties. Deprived of his objective, he turned his attention to Nottingham and sacked the city, though he did not attempt to hold it.

At length, her patience at an end, she sent a message asking Robert to attend her at Gloucester. When he joined her and Miles in the solar, she turned on them impatiently.

'This has to stop. The country is bleeding to death. Can we not bring Stephen to battle – force one decisive encounter and let God decide the outcome?'

Robert shook his head. 'We may have right on our side, but God will not support us in an act of outright folly. We do not have the numbers to match Stephen in the field. He can call upon the resources of the whole country in terms of men and supplies, and money from taxes to pay his mercenaries. Our only hope is to weaken his power base until we can meet him on equal terms.'

'But can we do that? How much longer must this war of attrition go on?'

'You know as well as I do that he who controls a castle controls the land around it, with the men and the supplies and the rents and taxes it supports. Every time we take a castle, we deprive Stephen of that income and add it to ours. Every time we lay waste a swathe of countryside, we remove that source of supply. Every time we sack a city we take away the trade and the taxes that it produces. That not only deprives the throne, it cuts off the income of the great men around it. Our best hope is that the earls who support Stephen's cause at present will tire of the damage to their interests and they will either come over to us, or at least withdraw their forces from Stephen's army. If your husband would bring his powers to our aid, things might be different, but as it is ...'

She ground her teeth. 'I have written again and again, but he will not leave Normandy until it is all under his control. You are in the right, of course. We have to wait. But we have one other hope. Bishop Henry is still working in our favour.'

Henry sent word that he was going to France to confer with King Louis and his mentor, Theobald of Blois. Theoretically Stephen was Louis's liegeman for the county of Normandy, and indeed he had acknowledged the position by arranging for his son Eustace to do homage. Theobald was, of course, brother to both Henry and Stephen. Perhaps, Henry suggested, they may be able to bring pressure to bear. He returned with the suggestion that Stephen should give way in favour of Matilda's son, the young Henry. She accepted with alacrity. Stephen flatly refused. They were at stalemate again.

Once again, she faced a winter of inactivity. As the weeks pass she grew increasingly short-tempered. Miles's small fiefdom was not enough to occupy her mind for long, and at night she was haunted by the images of devastated fields and starving people she saw whenever she left Gloucester. She was the cause of all this, through her determination to oust Stephen, and her conscience nagged at her unceasingly. She was almost tempted to give up and return to Anjou. It was only the steady support of Miles and Robert and letters of encouragement from Brian fitz Count that kept her in England.

At last, there was some good news. There were rumours

of further discontent among Stephen's barons. One of Robert's daughters was married to Ranulf of Chester. He and his half-brother, William of Roumare, had grievances over the distribution of lands belonging to their mother, Countess Lucy, who held great estates in Lincolnshire; but in spite of that he had up to now maintained his loyalty to Stephen. Now they heard that he and his brother were pressing their claim to the castle of Lincoln, which Stephen had garrisoned. It seemed, however, that matters had not come to open warfare as yet.

Christmas came again and she and Miles were invited to keep the festival with Robert and his family at Bristol. The twelve days were almost over when a messenger rode into the castle. When he was conducted into the great hall, where Robert and his guests were about to dine, Robert jumped to his feet.

'I know you! You're one of Ranulf's knights. What has happened?'

The newcomer bowed. 'Thorold of Saughall, at your service, sire.' He turned towards her and dropped to his knees. 'My lady, Lord Ranulph sent me to offer his pledge of fealty to you and your son.'

A shout of triumph went up from the assembled company, but her initial reaction was less enthusiastic. It infuriated her that she was expected to be grateful for something that should have been given her as of right. She said coolly, 'The offer comes late, but I accept it.'

Robert shot her a glance of annoyance, but she ignored it and stretched her hand to Thorold to kiss. She saw that he was taken aback by her response. He had expected a better welcome. His eyes swivelled to Robert and back to her, but he bent his head and kissed her hand. Then he rose and turned to Robert. 'My lord also bid me tell you that he is mustering his knights to attack the usurper and he asks you to join him with your forces.'

Robert signalled to a page. 'Wine for Sir Thorold.' Turning to the knight he went on, 'You have ridden hard, I can see. You will wish to rest and change your clothes. Before I let you go, can you tell us what has occurred to bring your lord to this decision?'

Thorold's weary face broke into a grin. 'I can, my lord, and it is a tale worth telling.'

'Then sit and tell it,' Robert commanded.

Thorold took the stool Robert indicated and swallowed a long draught of wine. He wiped his mouth on the back of his hand and said, 'You will know already that my lord and his brother lay claim to the castle of Lincoln. We went there intending to besiege it but the King – I beg your pardon, madam, old habits die hard – the usurper spoke the two lords fair and agreed that Lord William should have the title of Earl of Lincoln. That sounded good enough, until we realized that it did not include possession of the castle. Still, my lords pretended to be satisfied and Stephen withdrew to Windsor to keep Christmas, leaving the castle only lightly garrisoned.' He paused and took another swig of wine. 'At Lord William and Lord Ranulph's orders we pretended to draw back, too, but in fact we encamped close by. Then the two lords thought up a pretty ruse.' He grinned again and emptied his cup. At Robert's nod the cup was refilled and Thorold went on, 'It being the festive season, the troops of the garrison were keen to enjoy some of the celebrations. Well, sir, you know yourself how hard it is for young knights to be cooped up inside a castle with nothing much to do. So all those not on guard duty got into the habit of going into the town, to the alehouses. My lords waited until that happened and then they sent their two wives with gifts for the castellan's lady to offer their good wishes for Christmas.'

Robert started forward in his chair. 'Their wives? Lord Ranulph sent my sister into the lion's den?'

Thorold smiled easily. 'No need to worry, sir. The ladies came to no harm. When dusk came on, Lord Ranulph took me and two others with him to escort them home. He went unarmed and without a cloak, so the guards could see he carried no weapon except a simple eating knife. We were admitted to the solar where the ladies were sitting and Lord Ranulph went up to the castellan's wife as if to kiss her hand. Then he drew his knife and grabbed hold of her and held the knife to her throat and told all those standing by that if they did not lay down their weapons he would kill her. Of course, they had no option but to obey. We collected up their swords and tied their hands with their own belts; then we went out into the hall, where some of the garrison were eating and drinking, and we soon convinced them to lay down their weapons too. After that, we went to open the main gate. Some of the sentries tried to stop us, but we made short work of them and Lord William was waiting outside with a small force that he had brought up to the walls under cover of darkness.' He finished his wine and smacked his lips in appreciation. 'So there you have it, my lords and lady. I told you it was a tale worth telling.'

'So now, your lord and his brother are in full possession of the castle?' Robert said. 'In that case, what has brought you with such haste to ask my help?'

'Ah well,' Thorold said with a shrug. 'Getting the castle is one thing, keeping it is another. The citizens of Lincoln are loyal to Stephen and when they heard what had happened they immediately sent word to him. He has left his Christmas celebrations, called up his men and is preparing to besiege the castle. Lord Ranulph and his brother agreed that he would slip out with his men before Stephen closed the roads and ride for Chester, leaving

Lord William to hold the castle.'

'And my daughter?' Robert demanded. 'Did she return to Chester with her husband?'

'No, sire. It was deemed too dangerous for her to attempt the escape. The lady remains with Lord William and his wife.'

'And now he sends to me for aid,' Robert said grimly. 'Knowing that I cannot leave my daughter to the mercy of Stephen and his men.'

'I think he has more in mind than that,' Thorold said. 'He bade me tell you that the King – the usurper – has only a small force with him, thinking that the castle is but lightly held. He believes that if you and he join forces you can defeat him in open battle.'

'By God, Robert!' Miles broke in. 'This could be the chance we have been waiting for. A pitched battle with the weight of numbers on our side.'

'It is worth considering,' Robert agreed. 'Go to your rest, Sir Thorold. We will discuss this among ourselves and give you our answer in the morning.'

They withdrew to the solar and she turned to her brother. 'Robert, Miles is right. This is the chance we have been waiting for. We cannot let it slip.'

'Nor can we blunder into it without proper thought,' he responded.

Her patience, worn thin over the months, snapped. 'Oh, your caution is infuriating! Why can you not see that this is the time to act, now before it is too late?'

'I will act, if I think the time is right, but not before.'

'And if I order it, as your liege lady?'

He regarded her coldly. 'That would be a mistake. And you did ill to take Ranulph's offer of fealty so ungraciously. We need every ally we can get.'

'I spoke no more than truth! He should have pledged

211

his faith at the beginning. Am I to crawl to every petty lordling who decides his best interests will be served by coming over to my side?'

'You would do well to remember that if you ever wish to rule as queen you will depend on these "petty lordlings" as your vassals. Ranulph and William are powerful men. With them on our side the balance of forces is much more in our favour.'

'Then you will go with them, to face Stephen?'

'I will send Thorold back to tell Ranulph to come and pledge his fealty in person. Meanwhile, we will summon our forces. If I am satisfied with what he has to tell us, we will go.'

'Thank you!' She was aware that she had behaved badly but did not know how to make amends.

By next morning Bristol Castle was astir like an ants' nest kicked open by a careless foot. Messengers rode out in all directions. Robert was summoning all the forces he could muster. Miles went back to Gloucester to call up his men and send appeals to his allies in Wales. Sibyl, his wife, was the granddaughter of Gruffydd ap Llewelyn and her father was lord of Brecon. The army began to assemble; armoured knights from the households of Robert's tenants and liegemen; foot soldiers called from the fields and villages as part of the feudal levy; Welsh warriors, rough-looking men in red tunics, without armour and carrying bows and long lances, led by two of their princes, Meredydd and Cadwalader. Soon the castle precinct was crammed with men and horses and others were camped outside. Robert's cooks and servants ran hither and thither, in an effort to see everyone was provided for, and the great hall echoed with loud voices, while the smoke from the fire mingled with the stench of sweat and piss. Outside the air was loud with the clang of metal on metal and the rasp of steel on stone as the smiths worked to repair damaged armour and sharpen swords, and scented with the mingled odours of dung, both human and equine, of meat roasting over open fires, and the sharp tang of burnt bone as horses were shod.

Thorold returned to Chester and some days later Ranulph arrived to do homage. Matilda made an effort to be gracious, but could not resist remarking that it was a pity he did not follow his father-in-law's example and declare for her as soon as she reached England. She saw the colour surge into his face, but it was anger, not embarrassment. Robert had told her that he had a reputation as a proud and choleric man and she saw that this act of homage had not come easily to him. As soon as he decently could, he turned from her to confer with Robert, who questioned him keenly about the exact size of Stephen's army.

'I promise you, he has only a small force with him. When my men and I slipped out that night they were just making camp and I could tell from the number of fires that there were not many of them. I think he believes he can persuade William to yield the castle by offering him lands and honours elsewhere – or perhaps as he came straight from the Christmas feast he did not have time to recall all his troops. He has the citizens of the town on his side, of course, but they are unlikely to prove much use in a pitched battle.'

Robert gestured to one of his scribes, who spread a fresh sheet of parchment on the table. 'Show me the position of the castle and the layout of the land around it.'

Ranulph sketched rapidly. 'The castle occupies the top of the hill, with the cathedral. The west wall is also the west wall of the town. The ground drops away steeply towards the River Witham and the land between the town and the river is flat and good for a cavalry charge, except close by the river, were it is marshy.'

'How can we cross the river?'

'There is a ford here, a little to the south.'

She listened impatiently to further discussion until at last Robert said, 'Very well. We march tomorrow.'

In the great hall she called her household knights about her and bade them make ready, then turned to her ladies.

'Pack what is necessary for a journey. We shall be gone for a month, perhaps longer. I shall need a good, warm cloak – perhaps two—'

Robert, overhearing, interrupted her. 'You cannot mean to travel with us!'

'Why not? It will not be the first time I have travelled with an army.'

'But the danger! Suppose you were to be captured.'

'Then Stephen would have the dilemma of what to do with me. Anyway, you think we are assured of victory. I want to be there to see it. Once the battle is won, I should be there to accept the homage of the defeated.'

'Nothing is assured in battle. You know that as well as I do.'

'I am not so foolish as to place myself at the heart of the fighting. There must be some position, some point of high ground, where I can overlook the battlefield.'

He groaned and then grinned. 'Well, I know it is useless to argue with you. If you promise to stay well away ...'

'I will. You have my word.'

Next morning, as dawn broke, the vanguard, with Ranulph in command, rode out of the castle grounds and over the causeway. Following him came rank upon rank of infantry, archers with crossbows, men-at-arms with swords and lances, the Welsh with their longbows. Robert led the main division, mounted on a grey palfrey and followed by one of his squires leading his black destrier. With him were his household knights and after them came other groups of cavalry drawn from the minor lords who owed him fealty, and also from many who had been disinherited by Stephen and who had thrown in their lot with the Angevins. She followed, sitting sideways on a white palfrey, with her ladies behind her in three wagons, and after them ground and creaked other wagons loaded with supplies and the carts carrying the bakers and cooks and farriers and armourers and all the other essential impedimenta of an army on the march. Finally, Miles brought up the rear with another detachment of cavalry. The sun was high in the sky before all of them were on the road. They would be lucky to cover more than ten miles in a day. It would take them more than two weeks, following the old Fosse Way that tradition insisted was built by the Romans, to reach Lincoln.

On the first day of February they reached the high ridge which ran north/south through the Lincolnshire plain, divided halfway along its length by the cleft driven through it by the River Witham. Here they joined another ancient road running north from London and found a contingent of knights led by Brian fitz Count awaiting them. At Robert's order, they made camp around the village of Bracebridge, and she went to stand with him and Ranulph at the top of the escarpment looking down towards the river. On the far side and slightly below them the twin towers of Lincoln Castle and the cathedral crowned the top of a steep hill, with the town clustered at their feet, the whole surrounded by sturdy walls. On the plain below there were groups of tents flying pennants of many colours. Horses were tethered nearer to the river and the foreshortened figures of men moved among them.

At intervals around the walls of the castle they could pick out the outline of mangonels and the regular thud of missiles striking stone reverberated over the distance.

'Stephen has taken over the city,' Ranulph said. 'It is only the castle that is holding out.'

'Where is the ford you spoke of?' Robert asked.

Ranulph pointed. 'There, just below us. And there, further to the west, is the flat ground suitable for cavalry. I suspect Stephen will make his stand there, with the castle wall at his back.'

'Yes, that makes sense. We'll camp here tonight and prepare for battle on the morrow.'

She frowned. 'Stephen must know we are here. If his forces are as few as Ranulph said, he would be a fool to face us. What is to stop him packing up and slipping away during the night?'

'His honour,' Ranulph said. 'You remember that his father was branded a coward for leaving the crusaders outside Antioch? He will do anything rather than be shamed like that.'

'Of course,' she murmured. 'It was frequently spoken of when I was a child at the German court. But it was unjust, was it not? He went to Constantinople to seek help from the Emperor Alexios and when none was forthcoming he thought the cause was lost. How could he have known that Antioch would fall at last through the actions of a traitor who opened the gates?'

'And he did return to the Holy Land, and died there,' Robert added.

'None of that weighs with Stephen,' Ranulph asserted. 'I have been closer to him than either of you in recent years, and I have heard it said often that he will rather face a raging lion single handed than run away. He will wait to face us tomorrow, I warrant it.'

As they turned back to the village Miles joined them. 'I have been to the manor house. It's a poor enough place and the lord is a surly fellow, but they will find somewhere for the ladies to sleep and we can bed down in the hall. From the look of the weather we shall be glad of a roof over our heads tonight. Come, I'll show you.'

As he predicted, their welcome was less than warm and the fare was poor, tough meat and rough wine. In the women's room there were straw-stuffed mattresses where, she suspected, a number of undesirable creatures had made their homes. In the middle of the night they were jolted awake by a violent crash. Her ladies struggled up with cries of panic and one screamed. 'We are being attacked! God save us, the enemy are upon us.'

The room was illuminated by a brilliant flash and she said, 'Be quiet, you foolish girl. It is a thunderstorm, nothing more. Go back to sleep.' They lay down again but the one who screamed continued to whimper with fear. 'I said be quiet!' she repeated and the whimpers subsided.

She lay listening to the sound of heavy rain running off the thatch. The thunder and lightning continued most of the night and none of them slept very much.

She was up at dawn, but even so, going down to the hall she found it empty. The straw pallets on which the men slept had been stacked in a corner and there were the remains of a hasty breakfast on the table. The three ladies she had brought with her came in, scratching and yawning, and a sleepy maidservant brought them yesterday's bread and warm milk straight from the cow. They were still eating when Robert strode in. He was already wearing his gambeson, the padded jerkin which prevented his armour from chafing him and added an extra layer of protection.

He bowed and wished her good morrow and went on,

'Ranulph was right. Stephen is still there. He plans to face us.' His squires were at his heels, as always, and he turned to them. 'Bring my armour. Tell the groom to saddle Storm. Sound the call to arms!'

She followed him out of doors. The rain had stopped, but the roofs of the houses were still dripping and the ground was puddled. Trumpets sounded. Already men were tumbling out of their tents, or out of village houses where they had found refuge, pulling on helmets and buckling sword belts, half eaten crusts of bread still in their hands. Foot soldiers were struggling to their feet, rubbing chilled limbs. Robert's two squires came out of the house carrying his hauberk suspended on his lance. He ducked his head and they poured the glistening links over his shoulders in a chiming cascade. She had seen this so many times, on so many different battlefields. It always reminded her of a snake shedding its scaly skin, but in reverse. They bound the protective cuisses around his legs, buckled on his sword belt and handed him his mailed gloves. A groom led over his destrier, ready caparisoned and barded, and he vaulted up into the saddle. She was reminded of Geoffrey at the tournament to celebrate their betrothal – but that was just showing off. Robert was about to risk his life. She went to his side.

'Do not put yourself too much at risk, brother – for my sake if not for your own.'

He smiled down at her. 'Fear nothing. Today we will have victory.'

Brian rode over, ready armed, and she reached up to take his hand. 'Have a care, my dear friend. I should be lost without you.' Then, on an impulse, she pulled the kerchief from her throat and handed it to him. 'Wear this for me.' He lifted the delicate material to his face and kissed it, then tucked it into his sleeve.

'What can I fear, with this as my favour? Stay safe, my lady. We will bring you the usurper as your prisoner.'

Robert said, 'You will see all that happens from the hilltop where we stood last night. Do not come any closer.'

She smiled at the half-hidden plea in his eyes. 'I will wait here, with a few of my knights. I have told them who is to stay. They hate me for keeping them from the battle but if we should need to make a quick retreat ...'

'You will not need to,' he said firmly.

The ranks were forming, in the same order as on the march, and she stood aside as they passed her, following the old road down the hillside. Then she called her ladies and her attendant knights and they went together to the edge of the scarp. Below them the enemy camp was stirring. Horses were being watered and camp fires stirred into life. From the city came the sound of bells and she remembered it was Sunday. It was a day on which the Church forbade fighting, but it seemed that neither side was prepared to observe the prohibition.

They had to wait for some time before they saw the front ranks of their own army debouching onto the river bank. They reached the ford and then there was a halt. Horses and men milled about in indecision.

She turned to Alexander de Bohun, her faithful master-at-arms who had followed her in all her travels. She knew that the half-dozen knights she had kept with her resented being denied the chance to fight, but Alexander was different. He would not leave her side unless she ordered it.

'What is happening? Why don't they cross?'

'I should guess that the water is too high. Last night's rain has swelled the river.'

There was a flurry of activity below them.

'What are they doing?'

He screwed up his eyes. 'They are rolling up the horse's

caparisons, tucking them round the saddles. If the horses have to swim, the caparisons would impede their legs.'

As they watched, Ranulph urged his destrier into the river. By the middle of the ford the water was swirling round the animal's shoulders but he forged ahead and reached the far bank, shaking a shower of drops from his hide, which the early sun turned to crystal. The rest of Ranulph's knights followed and they formed up on the far side.

'That's all very well for the mounted men,' she commented. 'But what about the foot soldiers? They will find it hard to stand against the current.'

Now Robert rode his horse into the stream, but he halted in the deepest part and waved his knights forward. Some of them passed him but halted on his other side, others took positions between him and the nearer bank, until they formed a line across the river. Then each of them grounded the butt of his lance, so they formed a rough palisade reaching from side to side. The foot soldiers waded in, their weapons held above their heads with one hand, the other grasping for the lances which prevented them from being knocked off their feet and washed downstream.

Alexander nodded approvingly. 'Clever!'

She raised her eyes from the scene in the river and gasped. 'Look! Now they have seen us.'

Men were scurrying about like mice in the enemy camp. The sun caught flashes of metal as they pulled on their armour. A group of riders galloped up the road leading to the city gate and disappeared inside. 'Going to warn Stephen,' she said.

The river crossing proceeded slowly. It would take some time for all the men to get over. Her heart was beating unnaturally fast and she had to suppress an urge to shout at them to hurry.

'Hah!' Alexander gave a sharp cry of alarm and she saw a company of cavalry issue from the city gate and charge down towards the ford. Without thinking, she reached out and gripped his wrist, where his hand rested on the pommel of his sword. He glanced down briefly but made no move. 'No need to worry, my lady. See, Lord Ranulph is ready for them.'

Ranulph's men had already formed a defensive line and they heard the sound of his voice carried up on the clear air, giving the order to charge. The closely packed line of knights started forward. Horses, trained for battle and eager, broke into a gallop and when the two forces met the sound of metal crashing on metal reached the watchers on the hill. Stephen's men were outnumbered. There was a sharp skirmish and then they reined their horses about and galloped back to the safety of the city. Most of the men were over the river by then and Robert waved his knights on to join the others on the bank. Ranulph's men had returned, having seen off the opposition, and the column formed up again as before.

Stephen's army was marching out by then. Clearly the earlier panic had been replaced by discipline and the ranks formed up, as Ranulph predicted, with their backs to the city wall.

'Must be uncomfortable for them, knowing that William's men could sally out from the castle and take them in the rear,' Alexander commented.

She was studying the formations, trying to assess numbers. 'Ranulph was right. It is only a small force.'

'The fool!' Alexander said. 'He had enough warning. While our men were fording the river he could have got clear away and ridden north. Why face us, with the odds against him?'

'Pride,' she said. 'And fear of being shamed as his father was.'

The Angevin army was deploying opposite Stephen's. This was to be no untidy skirmish but a formal battle. Each force had three divisions. Ranulph and his men took the right flank, Robert was in the centre and Miles commanded the left. The Welsh were spread along the front of both wings. Opposite, Stephen's thin ranks of cavalry were reinforced by a citizen infantry of oddly assorted men and boys, poorly armed as far as she could judge from this distance. His left flank looked more formidable and shading her eyes she was able to make out the standard of its commander.

'See who is there, on the left?' She pointed.

Alexander growled. 'It's that whoreson mercenary, William of Ypres. I thought he was still in Normandy.'

'So did I.'

Stephen himself commanded the centre, with his household knights clustered about him. She could see his standard and the occasional flash as the sunlight struck a jewel in the crown he wore over his helmet. None of them were mounted, a clear signal that he intended to stand and fight to a finish. As they watched, one of his men climbed up onto a slight hillock and all those nearby turned to face him. From his gestures it was obvious that he was addressing them.

'Pre-battle speech. He's probably telling them what is likely to happen to their wives and children if they lose,' Alexander said. 'Why isn't Stephen doing it himself?'

'He's no orator,' she answered. 'I remember that from when we were both at my father's court. Very easy and affable under normal circumstances, but tongue-tied in more formal situations.'

As soon as the speaker finished Ranulph rode out to

the front of the Angevin ranks and delivered his own exhortation. He was followed by Robert, and from her brother's gestures she got the impression that he was referring to the commanders on the opposing side, in less than complimentary terms. The men responded with jeers and laughter. Condemned to inactivity she growled in frustration. 'Oh, have done! What purpose does it serve?'

'The men expect it,' Alexander said. 'They need something to get their blood up.'

She looked at him. 'Was it wise to put the Welsh in the front line?'

'From what I've heard, talking to their princes, they're a wild lot when the battle madness grabs them. They will rush in without thought for their own safety and can do a lot of damage before they're forced to retreat. You see those bows they carry? They don't use them at a distance, like a crossbow, but at short range. I'm told that from close to the arrows will pierce mail and leather and have been known to pin a knight's leg to his horse's side, through the saddle.'

Robert rode back to his place in the centre. The formal preparations were complete. A moment later a trumpet sounded and the Angevins raised a shout that reached easily over the distance. The Welsh infantry rushed forward, yelling like fiends. On both wings, Stephen's cavalry charged them. The fighting was fierce and brief and then the Welsh turned and ran back through their own ranks, leaving a number of bodies on the field.

'They are fleeing. Cowards!'

'No, clever tactics!' Alexander said. 'Stephen's cavalry are scattered now. It will take time for them to rein in and return to their formation. This is our moment!'

As he spoke, all three divisions of the Angevin cavalry spurred their horses towards the enemy. On

Stephen's right wing his knights were quickly pushed back or dispersed and Miles's men wheeled right to threaten the central ranks around the King. On the left, the mercenaries under William of Ypres put up a little more resistance to Ranulph's attack, but then there was a sudden reversal.

'Look!' she cried. 'D'Ypres is leaving the field, and his men are following. They are deserting!'

'They've seen that there is no chance of victory,' Alexander said. 'They have to choose between flight and a hopeless battle which will leave them either dead or prisoners. To my mind, they've made the sensible decision.'

With resistance on both wings at an end Stephen and his knights were surrounded, but they fought on fiercely and some of the local militia stood with them. Robert had kept some of his knights dismounted and they now waded in to engage in bitter hand-to-hand combat. Even from the height where they stood the watchers could hear the ring of metal on metal and see sparks fly up as sword met sword.

She craned her neck, struggling to see what was happening, but the mêlée of bodies was so tightly packed that it was impossible to distinguish man from man. Suddenly a cheer went up from the Angevins and the fighting stopped as if at a signal. All round the field men laid down their arms and submitted to being made prisoner. Others were running, some of them back into the city, some towards the river, in a desperate attempt to escape. They were pursued and cut down.

'That's it!' Alexander said. 'We have the victory.'

'Oh, praise God! Praise God!' She discovered that she was panting as if she had been in the midst of the fight. 'Is Stephen dead, do you think?' she asked. 'I hope not! I want to see him grovel!'

'They won't have killed him,' Alexander assured her.

'He's too valuable a prize.'

She stretched her arms, releasing the tension that had gripped her since the start of the battle. When she spoke her voice was unsteady. 'I think we might ride down now and congratulate our victorious commanders.'

By the time they reached the city the prisoners and the wounded had been taken into the castle. The Welsh were collecting their dead, but the field was strewn with bodies and men were scavenging amongst the debris for dropped weapons and any other items of value. Already the dogs and the crows had arrived. The river level had dropped and they were able to cross the ford without great difficulty, but as they did so one of her women gave a strangled cry. The current swept the body of a man across their path, and then two more. As they reached the far bank Matilda looked back and saw an upturned boat floating down towards them. Three men were clinging to the hull but they were carried out of sight and after them several more bodies floated past. It was obvious what had happened to the fugitives who fled in that direction. As they rode in through the city gate smoke was rising from several buildings and the ordinary soldiers were busily engaged in looting, the traditional reward of victory.

She was received at the castle gate by William of Roumare with a deep obeisance and conducted into the great hall. Robert and Miles were standing with Ranulph, wine cups in hand; but as she entered they turned and bowed.

'My lady, we have the victory. The usurper is conquered and nothing now stands in your way to the throne.' Her brother's voice was vivid with triumph.

She gave him her hand. 'My lord, you have fought well today. You all have, and be sure that you have my gratitude. You will find me generous when I finally come into my own.' She looked from him to Miles. 'You are not wounded, either of you?'

'A bruise or two, nothing more,' Miles assured her with a smile.

'Where is Brian?'

'Making sure the wounded are attended to.'

'Do we have many casualties?'

'None of note. Some minor wounds. We got off lightly.'

Brian came into the hall. 'The wounded are all in the chapel. The surgeon is with them.' He saw her and came to fall on his knees before her.

'Dear lady, my heart swells with joy to see you at last possessed of the royal authority which is yours by right of birth. May God be praised, who has brought the traitor Stephen low and raised you up to your rightful position.'

He kissed her hands, and it was more than the formal touch of a vassal. She felt a tremor somewhere deep inside her body, a sensation she had not expected to know again.

'Praise Him indeed.' She drew him to his feet. There were tears in his eyes, but in spite of that the light in them reminded her of the young man who rode beside her to her betrothal. 'And praise him for the loyal friends who have stood by me through these difficult years.'

'And will do so as long as God gives them life,' he responded.

She looked round the hall. 'Where is the usurper? You have not killed him?'

'No, he lives,' Robert said. 'But he was brought down by a blow to the head and he is still scarcely conscious.'

'Let me see him.'

He led her down the hall to the dais at the end, where the lord's table stood. Stephen was stretched out on it, with a surgeon bending over him. As she approached he shoved the man aside and struggled into a sitting position.

'I am a king! I should not be treated like this! It is not fitting that a king should be brought low by a treacherous blow. I am the Lord's anointed.' His voice broke, somewhere between tears and anger.

She looked at him and felt nothing but contempt, the same contempt she felt for Geoffrey when she saw him lying moaning in his own blood and excrement after the disaster at Le Sap. Men, she thought, are all the same – full of bravado when things are going well, self-pitying idiots when they are hurt. Most men, she corrected herself, thinking of Robert and Miles. There are exceptions.

'You are not a king. You are a usurper who stole the throne from me, Henry's rightful heir – to whom you once swore loyalty. Get down on your knees!' Two men-at-arms who were standing guard dragged him off the table and forced him to his knees in front of her. 'You will swear fealty to me, if you value your life.'

'Never! I am the anointed King. You cannot take my place.'

She raised her hand to strike him but Robert caught her wrist. 'Let be, for now. He hardly knows where he is. Any oath now would be worthless.'

For a moment she resisted, then she dropped her arm. 'Very well. I can wait.'

'Come, have a cup of wine. We have much to celebrate.'

Chairs were brought forward and she sat with Robert beside her. Miles said, 'I must look to the other prisoners.'

'How many have we taken?'

'Plenty, and some of high standing. Baldwin fitz Richard and Richard fitz Urse among them. They are both wounded but will recover.' He bowed. 'If you will excuse me, lady.'

She nodded permission and turned to Robert. 'How was Stephen captured?'

'With some difficulty. His knights fought valiantly, but he excelled them all. I have to admit, I admire him for his courage. He was outnumbered but fought on nobly until his sword broke in his hand with the force of his blows. Then a man nearby, one of the townsfolk, I think, handed him a battle-axe and he laid about him with that so ferociously that no one could get near him, until William Kahamnes got round behind him. He had lost his helmet in the struggle and William hit him over the head with a rock. It was a shameful way for one of his courage to be felled. I understand something of his distress now.'

She shook her head impatiently. She saw nothing to regret in the downfall of a traitor. 'Send William to me. I will see he is rewarded. But now, what are we to do with Stephen?'

'He must be kept prisoner until we can arrange your coronation. After that ... well, it will be up to you to decide. I dare say his brother Theobald will offer a good ransom for him. For the present, I think it would be unwise for him to travel. We don't want him to die on the journey. I suggest that you go back to Gloucester with Miles. I will stay here and see that everything is in order. I take it you are happy for William of Roumare to hold the castle?' She nodded agreement. 'As soon as Stephen is fit enough I will bring him to Gloucester and he can make his formal submission to you. After that, I think he will be safest housed at Bristol. There is no chance of him being rescued, or escaping, from there.'

It was agreed. That night there was a feast of celebration, with the best fare Roumare could contrive after weeks under siege. Next day, she summoned her knights and, escorted by Miles with his forces, she began her journey westward.

15

ENGLAND, 1141

SHE RETURNED TO Gloucester in triumph and was greeted with joy by Miles's wife and children. Robert arrived the next day, bringing Stephen with him, but before he presented him to her he asked for a private word.

'Be advised by me. Do not seek to humiliate Stephen.'

She was immediately irritated. 'Why not? He has stolen the throne and kept me from my rightful inheritance. He should be made to grovel.'

'No,' he said. 'That would not be wise.'

'Why? Why should I be careful of his pride?'

'Because, for one thing, he fought bravely. It was a dastardly blow that felled him from behind.'

Her lips curled. 'You men! You think courage in battle is the only thing that matters. For you, the ability to swing a sword wipes out all other failings.'

'That is not true. But courage deserves respect. There are more important reasons, however, to treat him carefully.'

'What reasons?'

'Whatever the rights and wrongs of the situation, he is an anointed king. For many people brutality towards him would come close to sacrilege.'

'He is an oath breaker and a usurper. No amount of holy oil can wipe out that sin.'

'You may be right, but think of this. When you are queen you will need the support and fealty of the men who now support Stephen. It will not make it easy for them to come over to our side if you show yourself arrogant and merciless.'

She stared at him. *Arrogant and merciless?* It was not the first time she had been charged with the sin of pride. Was that how men saw her?

More gently, he said, 'You might also consider that if the battle had gone differently I might now be in Stephen's position. Would you not wish me to be treated with the courtesy due to my rank?'

She saw him in her imagination, shackled and brought to his knees. She swallowed back her anger and nodded. 'Very well. Bring him to me. I want to see him.'

Stephen was brought in. His hands were manacled and his head was bandaged, but he carried himself proudly. Their eyes met and he made the slightest obeisance.

'Greetings, cousin.' They might from the tone of his voice be once again in her father's court. She clenched her jaw.

'I may be your cousin by blood. But in the eyes of God I am your queen, and you will address me as such.'

His gaze did not waver. 'That is yet to be decided.'

'It has been decided. God's judgement on you was manifested when you lost the battle.'

'I do not accept that. I am the crowned and anointed king. You are the rebellious subject who has riven the realm with conflict and brought destruction and starvation to its people. It is you who will ultimately have to answer to the judgement of God.'

She stepped closer to him and spat the words. 'Traitor! Oath breaker!'

'Your father absolved all who took that oath on his death bed. He knew you were not worthy to rule.'

She fought back the impulse to strike him. 'We shall see soon who is worthy. Once I am crowned we shall have to decide what is to become of you. Until then, you are my prisoner. Take him away!'

His guards hesitated and she saw they were unwilling to lay hands on him. 'I said, take the traitor away!'

He looked at her and the faint suggestion of a smile touched his lips. Then he bent his head very slightly and turned to the door. The two guards followed him out.

She turned to Robert. 'What will you do with him?'

'I shall take him to Bristol, as I said.'

'I want him close confined.'

'Trust me. I shall make sure he does not escape.'

She forced herself to be calm and moved away to sit at the table, beckoning him to sit beside her.

He said, 'So, what is our next move?'

'We must make sure that the bishops are on our side. I have already sent to Bishop Henry, asking him to convene a council of all the leading churchmen. I think we can be confident of his support.'

Robert frowned. 'I hope you are right.'

'Surely there is no doubt of that. He invited me to come to England, and he escorted me here from Arundel. Stephen may be his brother but he has obviously withdrawn his allegiance. He cannot forgive him for arresting those three bishops.'

'Yes, I know. I just have a feeling that Bishop Henry's allegiance is as changeable as the weather. All that matters to him is the power of the Church, and his standing within it.'

She met his eyes. 'Then we must offer him that power. He is already papal legate. He has to be convinced that I will never attempt to interfere with his jurisdiction in Church matters.'

He lifted an eyebrow. 'Are you prepared to accept that? Your husband the emperor spent most of his life struggling to maintain authority over the Church.'

'England is not Germany. If that is the price of Henry's support, so be it.'

Gloucester Castle became a magnet, drawing the great men of the realm to offer their allegiance. Mainly they were men whose fiefs were in the west, some of them already sworn supporters, others waverers who had waited to see which way the battle went. Brian fitz Count was one of the first to arrive, to her great pleasure. Among others who had been loyal from the start was Bernard, Bishop of St David's, who was once her mother's chancellor. But there were still many who held aloof, reluctant to break their oaths to Stephen, or unsure where their best interests lay.

News came from Normandy. Geoffrey, hearing of her success, had summoned a meeting of the nobles who held land there as well as in England, to determine where their allegiance should now lie. It seemed that their first reaction was to offer the overlordship to Theobald, Stephen's brother, but he had declined it and offered the dukedom instead to Geoffrey, on condition that Stephen be released from prison and given back the lands he once held during the reign of King Henry. Geoffrey wrote:

Be assured I have not accepted these conditions. Nonetheless, a number of castles have already submitted to me and I do not doubt but to have control over the whole duchy very soon. I have also concluded a truce with the two Beaumont twins, Robert and Waleran. Both have extensive lands on this side of the narrow seas as well as in England and will have to decide where their loyalty lies. So our cause progresses well and I look to see us undisputed rulers of England and Normandy very soon.

She crumpled the letter furiously. 'To Geoffrey! They offered the overlordship to Geoffrey. What business had they offering it to him? As Queen, Normandy belongs to me.'

She saw Brian and Miles exchange glances. Brian said gently, 'Nevertheless, it advances your cause to have your husband in control of Normandy. At the very least, it denies the resources of the duchy to Stephen and his supporters. Once you are crowned there will be time to establish your authority there.'

'Those men would make Geoffrey king, in preference to me,' she said bitterly. 'They loathe the idea of being ruled by a woman.'

'Then you must show them that you have all the qualities of a king,' Miles said. 'Let them see that you are the true-born daughter of the great Henry.'

She straightened her shoulders. 'You are right. I shall make them fear me, as they feared him. As for Geoffrey, he has Normandy now. It is all he cared about. He has no interest in ruling England.'

A message arrived from Bishop Henry. He did not offer immediate submission but had referred the matter to a higher authority, the Pope. Meanwhile, he asked her to meet him at Wherewell, just outside Winchester, to consider their position.

It was exactly a month from the day of the battle at

Lincoln when she rode, with her closest companions, through the gateway of the ancient abbey of Wherewell on its fertile island in the River Test. In good weather this would be a delightful setting, but that day the sun was obscured by low cloud and a chill drizzle was falling. She shivered in spite of herself, unable to banish the thought that the omens were inauspicious.

Brian, as always, sensed her mood. 'Henry could not have chosen a more suitable place for this meeting. You know that the abbey was founded by the wife of King Edgar, who founded the line of English kings and from whom, through your mother, you draw your own descent? It is fitting that this should be the place where the two royal lines, of Normandy and England, come together in your person.'

She caught his eye and smiled. 'You always have the right words to lift my spirits.'

'I speak no more than the truth. Trust me, this will be a great day.'

The abbey housed a sisterhood of Benedictine nuns and the mother abbess greeted her as she dismounted and conducted her to a private room, where a table set with delicacies stood in front of a cheerful fire.

'Pray refresh yourself, madam. Bishop Henry is already here. When you are ready I will take you to the chapter house, where he awaits you.'

A lay sister brought warm water, and when she had washed and eaten her ladies helped her out of her travelling clothes and arrayed her in a bliaut of sky blue silk, and a woollen overmantle in a deeper tone of the same colour, bordered with embroidery of gold thread and precious stones and lined with fur. She covered her hair with a veil of fine linen, held in place by a simple fillet of gold. The effect, as she intended, was impressive without overt pretensions to regality.

She entered the room with Robert at her left and Reginald at her right, reinforcing the family connection and demonstrating that, as Henry's sons, they endorsed her position as his rightful heir. Brian and Miles followed close behind. Bishop Henry came forward to lead her to a chair and took a seat facing her.

'My lady, it seems that God has favoured your cause and it ill behoves me to quarrel with that outcome. But there are certain considerations which need to be addressed before I can offer you my unqualified support.'

She bit back an irritable retort. 'What considerations are those, my lord?'

'You will be aware that when my brother took the throne he made certain promises, among them an undertaking to respect the authority of the Church and the dignity of its prelates. In that respect he has signally failed to keep his oath. By arresting Bishop Roger of Salisbury, Bishop Nigel of Ely and Bishop Alexander of Lincoln he made an unwarranted attack on the Church and by denying them the right to be tried by their peers in an ecclesiastical court he broke his oath to respect the Church's independence from lay authority. This is the matter upon which I require reassurance.'

'One moment, my lord,' Brian broke in. 'As you say, Stephen is your brother. I mean no disrespect, but you will understand that we also require reassurance. It seems surprising that you should turn against your own flesh and blood.'

Henry's lips tightened but he nodded. 'It is a reasonable question. I love my brother. But I am obliged to put my loyalty to God and his church above my loyalty to him.'

'So all you require of me is an oath not to meddle in the affairs of the Church?' she asked.

'Exactly so, my lady.'

'And if I give you that promise, you will acknowledge me as King Henry's rightful heir and Queen of England?'

'I will acknowledge your right to be queen, but until you have been crowned and anointed I cannot give you that title. I will, however, proclaim you as Lady of the English until such time as that can be accomplished.'

'Then I give you my oath that I will in all things connected with the Church consult with you and take your advice, particularly in the matter of the election of bishops and abbots. And you in turn will receive me in holy church as your lady and swear fealty to me?'

He went down on his knees. 'Madam, I will.'

Next morning she rode into Winchester, sitting sideways on her white palfrey. Since the birth of her children she had found this a more comfortable position, and besides she knew that to ride astride like a man might give offence to the bishops. She was dressed this time in white samite, the rich silk interwoven with threads of gold. Over this she wore a mantle of crimson trimmed with ermine and pearls and her veil was held in place by a jewelled coronet. In place of a page, Brian walked at her horse's bridle and Robert and Reginald rode behind her, with Miles following. Her household knights and Robert's formed a rearguard. At the gate of the city she was met by Bishop Henry and Turstin, the clerk of the royal treasury. Henry handed her the keys to Winchester Castle and Turstin the keys to the treasury, where the royal crown was kept. This ceremony over, she proceeded through the city streets and when they reached the square in front of the cathedral they found it crowded with people, who greeted her with cheers. Small children offered up posies of early spring flowers and mothers held up their babies for her to bless.

Outside the great west doors of the cathedral Brian lifted her down and she walked between Bishop Henry and Bishop Bernard into the nave. A procession formed, led by a canon carrying a crucifix and two boys with censors, so that she walked through a cloud of incense. Behind her, as well as her brothers and Brian and Miles, came five other bishops and a number of abbots. The cathedral was packed with people. Church dignitaries rubbed shoulders with local gentry and the burgers of the city and their wives, all wedged so close together that they could hardly move, though many of them contrived to bow or curtsey as she passed. She was reminded of her 12-year-old self walking to her wedding to the emperor, and for a moment she felt a constriction in her throat. A throne had been placed for her at the top of the chancel steps and when she was seated the choir began to sing Psalm 100. *'Make a joyful noise unto the Lord all ye lands. Serve the Lord with gladness; come before His presence with singing.'*

When the psalm was finished Bishop Henry moved to the chancel steps and faced the congregation. 'Beloved brothers and sisters, I present to you Matilda, the truly begotten daughter of our great King Henry, Empress of the Romans, and now Lady of the English and your rightful sovereign.'

A roar of acclamation arose from the packed congregation and voices called, 'Long live the Lady Matilda! God bless our lady!' The tightness in her throat was greater now and she forced herself to breathe deeply. *At last!* she said to herself. *This is the day I have waited for so long. At last I have my rightful place – and no one shall take it from me!*

When the ceremony was over she retired to Wherewell to hold council with the bishop, Robert and her other close friends.

'So, gentlemen. What is our next step?'

Robert said at once, 'We must get you crowned as soon as possible. Once that is done no one can dispute your position.'

'That will not be possible immediately,' Bishop Henry said.

'Why not?'

'To begin with, we must convince the archbishop. The coronation must be carried out by him or there will be room for doubts about its validity.'

'Where is Theobald?' she asked. 'Why has he not come to acknowledge me?'

'He sends word that he is much troubled in conscience and cannot commit himself to your support until he has first consulted with the anointed king and ascertained his wishes.'

She bit her lip. 'He knows me well, and I had thought to have his goodwill. He must know that in anointing Stephen he anointed an oath breaker and a usurper. What does he expect?'

'He has requested that he be permitted to visit Stephen. He hopes to win his consent to the change of ruler.'

'His consent?' Her anger flared up again. 'He is my prisoner. His consent, or otherwise, has no significance.'

'But if it serves to salve the archbishop's conscience …?'

'Very well. Let them meet, if that is what is needed. What more is there to do?'

'It is essential to convince the other bishops and leaders of the clergy of the rightness of your claim. Easter is approaching. I will invite them to a great conclave in Winchester and I do not doubt that when they learn of the promises you have made they will give their support.'

'Good. Can we then proceed to the coronation?'

'We need to win the consent of the Londoners.'

'Consent of the Londoners!' she exclaimed. 'Since when has the monarch required the consent of mere commoners for a coronation? It is not for them to give or withhold at their whim.'

'You must remember, my lady,' Henry said placatingly, 'that it is a long tradition, going back to the time of King Edgar, that the burghers of London should play some part in choosing the ruler. Besides which, when Stephen came to England to claim the throne, he made promises to them and gave them the right to form a commune. This gives them privileges that they will be reluctant to lose.'

She gritted her teeth. 'The concessions of a weak man who knew his claim was false!'

'Nevertheless,' Henry persisted, 'in order to reach Westminster Abbey for the coronation you will require their cooperation. We cannot risk antagonizing them at this juncture.'

She nodded reluctantly. 'Very well. Let them be sent for and I will speak with them.'

'They were invited to come to our meeting yesterday, but they begged time to consider the situation.'

'Consider? What is there for them to consider? Their queen requires their attendance. Is that not enough?'

'I think the bishop is making an important point,' Robert said quietly. 'Your position is not yet secure. If we need to conciliate these Londoners in order to get you crowned, that is what we must do. Anything else … any other measures you may think fit … can wait till later.'

She swallowed her growing irritation. 'Yes, you are right, as usual. Very well. When might it please these jumped up burghers to condescend to meet us?'

'I will send to them again,' Henry said. 'Now that you have been received by the Church I think they will not hesitate any longer.'

'There is another matter, more pressing perhaps than any of these.' Miles spoke for the first time. 'Stephen's queen, the other Matilda, still holds large areas of Kent and William of Ypres is with her. They present a major threat to any plans we may make to go to London.'

'It is vital that we control the Tower,' Robert said. 'Geoffrey de Mandeville was given custody of it by Stephen, together with the earldom of Essex. We need to win him over.'

'He's a time server,' Henry responded. 'His father was disinherited by the late King and he had a long struggle to regain his position. He will not risk going back to being a poor landless knight again. I think we can rely on him to see where power now lies.'

'Very well.' Robert flexed his shoulders. 'I shall open negotiations with him. Meanwhile, we need to consolidate our power. There are still those who have not made a formal submission. Some are determined to hold out for Stephen, others are wavering, waiting to see what happens next. Now that Matilda has been received by the Church as Lady of the English many of them will be ready to swear fealty. I suggest, madam, that you celebrate Easter in your castle at Oxford. We have heard that Robert d'Oilly is ready to surrender it to you. That is a central point, easily accessible from most parts of the country. We will proclaim that all those desirous of making their peace should wait upon you there. Meanwhile, we shall wait for the outcome of the council of churchmen which Bishop Henry is calling. Once we know for certain who is with us and who against us we shall be able to make plans.'

A few days later she set out with her entourage towards Oxford. The first night was to be spent at the abbey of Wilton, the convent where she spent five years of her childhood. As she rode through the villages the people came out of their houses to see her pass. Some cheered and called down blessings on her, but many watched in silence. Their faces were haggard; their children thin and ragged. Men stopped work in the fields to gaze, but many of the field strips were uncultivated, the weeds encroaching on the neighbouring strips which had been ploughed. The evidence of disease and starvation, which had killed so many, was everywhere.

She turned to Brian, who rode beside her. 'We have done this. We have wrought this desolation. Little wonder they see nothing to cheer.'

His eyes were compassionate but his tone was reassuring. 'There will be time to make all this good, once you are queen.'

When they reached Wilton a very different scene greeted them. Outside the gates a huge crowd waited to welcome her. Here the cheers were full-throated and the local dignitaries came to make their obeisance and offer gifts. She gazed around as she entered the abbey, trying to find something that reminded her of the 8-year-old child who left it on the way to her betrothal; but nothing seemed familiar. She was not sorry. Her memories, such as they were, were not happy ones.

The abbess greeted her. 'My lady, the Archbishop of Canterbury is here. He is waiting to meet you.'

'Archbishop Theobald! That is good news. I will go to him directly.'

When the first greetings were over Theobald requested a private audience and she dismissed her followers.

Alone with him she knelt to kiss his ring. 'Bless me, Father.'

'The blessings of God the Father, and of the Son and of the Holy Spirit be upon you, my child.' He raised her to her feet. 'It is many years since we last met.'

'It is and much has changed. I hoped to have your support for my claim to the throne.'

'I have never ceased to pray for you.'

'I am grateful to know that I have not incurred your anger, at least.' She paused. 'You told me once that I was guilty of the sin of pride. Do you think that it is pride that has driven me to take arms against my cousin?'

'That is something you must question your own conscience about.'

'I do not believe it is pride. I believe that I have right and justice on my side and that Stephen's usurpation was against the law of God. Did not He ordain that the daughters of Zelophehad should inherit their father's land? Is that not a powerful argument in my favour?'

'You are well read in the scriptures, as I recall. I do not doubt your right to the crown.'

'So why did you crown Stephen?'

'I did what seemed best for the country. Without a king the land was descending into chaos. You were far away in Anjou and gave no sign that you planned to return. Stephen was at hand and promised to restore order. Sadly, that is something he has failed to do.'

'Why then were you not present when I was proclaimed Lady of the English?'

'I crowned and anointed your cousin. It was a mistake. I admit that humbly and beg forgiveness from God and from you for my error. But it is done and cannot be undone, except with the consent of the man I crowned.'

'You believe that is possible?'

'I hope so. I believe I can convince Stephen that his defeat by your forces is a sign from God that he was crowned in error and that in order to make his peace with the Almighty he must renounce the crown.'

'And if he does, you will have no difficulty with crowning me in his place?'

'I understand that Bishop Henry has written to His Holiness the Pope asking for his opinion. If the answer is favourable, then I see no impediment.'

She chewed her lip in silence for a moment. 'Very well. Make arrangements with Lord Robert to be conducted to Bristol and given access to Stephen. If he can be persuaded, as you suggest, then we can only await the Pope's reply.'

As she continued her progress towards Oxford the crowds assembled to watch her pass grew by the hour. Local lords came with their retainers to pledge fealty and join the procession. Houses were decked out with banners and she and her followers were garlanded with flowers. At Reading the press of people in the streets was even greater than at Wilton and Robert d'Oilly, the custodian of Oxford Castle, came in person to offer her the keys.

The Easter celebrations were more joyful than any she could recall. Brian constituted himself master of ceremonies and there was no shortage of minstrels and jongleurs offering their services. Oxford Castle rang with the sound of music. There was feasting and dancing at night and hunting and hawking by day. Many of the greatest men in the land flocked to offer their allegiance and every corner of the castle and every inn in the city was packed with their followers. Chief among them was her uncle, David of Scotland, who had always been a loyal supporter, though the necessity of keeping control of his own border lands had prevented him from joining his forces with hers. One of the most surprising arrivals was that of William Pont de l'Arche, Stephen's former chamberlain. Old friends joined her too, among them Baldwin de Redvers and her stewards Robert de Courcey and Humphrey de Bohun.

When the celebrations were over and most of the guests had departed, Bishop Henry came to report on the council of churchmen that he had convened.

'I held separate meetings with the bishops, the abbots and the archdeacons. I pointed out to them that, aside from breaking his promise to protect the Church and respect the clergy, Stephen had failed in the most basic duty of a monarch – to keep peace in the land. I reminded them that from the time of his accession there have been constant uprisings, in many cases because he disinherited some men in order to reward his followers. So that all through his reign there was scarcely a month in which he did not have to ride from one end of the country to another to put down a new rebellion, with dire consequences to the prosperity of the nation and the lives of the inhabitants. I suggested that now he has been defeated and imprisoned the country must have a new ruler, and that therefore we should place our trust in the daughter of a king who was a great peacemaker.'

'And did they accept your arguments?' she asked.

'By the grace of God they did. And there is better news yet. The archbishop attended the meetings. As you know, he has been to visit Stephen in Bristol castle, and he reports that he is willing to renounce the throne and permit the anointment of a new ruler.'

She felt a rush of elation. 'Then nothing now stands in the way of my coronation!'

The bishop pursed his lips. 'There are yet two matters of concern. During the meeting a letter was received from Queen Matilda – I mean Stephen's wife. She denounced the proceedings and demanded the release of her husband.'

'Demanded?' Her lips curled in scorn. 'She can demand

all she likes. We will deal with her and her husband once I am crowned.'

'It is a matter to be considered,' Henry said. 'You cannot keep my brother in prison indefinitely.'

'Why not? My father kept his brother, Robert Curthose, in prison for the rest of his life after he defeated him.'

'It would be unwise to do that with Stephen. He still has supporters and if he was imprisoned they would never be reconciled to you. He would be the focus of repeated uprisings.'

'What do you suggest?' Robert asked.

'He might be offered the chance to return to his heredi-tary lands in Blois. If he will take an oath to remain there and not to foment discontent that might be the best solu-tion. Alternatively, we could suggest that he enters a monastery.'

'Very well.' She was growing impatient. 'That can all be decided later. You said there were two matters of concern.'

'The second, and more pressing, is the matter of the consent of the Londoners. At my invitation they sent a delegation to the conference, but at its conclu-sion they said that they still needed time to consider and to report back to their colleagues.' He pre-empted her angry response with a pacific smile. 'Now that they know that you have the backing of the Church, I am sure that they will soon decide to throw in their lot with us. Meanwhile, I suggest that you continue your progress towards the city, so that you will be on hand when they have made their decision.'

'We have been discussing that,' Robert said. 'Windsor is still in the hands of Stephen's men, so we propose to advance to St Alban's.'

'Very wise,' Henry agreed. He bowed to Matilda. 'A little patience, madam, and every obstacle will be removed.'

*

The court moved to St Alban's. She was welcomed with the same enthusiasm as in Wilton and Reading and she established herself in the abbey. Very soon after her arrival she was informed that a delegation of aldermen from London was waiting to attend on her. Before they were admitted, Robert took her to one side.

'Be politic. Remember that we need the assent of these men for your coronation. We must not antagonize them.'

The delegates entered, six men in middle age, robed in fur-lined cloaks and hung about with chains of gold. They bowed, but did not kneel. She regarded them stonily.

'Well, sirs? What would you with me?'

The eldest, apparently the leader, stepped forward. 'We come to offer you allegiance, madam, and to invite you to enter the city."

'Invite?' Her eyebrows went up. 'Since the whole of England is mine, what need have I of your invitation to enter my own city?'

Another man stepped up beside his companion. His look was meeker. 'What my friend means, my lady, is that we come to make arrangements for your reception into the city. We wish to greet you with all due ceremony.'

'Very well, then. Speak to my steward, Humphrey de Bohun. Make your arrangements with him.' She stood up. 'You may go.'

They bowed and backed out of the room, but not before she had seen them exchange angry glances.

She reached Westminster in mid-summer and entered Westminster Hall in solemn procession, but her triumphant mood was soon dashed.

'Stephen's queen and William of Ypres have raised the

men of Kent,' Robert reported. 'They are already within a few days' ride of London and are devastating the countryside as they advance. We must hurry the arrangements for the coronation.'

'It must be done properly,' Brian protested. 'If it is scanted it will seem we are afraid.'

'I agree,' she said. 'But it will be costly. Until now there has not been time to make full account of what there is in the royal treasury. I have sent for Turstin, so we should have his report soon.'

Turstin's account gave rise to considerable dismay. The treasury was much depleted. Stephen had been spendthrift in distributing largesse to his supporters. More importantly, in the anarchic situation with no central authority, taxes had not been collected, or had been pocketed by local lords. Her experience in Anjou and earlier in Germany came to her aid and for the next days she was occupied with administrative affairs. Her spirits were boosted by the appearance at court of Geoffrey de Mandeville. True to Bishop Henry's prediction he had seen where power now lay and came to swear fealty and offer her the keys to the Tower of London. As a reward she confirmed him as Earl of Essex.

King David was still with her, and one day he came to where she was working with a request.

'It is in connection with the bishopric of Durham. You will remember, perhaps, that the previous bishop, Geoffrey Rufus, died a month or so ago. I wish to have my chancellor, William Cummin, installed as bishop in his place. He was a pupil of Bishop Geoffrey's and has proved a loyal and able chancellor.'

'You want your man in Durham to reinforce your influence in the area, is that it?'

'Your cousin tried to wrest Cumbria from me, before

you arrived in England. But although I lost the battle at Northallerton, the one they are calling the battle of the Standard, I still control that area and I have kept the peace there. Which is more than can be said of much of the rest of England.'

'I know it, and I should like to reward you for the support you have given me. But there is opposition in the Church to the appointment of Cummin, is there not?'

'The local clergy do not like him, that is true.'

'Is it true that you have refused to allow them to bury Bishop Geoffrey until they accept Cummin?'

'It is one way of bringing pressure to bear.'

She compressed her lips. 'You know that I have given an undertaking not to interfere in church appointments? It was a condition of Bishop Henry's support.'

'Are you determined to abide by that undertaking? It seems to me that it significantly curtails royal power.'

'That is true. My first husband spent most of his life fighting to retain that control.'

'Then is it not time to assert your own authority? After all, you are queen in all but name now.'

She hesitated a moment longer. David was a powerful man and she needed to retain his support. Finally she nodded. 'So be it. I will sign the charter constituting Cummin Bishop of Durham.'

He smiled and kissed her hand. 'You are your father's daughter. He would have had no truck with such attempts to dilute his influence.'

A few days later she noticed that Bishop Henry was no longer at court. No one seemed to know where he had gone.

There was one obvious way of acquiring revenue. The city of London had not suffered as the rest of the country had from the constant fighting. Stephen's queen was

Matilda of Boulogne before her marriage and held lands in London and Kent as well as in France. The connection had served the Londoners well, with steady cross-Channel trade. Matilda sent for the wealthiest burghers. Many of them were the same men who came to her before and their attitude from the start was reserved, if not openly hostile. She seated herself on the dais at the end of the hall, behind the great table, the symbol of royal authority, as she recalled seeing her father sit to receive supplicants and give judgement.

She said, 'Gentlemen, the current unrest has greatly depleted the royal coffers and the coronation will require considerable expense. I look to you to make a significant contribution.'

The leader, whom she had mentally nicknamed 'pig face', bowed minimally. 'Naturally, we shall be happy to be of assistance. But Your Grace will be aware that we, too, have suffered in the current unrest. Trade has been badly hit. It has been impossible to move goods around the country without losing them to bandits or having them confiscated by local lords. Food has been hard to come by. We have been forced to import wheat, at great expense. Many of our citizens have fallen on hard times and we have had to support them out of charity. So we look to you, in your gracious benevolence, to ease the burden of taxation until we have had time to recover our losses.'

She regarded him for a moment in silence. His belly swelled proudly under a tunic of scarlet wool. Cloth that colour did not come cheap. His cloak was trimmed with fur and a heavy gold chain hung round his neck. His companions were accoutred in similar fashion and not one of them looked as if he had ever missed a meal in his life. She thought of the scrawny children and the haggard women she had seen as she travelled through the countryside.

Her mood became steely.

'I understand that the usurper Stephen gave you certain concessions with regard to the collection of taxes. You should know that I will have no truck with that. We shall revert to the system which was in place in my father's time and which served him well. You will be required to pay the same amount in tax that you paid in his day.'

A murmur ran through the group and glances of dismay went from eye to eye.

Pig face spoke again. 'Madam, it is impossible. Perhaps, when peace has been re-established and trade has picked up again, we may be able to find the sort of sums which were exacted from us in your father's day. But until that time we beg that you will excuse at least a part of the tax.'

The recent days and weeks had taken their toll. She was very tired, and now that the prize was almost within her grasp her nerves were strung as tight as a bow string. Her temper snapped. She rose to her feet.

'Traitorous dogs! You were among the first to rally to my cousin's support, because he wooed you with soft words and promises. You paid your taxes to him and, by God's blood, you shall pay as much to me.' Her voice sounded harsh and strident in her own ears. 'Get you gone and turn out those purses which are as fat as your bellies. Find what you owe, or you may find yourselves living at my expense in the Tower. Be gone, I say!'

They shuffled their feet and looked at each other. There was a mumble of protest, quickly stifled, and then they all backed away towards the door and there was an unseemly scramble to be first out of it.

Robert had been a silent spectator during the interview. Now he shook his head ruefully.

'Sister, I fear you have made a bad mistake in treating them so roughly. Their goodwill is essential until your rule is firmly established. It is only a few days now until the coronation. It would have been wiser to speak them fair until then.'

She rounded on him bitterly. 'Do you not understand? I am a woman. There are many, like those men who were here just now, who think because of that I shall be easily swayed and persuaded to grant them favours. I have to show them that I can be as firm, as steadfast, as any man. Many have yet to be convinced that a queen can rule. I have to be both king and queen to command their obedience.'

He frowned. 'Very well. What you say is true, but it will do no harm to let them see the gentleness of the woman as well as the ruthlessness of the King.'

'Listen,' she said. 'You have trained many a hawk to come to the fist. How is it done? By gentleness? No, by being harsh until it knows its master. If you offer food and then snatch it away it grows keener and more obedient, until it gets its reward. Kindness and gentleness come after obedience, not before. That is a lesson I learnt from the King my father.'

He sighed and shrugged. 'So be it. What is done cannot be undone. We must hope for the best. Stephen's wife and William of Ypres are ranging the countryside almost up to the city walls. I do not know how much longer we can hold them off.'

The date of the coronation was set for 25 July. On the evening before, she feasted her companions. The exhaustion that had assailed her in recent days had not eased its grip and, as a concession, she reclined on a couch instead of sitting at the table. The first course had just been brought in when they were all shocked into silence by a sudden clamour outside.

'What is going on?' Brian asked.

251

Robert left the table and strode to the window. 'They are ringing the bells. All the churches in the city are sounding their bells.'

'It is in celebration, no doubt,' Brian said. 'A way of welcoming the glad event tomorrow brings.'

Robert looked uneasy. 'Let us hope so.'

The door of the great hall crashed open and Alexander de Bohun, her master-at-arms, rushed in. 'Madam, you must fly! The citizens have opened the gates to your enemies. They have taken up arms themselves. I have seen them, streaming out in their hundreds, heading this way.'

She started up. 'Then they must be stopped. Sound the alarm! Call all my knights. Summon the men-at-arms. Arm yourselves, my lords!'

'It is too late!' Alexander cried. 'They will be upon us before we can organise our defence. You must leave at once.'

Robert had run to the door. Now he returned. 'It is true! The numbers are too great. We might beat off the citizens but if the ex-queen and her troops are behind them we have no hope. To horse, my lords! Our priority is to convey the Queen to safety. We will head for Oxford. Regroup there if we are separated.'

16

OXFORD AND WINCHESTER, 1141

'It is a setback but not a disaster.' Robert was addressing the royal council in the great hall of Oxford castle.
'Our departure may have been somewhat precipitate but
we were able to withdraw from London without losing
any of our forces. What matters now is to consolidate
our hold on the areas we still control before we make
another attempt to enter London. The ex-Queen and her
supporters must be brought to battle and defeated. Once
that is done the Londoners will soon return to their true
allegiance.'

In private he was less sanguine. 'We must appeal again
to your husband for his assistance. Fortunately, he seems
to be well situated in Normandy now.'

'He writes that he holds most of the key castles, but
he has yet to persuade King Louis to accept him as Duke.
Louis is besieging Toulouse at the moment, so his attention
is elsewhere and until he returns to Paris it is impossible
for Geoffrey to do homage for the duchy, assuming that
Louis is agreeable.'

'Nevertheless, he is the de facto ruler of the duchy.
Now, surely, is the time for him to throw his weight

behind your campaign.'

'I can only write and request his help. Whether it will be forthcoming only God knows.'

'Meanwhile you must act as though you were already crowned. It is time to establish your friends in positions of power wherever possible.'

'One thing above all else concerns me. I have not set eyes on Bishop Henry for many days now. Where is he?'

'My spies tell me he has returned to Winchester. I am greatly afraid that he is thinking of changing his allegiance once again.'

'That man!' Brian had been listening to the conversation. 'He is as variable as a weather cock, swinging whichever way the prevailing wind turns him.'

'We cannot afford to lose his support,' Matilda said. 'I will write to him and try to persuade him that he can never trust Stephen again, that his own reputation will never recover if he reneges on his commitment to us – whatever is necessary to keep him with us.'

Robert's expression was grim. 'Write by all means, but I fear recent events may have convinced him that he has thrown in his lot with the wrong side.' He did not refer to the affair of the Durham bishopric, but she knew that was in his mind.

She put her mind to ensuring the continuing loyalty of those who had come over to her side and to rewarding her most faithful friends. Miles became Earl of Hereford, Baldwin de Redvers was made Earl of Devon and William de Mohun Earl of Dorset.

She wished to signify her gratitude to Brian in a similar fashion, but when approached he shook his head with a smile.

'I have no desire for power and I have no heir to inherit a title, nor am I likely to have. All I wish for is the opportunity to serve you. As long as I hold Wallingford, that is enough.'

Geoffrey de Mandeville was one to whom she showed special favour, knowing how crucial his support was in London. In addition to confirming him as Earl of Essex she granted him the sheriffdom and justiciarship of London, Middlesex and Hertfordshire and promised him the castle of the Bishop of London at Bishop's Stortford, plus another he had recently built. She knew that the Londoners already resented the power of the feudal lords over the city and that de Mandeville regarded them as his mortal enemies. As part of the agreement she promised not to make any contract with the burgesses of the city without his consent. The thought of their discomfiture gave her pleasure.

Her husband's response to her plea for help was brought by three of his most loyal lieutenants, Jules de Mayenne, Pagan of Clairvaux and Guy of Sablé. They arrived with a small troop of 700 knights – a welcome addition to her forces but very far from the wholehearted support she hoped for. Over the month of July her allies assembled at Oxford, bringing their armies with them. King David had been north to gather his troops and now returned. Geoffrey de Mandeville and his brother-in-law Aubrey de Vere arrived. Her other adherents summoned their feudal levies and soon Oxford Castle was the centre of an armed camp of considerable size. Only Bishop Henry still held aloof.

'Go to him, Robert,' she ordered. 'Find out what the old fox is playing at. At all costs we must hold Winchester.'

Robert was soon back. 'Henry refused to give me a straight answer but I don't think we can trust him. My spies tell me he has had a meeting with Stephen's queen. No one knows what she has promised him but we can't afford to wait to find out.'

'I agree. Pass the orders. We advance on Winchester. We will require Bishop Henry's attendance, whether he wills it or not.'

There were two castles in Winchester, the royal castle at the south-western corner of the city walls and the bishop's castle of Wolvesey at the south-eastern corner. As her army prepared to advance word reached her that the bishop had laid siege to the former. There was no longer any doubt about where his allegiance now lay. After a brief council of war it was decided that Robert should lead an advance party into the city, while she waited outside the walls with the rest of the army. The gates were still open and she watched tensely as Robert and his knights rode through them. She expected to hear the clash of swords and the sounds of battle, but all remained quiet. After a wait that seemed endless, a herald rode back to her and fell to his knees beside her horse.

'Good tidings, my lady! The bishop has withdrawn his forces and retreated to Wolvesey. My lord Robert invites you to enter the city and take possession of the castle.'

Her reception into the city was very different from the one she received a few short months earlier. There were no cheering crowds to greet her. The streets were almost empty, the citizens hiding in their houses for fear of what was to follow. She rode into the castle courtyard and the castellan hastened to welcome her and conduct her to the royal apartments. Robert joined her a few minutes later.

'What of the bishop?' she asked. 'Is he holed up in Wolvesey?'

Robert shook his head grimly. 'The fox has eluded us. He rode out by the east gate as we entered by the west. He has left men in Wolvesey to defend it, but my guess is he is heading for London to join the Queen.'

She ground her teeth. 'The traitorous dog! God rot him! How can a man who breaks his faith so easily call himself a man of God? Well, we shall make him regret it. Lay siege to Wolvesey.'

'It is already done,' her brother replied. 'But it is a strong castle and well defended. It will not be reduced quickly.'

'I can wait!'

'Perhaps. But I have information that Matilda of Boulogne is advancing from London with William of Ypres and his mercenaries. We may find ourselves assailed from two sides. I suggest that we fortify Wherwell Abbey. It may be useful to have a stronghold outside the city in case of need.' He did not spell out the implications of the suggestion.

She frowned, recalling the peaceful atmosphere of the abbey and her courteous reception. 'It seems wrong to fortify a place dedicated to prayer and contemplation.'

'Desperate times require desperate measures. We cannot afford to be too particular at the moment.'

'Very well. Who will you put in charge of it?'

'John fitz Gilbert, your father's marshal. He's tough and experienced in building fortifications.'

His guess was proved correct. Within days the royalist army was at the gates. Robert and the earls sallied out with their knights in an attempt to drive them back, but they were overwhelmed by superior numbers and forced to retreat within the walls. The besiegers found themselves besieged. Looking out from the battlements, she was taken aback by the numbers encamped around them.

'How long can we hold out?'

'It is hard to say. Weeks, months perhaps. The city is well supplied. We can thank Bishop Henry for that.'

'Can we summon help from our allies? If we could

attack them from the rear ...'

'We gathered almost all the fighting men who owe loyalty to us at Oxford. Most of the barons left only a skeleton force to hold their castles. They will not be willing to commit them to a fight they cannot win.'

'So what do we do?'

'Hold on. Hope we can reduce Wolvesey and take any supplies they have. Hope that some of Queen Matilda's allies get tired of the siege and take themselves off.'

'What can we offer them to make them change their allegiance?'

He shook his head sombrely. 'Very little, as things stand at the moment.'

Worse news followed. D'Ypres had attacked her castle at Andover and burnt it and the town to the ground. The siege dragged on. With nothing to occupy her mind, Matilda sank into lethargy. She had never shaken off the weariness that beset her in the days leading up to the coronation, and the shock and disappointment of the abrupt reversal of fortune had left her empty and depressed. She wandered the battlements, gazing out in despair at the besieging forces; or sat slumped in her solar, snapping irritably at her ladies when they tried to distract her. As always, it was Brian who was her comforter. Robert and Miles were busy directing the siege and guarding against a sudden attack from outside, but Brian found time to sit with her, to talk and read. One afternoon they were sitting in a room at the top of one of the towers. The weather was heavy and overcast, with a threat of thunder in the air, which did nothing to lift her mood. He produced a beautifully bound book and offered it to her.

'I have been meaning to show you this. I acquired it while we were in London. It is a chansonnier, the songs and poems of William of Aquitaine whom they call the troubadour duke.'

She opened the book and turned the pages. They were exquisitely illuminated. 'William of Aquitaine? It is his granddaughter who is wed to Louis of France, is it not?' She handed the book back to him. 'Read something to me.'

He turned the pages and hesitated. 'This one is sad, but it is very beautiful.'

'Read it, then. It suits my mood.'

He had an expressive voice, as sweet when he read as when he sang. She closed her eyes and let the words calm her spirit.

The poem ended:

'I have given up all I loved so much,
Chivalry and pride;
And since it pleases God, I accept it all
That He may keep me by Him.
I enjoin my friends, upon my death,
All to come and do me great honour,
Since I have given joy and delight,
Far and near, and in my home.
Now I give up joy and delight,
Fine clothes and sable furs.

He closed the book and she sighed. 'How close that comes to what I feel!'

'I should not have chosen it,' he said. 'I should have found—'

He was interrupted by a sudden clamour from outside. She went to the window and leant out. The sounds were clearer now and among the noise she heard the shout of 'Fire!'

'Fire! Where? What is on fire?'

'Come up to the top of the tower,' he said. 'We shall see better from there.'

They ran up the narrow, twisting stair and came out on the roof. She leant on the parapet and strained her eyes over the city. 'Dear God! That is Hyde Abbey burning – and St Mary's nunnery. Who can have started it?'

'What is more to the point,' Brian said, 'who is going to put it out before the whole city goes up in flames?'

Below in the streets they could see men running hither and thither with buckets, but their efforts were puny compared to the fierceness of the flames. At that moment the storm which had been threatening all day broke with a flash of lightning and a tremendous crack of thunder. The heavens opened and rain poured down in torrents.

'You have your answer!' she said. 'God is with us, and he will punish whoever started the blaze that is destroying his holy places.'

Later Robert came to her, drenched to the skin and with his face smeared with ash.

'Is the fire out?'

'Yes, by the grace of God. But there has been great destruction.'

'I saw the abbey burning.'

'Yes, it has been gutted, and the great jewelled cross given by King Cnut has been destroyed.'

'That is nothing short of sacrilege!' Brian said. 'Do we know who started the fire?'

'Oh yes. It was started by firebrands thrown from the ramparts of Wolvesey Castle.'

'God will punish them,' she said. 'But why have they done it?'

'To deprive us of nourishment. I have not told you the worst of it. The city granary has been burnt to the ground.

It will not be many days now before there is no bread to be had.'

'They hope to starve us out. Can we get more supplies brought in? There is food enough in Bristol and Gloucester.'

'For sure, but I cannot see how we can get it past the blockade. I can send messengers ordering it. One or two of them might get through. But getting food wagons past the Queen's army will be nigh on impossible.'

'Her own men must be short of supplies by now, surely,' Brian suggested. 'They have been living off the countryside for weeks.'

Robert shook his head. 'They control the roads eastward. They have only to send to London for what they need.'

They fell silent. It was clear to all of them that their situation was dire and there seemed to be no remedy.

Next morning Robert brought worse news still. 'De Mandeville has deserted. He sneaked out through the postern with his men during the night.'

'Has he gone home, or joined the Queen?' Matilda asked.

'His banner is flying in the middle of her army.'

She sank into a chair. 'I gave him everything he asked for. Is there no faith in any man?'

Brian took her hand. 'You have your faithful friends, whom nothing can shake.'

She smiled at him wanly. 'I know it, and I thank God for you and Robert and Miles – and all those who have cleaved to me through good times and bad.'

As summer faded into autumn food began to run out. Rations were cut and cut again. Matilda was hungry all the time and the lack of nourishment exacerbated her weakness. Brian tried to feed her from his own plate but she refused. She saw how gaunt he had become, as had

Robert and Miles and all her other companions. There were rumours of rebellion among the citizens, who were said to be plotting to open the gates to the royalist army.

A day came when she sensed a change in the atmosphere. She could hear low-voiced discussions and there was a new sense of urgency. Then Robert came into her room.

'We have come to a decision. We cannot hold Winchester. We need to get out as soon as we can and head for Gloucester and Bristol.'

She lifted her head. 'Yield Winchester? But that is to admit defeat.'

'No. It is the only sensible way forward. We have a choice. We can stay here until starvation forces us to surrender, or we can retreat to Bristol and regroup our forces. There are still many who have come over to our side who once fought for Stephen – and most importantly we still have him as a prisoner. Sooner or later his wife will have to come to some agreement to secure his release.'

'You are right, as always. But it is easier said than done. How can we break through the enemy lines?'

'We need to create a diversion, something to draw some of d'Ypres's forces away. I have men who can slip through the enemy lines. I will send a message to John the Marshall at Wherwell, telling him to attack him from the rear. I shall call a council of all the earls tomorrow and explain our plan.'

The council met in sombre mood to hear Robert outline his strategy. Matilda listened with the rest, too disheartened to argue.

'It is plain that we cannot hold out much longer. The vital thing is to get the empress away to safety. Fitz Gilbert is going to mount an attack from Wherwell to create a diversion. We must seize the opportunity. Brian,

I am placing the empress in your charge. Reginald will come with you. Choose a small band of your most trusted knights and mount them on the fastest horses. I will make the first sortie with my men to clear a path for you. As soon as the way is clear you must make your break and ride like the wind. Head for John the Marshall's castle at Ludgershall and thence to Devizes. The main body of the army will follow under the command of Miles. I shall hold the line here as long as I can, until you are all out of the city, and then my men and I will bring up the rear. We shall reassemble at Bristol. The rest of you –' his gaze took in the assembled earls '– and you, my lord King –' this to David of Scotland '– will wish to head for your own strongholds, but be sure of one thing. This is not the end of our struggle. Once you have had a chance to regroup and recruit more men I will call another council to plan our next move. We move at dawn. Does anyone have any questions?'

There were a few discussions about the exact order in which the various forces were to leave but she sensed that there was a feeling of relief that the time of inactivity was over. Once the earls had dispersed, Robert came to her side.

'You will have to ride fast. Are you well enough?'

'I must be. Yes, have no worries on my behalf. You have chosen the most dangerous part for yourself.'

He shrugged the remark aside. 'You will need to ride astride, in man's attire. This is no time for modesty.'

'I understand that. Find me a young squire whose braies and chausses may fit me.'

When she retired to bed the requisite garments were laid out for her, together with a tunic that would reach to her knees. She slept little and was up as soon as the darkness outside her window turned to grey. Hawise came to help her dress, her eyes red with more than lack of sleep.

'Am I not to come with you, my lady?'

'No, child. You have never ridden a horse, I think? You could not keep up with the speed we must go. You must find Bertrand, my cook, and tell him that it is my order that he find you a place in his wagon. The wagons will be protected by the main army and bring you safe to Gloucester. We shall meet again there.'

She spoke with more confidence than she felt and Hawise was not reassured. The girl sniffed as she fumbled with the laces that fastened the unfamiliar chausses to the braies. When she was dressed she instructed Hawise to twist her hair into two plaits and fasten them on top of her head. Then she embraced her maid, who was now sobbing openly, and went down to the great hall, where Robert and Brian were waiting for her.

Robert nodded approval. 'Good. Now put this on.' He held out a tunic of chainmail and she bent her head and allowed him to slide it over her shoulders. She had helped Geoffrey to arm many a time, and the links were as fine as any smith could make them, but she was still astonished at the weight.

'Now this,' Robert said, holding out a mailed coif, such as a knight might wear under his helmet. It covered her head and neck and she thought suddenly that this must be how a snail feels inside its unyielding shell.

Brian held out his hand and led her to the door. The weight of the mail triggered a memory. When had she felt like this before? It came to her. It was when they dressed her for her betrothal to the emperor Henry, all those years ago. She felt then that she could scarcely walk under the weight of clothes and jewels they had loaded onto her. She dwelt on the recollection for a moment. It was easier to think of that, than to contemplate what lay ahead. There was a terrible, leaden despair at her heart which weighed her down more harshly than her armour.

The courtyard was crammed with men and horses. Girths were being tightened, bridles checked. Some men were already mounted and their horses snorted and sidled, eager to be off. Reginald brought her mount to the foot of the steps. It was not her usual white palfrey, but a big dun-coloured destrier who laid back his ears as she approached.

Robert took her hand. 'When Brian gives the order, you must ride like the wind and not look back. Do you understand me? Whatever happens you must keep going until you reach Ludgershall.'

She nodded, her throat tight. 'I understand. But dear brother, have a care for your own safety. If you are lost, so is our cause – and so am I.'

'Have no fear for me. I shall catch you up before you reach Gloucester.'

She reached up and kissed him on both cheeks. Then Brian helped her into the saddle and vaulted into his own. Orders were shouted, a horn sounded, and Robert, mounted on his coal-black destrier, led the way out of the castle. His men clattered after him and then her own knights, with Alexander de Bohun at their head, formed up around her, with Brian on her right and Reginald on her left. They rode through empty streets, though men stood in doorways and women peered from windows. There was no cheering; no one wished them Godspeed.

'They are glad to see the back of us,' she murmured and Brian nodded.

'Who can blame them?'

At the west gate there was such a press of men and horses that it was hard to make their way through. A sentry rushed down from one of the gate towers and panted out a message to Robert. He urged his horse along-side Brian's.

'All goes according to plan. Remember, as soon as you see a gap in the lines, go for it at the gallop.' He turned away. 'Ready, men? Open the gates!'

The massive gates opened with a groaning of hinges. She could see little at first, over the heads of the men and horses in front of her, then Robert spurred his horse forward and his knights followed and she saw the bridge over the moat and the road beyond. D'Ypres's army had not been caught by surprise. The road was barred by a solid line of armoured knights, their lances levelled, but Robert's men were well trained. As soon as they were clear of the bridge they formed themselves into a wedge with Robert at the tip. It was a technique learned from the knights returning from the crusades and well tried against the Saracen hordes. Riding at the gallop, they punched through the line of opposing men like a cross-bow bolt through leather, and as soon as the line broke they wheeled left and right, driving the enemy away from the road.

For a brief moment the way was clear and Brian shouted, 'Go!' Alexander was already spurring his horse into a gallop and his men followed. The big dun stallion started forward with such a leap that it almost unseated her and she had to grab the pommel of the saddle to stay on. They thundered over the bridge and for a moment she was surrounded by the sounds of battle, the clash of swords and the grinding of blades on armour, the shouts of men and the neighing of horses. She felt a whiplash of air on her cheek as an arrow narrowly missed her and behind her one of her escort cried out and swore, but there was no hesitation in their breakneck speed. Then they were clear and the road was open ahead of them, and they were galloping faster than she had ever ridden in her life. There was a time, when she was the young bride of the Emperor Henry, when she had revelled in the excitement of the chase. Even later she had enjoyed hunting with Geoffrey, but since the birth of her children she had not ridden like this. Now she found it hard to adjust to the long stride of the stallion. He was impetuous, eager to overtake the horses in front, and she had to grip the reins hard to hold him back. She had forgotten to put on gloves and very soon her fingers were blistered. She was half afraid that the horse would bolt with her, but Brian and Reginald were so close on either side that their knees brushed hers. The stallion laid back his ears, but he settled into a steady rhythm and she began to find her balance.

At the top of the first rise they paused for a moment to let the horses breathe and she twisted in the saddle to look back. The road was no longer clear, but had disappeared under a mêlèe of men and horses. For a moment she could not understand what was going on. Then she realized that the main army under Miles and the other earls had ridden out of the city and was now engaged in a desperate battle with the opposing forces. She scanned the confusion, trying to see a familiar banner, but it was impossible to tell friend from foe at this distance.

'Robert...?' she said. But at that instant at group of riders broke free from the mass and started up the road towards them.

Brian grabbed her rein and swung the horse's head round. 'Ride! No time for questions now.'

They galloped on until she felt that all the breath had been knocked out of her body and every muscle ached. Within minutes the folds of the downs hid everything behind them, so that they could not tell if they were pursued or not, but Brian did not wait to find out. They charged through the village of Stockbridge, scattering dogs and chickens and forcing women to snatch children from under their hoofs, and thundered across the bridge over the River Test.

Brian shouted across her to Reginald. 'There will be problems here. Too narrow, and the river is too deep to ford.'

'Bottleneck!' Reginald shouted back.

Once among the marshy fields of the river valley Brian slowed the pace a little, but they did not halt. They took the country lanes, skirting the still-smoking ruins of Andover, and reached Ludgershall Castle just after midday. By this time she was swaying in the saddle and Brian had to grip her arm to steady her. John the Marshall, given charge of the castle by her father, had enlarged and improved it and they rode into the spacious northern bailey with its watchtower and stone built living quarters. They were greeted with confusion. The steward rushed to her horse's side, babbling excuses for his lack of preparation. She was too weary to speak and Brian answered for her.

'The Empress understands. We know you had no warning of our arrival. Where is Sir John? Is he still at Wherwell?'

'No, sire.' The man shook his head as if struggling to take in what was happening. 'He is here, but in a parlous state. He is but newly arrived and sore wounded. But come inside. He will wish to greet you even so.'

She was so stiff that Brian had to almost drag her from her horse and support her up the steps into the great hall. Here there was more confusion, as servants and pages ran backwards and forwards. John fitz Gilbert was sitting on a stool, his head and one eye swathed in bandages, while his wife knelt at his side bathing his hands. She scrambled to her feet as they entered and sank into a curtsey.

'My lady, we did not expect ...'

'I know. It is no great matter.' With an effort she focused her mind. 'Tell me what has happened.'

'Bring a chair for the empress!' Brian ordered. 'And wine. Can you not see she is close to exhaustion?'

A chair was brought and a page offered wine and water. She sat wearily and repeated her question. 'You were at Wherwell. What happened?'

John's voice was cracked with pain and he was shaking. 'Madam, I fear I have let you down. Wherwell is lost.'

'What of that?' Her tone was bitter. 'So is Winchester, a far greater loss. But tell me how.'

'We sallied out, as Lord Robert asked, but we could not stand against d'Ypres's forces. We fought hard but we were forced back and took refuge in the church. That impious man ...' He broke off, breathing hard. 'He ordered his men to fire the church.'

'To fire a place of sanctuary!' Brian exclaimed in horror. 'Is there no end to that man's evil?'

'What did you do?' she asked.

'We held on as long as we could, but the heat was so great that the lead on the roof began to melt.' He raised a hand to the bandage round his head. 'Some fell on my face. My eye is gone, I fear. I remember little of what followed. Most of my men surrendered or were captured, but someone got me onto a horse and I was able to escape. I reached here only moments before you.'

'And the nuns?'

'All I know is that they fled screaming from the church. What happened to them afterwards I cannot tell you.'

She bowed her head. 'All this is at my door. I have much to answer for.'

Brian put a hand on her arm. 'The sin is d'Ypres's, not

269

yours. Do not distress yourself.' He straightened up and turned to John's wife. 'I know that all this has come upon you very suddenly, but we shall not trouble you for long. Tomorrow we ride on to Devizes. For today, the Empress is in great need of rest. Can you provide a bed and a woman to attend her?'

'Of course. Madam, if you will come with me?'

Matilda allowed herself to be led up to a room above the hall, where the great bed suggested that in quieter times this was the bedchamber of the lord and lady. Warm water was brought, and she was helped out of her mail and her man's clothes and her bruises and blisters were washed and anointed with a balm of some sort. By now her head was swimming and although she had eaten nothing since the previous day, and that a scanty meal, she was unable to swallow the broth that was brought to her. She climbed into the bed and fell into a supine state which was more like a trance than sleep, from which she was frequently jerked into wakefulness by the illusion that she was still on horseback and about to fall. Towards nightfall someone brought more broth and fresh bread and she managed to eat a little, and then at last fell properly asleep.

She was woken at dawn. 'Sir Brian begs that you will dress and be ready to ride again within the hour. He is anxious to reach Devizes as soon as possible.'

She swung her legs out of bed and cried out in pain. Every muscle in her body had stiffened. She had to grit her teeth to stand and when the woman sent to attend her tried to help her into her riding clothes, she almost broke down in tears. She staggered down the stairs to where Brian was waiting.

He regarded her with concern. 'Are you well enough to ride on?'

'I do not understand what is wrong with me. I have always been so strong but lately ...' She stopped and forced a smile. 'Of course I can ride. Let us be on our way.'

'You must eat something first,' he said, and she forced herself to swallow a few mouthfuls of bread and some small ale.

As soon as she had finished, he helped her onto the big destrier and they rode out of the castle gates, surrounded by her knights. After a few miles she felt that the stiffness was wearing off, but then the pain in her back grew worse and she could tell that the blisters on her thighs from friction with the saddle had burst. She clamped her jaws together to stop herself from crying out, but suddenly there was a buzzing in her ears and her vision grew hazy. Dimly she heard Brian at her side.

'Madam? What is amiss? Are you ...' Then in a loud command. 'Halt!'

The cavalcade stopped and he jumped from his horse and came to her side. He was just in time to catch her as she toppled from the saddle. She tried to stand, but her legs gave way and she collapsed into his arms.

'Forgive me! I am a burden to you. I have never believed myself weak but ...'

'It is a burden I shoulder willingly. I would carry you to the ends of the earth if need be.'

He lifted her in his arms and carried her to a grassy bank beside the road. She was dimly aware that he was issuing orders and there was a bustle of activity. Then she slipped into unconsciousness. When she came to he was leaning over her.

'Come. We have made a litter to be carried between two horses.'

The litter was a ramshackle affair. It seemed they had felled two saplings and somehow woven a mesh of leather belts and spare saddle girths between them and then padded them with their cloaks. He lifted her and laid her in it and wrapped another cloak tightly around her. 'There. Be at ease. We shall be safe in Devizes castle by nightfall.'

All through the journey she was only semi-conscious and when they reached Devizes she was carried upstairs and put to bed. That night she slept dreamlessly and when she woke the following morning her head had cleared and the pains in her muscles were less. Even so, she had to force herself to get out of bed. She allowed herself to be dressed in a borrowed gown and went down to the hall, where Brian and Reginald awaited her.

'What news?' she asked. 'Have Miles or Robert arrived?'

'Not yet,' Brian said. 'But it is early yet. We travelled fast and it will take them some time to catch up. We can rest now and wait for them.'

Devizes was one of the strongest castles in the country and had been under her control since John the Marshall took it from the mercenary Fitz Hubert. It was unlikely that William d'Ypres would attempt to attack it. She was safe, but the only thought in her mind was the fate of the companions she had left behind. She could not forget that brief glimpse of the desperate fighting on the road. She asked to be taken to a room from which she could watch the approaches to the castle. Brian sat with her and attempted to divert her with stories and poems, but even he found it hard to concentrate. It was well past midday when they saw three horsemen plodding towards the castle gate.

'Only three?' she said.

'Sent ahead with news for you, I expect.'

She hurried down to the hall and the three were

brought to her. They were unarmed and covered in mud. One had a deep cut across his forehead and the right arm of another hung useless, the sleeve stiff with blood. The third, the youngest, seemed unhurt but his staring eyes and white face told their own story. She recognized them as men-at-arms from Miles's household.

'What news?' she asked. 'Where are the others?'

The eldest bowed his head. 'I cannot tell you, my lady. Are there no others here?'

'You are the first. I don't understand. Did you flee from the battle?'

'Only when all was lost, my lady. I beg you to believe that.'

'All lost? What are you saying?'

'Forgive me, madam, for bringing bad news. The army is destroyed. To begin with it seemed we might break through and escape, but there were too many against us. The way ahead was blocked and the fighting spread out over the fields on either side. I fought until this happened –' He indicated the cut on his head '– then it bled so much that I could not see, and when I finally managed to staunch it the battle had passed on and there were only the wounded and the dead around me. I found Giles, here –' With a nod to the second man '– and helped to bind up his wound. Then we came across this lad. I don't think he is hurt but he hasn't spoken a word since we met up with him. Anyway, we decided our best course was to make for Ludgershall. It was no good trying to cross the river at Stockbridge. It was clear that the road there was controlled by the enemy. So we made our way across country, looking for another bridge, but there was none. In the end we had to swim for it. We had no choice. We threw down our weapons and swum for our lives. When we reached Ludgershall they told us you were on your way here, so we came on.' His shoulders sagged. 'You may brand us cowards. Perhaps we should have stayed and fought to the death.'

'No.' She spoke with unusual gentleness. 'What use to me are dead men? It was better to save yourselves than die uselessly. But tell me. Did you see what became of Sir Miles?'

'I saw him just before I was wounded. He was still fighting, but he had been unhorsed. I fear he may not have survived.'

She clenched her fists and bit back tears. 'We must pray that you are mistaken. And Lord Robert, what of him?'

'I do not know, my lady. He was with the rearguard. I did not see him.'

'Go and have your wounds tended and get some rest. Others may bring better news.'

All through the day the remnants of the army staggered in, bloodied and exhausted. To each group she put the same questions, but no one could give her any news of either Miles or Robert. It was almost dark when a lone rider came into the courtyard and almost fell from his weary horse. When he was brought before her she recognized him as one of Robert's household knights. He collapsed to his knees, and she bent over and shook him by the shoulder.

'Sir Richard? What has happened? Where is Lord Robert?'

'Lost!' His voice was a croak and he passed his tongue over cracked lips. She looked round for a page.

'Bring water! Can you not see this man is in desperate need?'

Brian was there already. He knelt by the knight and held a cup to his lips. He sipped, choked, then drained the cup. Brian helped him to a stool.

'Now,' he said. 'Tell us the worst.'

She felt a wave of cold despair engulf her. Miles and Robert both gone! Her closest friends and the rocks upon which she had founded her hopes.

With an effort Sir Richard straightened his shoulders. 'We held the road out of the city as long as we could, to allow the rest of the army to leave. Then we rode after you, but d'Ypres pursued us and when we got to Stockbridge we had to stand and fight.' He paused and Brian handed him a second cup. He moistened his lips and went on. 'It was carnage! The bridge was clogged with men and horses from the main army. Some men jumped into the river, but they were weighed down by their armour. I saw men drowning – and the bodies of those already dead. When Lord Robert saw what was happening he ordered us to block the road, to give the rest a chance to escape. There was a place where it narrowed, between two houses. We took our stand there and he ordered us to dismount and form a shield wall. We held them back for some time, but there were so many. For every man we killed or disabled, another took his place. Then they got archers up onto the roof of one of the houses and our own knights started to fall. In the end there were four of us, myself, Lord Robert and two others.'

His head sank down as if he would fall asleep where he sat. She leant towards him. 'Go on! Go on!'

He sat up and swallowed more water. 'I do not remember clearly what happened. Something hit me, here.' He raised a hand to his temple where a dark bruise covered the side of his face. 'I went down, but the last thing I saw was Lord Robert surrounded by four or five of the enemy. He yielded and gave up his sword and they took him away.'

'A prisoner!' She gasped with relief. 'Not dead, a prisoner?'

'He still lived when I last saw him.'

'How did you get away?' Brian asked gently.

'I think I lost consciousness. When I was next aware, the battle was over. Men were stripping the dead and looting the bodies. One came to me, thinking I was dead too, but I drew my dagger and thrust at him. I do not think I killed him but he staggered back and I got to my feet and ran. The bridge was clear by this time. I ran until I could run no further. It was getting dark and somehow I missed the road and found myself wandering among the marshes. In the end I lay down under a bush and I must have slept. A fisherman found me at dawn and took me back to his cottage. His wife let me sit by the fire and gave me some pottage, but she was afraid of what might happen if Stephen's men found me. She had seen riders searching the roads for fugitives and she would not let me stay long. I wandered for the rest of the day, trying to find my way. Several times I had to hide from Stephen's soldiers. Then, when I was almost exhausted, I found a riderless horse and managed to catch it. Some peasants put me on the right road. They told me they had seen you passing – but madam ...' He looked up at her as if startled by a sudden memory '... they told me you must be dead. They said you were carried in a coffin.'

'As you see, they were wrong. But I was very sick and carried in a litter. Finish your story.'

'There is little more to tell. I am truly sorry, my lady, not to be the bearer of better news.'

She exchanged glances with Brian. 'You have brought me more comfort than I expected. At least we know now that Lord Robert is alive. But what of your comrades? Did none of them survive?'

'I cannot tell. I saw the bodies of three but I did not stay to count the others. It may be that some were only wounded and have got away, as I did.'

'We must pray that they did. Go now. You have fought nobly.' She looked to her steward who was hovering nearby. 'See that his wounds are dressed and he is given food and drink and somewhere to sleep.'

'I will, madam.'

She looked from her position on the dais into the body of the hall. Already the space was almost filled with men, some of them asleep on straw palliases, others seated along the walls. Most of them showed evidence of freshly band-aged wounds; some groaned and whimpered, but there was little conversation. Pages and serving women moved among them, offering food and wine. Once again she caught Brian's eye. There was much to do. Tomorrow some sort of order must be wrested from the chaos of defeat. Devizes could not cope with all the wounded for long, and there might be others who had sought sanctuary elsewhere.

She said, 'Tomorrow we must go on to Gloucester. Those who are fit to travel will come with us. The rest must stay here until they are ready. Once we get there we can begin to make plans.'

He smiled at her. 'It is good to see you ready to take command again. But for tonight you must rest, or you will not be fit to travel yourself.'

She got up. 'You are right.' Then she turned back to him. 'They will not hurt Robert, will they?'

He shook his head. 'No. He is far too valuable a hostage to be harmed. They will want to negotiate a ransom.'

'I will pay whatever they ask.'

'I know that.' His expression grew sombre. 'But it may not be a matter of gold and silver.'

They travelled on as she had decreed, a slow-moving convoy of foot soldiers and horses and wagons carrying the wounded, protected on both flanks in case of ambush by those knights still able to ride and wield a lance. She travelled in one of the wagons, thankful that she did not have to ride. They were met at the gates of Gloucester Castle by Miles's wife, Sibyl. A messenger had been sent ahead to warn her of their arrival but he had been told to say nothing about the battle or its outcome. Sibyl curtsied as Matilda descended from the wagon, but her eyes were searching the ranks of knights escorting her.

'Welcome, my lady. We have longed for your return, though I know you would not be here if matters had gone as you expected. My husband...?'

She took the small woman by the hand. 'Let us go inside. I have much to tell you.'

She saw from Sibyl's face that she guessed the news was bad, but she was the wife of a warrior and descended from warriors and, without asking any more, she led her guest inside and sent servants running for wine and water.

'Pray, sit, my lady. I can see you are much fatigued. I have heard rumours of events at Winchester but I have no solid information. All is not well?'

'Not well. We have suffered a defeat at the hands of the usurper's forces.' She took Sibyl's hand again. 'I cannot tell you what has happened to Miles. He was last seen fighting bravely but I fear he could not have withstood the number of his enemies. It is possible he is a prisoner. If so, we shall ransom him.'

Sibyl lowered her eyes and said nothing for a moment. Her throat worked as she swallowed back tears. Then she said, 'We can only pray for that. But I know my husband. He would rather die than yield.'

She got up and began giving orders for the disposition of the wounded and the feeding of those able to eat.

Late the following evening a nervous page came to the solar where Matilda was sitting with Sibyl and Brian.

'Madam, they have sent a message from the gatehouse. A beggar is demanding entrance. He is claiming to be the Earl of Hereford and they are afraid to turn him away.'

She jumped to her feet. 'The Earl of Hereford! That is the title I bestowed on Miles not a month since. Do your people not know their own master?'

'Miles?' Sibyl rose too, staring at her. 'You think it is my husband?'

'Of course it is. Praise be to God! Go, boy. Tell them to bring their lord into the hall, before he has them whipped for disobedience.'

She ran down the stairs, Sibyl and Brian at her heels. As they reached the doors leading out of the hall they saw a little group of men crossing the courtyard. The page was in front and behind him two scared-looking guards supported a tattered figure who seemed hardly able to keep his feet. As she reached them it was not hard to understand why the guards, youngsters left behind when Miles took his army into the field, did not know him. His hair and beard were matted with filth and he was clad in a ragged tunic with a piece of sackcloth for a cloak. His feet were wrapped in rags in place of boots and he swayed as he walked like a man at the end of his strength.

She ran to him and would have thrown her arms round him, but he checked her with a formal bow and she recollected herself and gave him her hand to kiss. 'Oh, my dear, dear friend! God has preserved you. I thought we had lost you.'

He staggered and mumbled, 'It was close … too close.'

'Forgive us, Lord,' one of the guards babbled. 'We meant no disrespect.' Turning his eyes to her. 'We thought he was drunk.'

Sibyl stepped forward. 'Don't be afraid. You have done no more than your duty.' She stretched out her hand. 'Come, husband. Enter your castle, and welcome home.'

17

GLOUCESTER AND OXFORD, 1141-42

MILES'S STORY WAS much the same as those Matilda had already heard. Left for dead on the battlefield, he regained consciousness to find he had been stripped of his armour and everything of value. He managed to drag himself away and eventually found an isolated cottage.

'It belonged to an old widow woman. It's a familiar story. She dealt in simples and had been driven out of the village under suspicion of being a witch. She took me in and treated my wounds and let me lie by her fire. It was two days before I felt strong enough to go on. I was not sure whether d'Ypres might have laid siege to Ludgershall, or how much of the country was still in our hands, so I decided to head straight for Gloucester. I know now how it feels to beg my bread and sleep under hedges and I'm right glad to be home again!'

'And we to see you here,' she answered. 'If you can remember where the old woman lives we should reward her for helping you.'

'Yes, when times are more settled. But now we have more pressing business. Is Robert back in Bristol?'

'Robert was taken prisoner,' Brian said. 'We have yet to

find out where he is being held, and by whom.'

Miles drew a deep breath and compressed his lips. 'That puts a very different face on matters. His return must be our first priority. What of our other allies?'

'That remains to be discovered. They have been scattered. We need to send messengers to their homes to find out how they have fared.'

'And we must send someone to Bristol,' Matilda said. 'Robert's wife and family may not know yet what has happened. Also, we must find out how many of his men have survived. I need to be sure that Stephen is being kept secure.'

By the next day Miles was sufficiently recovered to ride to Bristol and a day later he returned with his report. 'Robert's son, Walter, was left in charge and he is a trustworthy fellow. The castle and its garrison are in good order, though only a small proportion of the men Robert took with him have got back safely.'

'And Stephen?'

'Fettered and in a dungeon. Robert treated him well when he was first made prisoner, gave him two rooms and access to a stretch of the battlements for fresh air, but lately he has been found wandering around the castle without permission. Walter concluded he was looking for a way of escape, so he has made sure of him.'

'Good!'

It took several weeks for the answers to come back from all their allies. David of Scotland was back in his stronghold in Cumbria, having been three times taken prisoner and forced to ransom himself. Ranulph of Chester, who arrived too late to play any useful part in the fighting, was back home and seemed to be prevaricating about which side to support. Several of the earls had been taken prisoner, including William of Salisbury and Humphrey de

Bohun, and were waiting to be ransomed. All her allies reported that though some of their men had found their way home, their numbers were greatly depleted. It was clear that there was little hope of a new campaign.

Brian sought her out. 'I come to ask your permission to return to Wallingford.'

She gasped. It was like a physical blow. 'You would leave me?'

He met her eyes and she saw that he was as distressed as she was. 'I must. It is imperative that we hold Wallingford and I cannot leave Boterell, my constable, to hold it on my behalf indefinitely. Believe me, I would stay at your side though the devil himself tried to drag me away, but I must do my duty.'

She swallowed. 'Is not your first duty to me?'

'That is why I must hold Wallingford for you. I cannot sit idly here while Stephen's Queen makes herself stronger at your expense. Please, you must understand that.'

'Yes, I understand.' She held out both her hands and he took them in his own. 'I wish … I could wish that there was some way we could … be more together.'

'Sadly, fate has decreed that we must tread separate paths.'

She longed to throw herself into his arms. It was many years since she had felt a man's arms around her, and most of the time she had not missed it. But now the desire to be held by him almost overpowered her. She raised her face to his. Any other man would understand the invitation, but whether he did or not, he did not take it. Instead he bent his head and kissed both her hands, then turned them over and kissed them again, his lips lingering in her palms. Then he stepped back and made a formal bow.

'God keep you, my lady. If He wills it we shall meet again soon.'

He turned and left the room and very soon afterwards she heard the sound of horsemen leaving the castle.

It was a blow she was ill prepared to deal with. The physical weakness which had dogged her since London, exacerbated by lack of food during the siege and her desperate ride, added to her feeling of despair. Alone at night, she berated herself. The crown had been within her grasp and she had lost it through a moment's bad temper. If she had placated the Londoners as Robert wished, the whole course of events would have been different. She remembered her first meeting with Theobald of Bec. He had warned her then that pride was her besetting sin. She had thought she had taken his words to heart, but now it was clear that they had not taken root there. For the first time, she questioned whether it was indeed God's will that she should rule England. Perhaps, after all, she was not fit. But with that thought came another: that Stephen was no more fitted to the role than she was. Perhaps God intended that neither of them should rule and if so, who was the chosen one? There was an obvious answer. Her son Henry must be King one day. It was her job to prepare the way for him.

A messenger brought a letter from Robert. He was being held in Rochester Castle by William d'Ypres. He had been offered wealth and influence if he was prepared to change sides and had refused. He was now trying to negotiate his ransom.

She sent emissaries to offer a large sum in gold. The offer was refused. Queen Matilda would settle for nothing less than an exchange of prisoners: Robert for her husband, the King.

'We cannot give Stephen up!' she protested. 'He is our only bargaining card. If we let him go we shall be back to exactly where we were before Lincoln.'

The response to her refusal was chilling. If she would not negotiate, Robert would be sent to Matilda's estates in Boulogne, into perpetual imprisonment.

She retaliated in kind. 'Tell her that if she were to do that, we shall send Stephen to Ireland and she will never see him again.'

Her councillors were more realistic. 'We have to give her Stephen,' Miles said 'Without Robert our cause is lost.'

Reluctantly she agreed, but the deal was not straight-forward. Robert argued that the life of a king is worth more than that of an earl, and therefore the other earls taken prisoner with him should be part of the exchange, but d'Ypres and the Queen refused. The earls must find their own ransoms. He did succeed, however, in one important matter. It was agreed that all land held by both factions before the rout of Winchester should remain in their possession. This meant that they still controlled most of the West Country with its vital resources in men and materials. Even then, there was still a lack of trust on both sides. Finally a deal was hammered out. Queen Matilda would bring her son Eustace and two of her barons to Bristol and they would remain there as hostages when Stephen was released. Once Stephen reached Winchester Robert would be released in his turn, but he would leave one of his sons, Roger, in Rochester as a surety for the Queen's freedom. Once she and the other hostages had rejoined Stephen, Roger would be released.

Matilda decided to move her court to Oxford. It was a royal castle, hers since Robert d'Oilly changed his allegiance and swore fealty to her. It was more central than Gloucester, so allowed for better communications with her allies, and it had the reputation of being impregnable. Moreover, it was closer to London, and she had not given up hope that one day she might return there to be crowned.

On 1 November Stephen rode out of Bristol Castle and was greeted with wild celebration when he reached Winchester. Robert joined her in Oxford two days later. She embraced him and searched his face. He was thinner, but otherwise unchanged.

'They have not misused you?'

'No. I have been well treated. But how are you? You are pale. I heard that you had been taken ill on the retreat from Winchester.'

'It is true. Had it not been for Brian and Reginald I should never have reached Devizes. But I am rested now, and much recovered.'

He looked sceptical, but appeared to accept her word. 'That is good, for we have much to discuss and plans to make. How do our powers stand at the moment?'

After a brief conference with herself and Miles and Reginald, his expression was more sombre.

'It seems we are in no condition to continue the fight at the moment. But winter is upon us so the campaigning season is over for this year. We must use the next months to rebuild our strength and see what new allies we can attract.'

Bishop Henry, they learned, was calling a council of Stephen's supporters, and any who had not yet renewed their allegiance, at Westminster. She sent Bernard, Bishop of St David's, who had remained loyal, to represent her. He returned looking grave.

'Henry has a letter from Pope Innocent, which he read out. His Holiness rebuked him for abandoning the King and instructed him to use all his efforts to secure his release. Well, that is all past history now, but Henry was able to use it as evidence that the Pope believes Stephen to be the rightful king.'

'So how does he justify changing his allegiance to me?'

'He said that he believed you would respect the freedom of the Church and that you pledged yourself to do so, but broke your promises. I pointed out that it was Stephen who violated that freedom, when he arrested the bishops, and that it was he, himself, who invited you to come to England to supplant him.' He sighed. 'I am afraid it was to no avail. Henry has told all those who once vowed their allegiance to you that their oaths are not binding, and he is threatening excommunication for anyone who continues to support you.'

'How many will abandon me now, with that threat hanging over them?' she wondered.

'Only those whose loyalty is not worth having,' Robert responded.

Brian wrote to her, assuring her of his continuing devotion. 'Pay no heed to Bishop Henry. He has a remarkable talent for discovering that duty points in the same direction as expediency. God will judge him accordingly in due course.'

The winter took a further toll on her health. Robert sent his physician to examine her. He diagnosed an excess of yellow bile and recommended bleeding, but that left her weaker than ever. She had one consolation. Rumour had it that Stephen had also been seriously ill and close to death. With the arrival of spring, she began to recover and early in Lent she summoned all her chief advisers to a council in Devizes. It had become increasingly clear that the losses they suffered at Winchester had not been recouped.

'If we are to have any chance to reclaiming the throne for our royal lady,' Robert said, 'we must have reinforcements, and I can think of only one way of finding them.' He turned to her. 'We must appeal to your husband, madam. He is well established in Normandy now. Is it not time he lent you some support?'

She sighed. The same thought had been in her mind for some time, but she was reluctant to make the attempt. 'We can try, but I do not hold out much hope. Geoffrey has made it abundantly clear that he has no interest in governing England. If he thought he might become king in his own right it might be different, but I think he sees it as demeaning to be simply the husband of the Queen.'

'Nevertheless, many of his Norman lords hold lands in this country as well. May they not be willing to persuade him?'

'Let us put it to the test. As soon as the sea crossing is viable I will send a deputation to discuss it with him.'

Lent passed and she celebrated Easter without any response from her husband. It was Whitsun before her emissaries returned, empty handed.

'Duke Geoffrey refuses to negotiate with us,' one reported. 'He said we are not men he knows and he will only discuss these matters with Lord Robert in person.'

'Damn him! It's just a delaying tactic,' she said. Then, to Robert, 'You will have to go to him.'

'I don't like leaving you. Suppose Stephen decides to make an attack while I am away?'

'He is still weak from his illness. We shall be safe for a while yet.'

'Just the same … Can we not send someone else?'

'I know my husband. Once he has made up his mind to something, nothing will change it. I do not understand why he is so determined that it has to be you, but if we want his help we will have to comply with his wishes. The sooner you leave, the sooner we will have his answer.'

Robert sailed from Wareham at the end of June, taking with him several family members of the earls who had transferred their allegiance to her since the battle of Lincoln, as surety for their continued loyalty. The weather seemed fair but that night a storm broke. She knelt in her bedroom and listened to the roaring of the wind, and prayed that God would bring her brother safely to harbour. With him gone she felt very much alone. Miles was in Gloucester and Brian in Wallingford. Humphrey de Bohan had negotiated his ransom and once again served as her steward, but he had his own estates at Trowbridge to administer. She had her servants and her ladies-in-waiting, including Hawise, who against all odds reached Gloucester safely, but she had never cared much for the company of women.

At last a messenger brought news from France. Robert wrote that several of his ships were wrecked but two of them made port, carrying him and his small band of household knights with their horses and equipment. Encouraging as this was, his next words made her stamp her foot with anger.

Your husband the Duke has made conditions for his assistance. There are several Norman lords who refuse to submit and hand over their castles to him. He wishes me to remain in Normandy and help him to reduce them. Only then will he consider sending the men we need. It seems I have no choice but to agree.

'I might have known!' she said aloud. 'Geoffrey's only concern is establishing his power in Normandy. He knows Robert is an able commander and he has deliberately inveigled him over there to help him. Who knows how long it will take to bring those recalcitrant vassals to heel?'

Another devastating blow followed soon after. Stephen had recovered and had attacked Wareham and stormed the castle. Without it they had no port for ships crossing the Channel. Communication with Robert in Normandy was now impossible.

She decided to return to Oxford, her safest stronghold. Robert d'Oilly still acted as her castellan there and though he originally supported Stephen, he had proved himself trustworthy. On her arrival, however, it disturbed her to see that he seemed to have aged since he came to her at Reading. He had a troublesome cough, which he tried unsuccessfully to suppress. His wife, Edith, was clearly worried about him, but he brushed her concerns aside.

As soon as she and her entourage had settled in, she called him to her. 'Since Stephen has taken the field again we must assume that he does not intend to stop at Wareham. There is no knowing where he may decide to strike next, but until Lord Robert returns from Normandy we cannot raise a sufficient force to oppose him. I do not imagine that he will attack us here in Oxford, but it is as well to be prepared. Is the castle well stocked for a possible siege?'

'It is, madam. But we do not need to depend entirely on our own provisions. The city is well defended inside its walls and we can always call on the resources to be found there.'

Her forecast of Stephen's intentions was proved mistaken. At the end of September she heard that he had left a garrison in Wareham and was advancing on Oxford with the rest of his army. She gave d'Oilly her instructions.

'There is no question of meeting him in the open field. We must prepare ourselves to withstand a siege. Our only hope is to hold out until Robert returns from Normandy.'

Stephen arrived sooner than they thought possible. From the top of St George's Tower she watched his army deploy on the far side of the Thames. The castle dominated the only bridge and at that distance they presented no threat. Her men on the ramparts greeted them with jeers and ribald jokes, and a shower of crossbow bolts, which fell short.

She turned to d'Oilly who stood beside her. 'Is there any other way across?'

'There is a ford a mile or two up river, but it is only passable in high summer when the water levels are low. Now, with the autumn rains, the river is in spate. Any man trying to cross now would be very foolhardy.'

Next morning a sentry on the tower raised the alarm. Stephen's men had crossed the river and were advancing on the city. Watching from the battlements as the enemy troops came closer, she turned to Edith. 'They must have swum the ford! Look! They and their horses are still wet. And Stephen is at their head, soaked to the skin!'

'Let us hope he contracts an ague from it,' the other woman remarked sourly.

D'Oilly was already mustering his knights in the courtyard below her and to her alarm she saw that he was preparing to ride out to face the advancing enemy. She scanned the field, assessing numbers.

'The fool!' she exclaimed. 'They must stay inside the walls. There are too many of them. Our knights will never be able to withstand an attack from so many.' She beckoned one of her squires. 'Run down to Sir Robert. Tell him I order him to remain within the walls.'

It was too late. Before the message could reach him, d'Oilly had led his men out and formed a defensive line in front of the city gates.

As she watched, Stephen gave the order to charge and his massed knights swept forward with their lances levelled. There was a brief skirmish, d'Oilly's men were forced back and the opposing knights rushed the city gate.

D'Oilly and his men broke and galloped for the safety of the castle. They reached it ahead of the enemy and the gates were slammed shut behind them, but Stephen's men were now in the city. Already she could see them spreading out through the streets, breaking down doors, rounding up prisoners, looting shops. Men and women ran for safety, many of them heading for the church. Some hammered on the castle gates but they remained firmly shut. A chorus of screams reached her ears. She turned away, sick not only with pity but with fear. Now that the enemy held the city, she and her men were bottled up in the castle with only their own limited resources to call upon.

'Smoke!' Edith cried. 'I smell smoke!'

She turned back. Smoke was curling up from some houses close to the city wall. It might have been an accident, a brazier overturned in the panic, a blacksmith's fire left unattended ... but then she saw a second plume of smoke closer at hand.

'May the wrath of God be upon him! He has fired the city.'

Most of the houses were of wood and the flames swept through them so rapidly that some of Stephen's soldiers were almost caught up in the conflagration. She watched as they and the citizens struggled to push their way out of the gates to escape. Soon the smoke was so thick that it was impossible to see what was happening and the inhabitants of the castle could only listen to the roar of the flames and the screams of the dying. By next morning the castle stood in the middle of a smouldering wasteland, encircled by the tents of the enemy. Only the moat, a tributary of the river diverted when the castle was built, prevented the flames from reaching the walls.

Over the next weeks Stephen built two counter-castles,

great mounds of earth and rock high enough to over-look the castle walls, and then they saw his men hauling throwing engines up to the top of them. She watched with growing despair. She had seen enough sieges to know what these instruments could do. The castle walls were strong, but for how long would they withstand the impact of the huge rocks that would be hurled against them? But strangely, the machines were not put to use. It seemed that Stephen had realized that all he needed to do was sit outside the walls until starvation forced them to surren-der. Every day she scanned the fields and roads beyond in the hope of seeing a relieving army, but no one came. They were so closely invested that it was impossible to get news from outside, or to send a message out.

At the base of the tower there was a small chapel dedicated to St George and d'Oilly's father, who built the castle, had endowed a college of monks to perform ser-vices there. She sent for the present incumbents, a dozen men of varying ages; some almost at the end of their lives, others who had barely finished their novitiate.

'My friends, I do not need to tell you that our situation is perilous. The usurper Stephen will stay until we either starve to death or surrender, and since you are trapped here just as we are you will share our fate. We desper-ately need rescue, but the only person with the strength and the men to do it is Lord Robert, who is at present in Normandy with my husband. It is possible, indeed likely, that he is unaware of the terrible straits in which we find ourselves. I need someone to carry a message to him. I am asking if two of you will volunteer to do that.'

They shifted uneasily and exchanged looks. She went on, 'I am asking you because two holy monks have a better chance of passing through the enemy lines and reaching the coast than any of my knights, no matter what disguise they might assume. And also because, even if you were to be captured, I do not believe even such an impious man as Stephen would do harm to men of the Church. Are there two among you who will offer themselves?'

There was another hesitation, then a young monk stepped forward. 'I will go.'

Immediately another slightly older joined him. 'And I.'

'I thank you both from the bottom of my heart. Here is what you must do. You must find your way to the coast – not to Wareham, which is in the hands of the enemy – but to some small fishing harbour. There you will have to persuade a shipmaster to take you across to Normandy. Once there you must enquire for the whereabouts of Lord Robert and Duke Geoffrey. Tell them what a perilous state we are in and beg them to hurry to our aid. I am certain that when he learns of this my husband will bring his forces to England.' She paused and drew a small package wrapped in cloth from under her cloak. 'I will not give you a letter, because if it was found on you it would incriminate you. But you will need money to bribe a mariner to set forth at this time of year. Take these ...' She unwrapped a pair of crucifixes and held them out. 'They are made of wood, but if you break them open you will find inside enough precious gems to pay for whatever you need. You must decide between you what story to tell if you are stopped. A mission of mercy, some holy pilgrimage – you will know better than I what to say.'

The older monk asked hesitantly, 'When do we leave?'

'Tonight. You can slip out of the postern gate under cover of darkness. I will see that you are given food for one day. After that you will have to fend for yourselves.'

She went to the postern to wish them Godspeed and watched them creep away into the night. There was no sound of a challenge but she had no means of knowing whether they had managed to slip through the lines, still less whether they would succeed in persuading a ship's captain to put to sea so late in the year. She told herself that if only word could be got to Geoffrey, he must come to her rescue. To have his wife a prisoner would be too great a shame, even if he cared so little for her person. She had done what she could. Now all that was left was hope.

As the weeks passed, rations were cut again and again. Every loaf of bread, every slice of bacon or ounce of cheese had to be hoarded and made to last as long as possible. Once again, hunger was her constant companion. Worse followed. It was the coldest winter in living memory. Night after night the temperature dropped; morning after morning they woke to find the world rimed with frost. Icicles hung from the ramparts; the courtyard was a sheet of ice which made walking treacherous; the moat, which had previously carried away the detritus from the garde-robes, froze over and mounds of frozen excrement built up beneath the walls. Then the snow came, covering the blackened remains of the city and half burying the tents of the investing troops. One day a sentry watching from the tower reported in amazement that the River Thames itself had frozen and men were walking about on it.

Inside the castle the very walls were icy to the touch. Firewood ran out and they had to resort to chopping up benches and tables to burn. No matter how many furs she wrapped around herself, she was always cold. Robert d'Oilly suffered more than any of them. He coughed constantly and the slightest effort made him wheeze and choke. Edith dosed him with warm wine sweetened with the last remnants of their honey, but to no avail. He took to his bed, struggling for breath. It was no surprise when Edith came to her one morning, her face drained of all emotion, and told her that he had passed away during the night.

She sent for Alexander de Bohun, her trusted master-at-arms, and gave him overall command of the defences. Next day he came to her where she was sitting with Edith, crouched over a brazier where a few embers gave off a little warmth.

'My lady, I have come to a decision but I need your agreement.'

'What decision?'

'I have taken an audit of the remaining provisions. Even if we halve the rations again we cannot hold out for more than a week. We need to surrender before we all starve to death.'

She lifted her head and gazed at him for a moment. She had known for days that it must come to this but she had tried to ignore it. The prospect was too terrible to contemplate. It was true that if they agreed to surrender it might be possible to negotiate terms. Stephen might be prepared to let most of the lesser men and women, the servants and grooms and others, go free. They would have no value for him. The knights might be able to arrange their own ransoms and Edith would probably be permitted to return to her family. It was her own fate that sent a shudder of fear through her. She would undoubtedly be made a prisoner and they had no captive of equal worth to exchange this time. She remembered how she gloated at the thought of Stephen fettered and in a dungeon. He would not have forgiven her for that humiliation and she could only expect similar treatment. She imagined herself, manacled and filthy, shut up in a place where no sunlight penetrated. Of course, Geoffrey would manage to either buy or force her release – but it might be many months before he succeeded. She had a presentiment that she would not survive very long in those conditions.

Alexander was still waiting for her response. She

nodded and said heavily, 'You are right. Surrender is the only option.'

'But there is one more vital attempt to be made before we do. When we yield the castle you must not be in it. It is imperative that Stephen does not capture you. I do not like to imagine what treatment you might have to endure at his hands. You have to leave before we surrender.'

She gave a brief, bitter laugh. 'Oh, and what am I supposed to do? Sprout wings and fly from the battlements?'

'No, but there is a way, if you are prepared to attempt it.'

'Go on.'

'We know that the river is frozen over, so much so that men can walk about on it. This is my idea. If you can slip out through the postern gate with three or four knights you might be able to cross the river on foot and make your way to Abingdon. There you would be able to find horses to take you to Wallingford, to Count Brian.'

'I would be seen and caught before I had gone a hundred steps.'

'Not necessarily. You would go at night, of course. If we could find a white cloak to cover you I believe you might not be seen against the snow.'

'I have just the thing you need.' Edith roused herself. 'Pure white and lined with squirrel fur. It would hide you and keep you warm.'

She looked from one to the other. 'Is it possible, do you think?'

'It's a chance,' Alexander said. 'Which is better than waiting here for Stephen to take you. And if the worst happened and you were seen and taken prisoner, you would be no worse off.'

She had her doubts about that. An unidentified fugitive, seen dimly through the darkness, might well be the target for a crossbow bolt or a lance thrust, and capture by the ordinary soldiers might involve greater humiliation than even Stephen would dare to subject her to. But it was a chance. Anything was better than sitting passively awaiting her fate.

'Very well. When do you suggest?'

'In three nights it will be dark of the moon. That gives the best chance of not being seen. Which of your knights will you take with you?'

She hesitated. Whoever she chose, she might be giving them a chance of freedom, but she would also be asking them to risk their lives. She might be too valuable a prize to be killed, but that would not be true of the men trying to protect her.

'I would prefer you to choose. Or ask for volunteers. Will you come yourself?'

'No. My place is here, if you will allow. I would gladly risk all to help you, you know that, but someone needs to be in command to negotiate with Stephen for the surrender terms.'

'Yes, of course, you are right. Well, ask my knights who will volunteer for this adventure.'

He came back an hour later with four men. She knew all her knights well, had observed their strengths and weaknesses over the months and years, and her first reaction was that these were the very four men she would have chosen. Sir Edwin was the oldest of the four, a big man who had been in her service since she first went to Anjou, not the most daring or skilful but steady and reliable; Sir Bertrand was clever, a wily man who was good at seeing a way round problems; the last two were Piet and Rollo, the boys she knighted after their escapade at Livarot. They had since proved themselves worthy of the honour, among her most daring and courageous knights.

She looked from one to another. 'My friends, I am asking you to undertake a perilous adventure on my behalf. I know you all, and know your loyalty. I trust myself to you entirely.'

She spoke with more confidence than she felt. That night it was not the prospect of capture that kept her awake, but the fear that the ice on the river might not be as thick as it seemed. She imagined it cracking beneath her feet, the cold water closing over her head as she was dragged under by her heavy garments. Almost any death seemed preferable to that.

Three nights later they assembled at the postern gate. She was wearing male attire again, the whole enveloped under Edith's white cloak, and her four escorts had also found white garments to cover their armour. She was shaking, partly from cold but also with fear. She had faced danger before, but always in the company of her knights and in daylight. It seemed that she was not as brave as she once thought. She clamped her jaws together to stop her teeth chattering.

Alexander came down from a window in the tower. 'God is with us. It is snowing heavily. Stephen's sentries will not be able to see more than a few yards in front of their faces.'

She turned to him. 'And may God be with you, too, my old friend. If it is in my power to set you free, you know I will do so.'

'I know it, madam. Now, go, and God speed you on your way.'

The door opened soundlessly. The hinges had been freshly greased. A flurry of snow whirled into her face and the cold made her catch her breath. Sir Edwin offered her his hand and they stepped out into a wilderness where every landmark was obscured and their feet sank into deep drifts with every step. She knew that they were facing towards the river, but between them and it were the ranks of enemy tents. Somehow they had to find their way between them, without alerting the guards. She comforted herself with the thought that all the men on duty must be more concerned with keeping warm than looking out for fugitives. It was the sort of night when no one in their right mind would be abroad.

They plodded forward, Bertrand in the lead and Edwin and herself following with the two young knights behind them. Glancing back she saw that already the snow was obscuring their footprints. The shape of a large tent loomed up ahead of them and Bertrand altered his course to pass between it and the next. The snow deadened all sound except the faint squeak of her boots as she stepped in it. They passed one line of tents and then another. She tried to remember how many ranks deep they were pitched. She must have looked out at them a hundred times, but she had never thought to count. A larger pavilion appeared ahead and once again Bertrand altered course. Then suddenly, from quite close by, a voice shouted a challenge.

'Who goes there?'

She stopped dead but Edwin shouted gruffly, 'Mind your own business and tend to your watch!'

His voice had the authority of an officer and for a moment is seemed the sentry was satisfied. They went on a little further, then behind them a trumpet sounded and they heard voices and the clash of armour. Lighted torches flared between the tents. Someone had called out the guard. Edwin reached out and grabbed her hand and the five of them ran, stumbling and sliding, in the direction of the river. Behind them they heard shouted questions and replies, but it seemed that no one had any clear idea of who, or what, had been challenged. They reached a steep slope down and Matilda clung tightly to Edwin as they slid down it; then they were on a level surface and the way ahead seemed clear. She realized with a shudder that they were actually walking on the frozen river. Bertrand came to her other side and steadied her elbow and they forged ahead. The shouting died down behind them and looking back they could see the torches criss-crossing the area around the tents, but no one followed them down to the river bank. She trudged on and once or twice the ice creaked under her weight, sending her heart pounding, but at last they reached the far bank and her two knights helped her up it.

Edwin said softly, 'I believe we are past the worst danger. The road must be just ahead of us, but we have a long walk. Are you strong enough, my lady?'

She was shivering, and the snow had got inside her boots, so that her feet were icy, but she nodded firmly. 'I am stronger than you think, sir. Let us go on.'

The walk turned into a nightmare. The wind blew the snow into her face and the air was so cold that she felt her lungs were freezing. Ice formed on her eyelashes, making it hard to see, and every step through the deep drifts required an effort. Bertrand saw that she was in difficulty and called a halt.

'We must try to shelter our lady from the worst of the storm. Edwin, you have the broadest back. You go first. Madam, if you will follow close behind him, he will keep the wind off your face. Rollo, Piet give her your arms on either side and help her along. I will bring up the rear.'

In this way she was able to stumble forward, step by step along what felt like an endless road, until at last Edwin said, 'I think I see houses ahead. It must be Abingdon.'

In the darkened streets the going was easier. The snow

had been trampled by many feet and the houses gave some shelter from the wind. No lights showed in any of them, but their passing was marked by the barking of dogs and eventually a door opened and a man with a lantern looked out.

'Who are you? What do you want? If you're after food you can forget it. Your soldiers have stripped us bare of every last crust.'

Edwin stepped forward. 'We are not from Stephen's army, old man, and we have not come to steal. We need horses and we will pay for them. Can you help us?'

'Horses? What do you think I am – the lord of the manor?'

She roused herself from a kind of stupor and said, 'Of course he can't. We must go to the abbey. If anyone has horses they will.'

A short distance further on the abbey gatehouse loomed up out of the blizzard. Edwin rang the great bell and thumped on the door, until a frightened face looked out through the grille.

'Who are you. Who dares make this disturbance in the middle of the night?'

She laid a hand on Edwin's arm and pressed him aside. 'It is I, Empress Matilda, Lady of the English and your rightful queen. I am in need of rest and shelter and horses to take me on my way. Let me in and inform the abbot.'

The eyes behind the grille swivelled from side to side, taking in the four knights who stood beside her. She understood the monk's indecision and pulled off a glove. 'Here, take this to your abbot.' She passed a ring through the grille. 'It is my seal. He will recognize it.'

The ring was grabbed and the cover of the grille slammed shut. They waited, stamping their feet and slapping their arms across their bodies to keep the blood flowing, until there was a scurry of movement and the heavy door swung open. The abbot was a tall man, lean and hollow cheeked. He bowed deeply, his hands hidden in the sleeves of his robes.

'My lady, please forgive us for keeping you waiting. You will understand that these are troubled times and your arrival is, to say the least, unexpected. But come in, please. You and your companions are most welcome to whatever help we can give you.'

They were conducted to the guest house, where a lay brother was already lighting the fire in the central hearth. Others brought warm wine and bread. She huddled by the fire, sipping the wine, suppressing a whimper as feeling came back into her frozen feet and fingers.

The abbot hovered, looking from one to the other. 'Forgive me, I do not understand why you are here. I heard that the Empress was in Oxford Castle and I understood that the siege was so complete that none could get in or out.'

'As you see, we have contrived to escape nonetheless,' Edwin said. 'The Empress is on her way to her castle at Wallingford.'

'But on such a night!' the abbot exclaimed. 'It is a miracle that you have reached here safely. We must thank Almighty God, who has preserved you.'

Matilda looked at him. He seemed flustered and ill at ease. That could be explained, of course, by their sudden arrival, but it occurred to her that he might well be a supporter of Stephen's claim to the throne rather than her own. It crossed her mind that he might even now have sent a rider to inform her enemy of her whereabouts. Bertrand appeared to be thinking along the same lines.

'Father, it is imperative that we reach Wallingford as soon as possible. Can you lend us horses to complete the journey?'

'Of course,' the abbot said, 'but surely you will rest awhile. Wait until the snow stops, or at least until dawn.'

She straightened in her seat. The idea of staying here in the warm, of lying down and going to sleep, was so inviting that it was hard to resist, but she said, 'No, Father. I thank you, but we must go on. Please arrange for the horses.'

A bell began to toll and the abbot turned to her. 'That is the bell for matins. I must officiate at the service. Please wait here and as soon as the service is over I will arrange for horses to be brought round.'

Edwin stepped between him and the door. 'No, Father. Our need is urgent and cannot wait, even upon the worship of the Lord. Please give orders for the horses to be brought, before you go to the chapel.'

She was still not sure whether the abbot's hesitation arose from genuine concern or from some ulterior motive, but he bowed reluctantly and called to a lay brother.

'Have five horses saddled and brought to the door of the guest house. Now, if you will permit me …?'

She gave her permission and thanked him for his hospitality. He left and shortly afterwards she heard the distant sound of the monks chanting the service. Then the lay brother reappeared to say that the horses were waiting. Reluctantly she got to her feet and pulled on her wet boots.

Rollo murmured to Bertrand, 'What's the hurry? We could have stayed here in the warm till morning.'

'And wait for Stephen's men to track us down?' the other man replied with some asperity.

The horses were not what the knights were used to. They were rouncies, basic nags for transporting men or materials, but they were better than walking. The storm had abated and it had stopped snowing, but the horses'

hoofs slipped and slid on the icy road. It was too dangerous to try to move fast. Edwin instructed Rollo and Piet
to hang back by a few hundred yards, to give warning of
any pursuit, but there was no sign of anyone on the road
behind them. It was still long before the winter dawn
when they saw the walls of Wallingford Castle outlined
against the stars. Her heart beat faster at the thought that
she would soon be reunited with Brian.

Edwin turned in his saddle and beckoned the two
younger men to catch up. 'Ride ahead and warn the sentries that the Empress is approaching.'

They kicked their horses into a canter, sending shards
of ice flying into the air. By the time she reached the castle
gatehouse, the gates were open and torches were moving
in the courtyard. As she rode under the archway a figure
came running towards her. Brian was still in his nightgown, with a cloak hastily thrown over it. He skidded to a
standstill at her stirrup and held up his hands.

'Praise God you are safe! But how have you got here?
We thought Stephen had you cooped up in Oxford.'

'Not any longer,' she said, and let herself slide from
the saddle into his waiting arms. For a moment he held
her close and she felt the warmth of his body through her
cloak. Then he set her on her feet, stood back and knelt in
the snow.

'Dear lady, welcome! A thousand welcomes!'

She raised him quickly. 'My friend, there is no need for
that. Let us go in and I will tell you how I escaped. And
give these noble gentlemen welcome. I owe my freedom to
their courage.'

Her feet were so numb that she stumbled as they
moved towards the door of the hall. Brian slipped his
arm round her waist and supported her, shouting orders.
'Warm wine! And see that these men are fed and given a

warm place to sleep.' Then, to her, 'Come up to the solar. We can talk there.'

She had never been to Wallingford before and she looked around the room with interest. A brazier smouldered in the centre and the walls were hung with tapestries woven with stories from the Bible. There were chairs with padded backs and arms and in one corner a writing desk, on which were pens and parchment and several beautifully bound books. It was the home of a scholar rather than a knight.

He led her to a chair and knelt before her, chafing her frozen hands in his. 'I have told my wife to stay in bed. She is not strong and the cold night air would be bad for her. If you permit, she will welcome you in the morning.'

'Of course,' she answered. She had forgotten he had a wife, and she was glad she was not present.

A sleepy page brought a flagon of warm wine and a platter of bread and cold meats. Brian drew a small table to her side and set the food and drink on it.

'Eat. I can see you are famished.'

She thought initially that she was too tired to eat, but after a mouthful or two hunger reasserted itself and she cleared the plate. When she had finished Brian said, 'Now, tell me. How have you escaped – and on such a night!'

He listened in silence as she told her story, his eyes fixed on her face. When she had finished he said, 'We knew, of course, about the burning of the city and the siege. You must not think I have been idle. I have mustered every man available and sent to all our friends for reinforcements. You will see in the morning how many have responded. But it is not enough. It has been eating at my heart to think what you were suffering, but I knew that if I attacked Stephen we must be defeated, and then he would take Wallingford as well. I felt that it was my

306

duty to keep this place safe for you as a refuge.'

'You were right. There would be no point in throwing away your men and perhaps your own life in a useless attempt. If only Robert were not in Normandy! He would have been able to bring Stephen to battle and relieve us.'

He sat back and looked at her in surprise. 'Robert is in England. You did not know?'

'How should I? Robert, in England? Since when? Where is he?'

'He has been back for some time. He is in Cirencester assembling a force to march against Stephen.'

She gazed at him in silence for a moment. Robert had been in England for weeks, and had not brought his troops to her aid. It was too much to take in at once. Then a fresh thought occurred to her.

'And my husband? Is he with Robert?'

'I have heard nothing about that. I assume he is not. Perhaps there are matters of importance that detain him in Normandy.'

Their eyes met and she knew that the same thought was in both their minds. If he had been in Geoffrey's place he would have sold Normandy to the devil, and Anjou into the bargain, in order to save her.

Suddenly the exertions of the night overwhelmed her. She sighed deeply. 'So, what next?'

'Tomorrow you must set out for Devizes. You will be safe from Stephen there. I will provide you with horses and a strong escort.'

'Will you come with me?'

He shook his head regretfully. 'You know I cannot. Once Stephen realizes that you are not in Oxford he will search every road and village for you, and the first place he will think of is here. I have to stay to see to the defences.'

She nodded wearily. 'Do you think there will ever come a time when we can sit quietly and enjoy each other's company without the threat of danger?'

He touched her hand. 'God willing, the day will come. But now you must sleep. I have told two of my wife's women to attend you. Let me take you to your room.'

She leant on his arm as he took her up the winding stair to a room in one of the towers. At the door he kissed her hand and wished her goodnight. She hardly registered the faces or the names of the two women who awaited her, and almost before they had undressed her she was asleep.

18

DEVIZES, 1143-45

She reached Devizes next day and Robert arrived the day after. He strode into the great hall where she awaited him, brushing the snow from the shoulders of his cloak, bowed and kissed her on both cheeks.

'Sister, I am rejoiced to see you safe and well.'

'It is thanks to my own loyal knights and to Brian fitz Count,' she replied. She was glad to see him, but his failure to come immediately to her aid still rankled.

He recognized the coolness in her tone. 'You wonder why I did not come straight to Oxford. It was necessary to recapture Wareham first. I gave the garrison an ultimatum. They could appeal to Stephen for aid and I would wait for thirty days. If he did not come within that time then they would yield the castle to me without a fight. In this way I hoped to draw him away from Oxford, or at least to divide his forces, but he did not take the bait. I had no option but to wait out the thirty days. Then I attacked two castles belonging to his supporters, with the same objective, but still he persisted with his siege. I have even now come from Cirencester, where I have been mustering a force to relieve you. But here you are, unharmed, praise be to God! Has Oxford yielded?'

'Yes. There was no choice. We agreed that once I was out of danger they would make terms. I do not know yet what those terms were.'

He grimaced. 'It is a loss – but it is not insuperable.'

She voiced the thought which was uppermost in her mind. 'Geoffrey has not come with you.'

'No, God rot him! He had me trailing around Normandy like a hound on a leash to one castle after another. We reduced ten of them. Ten! And then he had the gall to say that he does not feel secure enough as yet to leave. But we have gained something. He sent four hundred knights back with me – and something else. I have a surprise for you.'

'A surprise?'

'Wait.'

He strode to the door and shouted an order. A moment later one of his squires appeared, bringing with him a young boy. It was a moment before she recognized who it was.

'Henry?'

Robert gave the lad a light cuff to the back of the head. 'Go to your mother, boy, and ask her blessing.'

Henry advanced and knelt before her. 'Bless me, Lady Mother. My father greets you by me and wishes you health and success.'

It was a speech made from memory, but delivered with some grace. She laid her hand on his head. 'The blessing of God upon you, my son.' She leaned down and raised him to his feet. They looked at each other and she experienced a sharp pang of regret and guilt. When he was a small child in Anjou he was her favourite and they were close. Now he looked at her as if she were a stranger, whose face was familiar but whose name he could not quite recall. He was eight when she left for England. He was eleven now. At his young age, three years was a long time.

She studied him as he stood before her. He was not tall for his age, but sturdy and solidly built. His head seemed a little too large for his body and his hair, which she remembered as fair, had now taken on the russet tones of his father's. His face was freckled and he would never merit Geoffrey's appellation *'le bel'*, but that was no source of regret. It was her own father she saw reflected in his square jaw and lively dark eyes.

She smiled at him and kissed him on the brow. 'Welcome to England, Henry. It is time you got to know the country of which you will one day be king.'

He tilted his head. 'Are you a queen now?'

'I have been a queen since I was eight years old, and an empress from the age of twelve,' she reminded him.

'But are you Queen of England?'

'Not … yet. That is still to be decided.'

'Father says King Stephen is too strong for you. He said he has defeated you in battle.'

'The only time we met him face to face on the field of battle, at Lincoln, we were victorious.'

'But you lost at Winchester.'

'Your father might also have pointed out to you,' Robert cut in, 'that one battle either way does not determine the outcome of a campaign. Your mother is the rightful heir to your grandfather King Henry.'

Henry jutted his jaw pugnaciously. 'When I am old enough I shall defeat Stephen and put you on the throne, madam.'

She felt a catch in her throat. 'That may be, my son. God will determine the final outcome.' She dragged her thoughts back to domestic matters. 'You must be hungry – both of you. Sit. I will send for food and wine.'

Later, when Henry had gone to explore the castle in the care of Robert's squire, she sat with her half-brother in the solar. Together they reviewed their position and the strength of their forces.

She said, 'I fear for Brian in Wallingford. Once Stephen is assured of Oxford he may decide to attack there.'

'Brian has withstood a siege before now and he will be well prepared. If that does happen, then it will give us the opportunity for a counter attack, though we are hardly ready. But the season is late for fighting and this terrible weather may well dissuade him from continuing the campaign.'

'Let us pray so.'

Robert's prediction proved correct. Stephen contented himself with the possession of Oxford and settled in to celebrate Christmas there. She sent emissaries to negotiate the release of her remaining knights. Many of them had already arranged their own ransom, but it cost her more than she could well afford to redeem Alexander de Bohun and the rest.

The festival was too close to allow for elaborate preparations but she feasted her followers as richly as she could and there were plenty of musicians and entertainers anxious to offer their services. It was a subdued celebration, but one where she had the opportunity to give thanks for her preservation and feel some hope for the future.

When the twelve days were over, the question arose of what should be done with young Henry. She turned to Robert for advice.

'I suggest I take him back with me to Bristol. As you know, I have put Walter in Wareham and now Roger has charge of Bristol. He has a son much the same age as Henry. He is being taught by Master Matthew, an extremely learned man, and Roger is pleased with his boy's progress.

Henry can join him, and of course they will both have the benefit of lessons from my master-at-arms in the knightly skills. Bristol is the most secure stronghold in the kingdom, so you need have no fear for the boy's safety.'

Henry greeted the suggestion with fury. 'I will not go back to studying frowsty old books! I will stay here and help you beat Stephen.'

She looked at him severely. 'You will do exactly as you are told. I am your liege lady, as well as your mother, and you owe obedience on both counts.' Then she softened her manner. 'Listen to me. One day you will be king. If you are to be a great king, like your grandfather, you must learn from his example. He was not only a great warrior, he was a man of learning. A king must be more than a leader in battle. He needs to understand the hearts and minds of men. He has to know who he can trust and who must be closely watched; who to reward and who to punish. He has to make decrees and give charters and administer justice. Those frowsty books you speak of contain the wisdom of great men of the past. It is through studying them that you will prepare yourself for the tasks ahead of you. And do not worry, you will have ample opportunity to practise all the knightly skills you need. Your Uncle Robert has some of the best swordsmen and archers and riders in the country in his service.' She took his face between her hands. 'If you want to help me overcome the usurper, you could not find a better way to prepare yourself.'

He hesitated, frowning, then conceded. 'I shall obey you in all things, Lady Mother.'.

It was February, the month of Matilda's birth. She was forty years old, and she had had enough of warfare. Stephen remained entrenched in Oxford and London, but all the lands to the west, in a triangle with its apex

313

at Worcester and its sides extending to Exeter on the one hand and to Marlborough on the other, acknowledged her as their suzeraine, and Brian fitz Count still held out in Wallingford. Over the months that followed she brought to bear the skills she learned as the consort of the emperor and later as Countess of Anjou, skills of administration and the dispensation of justice. She appointed sheriffs and collected revenues and was able to settle her household knights and other followers on demesne lands of her own. The country was not at peace. The war of attrition continued, with each side raiding the other's lands to replenish their own stocks of food and materials or to deny them to the enemy. From time to time Stephen launched attacks on the castles of her supporters and from time to time his own supporters rebelled against him, but she was content to leave the fighting to others and play a waiting game.

The first real attack came in the summer, when Stephen decided to make another attempt on Wareham. Robert had made sure of the only port they possessed and strengthened the defences, and Stephen turned instead on Salisbury. En route he stopped at Wilton Abbey, dispossessing the nuns and fortifying it. She learned of the events that followed when her brother rode into Devizes with a strong force of knights.

'We almost had him!' he exclaimed between gulps of wine. 'I thought we were going to have a repeat of Lincoln but the whoreson got away.'

'What happened?' she asked. 'Tell me from the beginning.'

'We made a surprise attack at dawn. Stephen came out to face us and the numbers were about even, but I ordered a charge and we split his forces, just as we did at Lincoln. That was when I thought we were going to

314

capture him. But he'd learned from his mistake. He didn't wait to fight it out this time, but called his knights to him and galloped off the field. I followed, of course, but his steward, Martell, chose to fight a rearguard action. We captured him, but by that time Stephen was well away.'

'Martell? He's a powerful man. I remember he served my father when he was alive and he's been one of Stephen's most loyal supporters. He will make a valuable hostage.'

'Very true. It will be interesting to see what Stephen is prepared to offer in exchange. What do you want me to do with him?'

'Send him to Brian fitz Count at Wallingford. He has a strong prison within the castle and Martell will be on hand if Stephen comes to an agreement.'

'Very well. Let us see what comes of this.'

'Wilton,' she murmured. 'You know I was educated there for a while? What has happened to the convent now?'

'Burnt to the ground, I'm afraid.'

'Well, I shall not shed any tears for that.'

Messengers plied backwards and forwards between herself and Stephen. He wanted Martell back and offered a large sum of money.

'Tell him you don't want money,' Robert advised. 'Tell him you want Sherbourne Castle and will not settle for anything else.'

'Sherbourne? Stephen is desperate to get as many castles under his control as he can. He won't give one up for anyone's sake.'

'Martell sacrificed his own liberty to save him. If he has any decency he'll do anything he can to free him.'

'I doubt it very much.'

She was wrong. After further negotiations Stephen reluctantly handed over control of the castle and Martell was released.

Soon Stephen had other troubles on his mind. Brian wrote from Wallingford:

It seems de Mandeville has got his just deserts. Stephen has had him arrested on suspicion of plotting treason. I do not know if the charge has any basis, but I would not put it past de Mandeville after the way he behaved to you. On the other hand, it could just be a pretext, so Stephen can get his hands on de Mandeville's castles. Either way, it has done Stephen's reputation no good with his barons. He arrested de Mandeville when he attended court at St Alban's, which is just the kind of treacherous and underhand action we have learned to expect. He may have strengthened his position temporarily but in the long term it will turn men against him.

Events proved his predictions correct. She had her spies, merchants and travelling minstrels and wandering friars – or men in those guises – who reported back to her what was happening in the enemy territories. De Mandeville had handed over his castles, including the Tower of London, to gain his freedom, but on his release he immediately repudiated his allegiance to Stephen and retreated to the fen country of East Anglia, where he fortified the abbey of Ramsey. Stephen was forced to abandon any attempts to make incursions into Matilda's territory while he dealt with this new rebellion. The rest of the summer passed quietly.

Henry came to visit her in Devizes from time to time. He was reconciled to his life in Bristol, had made friends and spoke highly of his teachers – even including Master Matthew. She quizzed him about his lessons and gave him texts in Latin to translate for her. He was proficient, if inclined to make errors through impatience, and she was pleased to find that he could sustain an intelligent discussion about the subject afterwards. While he was with her she arranged for him to take oaths of fealty from her vassal lords, in preparation for the day when he would inherit her powers. She began to instruct him in the skills he would require when he came to rule, skills which she herself learned from her father. He listened attentively, but at the first opportunity he was off to the stables and the tilt yard with the boys training as squires under her household knights. She watched him demonstrate his horsemanship and skill with the lance and sword. He was at ease with the other boys, and with her knights, relaxed and friendly without compromising the dignity of his rank. It was a talent she had never been able to master.

Men disinherited by Stephen or displaced by the fighting gravitated to her court. Thanks to the agreement extracted from Stephen before his release, that all the conquered lands should remain with their current overlord, she was able to settle them on new estates. She was surrounded now by men who owed their position and prosperity to her. She saw less, however, of her closest friends and supporters. Robert ranged the countryside, checking their defences and raiding where he saw opportunity. Miles had his own earldom to administer now and Brian would not leave Wallingford, though they were in regular communication by letter. There was a cell of monks affiliated to the abbey of Bec at Ogbourne, not far from Wallingford. The monks travelled regularly between there and the mother house in Anjou, via monasteries at Chisenbury and Brixton Deverill and the port of Wareham, and they were happy to carry letters and unlikely to be the target of the robber bands that roamed the countryside.

Brian wrote that he was preparing a treatise setting out in detail her claim to the throne:

I am in correspondence with Gilbert Foliot, the abbot of Gloucester, and one of the most learned men of our time. He approves of my arguments and is supportive of our enterprise.

She smiled as she read this, remembering his room at Wallingford; the room of a scholar rather than a warrior.

At the end of September there was a new development. News arrived of the death of Pope Innocent II. This meant that Bishop Henry's legateship lapsed, unless he could persuade the new Pope to reappoint him. It pleased her that Archbishop Theobold was now the chief authority in the English church. She had always respected him as a man of integrity, far better to deal with than the devious Henry.

When Christmas approached she made elaborate preparations. This time there would be no repetition of the previous year's low-key celebrations. She had attracted to her court not only men of influence and learning but musicians and troubadours – and cooks. She was determined not to be restricted to the prevailing cuisine of bread and roast meat, lacking any kind of sauce. This year there would be a feast to remember.

She was leaving the chapel after mass on Christmas morning when a rider clattered into the courtyard and fell on his knees before her. She recognized him as one of Miles's men and the look on his face told her at once that he was not the bearer of good news. She hauled him to his feet.

'What is it? Is Gloucester under attack? Surely even a man as godless as Stephen ...'

The young man shook his head wildly. There were tears in his eyes. 'No, my lady, it is worse than that. Sir Miles is dead.'

'Dead? Miles? How?'

'It was an accident. Yesterday we went out to hunt boar. You know how it is … you hear a movement in the undergrowth … it is impossible to see properly. Someone let loose an arrow. It hit him in the chest. At first he tried to make light of it. Then he began to cough blood and before we could carry him to a physician he was dead.' He dropped his gaze. 'Forgive me, my lady. My tongue runs away with me.'

She turned away and headed back into the chapel. Her attendants tried to follow but she waved them away. 'See that this man is fed and rested …'

Inside, she sank to her knees before the altar and buried her face in her hands. Miles! The man who was like a father to her; who took her into his home and made her feel that it was her own; who had risked his life for her in battle again and again. Then a terrible thought struck her. He had written not long ago that he had been excommunicated by the Bishop of Hereford for plundering a local church. It was a matter of necessity, to provide desperately need funds to pay his men, but it was a sin nonetheless. What help was there now for his immortal soul? She prostrated herself and sobbed convulsively.

There would be no Christmas celebrations this year after all.

With the New Year came better news. Geoffrey had finally succeeded in taking Rouen and made himself the undisputed master of Normandy. There was, however, a sting in the tail. He wanted young Henry back with him. She understood the need for this. Henry must be known to all Geoffrey's vassals as the heir and their future liege lord, and he must take oaths of fealty from them. Also, he needed to begin to learn the complexities of governing a large and disparate dukedom. She consoled herself for his

319

loss with the thought that at least he had a secure inheritance on that side of the narrow seas. For her the parting was a wrench but he went gladly, eager to take up his new position.

Brian wrote from Wallingford:

I have received threats of excommunication from Bishop Henry, as punishment for diverting a train of merchandise on its way to Winchester for the sustenance of my garrison. As you well know, in the current disturbed condition of the country much land is not under cultivation and normal taxes and tithes cannot be collected. I often have great difficulty in obtaining supplies to feed the men I must keep for the necessary defence of the castle, and for that reason I have to resort to taking them from those who can better afford their loss.

I have written to Henry pointing out that there was a time when he himself ordered all the great men of the realm to give their oath of allegiance to you, and I have added a list of the names of all those who so swore at his behest. I further told him that, had he maintained his oath instead of reneging on it, the country might now be at peace under your rule and therefore the current state of unrest is largely his own responsibility. In short, I maintained that his only grounds for quarrel with me is that I have refused to change my allegiance as often and as easily as he has.

I do not expect to hear any further threats from that quarter.

She admired his courage and his scholarship in her defence but she was still anxious for him, remembering that Miles was not in a state of grace when he died. There was nothing she could do to provide Brian with the supplies he so desperately needed, but she could do something for the care of his immortal soul. She owned the manor of Blewberry, which was not far from Wallingford. She sent a charter to the monks of the abbey of Reading, gifting the manor to them, with the provision that it was for the good of the souls of her ancestors and for the love and loyal service of Brian fitz Count.

There was no end to the unrest that plagued the country. Robert tried to take the castle of Malmesbury but was driven off by a surprise attack from Stephen, who went on to besiege Robert's castle at Tetbury. Robert called up his Welsh allies and also requested the help of Roger of Hereford, Miles's son. In response Stephen relinquished Tetbury and attacked Roger's castle at Winchcombe, which was forced to surrender. As the summer progressed Stephen's incursions into the Angevin territory in the West Country grew increasingly frequent. In September there was a further blow. News came that Geoffrey de Mandeville, who had until now been holding out in the fen country, had been killed by an arrow in the head. She could not feel any regret for him, after his desertion at Winchester, but the collapse of his rebellion meant that Stephen was now free to concentrate his efforts on her own territory.

There was one small success. One of her allies, William Peverill of Dover, had established himself at Cricklade on the Thames and was carrying out a campaign of harassment along Stephen's lines of communication. He arrived unexpectedly at Devizes, bringing with him a prisoner.

'I have brought you Walter de Pinkney, my lady. He is the castellan of Malmesbury.'

'Malmesbury! Has the castle fallen?'

'Alas, no. Walter made the mistake of venturing outside

with only a small retinue. I got wind of it and set an ambush. But now that we have him I feel sure that he can be persuaded to hand it over.'

She ordered de Pinkney to be chained up in her dungeon and William left. She knew what was expected of her. If he would not willingly yield the castle in order to obtain his freedom he must be tortured until he did, but her soul revolted against the idea. Once, a few years ago, she rejoiced to think of Stephen in fetters. But this man's only fault was loyalty to his sovereign lord and she had to admire his courage. She let him starve for a day or two, then had him brought before her. He was filthy. His lips were cracked from thirst and his wrists and ankles covered in sores from the shackles, but he faced her with defiance.

Hugh, her chief gaoler, murmured, 'Let me have him, madam. I'll persuade him of his folly in refusing.'

She shook her head. 'Take him away. Keep him shackled, on bread and water. We'll see how long he can hold out.'

John the Marshall paid one of his regular calls and she put her dilemma to him.

'Threaten him with execution,' was his advice. 'It's remarkable how quickly a man can change his mind when he feels the noose around his neck.'

But even that seemed too barbaric, and while she hesitated word came that Stephen had reinforced the garrison at Malmesbury and appointed a new castellan.

'What do you wish me to do with the prisoner?' Hugh asked.

She shrugged. 'Set him free. He's no use to us now.'

Malmesbury continued to be a thorn in the side of the Angevin forces. As the year drew to an end, their position looked increasingly insecure.

*

With the coming of spring Robert came to visit her, to discuss their strategy for the new fighting season.

'Peverill wishes to relinquish Cricklade and hand it over to someone else.'

'Why?'

'As far as I can discover something happened over the winter to make him feel he was endangering his immortal soul. He wants to go on pilgrimage.'

She nodded wryly. 'I can understand that. Perhaps it is something we should all consider. Meanwhile, who will you put in his place?'

'I've sent Philip.'

She raised an eyebrow. 'Is that wise?'

Philip was Robert's third son and she had never taken to him. He was an impatient young man with a hasty temper, given to black-browed sulks when thwarted.

'It will keep him occupied,' Robert said. 'It's time he took on some responsibility. Walter has Wareham and Roger is in holy orders, so he is the obvious candidate. He has been pressing me all winter to make a push towards Oxford, to take the fight into Stephen's territory and put him on the defensive. Cricklade is a good forward base for an advance in that direction.'

'Very well,' she agreed. 'You are the best judge.'

Sometime later he wrote to tell her that Philip had identified what he regarded as the ideal site for a new castle, on the top of a hill known locally as Faringdon Clump, a place which had, in Robert's words, 'been fortified since ancient times but has now fallen into disrepair'. He was going there to see for himself. His next letter told her that he had approved the choice and started the building of a strong fortification.

In midsummer he visited her again, looking more optimistic than he had for months.

'Faringdon is finished and it is a good piece of work. The hill is very steep and we have encircled the summit with a ditch and a palisade and built a strong keep. It will withstand any attack.'

'Who has charge of it?' she asked.

'Brian de Soulis. He's reliable and I've given him some of my best men for the garrison. He should be able to keep Stephen's forces busy and away from us.'

Robert was still at Devizes when a messenger brought word from Philip that Stephen had assembled a very powerful force, including the London militia, who had never wavered in their hostility to the empress, and marched against Faringdon.

He is building a counter castle to protect his men and I am greatly afraid that when it is finished it will overlook the walls. If he brings up throwing machines de Soulis will not be able to hold out. It is imperative that you march to our aid immediately, or all our labour will be undone.

Robert threw the letter aside. 'March to his aid immediately! He knows how thinly our forces are spread now. It will take days before I can call in enough men to risk an attack.'

He sent riders all over the county and beyond, summoning his vassals to bring their levies to Devizes. The reinforcements trickled in but it was days before all of them arrived. Meanwhile they received increasingly desperate appeals from Philip. Stephen's mangonels were steadily reducing the turf palisade to dust and his archers were able to fire over the top of it and had killed a number of the defenders.

Robert was about to set out when another rider galloped into the courtyard. Robert took the letter and turned back into the hall. She watched as he read and saw the colour drain from his face. He sank down on a stool and dropped the parchment on the rushes.

She knelt at his side and laid a hand on his arm. 'Brother, what is it? Are you ill?' He shook his head wordlessly. 'Tell me. Is Faringdon lost?'

'Worse.' His voice was a strangled croak. 'Philip ...'

'Dead?'

'No. That could be borne, but this ... He has defected to Stephen. My own son!' He choked and fell silent.

She reached down and picked up the letter.

I have to inform you of the loss of both Faringdon and Cricklade. The condition of the men in Faringdon having become desperate, and there being no sign of help from you, de Soulis sent a messenger to me in secret to tell me that he had made a treaty with Stephen to surrender the castle and had been offered generous terms. Since you have neglected to respond to my appeals for aid, knowing how desperate the position was, I have concluded that our cause is doomed to failure. It therefore seemed prudent to make my peace on the best terms I could get. Accordingly, I sent an embassy to King Stephen, offering to resign Cricklade to him, and my offer has been accepted in the most noble and generous manner. I am to have the control of several castles with their land and revenues. I have pledged my faith to the King and I shall henceforth serve him loyally as my liege lord.

She took her brother's hand. 'He will soon discover his mistake. Stephen has proved himself faithless again and again. Look how he treated de Mandeville after he

325

changed his allegiance. Trust me, before long Philip will be back, begging you on his knees for forgiveness.'

He heaved a deep sigh. 'Perhaps. It must be as God wills, I suppose.' He hauled himself to his feet. 'I had best countermand the orders I have given and send these men ...' He stopped suddenly and she saw him wince and clasp his left arm with his right hand.

'What is it? You are ill. Let me send for the physician.'

He breathed deeply and shook his head. 'No, no. It is nothing. A strained muscle, nothing more.' Before she could say anything else he strode out of the hall and began issuing orders.

Over the next months they learned that Philip was not the only one to defect. Many of the barons who had come over to her cause when she seemed to be in the ascendant now decided that their best interests lay in submitting to Stephen. Most painful of all, Philip, with the zeal of a convert, was carrying out a violent campaign against any weak spots around the margins of his father's land and earning himself a reputation for brutality surpassing even the cruel norms of warfare. Increasingly, she doubted the rightness of her struggle.

'It would have been better for the country if I had stayed in Anjou and not pressed my claim to the throne,' she said to Robert at their next meeting.

'No! You must never think that. Your cause is right in the eyes of God.'

'But look at the destruction we have wrought between us. Look at the suffering of the people.'

'Look instead at your own lands, here in the west. Here the land is at peace, the folk go about their work as they have always done, and you are known as a just ruler who respects the laws and keeps her oaths. That is not so with Stephen. Since he first seized the throne the country has been torn apart by rebellion and unrest. It was his failure to keep the peace that first impelled the bishops to invite you to take the crown. He is known throughout the land as a man who cannot be trusted, who considers only his own advantage and not the obligations he owes to his subjects. If we had prevailed, if Bishop Henry had not forsworn himself, the country would long ago have been at peace under your rule.'

And if I had not antagonized the Londoners... She thought it but did not speak it aloud. Instead she said, 'So, what can we do now?'

'Only hold on and wait for those who have turned against us to find out their mistake. It will happen, I assure you.'

Before the year ended they had news from Rome which had the potential to alter the balance of power. Pope Eugenius had promulgated a bull declaring a new crusade. The question now was, how many English lords would heed the call and leave the country, taking their knights and men-at-arms with them?

19

DEVIZES, 1146-48

ANOTHER WINTER PASSED and in the spring they learned of yet another defection. Ranulph of Chester, who had never committed himself wholly to her cause, signed a treaty with Stephen. It was a great loss. He controlled huge tracts of land in the north-west and now offered all those resources to the King on condition that Stephen helped him against the north Welsh, who were harrying his borders. As an earnest of his loyalty he joined Stephen in his campaign. They attacked and took Bedford and turned against Wallingford. But once again Brian and his loyal constable, William Boterell, held out and the great castle proved impregnable.

Robert rode in, looking triumphant. 'I knew this must happen. Did I not tell you that Stephen cannot be relied upon to keep his word? He has refused to send his troops into Wales, as he agreed with Ranulph, and demanded hostages from him as a pledge of good faith. Ranulph has refused so now they are at loggerheads.'

Not long afterwards they heard that Ranulph had been arrested on suspicion of treason. Brian wrote to her:

It is an infamous deed and one quite in keeping with Stephen's character. I have heard that Ranulph attended his court with only a small following, suspecting no treachery, and was seized by some of Stephen's men and thrown into prison.

Rumours reached her that Ranulph's men had started to attack Stephen's properties in the north and then that Ranulph himself had been forced to hand over his castle of Lincoln in order to obtain his release. Within days an embassy from him arrived in Devizes. He was willing to renew his pledge of allegiance to her and promised her his loyal support from now on. He came south to take the oath of fealty and then returned northwards in an attempt to regain his lost castles.

She called in her closest advisers, Robert and Reginald of Cornwall, her two half-brothers; John Marshall and Patrick of Salisbury.

'I have been greatly troubled in mind for some time about the devastation these wars are wreaking on the common people. I have decided that we must make one last attempt to negotiate with Stephen. Reginald, you have always shown yourself a wise councillor and adept at argument. Will you undertake this mission, if we can agree a safe conduct for you and some of your men?'

'I will do it, madam,' he agreed, 'but I have little hope of success. What do you wish me to say on your behalf?'

'You must press on Stephen the rightness of the Empress's claims and demand that he renounce the throne,' John said.

'No, that will not work. The argument has been made too many times. Tell him that if he will agree to name Henry as his heir, instead of his own son Eustace, I will quit England and leave him to rule in peace for the space of his lifetime.'

There was considerable argument over this approach but she remained adamant and in the end Reginald agreed to act as her ambassador. Messages were sent to Stephen in Oxford and he agreed a safe conduct for the deputation. Reginald set out with a small band of knights.

The next day one of those knights rode back into the castle, bloody and dishevelled, and begged an urgent interview.

'My lady, we were ambushed and attacked. Earl Reginald is a prisoner.'

'Attacked? By whom? Surely Stephen is not base enough to renege on his own safe conduct.'

'No, madam. Not King Stephen's men. It was ...' He licked his lips and swallowed as if he had difficulty pronouncing the words. 'It was Philip of Gloucester, Earl Robert's son.'

'Philip? Philip has attacked and taken Reginald prisoner? With what object?'

'Ransom, madam. He set me free and sent me to tell you that in return for your brother's freedom he demands that his father hand over Bristol Castle.'

'Bristol! That is the heart of his father's power. He could never relinquish it.'

'I am instructed to tell you that if his father does not comply, your brother's life will be forfeit.'

She turned away, pressing her hand to her mouth. 'God rot that man! He deserves no mercy either here or in hell, where he will surely go.' After a moment she recovered herself and said, 'Go to the kitchen and get yourself food and drink. Find my physician to tend your wounds. I need time to think.'

For some time she paced the chamber, gnawing her fingers as she struggled to make sense of what she had been told. Then she sent for Alexander de Bohun and told him what had happened.

'Philip is Stephen's man since he defected. Stephen has given his word for the safety of Earl Reginald and it is against his honour to allow harm to come to him. I shall write a letter to him and you must convey it. Tell Stephen that it is for him to bring Philip under control and make him yield up his hostages.'

Stephen, to his credit, acted at once and within days Alexander was able to return and report that Reginald had been freed and Philip was now under his lord's extreme displeasure. That was the limit of his good intentions, however. Reginald returned, having achieved nothing.

'I put our case as forcibly as I could, but Stephen is adamant. He will never relinquish the throne, nor will he accept Henry as his heir.'

She bowed her head. 'So be it. The struggle goes on.'

Reports came to her from Ranulph. He had attacked Lincoln in an attempt to repossess it but had been driven back. He then turned his attention to Coventry and laid siege to it. Stephen marched to the garrison's relief and briefly there seemed to be hope of the victory she had striven for for so long. She learned that Stephen had been wounded in the fighting; but almost at once a new report told her that the wound was slight and he had recovered and routed Ranulph. He had knighted his son Eustace, who had shown himself an able warrior in his father's cause.

Then a serious blow came from an unexpected quarter. Jocelyn, Bishop of Salisbury, arrived at Devizes.

'It is a matter of the rightful possession of this castle,' he began.

'What do you mean? Devizes is mine.'

'Not so, madam. You know as well as I do that it was

originally built by Roger, my predecessor as bishop. It was expropriated by Stephen when Roger fell from grace, but it should by rights belong now to me.'

'You are asking me to give up Devizes to you?' She stared at him in disbelief. 'That is out of the question. It is the centre of my power, my most vital stronghold.'

Jocelyn's bland expression did not change. 'I simply state what is the legal position. I require you to hand over Devizes and if you refuse I shall appeal to the Pope to adjudicate. I have no doubt he will find in my favour.'

She succeeded in persuading him to give her time to think, and he left, promising to return in a few days. She was distraught. Devizes was vital to her. She had no other stronghold to go to and it was her only secure foothold in the country. Eventually a possible compromise occurred to her. She wrote to Jocelyn, offering to augment the prebend due to the church of Heytesbury, which was within the diocese of Salisbury. She had already given the two priests that served the church a generous endowment but she now offered to add twenty-eight acres of land, with pasture for 100 sheep, ten oxen, two cows and two horses. It seemed at the time that the bishop was satisfied and she heard no more.

Christmas came again and she kept it with as much state as she could muster. Then she heard that Stephen, to emphasize his supremacy, had held a ceremonial crown wearing in the city of Lincoln. It was a bitter reminder of the reversal of fortunes since the day of triumph when he became her prisoner.

She was reading in her private chamber, trying to find some consolation in the work of Peter Abelard, when she heard the sound of horses clattering into the courtyard below. From the window she saw a large party of knights, but their colours were unfamiliar to her. Then one rider detached himself from the rest and dismounted from a magnificent chestnut destrier and she caught her breath.

'Henry?'

By the time she had run down the winding stair, he was in the great hall. He bowed and then came closer to kneel at her feet.

'Lady Mother, I am happy to see you again. Please give me your blessing.'

She spoke the words automatically and pulled him to his feet. 'Henry, what are you doing here? You gave no notice of your coming.'

'I did not want to risk being stopped at the coast. Are you not pleased to see me?'

'It is always a joy to see you, but you have come at a dangerous time. You should not have risked yourself.'

'It was no risk. I come well prepared and with a large escort.'

'Who are these men?'

'Mercenaries for the most part. I have promised them rich pickings when I am victorious.'

'Victorious? You cannot mean to pit yourself against Stephen's army.'

'Of course. That is why I am here. I heard in Normandy that things were going badly for you and I thought it was time I took a hand.'

She stared at him. He was what … fourteen, now. In the two years since he left he had grown from a boy to a young man. His shoulders were muscular under his tunic and there was the first hint of a beard among the freckles on his face. She remembered how impetuous he always was as a child. It was clear that he had not changed in that respect.

'Henry, do you have your father's permission to be here?'

He shrugged and turned away. 'I didn't ask. He was away from Rouen, teaching some upstart vassal a lesson.'

'So you have come with what … a handful of mercenaries … expecting to do what?'

'I shall begin with Cricklade. I heard how treacherously it was handed over to Stephen. I mean to teach Philip a lesson.'

For a moment she almost laughed. 'My dear boy, you have no idea what you are saying. Philip of Gloucester is a traitor and a renegade, but he is also a most formidable commander, well seasoned in battle.'

He moved away. 'I do not care about his reputation. He should be punished for what he has done. God will fight on our side. My men are tired and hungry. Will you give orders for them to be fed and found accommodation?'

She did as he asked. His band of followers was not as numerous as he would have her believe and her heart sank as she looked them over. She sent a rider to Bristol to inform Robert of Henry's arrival. Robert arrived the next day and there was a furious argument. He made the mistake of forbidding Henry outright to leave Devizes and threatened to inform Geoffrey in Normandy of his son's disobedience. Henry flew into a rage and before she could intervene he summoned his men, ordered his horse to be saddled and rode out of the gates.

'Go after him, Robert,' she begged. 'There is no knowing what his intentions are, but he spoke of attacking Cricklade.'

'Then the boy is a fool,' Robert responded, 'and he will have to learn the consequences of his foolishness.'

'Even if it means his death?'

'They won't kill him! He's far too valuable as a hostage. But if he's captured we may have to give up more than we should like to get him back. I can't afford to risk my men on a fool's errand like this. God's blood! Why hasn't Geoffrey taught the boy some sense?'

For the first time she noticed that he had aged since the shock of Philip's desertion. His hair was liberally flecked with grey and his eyes were more deeply sunken, surrounded by fine lines from screwing them up against wind and sun. It occurred to her that she had never asked him when he was born, or who his mother was. He must, she knew, be at least ten years older than she was. That was not an age to be spending all day in the saddle in full armour and leading men into battle. She did not press him further.

She endured days of anguished suspense until one of her spies reported that Henry had been driven back from Cricklade but was now laying siege to Purton. Not long after that a bedraggled train of riders re-entered her castle, with Henry at its head. There were far fewer of them than when he arrived. He was unhurt, but exhausted and, she could see, close to tears. She waited until he had washed and eaten before she questioned him.

'Those whoreson Flemish mercenaries!' he exclaimed bitterly. 'They broke and ran at the first charge. I offered them riches and honour and they deserted me when I most needed them.'

'It is in the nature of such men,' she said. 'They serve only for pay and if they do not see any chance of victory they will not fight. If you are ever to be successful in battle you must gather to yourself men who fight from loyalty and conviction, men who will lay down their lives in a cause they believe is just. It takes time to build that kind of trust. It cannot be bought.'

He looked up at her, his face haggard and his eyes red. 'I cannot even buy them. I have no money to pay them. They came with me on the promise of reward and now I have nothing to give them.'

She shook her head in despair. 'You foolish child! What do you expect to happen now? These are dangerous men and you will have to pay them off somehow.'

'Then you must give me the money,' he said.

'I do not have the money to waste on your rash enterprises. Do you not realize how much my revenues have been diminished over the last years? I could not pay your men, even if I wanted to. You have put your head into this trap. Now you must find your own way out of it.'

'Then I shall ask Uncle Robert.'

'You can ask. I doubt if you will get the reply you hope for.'

He rode off to Bristol the next day, while his mercenaries, those that remained, caroused at her expense and picked fights with her own knights. Then Robert arrived, grim-faced.

'What has happened? You have not agreed to pay his men?'

'I have not. I need all my money to pay my own men, and he needs to learn that he cannot expect either of us to rescue him from his own foolhardiness.'

'So where is he now?'

He gave a mirthless laugh. 'He has gone to appeal to his cousin Stephen for succour!'

'To Stephen? Is he mad?'

'Perhaps not. Whatever Stephen's faults, he has a reputation for generosity towards those who appeal to him. And it would be worth his while to pay off Henry's debts, just to get him out of the country.'

He was right. Henry returned triumphant. 'Cousin Stephen received me warmly and entertained me most nobly. He is a man of great generosity. He has given me enough money to pay my men and to spare.'

'Does that mean you accept his right to the throne and will not fight for your inheritance?'

'Oh no.' He looked as if the answer was obvious. 'He understands that I still maintain my rights and shall strive to establish them. It is an agreement between gallant adversaries, in the spirit of knighthood.'

Her anger evaporated in an upsurge of tender pride. She reached for his hand. 'So, now you can pay your men and send them packing and we can sit down together and attend to the business of the realm – such as it is at present.'

He stayed with her for a month, but Geoffrey sent messages demanding his return and he left in the middle of May. Later he wrote to say that on Ascension Day he visited the convent of Bec-Hellouin and was received with great ceremony and acclamation.

There was less fighting that summer. Many of the nobles had heeded the call to join the crusade and others had simply tired of the struggle and were licking their wounds in their own castles. She heard that Stephen was pressing the Pope to allow Eustace to be crowned in his own lifetime. It was a custom often adopted in France but it had never been done in England and Eugenius refused. It was a small victory.

Geoffrey wrote from Rouen.

My dear wife,

You will know by now that I am firmly established both as Duke of Normandy and Count of Anjou. It is a great victory, but the control and administration of such a large domain requires me to spend a great deal of time travelling around from one castle to another. I remember well the great help you were to me in the early days of our marriage, with your unrivalled knowledge and experience in these matters. I need someone to act in my stead while I am away and there is no one so suited to the role as you are.

I would also remind you that you have three sons, two of whom have not seen their mother for ten years. You have a duty as a mother, as well as a wife; both of which you have failed to fulfil.

It seems to me that your struggle to establish yourself as Queen of England has come to nothing and that matters are no nearer to being resolved than they were when you left Normandy. Would it not be better, for you as well as for your children, to return here and take up your rightful position at my side, as Duchess of Normandy?

The letter evoked a turmoil of emotions. Her first reaction was anger. She was tempted to write back pointing out that the failure of her hopes in England was in large part due to his lack of support. But Geoffrey's accusation that she had failed in her duty as a mother hit home. She had given a great deal of her attention to Henry, but over recent years she had thought less and less about her other sons. It was a failing – perhaps a sin – and it should be remedied. Then, there was the prospect of life as Duchess of Normandy to consider. To go back would mean an end to her hopes, but it would mean the end of warfare; and an end to the burden of guilt she carried for the suffering of the common people. She had no doubt that there was useful work she could do in helping to settle the duchy peacefully after years of upheaval. She could bring justice and good governance to the whole of Normandy and Anjou, rather than the small part of England that was all she currently controlled. There was one consideration, however, that outweighed the rest. If she left, it would be an end to the hopes of the men who had supported her and who had become her friends. Most importantly, it would mean abandoning her brothers, and she did not like to imagine what Robert would say. And, most crucial of all, it would mean abandoning Henry's prospect of one day inheriting the throne.

As the months passed, with no change in the balance of power, she found her thoughts returning to the prospect of a retreat to Normandy more and more frequently. Then came a message that seemed to her a direct indication of the will of God. Jocelyn of Salisbury wrote to her. The Pope supported his claim to Devizes Castle and she was threatened with excommunication if she refused.

It was a dank, grey day in November when Roger of Gloucester rode into her castle. She was sitting in her private chamber reading and as soon as he was announced she knew what he had come to say. He made the conventional obeisance and murmured, 'Heavy news, my lady.'

'Your father?'

He swallowed and cleared his throat, as if to speak the word was a struggle. 'Dead, madam.'

She clasped a hand to her own throat, but whether it was to stifle a sob or because she suddenly found it hard to draw breath she could not tell. 'How?'

'It was quick. He did not suffer long. We had been sitting at dinner. He was laughing at the antics of a juggler. Then he got up and seemed to shudder, clutched at his chest and fell to the ground. When I reached him he was insensible. We carried him to his bed and called the physician, but he said there was nothing to be done.'

'Tell me,' she leant towards him. 'Was he in a state of grace?'

'He was, madam. We sent for the chaplain and he

conducted the last rites and just at that moment my father seemed to rouse. He opened his eyes and whispered the words of confession, and then he fell back, and his soul fled to Him who made it.'

Tears were on her cheeks but they were tears of relief. 'Where he will be received and set among the warriors of God.'

'I pray so, my lady.'

She was silent for a moment. Then she rose to her feet. 'I should like to go to the chapel and pray for him. Will you come with me?'

'Most willingly.'

She sent for her own chaplain and together they repeated the prayers for the soul of the departed. She did not weep. As with the death of her first husband, the emperor, and the death of her father, this was a grief beyond the comfort of tears.

Next day she rode with Roger to Bristol for Robert's funeral. All his family were gathered there. Mabel, the old antagonism between them long forgotten, was stoic and dignified. Robert's sons were all there, except of course for Philip. His daughters had journeyed from distant parts of the kingdom. Matilda, her namesake, the wife of Ranulph of Chester, arrived with her husband and children; and Mabel, whom she remembered as a shy girl, was now the wife of Aubrey de Vere. Reginald was present, of course, and to her great comfort, Brian fitz Count had left Wallingford to join the mourners.

Robert's eldest son, Walter, would inherit the earldom, but Matilda knew already that he was not a warrior like his father. In fact, he had the reputation of preferring the bedchamber to the battlefield and she had her own private thoughts about the kind of company he kept there. Roger had his career to make in the Church and the rest were still boys. None of them had shown any sign of their father's drive and ambition. They would have no interest in fighting for her cause.

In procession they followed the coffin, draped in a white pall, to the Priory of St James, while the priests chanted the *miserere* and *de profundis*. The funeral mass was celebrated and at the end Robert's destrier, fully caparisoned, was led up to the altar by one of his squires and offered to the officiating priest. It would be redeemed later by Walter for a cash donation. Finally Robert's body was lowered into the tomb prepared for it. Then they returned to the castle for the funerary feast.

When the meal was over she rose and the chatter in the hall died down.

'My friends, we have lost a noble spirit, a man of courage and integrity unsurpassed by any in the land. He was to you a husband, a father, a brother, a grandfather. To me, as well as a brother, he was my dear friend and my most loyal supporter, without whom I could never have laid claim to my rightful heritage. He fought many battles on my behalf at risk of his life and laid out much in treasure and time, and my gratitude to him is boundless and without end. But he is gone, and the world for all of us is changed. The time has come for me to embrace that change. The country has been troubled with war and dissent for too long. I intend very soon to return to Normandy and pass the rest of my days, if God wills, in peace.' A murmur of consternation ran round the hall and she had to raise her voice to speak over it. 'Do not think, therefore, that I have relinquished my right to the crown. I intend instead to pass it to my son Henry, who is the legitimate heir. He is almost of an age to prosecute the quest on his own account and when he returns to claim his birthright I know all of you will support him. Many

341

of you have already accepted him as your liege lord and sworn the oath of fealty. Those who have not will, I know, hasten to do so when the time is right. So now I bid you all farewell. I thank you for your unfailing support and I shall remember you all in my prayers, as I hope you will do for me.'

She sat. A few voices were raised in protest, asking her to stay, but they quickly fell silent. She sensed a relief among all those gathered. They, too, had had enough of war. Soon she left them to their wine and their memories and went up to her bedchamber.

Next morning, as she prepared to leave, Brian asked her permission to ride with her to Devizes instead of returning to Wallingford. She gave it gladly. As they rode he entertained her with stories and poems, as he did on that long ride to Rouen for her betrothal, and after dinner that night he sang for her, the song of the lovesick knight which he composed for her on that far off evening. Listening, she thought that perhaps at last the day had come for which she had longed, when they could sit together in peace and enjoy each other's company.

Next morning he asked to speak with her alone. She dismissed her attendants with a trembling around her heart which might be either hope or fear. She offered him a seat beside her and noticed for the first time that he, too, had aged. The hair at his temples was grey and there was a stiffness in the way he moved that she did not recall seeing before.

He said, 'You are quite determined to return to Normandy?'

'Yes. There is no place for me here now. I must hand this castle back to the Church or risk my immortal soul. With Miles and Robert gone, I cannot go back to Bristol or Gloucester, and Oxford is lost. Where else could I go …

unless—' She made her tone deliberately light '—I were to come and live with you in Wallingford.'

He did not smile. 'That would not be possible, for I shall not be there.'

'Not there?'

'Since you are returning to Normandy you have no further need of me to guard Wallingford for you. William Boterell is well able to keep it safe. This frees me to follow a course I have long contemplated. I intend to enter a monastery. I have already spoken with the abbot of Reading and he is happy to receive me. I need only your permission.'

'A monastery? But your wife...?'

'She has already entered the convent of Oakwood. You know that our marriage was never more than a match arranged by your father to give me, a landless knight, the rank and resources to sustain myself in the company of men like your brothers. It was never consummated. Hence I have no sons to inherit and when I die the honour of Wallingford will return to the crown. God willing that will mean to Henry. I should like to spend what time I have left in study and contemplation. Will you allow it?'

It was the final blow. She had to swallow hard before she could speak. 'You know I will do anything to give you ease and pleasure. You have been to me a tower of strength and it would ill become me to prevent you from pursuing the health of your own soul.'

He bowed his head. 'Thank you.'

She was silent for a moment, struggling to comprehend what his decision meant. 'I suppose ... I suppose, then, this is the last time we shall meet.'

'On this side of the grave, unless God wills otherwise.'

'I shall pray for you.'

'And I for you, and for your son. May we both live to

343

see him installed in his rightful place.'

'Amen.'

He got up. 'I bid you farewell, my lady.'

She rose too and he went down on his knees and kissed her hands for the last time. 'God go with you, queen of my heart.'

'And with you, my dear, my dearest friend.'

He stood, bowed and went quietly out of the room.

20

WESTMINSTER ABBEY, 19 DECEMBER 1154

THE TRUMPETS SOUND and the procession begins to move down the long nave from the great west door. She leans forward from her seat in the choir stalls to watch her son moving to his coronation. Henry looks magnificent. He is dressed in a crimson surcoat and his chestnut hair glows in the light of hundreds of candles. He will never have his father's height or his father's beauty, but his whole presence radiates energy and power. His expression is open and benign as he looks from side to side and nods in recognition of the bows and curtseys; but she knows him well enough to understand that behind that friendly gaze he is taking note of who is present and who has chosen to stay away. He is twenty-one years old but already well acquainted with the necessities of rule – thanks to her teaching. He will make a good king, she thinks. He will be able to heal the wounds of the past decade and a half of strife and bring the warring elements together.

She is less confident about the woman at his side. Eleanor of Aquitaine is undoubtedly a splendid catch, but she is eleven years older than Henry. She reminds herself ruefully that she should not consider that as a necessary impediment, since there was almost the same age difference between herself and Geoffrey; but whereas she had been a widow, Eleanor is the divorced wife of the King of France, put aside because after fifteen years of marriage she has born him only daughters. It is vital that she bears Henry sons. There must not be a repetition of the conflict caused by her own father's death, leaving only a daughter as his heir. The marriage has scandalized Europe, coming as it did only eight weeks after Eleanor's final parting from Louis. As soon as she was free she rode at top speed to Poitiers to join Henry and they were married within weeks. It has never been clear to her whether they had planned it together when they met in Paris the previous year, or whether it had been an impulsive decision on Eleanor's part. Whichever it was, Henry is besotted with her. Or is he besotted with the vast tract of territory she brings under his rule? Watching them as they make their slow way towards the high altar, she reflects on the twists of fortune that have meant that the boy who, at his birth, stood to inherit no more than the county of Anjou, now rules an empire that stretches from the borders of Scotland in the north to the Pyrenees in the south.

It has not happened quickly or easily. Henry had been forced to fight for his inheritance on both sides of the Channel. It had seemed for a few months that Normandy was secure, after King Louis accepted his homage and confirmed him as his father's heir, but no one expected him to inherit the title so soon. Geoffrey's death had been as sudden and as unexpected as her own father's, and from similar causes. Meanwhile Henry had been determined to continue the fight for the English crown. His first expedition had gained him little, except his knighting at the hands of his uncle, David of Scotland, but the English lords who had supported her had continued the struggle and begged him to return. Finally, in the depths of winter in 1153 he had braved the narrow seas with a small but loyal force and had set about a campaign of harassment against Stephen's castles. He had won new allies by offering generous rewards in terms of land and influence, and by avoiding pitched battle had made himself a thorn in Stephen's side. It was fitting, she thinks, that the final confrontation took place outside Wallingford, which Stephen was besieging yet again. Brian was no longer there to defend it, of course. He did not live long after retiring to Reading Abbey and she suspects now that he already knew that death was approaching when he made the decision. But Wallingford was still stoutly held by William Boterell, aided by Miles's son Roger, and Henry had marched to its relief. It was at that point that the great lords of England finally decided that they had had their fill of warfare and turned to the men of the Church to broker a peace deal. Henry and Stephen met face to face on either side of a stream and, as Henry told her later with a wry smile, complained bitterly about the disloyalty of their respective allies. In the end it was Theobald of Bec and Henry of Winchester who hammered out a deal by which Stephen agreed to disinherit his son Eustace and adopt Henry as his heir. Even then, it might not have been the end of hostilities. Eustace was understandably furious and would have continued the fight, if he had not died suddenly a few months later – a final proof, to her mind, of the legitimacy of Henry's succession and the favour of God. It was not to be expected, however, that Henry would inherit so soon. Indeed for a desperate week or two in October of that year she had feared that all her hopes might yet come to nothing when Henry fell dangerously ill – but in the end it was Stephen who died and Henry recovered to assume the role she had always envisaged for him.

The procession has reached the high altar now and the

archbishop turns to the congregation.

'I here present you Henry, son of the Duke of Normandy and the Empress Matilda, grandson of King Henry the First, and your undoubted King. Wherefore, all you who have come to do your homage, are you willing to do the same?'

The cathedral rings with the shout, 'We are. We wish it.'

The coronation mass begins. It pleases her that it is conducted by Theobald. He has been a constant presence in her life, and, though he always refused to renege on his loyalty to the man he had anointed as king, she respects his integrity. She has reason to be grateful to him. During the period between Stephen's death and Henry's return from Normandy, when bad weather prevented him from crossing, Theobald acted as regent and kept the throne secure. It is just as well that Henry of Winchester has chosen to go into exile at Cluny. It would have galled her to watch him perform the ceremony. And now, the moment of anointing approaches. Theobald takes the filigreed spoon from an acolyte and marks the sign of the cross on Henry's hands, brow and breast. She finds that she is trembling and her vision is misted with tears. The actual coronation follows and it is the crown which was once worn by her first husband the emperor, which she brought with her when she fled Germany, which is set upon her son's head. Solid gold and set with precious gems, it is so heavy that it has to be supported on either side by pages holding silver rods.

The ceremony is almost over. She looks round at the assembled nobles. There are a few familiar faces, but not many. Reginald, her half-brother, is here, the last survivor of the band of friends who gathered round her when she arrived in England. He is steady and sensible and

Henry listens to his advice. Ranulph of Chester is here, a staunch ally these days; and Robert Beaumont, the Earl of Leicester, once a favourite of her father's and later a supporter of Stephen, but now reconciled to Henry. Most of the men closest to Henry now are newcomers. Henry is following his grandfather's example and promoting talent and ability over noble birth. Like that young clerk in the front rank there – Thomas Becket, one of Theobald's acolytes. Henry has shown him favour. A good choice, she thinks.

She eases her position. Once she could sit upright without moving for hours if the occasion demanded it, but lately her bones begin to ache after a while. Her mind drifts to the small house in the grounds of the convent of Bec, where she has made her home since her husband's death. It was a wonderful relief after the bustle and noise of Rouen. If she imagined that her life would be peaceful when she left England she was sadly mistaken. First as Geoffrey's vice regent and then after his death as Henry's, she has been responsible for the safety of Normandy and the smooth running of its administration. There was a time, when Henry was absent in England, when the whole duchy had been imperilled and she had feared that they might lose both the crown and the dukedom. King Louis, incensed by Henry's marriage to his ex-wife, was hovering on her borders, ready to take advantage of any sign of weakness, and she had turbulent barons to deal with in every corner of both Normandy and Anjou. By the grace of God, Henry had returned with the promise of the English throne secured and quickly quelled the opposition, but she looks back on it now as one of the dark times in her life. She straightens her back. All that is behind her now. Henry is King and he has good men around him – and a wife to turn to for council. Her part in the affairs of state is over. Maybe now she will be free to enjoy the peace of the abbey and devote herself to prayer and good works.

The mass is complete and the new King and Queen have been crowned. They rise from their thrones and process down the nave. She watches Eleanor and remembers suddenly how heavy the crown felt when she herself was crowned Queen of the Germans and how hard it was to walk elegantly in the heavy robes. Eleanor seems to be managing it without difficulty, but then she is a mature woman, and she herself was only twelve. It crosses her mind that Eleanor may be a queen twice over, but she will never be able to call herself Empress – or Lady of the English, for that matter.

The procession reaches the end of the nave and the great doors are thrown open, admitting the noise of the crowd waiting outside. One voice rings out clearly above the general hubbub. 'Long live the King!' Immediately the cry is taken up outside and then inside the cathedral and the great building echoes to the sound. 'Long live the King! *Long live the King!*'

POSTSCRIPT

MATILDA LIVED ON for another thirteen years, during which time she remained active in state affairs. She maintained contact with Frederick Barbarossa, the new German Emperor, and tried to mediate between her son and Archbishop Thomas Becket when their relationship soured. She also became known for her pious gifts to religious foundations and for her charity to the poor. Stephen of Rouen, a monk of Bec, praised her as 'a generous benefactor to the Church, pious, merciful and intelligent'.

She died on 10 September 1167 and was buried under the high altar in the abbey of Bec. The inscription on her tomb reads as follows:

Great by birth, greater by marriage, greatest in her offspring,
Here lies the daughter, wife and mother of Henry.